All She Ever Needed

Lora Logan

ISBN 978-1-912768-28-8

Published 2019
Published by Black Velvet Seductions Publishing

All She Ever Needed Copyright 2019 Lora Logan
Cover design Copyright 2019 Jessica Greeley

Acknowledgements

For my husband, who is the best part of my every day.
My parents, who taught me that I can be anything I want to be.
My sisters; my best friends.
Juniper, Sommer, Randy, Darnetta, JW & Conley.
My fabulous street team for all of your input and suggestions.
My amazing editors; Ansley Blackstock and Jane Spencer.
Richard Savage and the Black Velvet Seductions team for showing me the ropes and holding my hand.
And to the readers! Thank you for bringing these characters to life! I hope you enjoy.

Flame and *Goodbye to May*
lyrics and original music by
Michael S. Fletcher. www.mikesfletcher.com Copyright 2018

Chapter One

I landed on my butt with a thud, still holding the tray of food high above my head. Somehow, I managed to balance the plates which were overflowing with burgers and onion petals. The ramekin, however, hit the ground before I did, and splashed my bare legs, covering me in the sticky mayonnaise-based special sauce.

"Good save, Becca!" Amelia grabbed my tray and set it back on the counter, then held her hands out to help me up. She's a good friend. The rest of the kitchen staff just clapped at my little display, which was most likely a slow-motion river dance style of a fall. I took a brief bow, straightened up and grabbed the tray.

"Did I just hear Jameson is back?" I leaned into Amelia and whispered the words—not everyone needed to know the reason I'd taken a swan dive across the cold tile of the kitchen floor.

"Yes, and what is it about him that makes you turn into a completely awkward"—she paused, searching for the right word—"whatever *this* is?" Her fingers pulled at the special sauce which was apparently caking layers of my hair together.

Mortification struck me instantaneously. "Like, tonight?!"

Not tonight, please, not tonight!

"Tonight," she deadpanned. "You may want to think about doing something about…all this." She motioned toward my sticky, disheveled appearance. "And, if you've got enough time in the bathroom, I don't know, maybe stop acting like a crazy person."

Despite the hard time she was currently giving me, Amelia had easily been the best part about working at Maggie's for the past two years. At twenty-four, she was a few years older than me, and instantly became the older sister I always wanted. At five foot two and maybe a hundred pounds, she was the sweetest, wildest person I'd ever met. Half Greek and half Armenian, she was stunning on her worst day. If she was supposed to be at work at five, they told her to be there at four. She was an hour late wherever she went, but the life of the party everywhere. When I needed a good shopping partner, and had a good ten hours to spare, she was my girl.

"Ha!" I laughed bitterly as I shoved the tray of burgers at her. "Table twelve, please?"

Smiling, she accepted the tray while I hightailed it to the bathroom. She had a small point. Something about Jameson did seem to bring out every ounce of awkwardness that resided in each individual strand of my DNA.

Frantically, I pulled paper towels from the dispenser and wet them, then scrubbed them up and down my legs. Once satisfied, I looked at my reflection and was horrified to see the sauce hadn't just managed to ricochet across my legs; I also had specks of it decorating my "Maggie's" T-shirt.

Of course, they just had to order extra sauce!

What was my deal with Jameson anyway? Yes, he was gorgeous—strong tattooed arms, wavy, dark, wild hair, and a devilish grin. I just wanted to stare at him. Unfortunately, talking to him was much more of a challenge. As much as I didn't want my mind to go there, it immediately flashed to the first time I'd met him—my first day at Maggie's.

My attraction to Jameson was instantaneous. So instantaneous, in fact, that I'd felt him before I saw him. While I'd heard of that type of attraction before, I never would have believed it until I experienced it myself. I was busy straightening and re-straightening the menus at the hostess stand when something caught my attention—a dropping feeling in my stomach, and an almost anxious curiosity at who was coming around the corner. When our eyes met I thought the dropping in my stomach must have made an actual sound because he was watching me just as intently. I fidgeted nervously with my short jean shorts and the Maggie's T-shirt, which was just a bit too tight across my chest. At least, since I wasn't serving, I was able to keep my sandy blonde hair down, where it fell just below my shoulders, instead of having to keep it up in a sloppy ponytail.

"You new?" He gave me a sideways, disinterested glance.

"Um, yeah. I mean, I've worked for restaurants before...just not this one?"

Why did that last part come out like a question?

A smile etched across his face as he passed me, heading toward the front door, where he remained for the rest of the night. As a bouncer, he arrived later in the evening and checked IDs. Maggie's was a restaurant, but after nine p.m. it was much more about the bar. There were always a few fights, and people needing to be unceremoniously taken outside. Maybe it was the way he looked, or maybe he just had a way about him, but people usually calmed down when Jameson got involved. A lot of the bouncers at Maggie's were on the eager side when it came it getting in the middle of an altercation, but Jameson handled it differently, usually walking the offending parties outside without needing to get nasty.

Maybe I'd done a terrible job of hiding it, but Amelia picked up on the fact that I had a thing for him pretty quickly. On one particular day, she winked at him when we caught him eyeing us from his post, and I immediately complained that I wished I had as much courage as her. She never had a hard time being bold, and it was something I'd always admired about her. When she didn't understand what I meant, I explained that the ability to wink was not something I'd been granted. When pressed, I attempted to show her what I meant. Suffice it to say, my attempt at winking at someone resulted in the nearly involuntary movement of the entire left side of my face. With my nostrils flaring and one side of my lips puckered up—it was not a pretty picture. So naturally, that would be the moment Jameson walked up to us to say something.

Whatever it was he'd planned on saying would never be known, since as soon as he saw me he laughed and headed back to his spot up front. And that is how my time with Jameson went. Often, I'd feel his eyes on me, and whenever I looked his way he'd simply wink at me and go back to work. Never once did the butterflies stop putting on a show in my belly when he was near, and despite the fact that it seemed like he felt it too, our interactions never went past a few words here and there.

By the time I worked up enough courage to have an actual conversation with him, he was gone. In an attempt to act complacent, I didn't ask a lot of questions, but from what I heard he was busy with a rock band he was putting together.

Over the past year, the what-ifs had bothered me. Never had I felt a connection with anyone like I did with Jameson. But now, as I stood in the bathroom of Maggie's, covered in special sauce, he was back. Would we still have that same connection? More importantly, had I gotten over whatever spell he seemed to cast over me?

Chapter Two

Somewhere in the galaxy a divine miracle or some one-hundred-and-fifty-year eclipse took place, and I managed to get cut before running into Jameson. As excited as I was to see him, I'd much prefer it to be on my own terms, with my clothing and hair free of the debris and smells of Maggie's. Leaving early meant I had time to run home and shower before meeting Amelia at her house.

"Why exactly did I agree to get ready at your place?" I asked as I scanned her bedroom.

I'd only made it to her bedroom door before being completely overwhelmed with the mess that was Amelia preparing to go anywhere. Technically, she lived with her aunt and uncle, but they had given her the entire main floor of the house and renovated the basement to be their apartment. It even had a separate entrance, although I'm not sure why because every time I was there they were all upstairs.

Since her bedroom was the master it was impressive in size. Taking up the middle of the room was a four-poster king size bed that at that moment held more clothes than the walk-in closet.

"Hey!" She popped her head out of her en-suite bathroom.

"I'll be ready in ten minutes." She winked slyly and disappeared back inside.

That comment was laughable considering she still had her long thick hair up in a sloppy bun on the top of her head. I was pretty sure she'd never walked to her mailbox without straightening her hair, let alone actually go out for the evening.

We spent the next twenty minutes searching for the perfect black bra to wear under her other black bra. Apparently, for the less endowed, there is an art to wearing two bras to maximize cleavage. This isn't the type of thing I've ever had to worry about being that I was a big C—

okay, D—by my freshman year in high school.

"Why don't you pick out something of mine to wear?" She looked me up and down with disapproval.

"Milly!" I only called her that when she was really getting on my nerves. Mostly because one of our previous managers at Maggie's was named Milly, and she'd been a flaming bitch, but also because four syllables is too many when you're trying to yell at someone in exasperation. "Seriously?" I looked down at the outfit I'd spent twenty minutes picking out. "It's midnight, and I have two feet and twenty pounds on your skinny behind. Let's go!"

Thirty minutes later I looked at my reflection in her full-length mirror and conceded that I seriously needed to listen to her more often. If there's one thing I can pull off it's a mini-skirt, and I felt good in this gold sparkly one, teamed with a white low-cut top with spaghetti straps. The real winner was the shoes. Aren't they always? Three inches taller is a lot of fun—before you start drinking, of course.

"So... did Jameson show tonight?" I looked away from her as soon as the words left my mouth. I didn't have to see her to know she'd been waiting this entire time for me to bring him up.

"Yeah, just after you left, you big freaking chicken!" She laughed while nudging me with her elbow. "He was looking all over for you, too."

"Shut up! He wasn't!" As much as I'd have liked to believe that was the case, I wasn't falling for her teasing.

"Mmm hmm... I guess we'll see, won't we?"

What was that supposed to mean?

Chapter Three

It was after one a.m. by the time we pulled into the garage and made our way to Iron City, Over-The-Rhine's newest reinvention. This area used to be a real dump, but with years of work the city had really started to bring back what once was the "new New York". I wouldn't walk around this place by myself, but generally speaking it's the ones involved in drug deals who end up getting shot.

"Milly! Line!" As usual, she was dragging me to the front, bypassing everyone patiently waiting to get in.

I swear she has more energy than the Energizer Bunny. Despite her short black dress and three-inch heels, she led me through the crowd, her hair swaying back and forth with her excited gait.

"Hey, Jeremy!" Amelia skipped toward the bouncer and gave him a hug and a kiss on the cheek. Jeremy looked just as you'd expect a bouncer to look like in the newest swank club in the area—dark, smoldering eyes, and lips which held no smile until Amelia made her way to him. Dressed in black dress pants and a long sleeve collared black shirt, it was pretty obvious he was not someone to fuck with. Aside from his arms and shoulders attempting to bust from his sleeves, he also had that intimidating thousand-yard stare.

"Jeremy this is Becca. Becca, Jeremy." Amelia motioned excitedly between the two of us.

I nodded at Jeremy and stuck my arm out to shake his hand, but instead he took my hand, pulled it to his mouth, and delicately kissed it. Like a practiced flirt, he had no shame as his eyes surveyed me.

"Try to stay out of trouble, girls." He grinned his warning at me and held onto my hand a little longer than necessary as Amelia pulled me into the bar.

Iron City has the industrial, warehouse feel you'd expect, given the name of the place. The floors are cold concrete and the ceiling is completely exposed with pipes and ducts dropping down beside high hanging fluorescent lighting. The bar itself, which takes up the entire left wall has no stools, just the words, "LOADING ZONE" stamped in construction yellow across the floor. The wall behind the bar is dark brick, with endless steel shelves holding various bottles of liquor. At the end of the bar are concrete stairs with steel handrails leading up to the second-floor overlook, which, while small, gives the perfect view of the vintage stage that takes up the entire back wall of the club. If we'd gotten there early enough, which obviously we hadn't, we'd have been able to actually sit down in one of the long eight-seater steel tables with the backless leather barstools.

The place was packed. This is always fun since I'm too short to see over the crowd. Our method of choice is to find the biggest guy going in the direction we want to go in, grab on to him, and let him carve a path through the crowd. As per protocol, off to the bar we went, our guide leading the way.

"Two vodka and Red Bulls please," Amelia yelled over the hard rock music that Iron City is known for.

"Before you say it, don't! You can afford to live a little tonight," Amelia shouted before I could interject.

"Here's to you, my love!" she shouted over the noise, and she held up her drink. "You may be leaving me for Providence, but you'd better believe I'll be joining you in a year! Then we can get our apartment, find rich Ivy League husbands and live happily ever after," she insisted with a toothy grin.

"I'll drink to that! But enough with the talk of me leaving! We have two months before I go, and we're gonna make the most of it!"

Generally speaking, Amelia hadn't been able to talk much about me leaving for school in Providence without tearing up. Our plan had been to go together, but when her uncle got sick our grandiose ideations had taken a backseat.

Before I could think much more about it, we made our way toward the stage, just in time to hear them introduce the next act. In places like this it's hard to hear much of anything, but I was able to make out the band they were introducing. The nerd in me appreciated the name: The Metalloids.

The room was so thick with smoke that you could cut the air with a knife, but when I saw four guys walk out on stage, my eyes immediately went to one in particular. My jaw dropped when I saw it was Jameson.

The romantic in me quickly noted that I could now add bassist to his list of sexy attributes. With the lights and the number of people in the crowd I doubted very seriously that he was able to recognize me. Occasionally, I would look his way and our eyes would meet. Then again, maybe he was just staring off into the crowd and not really seeing me. He looked better than I'd remembered. Maybe it was the musician side of him I found so appealing, or maybe it was just him, but there is nothing quite like seeing someone completely in their element. It was pretty obvious he belonged on that stage. Some of the songs they played were covers, so we sang along with the ones we knew, and danced to the ones we didn't. Before I knew it, Jeremy was bringing us more vodka and Red Bulls.

"Thanks, Jeremy!" Amelia hugged him, but he didn't take his eyes off me.

"Now, why is it Amelia here gives me a hug for a thank you, but all I get from you is a smile?"

He winked, and my look of betrayal immediately landed on Amelia.

"I didn't tell him!" she laughed, innocently holding her hands in the air.

I looked back at Jeremy who was looking at me with a confused expression, and from the corner of my eye I could make out Amelia grinning. She was perpetually trying to hook me up with a random someone.

"Thank you, Jeremy." I smiled up at him and went in for the asexual side hug, but he quickly grabbed me by my hips and slid me around so I was giving him a full on frontal hug, while his fingers played across the delicate bare skin of my sides. Okay, so he smelled good, I'll give him that.

Once again, he held on to me a little longer than necessary before he let me go, still keeping ahold of my hand. He leaned down to talk to me, but to be heard over the music he had to put his face pretty much against the side of mine.

"I gotta get back to work. I'll talk to you a little later?"

"Yeah, we'll be here," I said, putting a little distance between us.

I'm not sure why but something felt off and it wasn't until I looked at the stage that I figured out what it was. There was Jameson, glaring a hole through Jeremy's head. Kinda funny really, or maybe that was the vodka and Red Bull.

As soon as Jeremy left Amelia was dragging me up the concrete stairs to the second-floor overlook.

"Why didn't you tell me he was going to be here?" I gaped.

"Must have slipped my mind." She grinned toward the stage without looking at me.

"I'm thinking it had a little more to do with the fact that you couldn't keep your eyes off the lead singer," I teased.

"Speaking of lead singer…" Amelia was heading back downstairs after noticing the band was taking a break.

Usually, I have a hard time standing around by myself with nobody to talk to, but then I'm used to this sort of thing with Amelia. She is easy to entertain, and tends to make herself the center of attention wherever she is, whereas I, on the other hand, don't always enjoy being in that kind of place.

It was then that I saw Jameson coming up the stairs toward me. Damn the grin I couldn't get off of my face! So it wasn't the bass that made him so sexy—it was just him.

"Becca."

Damn, even the way he says my name is sexy!

Something about his eyes just penetrated through me and all the breath in my lungs escaped me. I could only stare.

"How have you been?" he asked.

Crap, I forgot to respond, didn't I?

"Good, good. How you've been?" I shook my head back and forth. "I mean, how *have* you been?"

He laughed at me (again).

"Oh hey, I've been working on that whole winking thing," I said reassuringly.

"So, how's that going for you?" he laughed.

"Not well."

Why can't I stop grinning?

Being awkward has its downsides, but at least drunken awkward wouldn't hit me until later.

"You look beautiful, but then you are beautiful no matter what you are wearing. But that… that… is gorgeous." He looked me up and down in a seriously sexy, and not at all creepy way.

"Thank you," was all I managed. I couldn't think of a thing to say, but, God help me, I couldn't look away.

"So how well do you know Jeremy?" He was suddenly more serious.

"Who?" I asked with a blank expression. "Oh! Bouncer Jeremy!" I said after the realization hit me. "I don't know him really. Amelia—you know Amelia; she knows everyone."

The months since I'd last seen him were suddenly erased, and without fail I was right back where I'd been before—stupidly wordless and unable to stop staring. He looked the same, but different somehow. He wasn't your traditional pretty boy, not at all. It wasn't just his forearm tattoo that gave him more of a bad boy look, but also something about his wavy dark hair and perpetual five o'clock shadow. Effortlessly sexy. Hollister could try to create this kind of man, but nothing could compete with someone who comes by it naturally. He has the smallest hook-shaped white scar by his left eye and never have I looked at him and not had the urge to trace it with my finger. I wondered how he got it, but wherever it came from it was right to be there. It made him... him.

I wasn't sure if it had been ten seconds or two minutes that I'd been staring at him, taking him in, and saying nothing. But suddenly I caught myself, and I was much more conscious of him staring at me, too. His eyes were drawn to my lips and to the fact that when I'm nervous, or thinking hard on something, I tend to bite down on the nail of my index finger.

"Where have you been?" I ask, with far more emotion than I intended.

He had started to open his mouth to answer my question, when we both became aware that the band's break was over and the rest of them were on stage waiting to start their next set. Jameson just smiled and took off down the stairs, leaving me still dazed.

Abruptly needing a purpose, I made my way back down to the main throes of the club and found Amelia.

"Please tell me you are taking that boy home with you tonight!" she grinned.

Thankfully, there was no chance to acknowledge that statement because the club was officially overflowing with people.

There's a girl code in situations like these, because with all the people there it can be difficult to even figure out who has come up behind you dancing. The responsibility then falls to the best friend to either discreetly give the thumbs up, or grab hold of your hand and pull you away from the offender. That night there wasn't a single guy that could distract me from Jameson and his world, which was quite obviously his music.

Very quickly the place had gotten out of control and it was too much. In the chaos of so many people we had become separated from each other; Amelia ending up against the stage, while I was being pushed in the opposite direction.

The guy next to me must have spilled his drink on someone, or some other inadmissible crime, because another guy turned around and laid him out with one punch square to the jaw. I jumped back, trying to stay separate from the chaos, but like chaos often does, it spread like a wildfire.

"Becca!" Amelia yelled. "Time to go!"

She caught up with me, grabbed my hand, and led me to the door.

I looked back at the stage, disappointed that this was how the night would be ending. The only way I knew to find Jameson was if he'd be playing here again. I sent him a small wave, doubting he'd be able to see it through all the people and the smoke of the club.

Chapter Four

Like it or not, the sun streaming through my bedroom curtains and blinding my eyes was getting my butt out of bed. I glanced over at my bedside table; the glowing red numbers told me it was eleven thirty am. I am not a morning person, not even a little bit. I was lying flat on my back in the middle of an overabundance of feather comforters and pillows, willing myself to get out of bed, when my phone chirped. I reached for it and stared at the number, but I didn't recognize it. Who was texting me?

>When might I be seeing you again?

Interesting. I sent a quick text to Amelia asking if she'd given my number to Jeremy. He was cute, but I wasn't about to start dating someone when I would be leaving for Providence in two months.
Shit, no response from Amelia.
I was getting impatient.

>That all depends…

I realized I'd been holding my breath. No way was this Jameson texting me. I needed to get it in my head that it was just Jeremy, and another one of Amelia's ill-fated matchmaking attempts.
It's just Jeremy, don't get excited. It's just Jeremy.

>Depends on?

>Who exactly it is I'm talking to!

>I'll give you a hint. Sexy as hell, smart, and a great sense of humor.

>Hmmm... I'm thinking this is a wrong number text 'cause I don't know anyone like that!

>HaHa. It's Jameson.

Holy Shit!
That last text got my butt out of bed with a quickness. Thank God the Jetsons's predictions of all telecommunications being done through video never came to fruition because I couldn't get the grin off my face! Immediately, I felt the need to move. As I paced around my bedroom, I tried to think of something remotely interesting to say.

>That's odd, I don't remember giving you my number! You my new stalker?

Fingers crossed he didn't take that one the wrong way. He could stalk me any day of the week!

>Nah, one restraining order is enough.

I wondered if we were still joking around. He had disappeared for nearly a year after all. What could I say back to that?

>That was a joke, Becca. Lol. In all seriousness, Amelia gave me your number. I know you're leaving soon but I was hoping we might continue our conversation from last night.

>Sure

I knew that was a lame response.

>Great, I'll pick you up from Maggie's tonight. 10:00?

>I'll see you then.

I spent the next few hours trying to figure out what to wear, what to say and how to act, and talking myself in and out of this date repeatedly. Honestly, I'm not sure there was any argument I could have given myself that would have kept me from seeing Jameson. Although my brain knew better—I was leaving, and the last thing I needed to do was get involved with someone.

It was the slowest night ever at work. We were busy, as we pretty much always were, and usually that would make the night go by a little quicker. Tonight, though, there was way too much nervous excitement flowing through me to think about anything other than Jameson.

"Stop looking at the clock!" Amelia teased. She knew exactly where my mind was, and in my opinion, she was a bit overly excited about my date.

"You put that C on L!" she whisper-yelled in my direction as she made her way back to the bar to pick up the drinks for one of the tables she was serving.

I shushed her as I laughed to myself. It's not like anyone would know what the hell we were talking about. Putting the C on L meant to put the cock on lock. Classy, I know, but Amelia was always making up some crazy random shit, and that one had stuck.

Just before ten, I begged my manager to cut me. The place was still busy but starting to slow down. I went to the bathroom and changed into some jean shorts, flip-flops, and an army green tank top. I retouched my makeup and brushed my hair out. My hair has a small amount of wave to it, and I was thankful it still looked halfway decent.

As I swung the door open I nearly ran face first into Amelia.

"Excited much?" She raised her eyebrows suggestively.

"Good?" I pointed at my outfit with uncertainty.

Amelia stepped toward me and unbuttoned the first two buttons of my tank top, revealing a little thing I like to call "classy cleavage". Enough to be like "Hey, I'm down here check me out", but not so much as to look like I'm trying to attract everyone to my goods.

"Better!" She took a step back and looked me up and down.

Before I had a chance to appraise and decide if "classy cleavage" was the plan for tonight, Jameson stepped into the hallway.

"Hey Amelia, Becca…" Jameson said, his eyes never leaving me.

I tried to hide the grin on my face, but I couldn't help but bask in the attention he showed me. Amelia was beautiful and never lacked any attention from men. Her looks, combined with her outgoing personality, seemed to attract them easily. Maybe I was showing a lack of confidence here, but I would have expected Jameson to go after a girl like her. Instead, it was me.

"Ready?" He held his hand out to me.

"Sure." I smiled and easily accepted his hand. I swear, just touching him made me giddy. "So, where are you taking me?"

We left Maggie's under the watchful eyes of nearly every employee and climbed into his older black Chevy SUV.

"It's a surprise," he teased as he opened the car door for me.

Surprisingly, I was able to give him my "not amused" face, despite the gorgeous grin he was giving me.

"Let's just say I'm sending you off in style." The mischievous glint in his eyes is unmistakable.

Not that I'd expected any less, but he looked incredibly hot in his worn-out jeans, black boots, and black T-shirt. His clothes might have seemed plain, if it weren't for the vivid, colorful tattoos that covered his arms. My eyes caught one in particular, on the inside of his right forearm. It was difficult to see from the angle I was seated at, but it appeared to be a hummingbird wrapped in thorns, struggling to break through.

"Your tattoos are so vibrant." My fingers danced across the lines of the hummingbird.

When our skin made contact, I immediately felt a surge of electricity, so much so that my immediate reaction was to pull away. I gave myself an imaginary pat on the back for maintaining some control over my awkwardness and managed to keep the contact.

"Does this one mean something?" I asked, my eyes never leaving the tattoo.

Immediately I remember reading an article somewhere about that being one of the most annoying questions to ask someone who has a tattoo. Of course, it meant something, either that or they were just a complete idiot for picking some random tattoo out of an artist's portfolio.

"That's a story for another day," he replied.

I removed my hand from his forearm and regretted my question. He looked over at me, smiled, and rested his hand on my thigh.

"So how you feeling about leaving for school?"

Somehow, I had to allow some of the blood in my body to flow from my thigh back to my brain. It was difficult to focus on anything when every part of my body was completely focused on his hand on my leg. I felt like a teenager, but something about Jameson was different.

"Pretty good, for the most part." My breath hitched in my throat as his fingers traced small circles on my upper thigh.

"Becoming a chef is something I've wanted for a long time, but I just wasn't able to make it happen until now."

"And Providence has the best school for that?" Jameson asked with an honest curiosity.

I nodded.

"You were going to school locally, right?" He glanced briefly at me before returning his eyes to the road.

"Yes, Cincinnati State. Their culinary program is good, and it's been nice being near family…but Johnson & Wales University? Amazing. That's where I want to be, and where I want to learn. The professors are the best in the country. And Providence? I'm not sure there's any place I would rather be."

As I looked out the window I could see the lights of Cincinnati and felt my first real twinge of sadness for what I'd be leaving behind.

"You taking me to Queen City Sausage?" I asked him teasingly as I nodded toward the brightly-lit billboard.

"Yes, there's something I need to tell you about my kielbasa," he replied with a serious look on his face.

It took me a minute to figure out if he was joking, but he suddenly burst out laughing.

Relieved, and a little saddened I wouldn't be learning more about his kielbasa, we made our way to Over-the-Rhine.

"First, we will be going through Skyline to get a couple four-ways and coneys that you can only get in Cincinnati. But, I'm not taking you on a date to Skyline, so we're going to take them with us to The Brewery, where we can put back some of Cincinnati's local brews, followed by the best ice cream—"

"Graters!" I yelled out, a little overly excited for the best ice cream ever!

"Exactly. Sound good?"

"Perfect!" I smiled.

The Brewery is the type of place you can bring your own food, but you have to buy their beer. It was crowded with people, but we managed to find a high-top table near the back. The walls were adorned with photos and newspaper clippings of everything from the World Series to the floods, and it housed the most extensive collection of baseball and football memorabilia from our local teams. After we finished off our Cincinnati chili we decided to do the local brewery tour, which consisted of drinking one bottle from each of the local breweries. After that, we left the notion of local beers behind and went the more global route.

The best thing about craft beer is that it usually has a much higher alcohol content than domestic beer, so my nerves went out the window.

"So, what about you? You ready to get out of Cincy and go to Seattle…or wherever it is musicians go when they are ready to hit the big time?"

"Think I'm ready for the 'big time'?" His head tipped back in a laugh at my choice of wording.

"I do!" I grinned, leaning closer to him from across the small table. "I may have been marginally impressed when I saw you play." I tried to downplay the ego boost I had just given him.

"Only marginally impressed?" The little glimmer in his eye let me know he wasn't buying it.

"Alright, fine!" I scoffed. "You guys were really good."

The distance between us nearly evaporated as he leaned in so much that I thought he might kiss me from across the table.

"Maybe you could check out another one of my shows before you head off to school." He pushed a stray lock of hair from my face and tucked it behind my ear.

I nodded as the tingles worked their way across my face. Why did his touch have such an effect on me?

"You ready for that ice cream?"

As soon as he mentioned ice cream, all I could do was think about my belly full of beer, and apparently I have no control over my facial expressions because he said, "I know, right? I think we should have done the ice cream before the beer."

I shook my head regretfully. As much as I love ice cream, there was no way I could eat any now.

"I'm pretty sure they are closed by now." I glanced at the time on my phone.

"Maybe I have connections…" His lips cocked to the side teasingly.

"Oh wow! You might just be approaching dream guy status." I laughed.

We got up from our table and headed to the door, and I felt bad that since he drove it was me who had done most of the drinking. I wasn't drunk, but I had a warm buzz about me that just made me relax. It was a relief really, because I often end up getting all awkward with nerves on first dates.

As we walked, Jameson put his hand on the small of my back, and I silently tried to figure out if I had to wait on him to make the first move.

When we got to the car I leaned against it and looked up at the night's sky.

"I love the nighttime in the summer." I smiled to myself as I took in the few stars visible through the lights of the city.

Jameson had come to the passenger side door to open it for me but stopped short as he watched me gazing at the stars. He leaned against the car next to me so our shoulders were touching.

"My aunt has always told me that life is full of moments where you need to just stop and breathe it all in." He looked from me up to the night sky.

"This is one of those moments." I turned my head and looked up at him.

"Definitely." He turned back to me and smiled.

Jameson moved his head toward mine and watched my eyes intently as he went in for a kiss, as if waiting to see if I would move away from him. Instead, I moved closer, impatient at how long it had taken him to kiss me.

His lips were tentative, but after a moment our mouths parted in unison and his tongue brushed across mine, our warm breath mingling and creating a charged passion. From our sideways position it was only our mouths that touched. Both of us wanting more contact we moved at the same time, bringing our bodies closer and our chests flush against each other. His hand went to my hip and my body surged with the electricity of his touch. From the way he touched me I knew he felt it too. I could feel the hunger inside him as he grasped my hip with his hand.

Jameson pulled away first, and I silently cursed the fact I lived with my family and couldn't offer for him to come hang out and "watch a movie".

Chapter Five

If I could pick a time of my life to freeze, I would happily live forever in the moments I spent with Jameson over the next month.

When I wasn't with him, I was thinking about him. Suddenly going to work was much more exciting because he'd resumed his previous position as a bouncer. The best part about working together was catching him watching me. He would wink when he noticed me.

I thought we weren't making it too obvious, until one of my coworkers totally called me out on it.

"How long have you two been a couple?" Her eyes went from me to Jameson, who was thankfully out of earshot.

"Wait, what? We aren't a couple."

"Uh huh… Have you told him that yet? That boy has got it bad for you."

I could feel the heat come to my face, but it wasn't embarrassment that did it. Somehow just talking about him warmed my flesh and made my heart beat a bit faster. Her observation did bother me though. Not because I didn't want people to know about Jameson and me, but because I was so busy being wrapped up in the moment that, before I'd had a chance to stop it, I had completely fallen for him.

Jameson was more than I thought possible in another human being. He was so talented, yet so humble. I could watch him onstage forever. Something about him seemed to naturally draw people in, and when they saw him perform they knew he was something special – something that couldn't be contained in a small club like Iron City. He was intelligent as well as artistic; we could discuss anything from religion to politics. Even when we had differing opinions we debated without arguing. His rough, tattooed exterior only made his sweet, sensitive side that much more appealing. The way he held my face when he kissed me made me more content than I'd ever been. He brought me flowers and listened to me go on and on about my grandiose plans for opening my own restaurant one day. For a moment I might have thought he was perfect. He encouraged me to go to Providence to pursue my dreams, and never once asked me to stay. I wouldn't, but there is something to be said about being asked not to leave. I wanted to encourage him to come with me, but whenever I tried to talk about him leaving Cincinnati and pursuing his music career he shut me down—this was where his family was, and where he belonged.

With less than a week to go before I left for Providence, my time with Jameson quickly went from living in the moment to a constant fear of the future and what I was leaving behind.

Chapter Six

The reminder chirp on my phone interrupted my thoughts, and I reached across the feathered layers to my bedside table.

>You're off today, right?

>Yes…

>Great! I'll pick you up in an hour. We won't be back until late tonight. Bring a change of clothes & swimsuit.

>Seriously?

>Seriously.

I wasn't sure whether to be excited or scared, so I went with both. My little plot to stay away from Jameson had died after I'd seen him. It didn't matter what happened between us this summer. I was leaving in September so I might as well have some fun in the meantime.

At nine thirty am, Jameson pulled up to my apartment. With the early hour and the secretive plans for our day, I was nervous about the idea of him meeting my family, so I was thankful when he texted me.

>I'm here but forgot to tell you to bring shoes you can hike in. Need help?

>Nope, I'm good. Be down in a sec.

I walked out into the cool morning air to find Jameson leaning against his SUV, wearing long khaki cargo shorts with a blue fitted Under Armour T-shirt that gave me way too many ideas for such an early hour.

"Good morning." He gave me his signature mischievous smile.

"Morning." I looked up at him, and then back down to his hands which held two insulated cups of my own personal heroin, Starbucks.

"One for me?" I asked innocently.

"Yes, sorry—for you." He handed me one of the steaming cups of heaven.

"Thank you." I inhaled through the lid. "You might not be so bad after all," I teased.

He held my door open and I threw my small bag into the backseat. We were on our way and I was thankful I'd decided to bring my oversized gray sweater to throw on over my short jean shorts and blue tank top. The sweater, while a bit too large, reminded me of one my grandpa used to wear when I was a kid, and despite the years that had passed, it made me feel closer to him.

We spent our drive in comfortable silence, or maybe that was just because it was way too early for me to even entertain the idea of conversation. Instead, I took in the sights of the rock-covered hills that lined the highways through Ohio into Kentucky, and we took turns playing our favorite music through the crappy car speakers. With the sun in my face and the wind from the open windows, I felt completely content with this moment in my life.

After a few hours, we arrived at the caves, and he made me pick which path we should take. With me this is never a good idea because I've always been prone to take the pretty route, not thinking about where I'm going or where I'll end up.

We hiked for about an hour, and before long we were off by ourselves. Suddenly, he pulled me by the hand at took me between the narrow walls of the caves.

"Where are we going?" I trailed behind him, laughing.

He came to an abrupt halt and stepped through a small opening.

Suddenly he pulled me into his body, spinning me roughly so I was backed against the wall. I was enclosed in his arms as he looked at me with determined eyes.

"I just wanted to tell you—"

He paused, caressing my cheeks with his thumbs. As though he'd lost his thought, he ran them down across my bottom lip and kissed me. He was slow and gentle at first, taking my bottom lip and sucking it.

I felt like all the heat in the cave was sucked out and poured inside me. My entire body tingled from my toes to the top of my head, and suddenly I felt like the rest of the world had stopped—it was only us. My stomach burned and my whole body ached with a tangible need that could no longer be ignored. I know that nothing but him could take away this burning inside.

A kiss that had started out innocent soon had us both panting, out of air. I could feel his desperation as much as I could feel my own. The need to touch him and feel his skin on mine was overwhelming. I slid my hands up his broad chest. When he stopped kissing me I moaned at the loss. My eyes fluttered open to see him watching me. With our eyes locked on each other my skin was hyperaware. He slowly slid his hand down my side so his palm was flush against my upper thigh. I could no longer hide my shudders of pleasure as he caressed my face, and then my bottom lip, with the pad of his thumb. I could kiss him forever, but when he slowly moved his hand up the length of my thigh and under my shorts I lost all thought and was nothing but sensation.

His fingers stroked me through the thin fabric of my panties. He kissed me, continuing his assault while I shuddered, on the edge between heaven and hell. He pulled back from me and I leaned forward trying to prevent him from breaking contact. He looked at me with hooded eyes and exerted even more pressure across my folds. Involuntarily, I arched my back giving him permission to push my panties to the side and slide one long finger inside me. Without realizing what I was doing a moan escaped my lips, and he quickly kissed me to keep the noise from carrying into the narrow corridors of the cave. Slowly he continued to search and feel me, his finger deep inside, building an endless fire only he could extinguish.

He stopped our kiss, but continued his taunting, staring into my soul. He placed his hand back on my jaw, resting his index finger on my parted lips. I bit down when he slipped a second finger inside me. He didn't look away from my eyes while his fingers took me near the edge. His hand left my mouth and covered my breast, finding my pert nipple. I reached for him, feeling his hard shaft straining against the confines of his pants. Greedily and uncharacteristically, I felt the length of him through the fabric, and began working his shaft with as much focus as I could muster. I couldn't concentrate on what I was doing as I felt myself getting hotter, ready to explode. He picked up his rhythm and I fell apart. Caught up in the intensity of my orgasm, I cried out. Jameson quickly found my mouth with his and stifled my cries of pleasure. Despite my climax, he continued to slowly explore me, as my body contracted against his fingers.

"I want you," I told him breathlessly.

Before he could move or respond voices echoed through the cave. Thankfully, he came to his senses first. He already had my clothes back into place and had righted himself before I even realized what was occurring. Then he took my hand and he pulled me back onto the wooded path, to the reality that is my life. Jameson grinned at what nearly was, but like the cool air, the reality of our situation hit me.

My tone was full of regret. "What are we doing? I'm leaving."

Jameson stopped walking and looked at me, his features lined with all the grief that I felt too.

Our ride back was nearly silent. I couldn't change what I'd said any more than I could change the fact that I was leaving. Just before I was ready to get out of the car he grabbed my arm from across the console.

"Becca, I have to say this. You don't have to say anything but just listen to me. I know you're leaving, and I wouldn't ask you to stay. But I want you to know I love you. I want to be selfish and keep you for myself."

I sat there, stunned, near the point of tears. This was all happening too quickly. Instead of trying to figure out what I was feeling or what to say I held his cheeks and kissed him.

Chapter Seven

After our trip to the caves, I didn't respond to Jameson's calls or text messages. I just didn't know what to say. When he told me he loved me, while it felt amazing, it was also overwhelming. I couldn't allow myself to think too much about the fact that I was leaving, and he wouldn't be coming with me. Thinking about being without him caused my stomach to flip and something that felt like flight or fight overwhelmed my senses. I had to remind myself that I didn't want to stay here in Cincinnati and be a waitress for the rest of my life. What I wanted meant leaving this place behind, and going to school in Rhode Island.

"What is going on with you today? You look like your puppy died." Amelia grabbed my hand to stop me from endlessly thumping my pen against the waitress station.

"Sorry," I said, snapping back to reality.

"What's going on? You and Jameson have a fight?" Her expression sincere.

"Yes… I mean no… He told me he loved me." I whispered the last part, not wanting anyone to overhear us.

"Oh." I love Amelia, she understands me. "So you're freaking out?" she asked sympathetically.

"A little bit." My wide eyes searched hers.

Amelia grabbed my hand and pulled me back to a table next to the bar where the employees take breaks when we have time. We sat down and leaned close to each other so nobody would overhear us.

"Are you freaking out because it's too soon and he eeked you out? Or are you scared because you love him, too?" she asked for clarification.

I thought for a minute, trying to figure out how I felt.

"Both, I think." I am nothing if not honest, but hearing myself admit something like that filled me with a certain level of fear.

"Alright, that's okay." She patted my knee reassuringly.

When I looked away she grabbed my hand.

"You can't help who you love, Becca. Enjoy the time you have left here, and then figure out what you want to do."

Before I could respond, Jameson walked by and caught our attention. He looked distraught, and I immediately felt bad for ignoring him. I couldn't begin to imagine how he felt right now. If I told someone I loved them, and they said nothing and then ignored me for two days, I'd be freaking out. I hated the fact that I had put him in that situation, but what was I supposed to do here? What I felt or what I wanted seemed impossible, and saying those words only made it more real.

A busy night left all words unsaid as I served table after table of people and tried to put on my best happy face.

By eleven p.m. we had finally slowed down. I grabbed an empty lemon pan from behind the bar and made my way to the walk-in cooler to restock it.

I watched the door close behind me then searched the shelves for the lemons, which never seemed to be in their allotted place when I needed them. I rubbed my arms to fight off the cold that hit me quickly because I'd been running around like a crazy person for the last few hours. I shook my head and I attempted to ignore my ever-constant fear of being locked in the cooler.

When I heard the door open I didn't think to look because someone was always running in and out for one thing or another.

"Hey," Said a voice.

I looked over to find Jameson standing in the doorway.

"Hey."

My voice gave away my guilty feelings.

"Look, I'm sorry for what I said. I shouldn't have told you that; it was stupid."

The torment was evident on his face, and made me feel like an asshole all over again.

"No, I'm sorry. I shouldn't have avoided you."

Maybe that wasn't the best response, but I still hadn't completely figured out how I felt. How could I explain it to him when I couldn't even really understand it myself?

Jameson took a few steps toward me and waited for a second before gently pulling my ponytail back and tipping my face up to him.

"So, you're done avoiding me?"

His smile was contagious, and I couldn't help but return it.

I nodded, his hand holding my ponytail all the while.

"Okay, good. You want to do something after work? Everyone is going to O'Malley's."

Blah.

"I don't know about O'Malley's. I'm kind of in the mood to just chill."

"Movie at my place?" His smile was devious; whether that was because he was up to no good, or just trying to get me to agree, I don't know. Whatever, it was working.

"Sounds good."

Chapter Eight

It was close to one a.m. by the time Jameson and I got out of work. Working in a restaurant and bar we really lived by a different clock than everyone else. Most of us got up around one or two p.m., went into work around four or five, worked until midnight or one a.m., and partied 'til around four or five.

I was already tired, so I let Jameson drive us to his place while I texted my mom, who still insisted on knowing if I was going to be out all night.

Jameson lived in an old house that had been converted into two apartments. It had a small covered porch the two residents shared, one side housing ornate patio furnishings, while the other held a worn-out brown love seat.

"I'm guessing this is your decorating?" I pointed to the love seat as I smiled at him.

"What? You don't like it? What could be better than being outside AND being on a couch?"

I laughed at his masculine take on outdoor furnishings as he opened the front door and gestured for me to go first.

As soon as he flipped on the light I was immediately drawn to a piece of art hanging on the far wall of his living room. I made my way to it to take a closer look, and examined what appeared to be a huge framed sheet of music. It was the size of a big flat-screen TV, and from the little bit I know about reading music it appeared to be a score for several instruments. The paper was yellow, but what drew the eye were all the black dots that made up the notes.

"You like?" he asked from behind me.

"Love." I smiled to myself.

Maybe it was because I'd grown up with a musician for a father, but I couldn't get over the fact that Jameson had such an interesting piece in his living room. Immediately it made me want to do something like this for my dad, who would certainly appreciate it.

I looked at the bottom left of the print where the letters JMC were scribbled.

Startled, I turned around to face him.

"You did this?" The surprise was apparent on my face.

He laughed and grabbed the front of my jean shorts playfully, his fingertips grazing my skin.

"Why so surprised?" He held my gaze.

"It's just... I don't know. I knew you played, obviously, but I didn't know you write, too."

"That's just one song, my favorite. At least so far."

He stared up at his work, then quickly looked away and headed to his kitchen to grab us a couple beers.

I sat down on his couch, and thought for a moment about the stark differences between men's and women's apartments. There was nothing wrong with it, but besides the print on his wall, there were little to no decorations. The place was relatively clean and clutter-free, not something I'd expect when we hadn't talked about coming here until we were both at work.

The house, while it needed a little updating, had beautiful crown molding around the doors and windows, and in the right hands, could be restored to its original beauty.

After a few minutes, Jameson returned from changing his clothes and sat down next to me on the couch. We flipped through the movies on demand.

"Horror?"

He clicked through the genre selections.

A moment passed with me lost in thought.

"Come here, fidgets."

He wrapped his arms around my waist and slid me closer to him.

He was sitting with his body facing me, so when he pulled me to him my back rested against his chest. I didn't even realize I'd been fidgeting, but could easily believe it, because my nerves were getting the best of me.

He kept his hand on my waist, with one of his fingers, having unintentionally slipped below my shirt, resting against my skin.

He pulled his hand holding the remote free and continued to scan through the movie categories.

"Action?"

He looked down at me as the hand that held my hip caressed my skin.

I tried to keep still as my body wanted to press against him, loving the feel of his skin on my own. Instead, I made a face at the action suggestion and he continued.

"Suspense?"

As he spoke his hand went higher and stroked the sensitive skin around my navel.

"Comedy?" he suggested when I didn't answer. His hand climbed higher on my waist until his fingertips skimmed across my ribs to the edge of my bra.

His touch left behind a burning, tingling sensation that spread across my body—such a simple touch, yet such a strong effect.

He moved my hair to one shoulder, his mouth only inches from my neck.

"Drama?"

The words were spoken so close to my skin I could feel the heat from his mouth, making me squirm slightly against him.

Still, I said nothing, somehow fearing my words might make him stop.

His lips brushed across the skin on my neck, and without realizing it I pushed back against him bringing his lips closer to my skin.

I turned my head, giving him more exposure to my neck, and his soft lips brushed my skin again. As I felt the wetness of his tongue I couldn't keep my body still and I pressed against him wanting more. Slowly he kissed and sucked on my nape, his hand soft against the skin of my belly but his grasp firmer, as if he, too, was overcome with want.

"Romance?" he said against my neck, his breathing a bit more labored.

I pulled myself up and he looked at me questioningly as I stood and faced him. For the first time in forever I felt comfortable taking the lead and I sat on his lap facing him, my legs bent at the knees and resting on either side.

The surprise registered on his face, but before I could think more of it I took control, leaned into him and kissed his lips.

His hands immediately went to my waist and he pulled my hips closer to him.

His mouth tasted like mint, and his cologne smelled like the woods on a fall day, with a hint of some mysterious spice I imagine could only be found in some foreign country. All my muscles clenched with desire and as I rocked my hips against him I felt him harden beneath me.

His mouth moved to my neck once again and tingles filled my body. I grabbed onto his thick wavy hair, unable to control the slow grinding of my hips as his teeth delicately pulled on the skin of my neck.

He slid his hands under my shirt and pulled it over my head, leaving me wearing just my bra and shorts. Before I could respond or feel self-conscious, his mouth found my breast and his tongue lapped across my nipple through the thin fabric of my blue sheer lace bra.

I couldn't keep the small moans from escaping as my nipple grew hard against his tongue. I let go of his hair to reach around my back and undo the clasp of my bra.

He pulled the straps from my arms and looked up at me, his gaze holding mine firmly. For a moment I thought he was going to say something but he just watched me as his fingers trailed up my hips. Goosebumps covered my skin as his fingers went higher, sliding across my ribs to my breasts.

"Beautiful," he said, before he took one of my nipples in his mouth gently sucking it until all the blood in my body rushed to them creating a painful want.

When I rolled my hips against him again his hands immediately went to the back of my thighs and slid slowly beneath my shorts to the curve of my ass. As soon as he touched me I felt him grow fully hard beneath me, and without a choice I rocked against him steadily, needing to feel his hard flesh against me.

"Stand up for me." His voice was nearly a whisper.

Not wanting to break our contact I stood reluctantly, covering my bare breasts with my forearms.

Silently he undid the button of my jean shorts and slid them down my legs. I congratulated myself for having the forethought to wear a matching bra and panty set.

I took a step toward him, ready to resume where we left off but his hand went to my hips and slowly pulled my panties down my legs, exposing me completely to him.

Once he had my panties off he just looked at me, taking in my nakedness in front of him.

"Don't cover yourself up." He moved my arms.

"You're gorgeous." He pulled my body toward him so I was once again straddling his lap.

He leaned into me and kissed me passionately, his tongue exploring my mouth as his hands grasped my bare ass. He broke our contact only long enough to pull his shirt over his head and throw it on the floor next to my clothing.

I ran my hands across his chest and felt the firmness of his muscles. I wanted to complain that I was the only one naked, but before the words could leave my mouth I felt his fingers slide down my belly and lower, finding my wet folds. It was almost embarrassing how wet I was, but that had everything to do with how he was touching me, and how intensely my body was responding to him. His pace quickened, and his fingers slid across my clit to my opening without actually moving inside me.

"You're so wet," he said against my neck, his voice strained.

"Lose these."

I pulled on his knee-length nylon shorts. I had to concentrate on the words just to get them out of my mouth. This neediness was not a familiar feeling but I desperately wanted to feel him inside me, as if the past month had been nothing more than constant foreplay.

"Not yet." His eyes roamed lazily across my body. "I'm not done looking at you yet."

"Please?" I asked in a whisper as I delivered brief kisses to his lips. My hands held his hips, as my fingertips dipped slightly into his waistband.

His breath hitched in response, his chest rising and back arching, letting me know my touch affected him too.

He pulled my hips up breaking our connection, and he lifted himself from the couch just enough to pull his shorts down.

I felt his cock spring free fully hard from our intense foreplay, and when I went back to my position on his lap feeling him against me was too much.

"The bedroom." He made a halfhearted effort for us to move.

"No." I slid my body against his.

His breath hooked as I moved my hips, slowly letting his hard cock move down my belly before it slid between my legs.

He closed his eyes, his head resting on the back of the couch, and I took his cock in my hand, working it slowly, feeling the hardness of it.

He let out a sharp breath as my finger slid across his tip, feeling a single bead of moisture there.

With that touch, he straightened, wrapped his arms completely around me and pulled me flush against him. His kisses were urgent now, dominating me, but never overpowering.

He shifted beneath me and I pulled my hips up as he took his cock in his hand and slid it against the wetness that existed between us. Moans escaped both our mouths as he slid against my heat, and I knew if he never pushed himself inside me I would come just from what he was doing in that moment.

His cock rested at my opening as if waiting for permission, and I pushed down on him, my body giving the answer.

Slowly he pushed inside me, just the head filling me. I gasped audibly. I closed my eyes at the sweet pain of it and his hand went to my mouth, his thumb pressing gently against my bottom lip.

"Look at me," he said, his words coming out with difficulty.

Our eyes locked as he pushed deeper inside me, slowly expanding me to accommodate his impressive length and girth.

We both let out a moan once he was completely inside me, and I slid up and down on him, controlling our pace.

His hands went to my breasts, and he gently groped and pulled on my hard nipples, while my hands instinctually left his shoulders, going to his hair where I couldn't help but pull gently.

Our quiet moans and labored breaths filled the room until my orgasm started to build more and more, making my moans difficult to control. I fought the urge to allow my eyes to roll back in my head, wanting too badly to see the ecstasy that riddled his every feature.

Nearing the point of losing all control my head dropped back and my grasp tightened on his hair. As I became completely lost in the moment Jameson kept our momentum going, setting the pace when it became too overwhelming for me to do so.

His hand slid across my belly, and my reaction to him was so strong I jumped. His finger circled my belly button before he went lower, sliding his finger to my clit and working it in circles.

"Oh my God!" I cried at the onslaught of sensations working through my body.

Close to orgasm, I regained enough control of myself to quicken our pace. I leaned up enough so he nearly came out of me before pushing myself down on him again, letting him fill me completely with one thrust. His gasps let me know he liked what I was doing, and I repeated it, each time coming down harder on his cock.

My game quickly came to an end when his fingers worked across my clit so quickly it was as if they were vibrating against me. My moans filled the room, but I was lost in what he was doing to me, not caring if the neighbors could hear me.

I could feel him twitching just slightly inside me, and his breath let me know he was close. I tried to pull away from him just enough, so I could hold off and wait for him, but that only brought about a new determination from him. He pumped faster as his fingers continued taking me higher.

Before I even realized it, I was coming, milking him as my fingers grabbed and scratched his shoulders. Despite my orgasm, he pumped faster, and when I opened my eyes he was watching me.

His face contorted obviously trying to hold onto the last of himself.

"Fuck! What are you doing to me?"

I smiled at his question, liking the effect I had on him. I flexed against him and watched his features twist with pleasure as my breasts bounced against him.

"Mmm, slow down, baby." His words were labored as his hands returned to my hips, forcing to slow our pace. "I just want to stay right here." His hand went between us, feeling the wetness and the friction of where our bodies connected.

Like two magnets our mouths found each other again, and his pace slowed to match that of his kisses—slow, electrifying, and perfect.

"I need you in my bed." His eyes shot open with a newfound determination.

I shook my head no and flexed against him, letting him know I wasn't ready to be without him.

"Uh huh." He nodded his head playfully at me.

When he started to shift his body toward the edge of the couch I held on tightly, pretending I had the strength to keep him where I wanted him. He laughed playfully as he stood, taking me with him. I wrapped my legs around him and clasped him to me as he started to walk us down the hallway before stopping briefly to kick off his shorts that were still wrapped around one ankle. I couldn't help but laugh as he shook one of his legs to lose the fabric.

"Oh, you think that's funny, do you?" Once we'd reached his room he dropped me onto his bed, and we both hissed as our bodies detached in the process.

I laughed slightly as he stood above me, his naked skin slightly visible, thanks to a light that had been left on in the hall. His cock stood hard and ready, and I tried unsuccessfully to keep my eyes from locking on it.

"I like your bed."

I spread out my arms, feeling the soft blankets beneath me.

"Oh yeah?"

He knelt on the bed and leaned over me, his arms holding his weight above me as he looked down into my eyes.

"I like you in my bed."

His face came closer to mine as his fingers trailed up my leg. I tried to stay still, fighting my muscles and their demands to spasm at his touch.

"Becca," he whispered against my mouth, before his lips connected with mine. His tongue dipped into my mouth just as his fingers found my opening and pushed inside.

"Jameson." I whimpered his name in response.

Slowly he stretched out his body on top of mine, keeping his weight on one elbow next to my shoulder. His hard cock lay across my hip, and my hands went to his hair and pulled him tighter against me.

"Please." My voice was so thick with need I barely recognized it.

He grabbed his hard length and slid it against my wet folds. My body was so ready for him he was completely inside me with one swift thrust, rocking my every nerve ending. He took my hands, pulled my arms over my head and held them together with one hand. This time he controlled the pace, and he watched as I moaned with pleasure, taking all of him with every rock of his hips. He created a painful want inside me that left me begging for release when he toyed with me, bringing me to the edge, before slowing down. I was putty beneath him, paying for my own indiscretions when it was me who had controlled our pace.

"You gonna come for me, baby?" I loved the way the words left his mouth, strained and desperate.

"Yes. Yes!" I begged without an ounce of propriety.

"Yeah?" He picked up his pace.

My body burned with unshed desire, building unrelentingly at his touch.

"Mmm, yes!" My eyes squeezed shut, unable to comprehend the onslaught of feeling that radiated across my entire body.

Feeling him twitch inside me quickened my breathing and my lungs greedily huffed for air as moans echoed from my mouth without restraint.

"Look at me."

I opened my eyes at his command and within seconds came apart. His body tensed and he was spilling his hot juices inside me, calling my name before my body had released me from the grips of my orgasm.

"Let's just stay like this for a minute." He looked at me hopefully.

Happily, I stayed there and kissed him before closing my eyes, blissfully spent.

"What am I going to do when you're gone?" And just like that, I felt a little stabbing pain to my heart.

I have to go but ask me to stay.

"You could always come with me…" I chanced after a few moments of silence, completely afraid of what his reaction would be.

Chapter Nine

I left early. I'm not exactly sure what I was thinking, but I'm sure it's safe to say I'm a huge freakin' chicken. It would be foolish to think my family bought my brilliant explanation I fed them about wanting to get in a day early to get settled. I texted Jameson and fed him the same line, knowing very well he'd be asleep and wouldn't get the message until I was well on my way. I admit it was a chicken shit move, and, lucky me, I had a fourteen-hour drive to beat myself up over it. Cowardly or not, it was necessary. Going to Providence was the best thing I could do, and in doing so I'd be able to turn my dream into a reality. I would have my own restaurant. I was making the life for myself that I always wanted. Finding Jameson had not been planned, and I wasn't ready to be all about someone else. I needed to establish my life first.

Sadly, I couldn't lie to myself and say the butterflies in my stomach were just nerves and excitement about this new chapter of my life about to begin. I was excited, but moreover I couldn't get the images of last night out of my mind. I couldn't think about him without feeling that now common drop in my stomach—the butterflies that engulfed me every time I thought of him, his mouth on my lips, his hands touching every part of me.

FOCUS. You can't get what you want out of life when you're too distracted to accomplish your own goals.

Needless to say, I spent the trip fighting with myself, contemplating turning around, and ignoring the onslaught of calls and text messages. I just texted my family frequently enough to ensure they weren't envisioning me in a ditch somewhere.

Every time my phone beeped my heart fell into my stomach. I wanted nothing more than to hear his voice, despite it being less than twenty-four hours since I'd been in bed next to him. Every time I felt the temptation

I fought it away, knowing that just the sound of his voice could result in me turning around and heading right back to him.

Fourteen or so hours later, I'd made it. As much as I wanted to explore, making it to my dorm was all I had left in me.

My dorm was more or less on the Brown University campus, a building JWU had rented out due to the overflow of students. It wasn't close to most of my classes but I had picked it due to it being so close to Thayer Street and downtown Providence. The building itself was old and had great, albeit rundown, architecture. Entering my new place I followed the narrow hallway past a tiny airplane size bathroom to the left and a single bedroom to the right before reaching the end where the largest room sat. Despite having arrived early my first roommate, or at least her stuff, had arrived and claimed the single room. I looked over the larger room, which had two extra-long twin beds, with mattresses that could possibly be as old as the building itself and were exactly what you would expect to see in a prison cell. There were two wooden desks with matching chairs sitting next to each bed. At least the room had two large windows, one facing the front of the building, and the other looking off to the side over the trees. I decided to settle on the side with the view of the trees.

The endless cappuccinos or Red Bulls, or the Vivarin I had kept popping to stay awake—or the combination—had left me with one hell of a caffeine buzz. Even though I'd stopped driving, my mind's eye continued to play the sight of the road, over and over again, until I developed a fun case of tunnel vision. I was immediately thankful I decided to bring along my oversized feather comforter, and after a quick, awkward shower, I lay down and passed out.

Chapter Ten

I awoke the next day in an almost immediate state of panic. It took me a good thirty seconds to figure out where exactly I was, and then another ten seconds after that to feel completely overwhelmed with where I'd found myself.

What did I do? I can't do this alone; I don't know a single person here.

Jameson, my family, Amelia—all eight hundred miles away, but it might as well have been a million. I did the one thing I knew to do in that moment—I called Jameson. I had planned on calling him in the morning anyway, knowing I needed to let him know why I left like I did, but waking like this brought it about much more abruptly.

"Sweetheart, breathe, you're okay. Breathe, you're going to be fine," he reassured me.

Hearing him call me "sweetheart" made me cry harder. I missed him and I wanted to be there with him, not hours away.

I was sitting on the bare mattress, my head virtually between my knees.

"You are there because it is the best school for what you want to do. It's not forever, and you can come visit whenever you want. You're going to get your degree, and then you can come back here and open your restaurant in OTR. You're alright, Becca."

He was so confident and sure of everything he said, I wished he was there sitting next to me and telling me all this. I almost said as much when he spoke again.

"Have you met your new roommate yet?"

"No!" It sounded way more pathetic and whiney than I intended it to. I didn't want to meet my new roommate while I was curled up in a human ball crying all over myself.

"Alright, Becca, you don't want to be crying and snotting when you meet your roommate, do you?"

"I'm totally not snotting!" I choked out, half laughing, half serious. Alright, I was totally ugly crying and sniffing all over the phone.

He laughed at my obvious downplaying of my emotions.

"Go take a shower, check your mail, and get a coffee. You've been on the road, you're not feeling completely like yourself. Call me when you get back."

"Alright." He was starting to get through to me. I got up from my bed and started to pace, checking out my new surroundings.

"Wait, why am I checking my mail?" I asked.

"I might have sent you something."

"You might have?" I teased.

"Yes, maybe. If you are a good girl and do what I tell you…" he added playfully.

"Do you have a gig tonight?" I asked in a much calmer, much more composed voice.

"Yes, I'm playing at Iron City at about ten thirty, so go get your stuff done, and call me when you get back."

"Alright, I will. Thank you." I paused momentarily. "I miss you already." It wasn't all that I wanted to say.

"I know. I miss you, too. I'll talk to you later tonight."

"Tonight." I smiled into the phone.

A battle of wills ensued. Neither of us wanted to hang up.

Chapter Eleven

After our conversation, I felt much more optimistic about being here and going after what I wanted. Of course, I wanted to rush down the stairs to check my mail, but I decided to listen to him, and dug through my boxes to retrieve my shower stuff and some clean clothes.

While the bathroom was tiny it didn't escape my attention how lucky I was to have one in my room. I let the warm water run down my hair and across my face, and calm the anxieties inside me. I had waited for this moment, and here I was, exactly where I wanted to be.

Jameson, knowing me well, had sent me the most perfect gift anyone could have gotten me—Korin knives. To many, it wouldn't seem like an amazing gift, but to an aspiring chef, the perfect knives made all the difference. And because he is who he is, he'd had them shipped directly to my dorm so they would be here when I arrived.

I looked around at the blank walls and meager furniture and reminded myself it's a clean slate.

I can do this.

In an attempt to busy myself, I started looking through the bags of stuff I'd messily packed in my haste. Deciding it would do me some good to make this place feel a bit more like home, I spent the next few hours unpacking and decorating. I managed to turn my meager bed into a pretty comfortable one, thanks to five hundred thread count sheets and an overabundance of pillows and a feather comforter.

I didn't get to call Jameson before his gig as I had hoped because my new roommate, Kera, arrived with her entourage of family members. Kera appeared to be as nervous as I was, which strangely made me feel more at ease. After we made our introductions they invited me to go have dinner with them, and I accepted in the hope that distracting myself would be a benefit.

Being with Kera and her family made me miss mine that much more. Kera was about five foot four with a slender build, and red hair and green eyes that matched her mother and older brother. She and her brother shared a closeness that was evident. They laughed at each other's jokes that nobody else at the table seemed to get.

Without realizing what I was doing I mindlessly scraped my fork across my plate, playing with what was left of my chicken parmesan. I should have spent more time with my family before I left, but in the little time I'd had at home I couldn't keep my distance from Jameson. I didn't regret a second of my time with him but I never could have imagined how all-encompassing our short relationship would end up being.

My phone vibrated and I nearly jumped out of my skin, unable to dig it out of my pocket quickly enough.

>How's Providence?

Almost immediately my phone vibrated again, another message from Jameson.

>I miss you.

"What's got you so happy all of a sudden?" Kera asked, bringing the attention of everyone at the table on me.

"Oh." I blushed. "Just... someone back home."

"A boyfriend?" Kera's grin was wide as she asked excitedly.

"Oh, I don't know... not sure how I feel about the whole long-distance thing," I replied, hoping it would take the attention off me.

"See Kera, that's what I was trying to tell you!" her dad said excitedly while pointing his meatball-covered fork at her. "You can't start the next chapter of your life when you are holding onto the past!"

Kera reacted with an eye-roll, then she looked at her mother for support.

"He's right, I'm afraid. You can't create the future you want for yourself when you're holding onto someone who is going in a different direction."

I felt responsible for Kera's dinnertime lecture, but worse than that, their words, while painful, were true.

"It could be worse!" I said, stealing everyone's attention. "We could be two single girls looking for a kegger!" I added.

A moment of silence passed before everyone started laughing, and I breathed a quick sigh of relief that after only just meeting them I already felt comfortable.

I looked down at my phone and ran my fingers across the screen. I missed Jameson so much, but how long could I hold onto something that could never be?

Chapter Twelve

Over the next few days, I made a pretty ineffective attempt at diving into my new college life. I knew the importance of getting off to a good start but found myself texting and emailing Jameson every chance I had. The more I talked to him, the more I wanted to be there and not here. It didn't take long for me to realize I couldn't be in both places at the same time. It was the end for Jameson and me—at least that is what I kept telling myself. There was no way for me to focus on what I wanted while longing for what I couldn't have. I couldn't say the idea of a long-distance relationship hadn't crossed my mind, but I knew it was too unrealistic. It would never work. He has his band, and I refused to think about all the women that went along with that. I wouldn't lose my focus on my own dreams. I would make this happen, just without him.

Despite my best efforts to listen to the lecture playing out before me, I was watching the clock. Admittedly, business classes, while important, were far too hands-off for me. I did much better when my hands were busy, hence my love for cooking.

It was just before noon, and Jameson was going to call me at any moment. Generally, it was a conversation I looked forward to every day, but all too quickly I'd realized it was more than just something I looked forward to— it was something I relied on. As pathetic as it was to admit, I woke up every day willing to push through until noon when I got to talk to him. After that it was the final push through classes and dinner until I could talk to him again. Everything happened around me, but nothing happened *to* me, because I was too busy with my head in my phone, texting and missing him, while everyone else was actually participating in their lives.

A shuffling around the room alerted me to the fact that class had been dismissed.

I piled my book and notebook into my oversized purse and was heading toward the door when I felt my phone vibrating in my pocket. I had to fight the urge to let the call go to voicemail.

"Hello?" I answered.

"Becca!" His voice always held the same sweet, excited tone, as if it had been weeks since we'd last spoke.

"Hey," I said, the dread I felt intentionally disguising itself as boredom.

"How are you doing?" His voice was now tentative and questioning, and knowing him as I did, I could imagine the confusion that would be lining the features of his face.

I paused, not sure how to answer that question.

"I'm just leaving class," I said, avoiding his question.

Now it was him who paused.

I walked down the street looking for somewhere private to have this conversation. Finally, I settled on a small park with a few benches and a solitary fountain.

"What's going on, Becca?"

Did he know me so well that he had me figured out after just a few words? The tears were already threatening to fall as I tried to focus on what it was I needed to say.

"Things have just gone so fast for us," I said.

True, but a total lie. Things had moved quickly, but I was just as wrapped up as he was. I could pretend that his telling me he loved me scared me, but really I was scared because I knew I loved him too.

I could hear him exhale through the phone, and I held my breath waiting for his response.

"I didn't want to push you, Becca. I guess sometimes I have a hard time not saying exactly what it is I'm thinking."

"You didn't push me—I just—I can't be in two places at once all the time." When he said nothing, I continued. "I can't be here but have my thoughts tangled up in you."

"Becca—" His tone held so much I couldn't bear to hear the words that were going to come next.

"I just can't, Jameson," I interrupted.

Another exhale came from his end of the line, and in my mind I could clearly see his hand going to his dark wavy hair and running his fingers through it in frustration. I missed him, and I missed tracing my fingers across the bold colors of his forearm tattoo—the hummingbird with the thorns that he never had told me the meaning of. I missed the roughness of his five o'clock shadow abrading my neck as he kissed his way down from my ear to my chest.

"Alright."

Alright? That's it? Why does that instantly piss me off?

"Alright," I repeated. There was nothing else to say.

I waited until he hung up the phone, unable to be the first to do so. It struck me as odd that for the last few weeks, like a couple teenagers, we never could hang up. Usually, it was me that had to give in, but this time it was him, and this time would be the last time.

Refusing to allow myself to wallow, I got up and headed to my next class. Even though I was going to be late I wasn't about to go home and feel sorry for myself. My resolve, however, seemed to diminish further with each step, and the tears that I refused to allow to fall did so of their own volition. It seemed as though there was no right or wrong answer. As much as I wanted to focus solely on school, what good did it do if not being *with* Jameson didn't change the fact that he consumed my every waking thought?

Chapter Thirteen

My easiest, yet most annoying, class so far had to be professional development. The combination of having to learn about things I already knew, and the monotone voice of my professor, resulted in my near-constant inability to pay attention. The upside was I had a semester behind me already. Absently, I scrolled through the contacts on my phone. I lied to myself, acting as if this was a mindless task since I couldn't seem to focus on "Choosing Professional References", yet another chapter in this two-hundred-dollar textbook that could be easily be considered common sense. I stopped at Jameson's name. I'd started and then deleted at least a hundred text messages.

If I'd hit the send button, would he have responded? If he hadn't, what would it have meant? Had he moved on and found someone else? Or maybe he would have responded, thinking of me as little more than a girl from his past he'd spent one summer with. Maybe that's all it ever was: a moment in time that was exactly what it was supposed to be—a relationship that could only survive in the past, like a memory. Even the thought inflicted a certain amount of pain.

Didn't he miss me as I missed him? One text message was all he'd ever sent me. Two words— *Still here*. What did it even mean? I'd written a million responses that never met the send button, and spent more time analyzing those two words than any paper I'd written during my entire first semester. Ultimately, I'd only ever been able to come to one conclusion, and it was his text message that led me there. He was there, and I was here. It wasn't just the miles that separated us, but the trajectory of life, plain and simple. Our lives were not the same.

I refocused myself on the professor and reminded myself why I was here. My personal pep talk echoed through my mind, and I vowed to stay busy at all costs. Idle time led to thoughts of Jameson.

When my class ended I walked the now familiar streets back to my side of town. Like many things, my walk was now part of my routine, but slowly the stores that were once a blur began to come into focus. The endless flyers for frat parties seemed just a little more intriguing, and all the faces that were once blank were starting to show their features. I wouldn't allow myself to think of Jameson anymore, hoping stupidly he'd come here to see me. Instead of home, I headed to a local soup kitchen and spent the rest of the day's free time thinking about someone other than myself (and Jameson).

***

I stared at the mound of books covering the surface of my bed, flipping the eraser end of my pencil on the book I'd been unsuccessfully trying to read for the last hour. I caught Kera's stare from the other side of the room.

"Sorry." I realized I'd probably been driving her crazy with my preoccupied pencil thumping.

After a few more moments of silence, I asked, "You want to go do something?"

"You mean other than studying?" she asked, now more interested.

"Yes."

"Thank God!" she exclaimed. "Does this mean you're finally over J—"

"Don't! Don't say his name! I'm sick of hearing myself talk about him."

I knew she had got to be sick of hearing about him. God love her, she'd been listening to me stammer and cry about him for the last few months. In all fairness, I'd really only cried and stammered for about a month. The next couple of months were really just full of me bringing him up on occasion, and her bringing him up when it was obvious he was running circles in my mind. It's crazy how quickly you get to know someone when you are sharing such close quarters. She didn't understand why I'm so opposed to the long-distance thing, and why I'd not been interested in dating anyone here. Honestly, she was about as much of a social butterfly as I'd been.

"So, what should we do?" I ask.

"It's Friday... frat party?"

The interesting thing about frat parties is: A, there is no shortage, and B, they literally come pick you up from your dorm and walk you (with a big crowd of eager freshmen) to the frat house. I'd be lying if

I said I didn't feel a little awkward. This was my first official frat party and I was following a bunch of giddy girls dressed like they were headed to a nightclub in Miami, not Providence in October.

Despite also being a junior, Kera had never been to one either, and we'd decided it was an important rite of passage for anyone who goes away to school. So we followed our herd to one of the residential streets off campus and an old three-story house converted into a frat house.

We paid five bucks for our red solo cup and unlimited trips to the kegs strewn about. That was if we could make our way through the crowds of endless people packing every single room of the place. Kera clung to my hoodie as I made my way through the house to find the nearest keg, which in this case was the kitchen. Before I was able to take my first drink—

"COPS, COPS, COPS!!!" someone yelled, and people immediately scattered. Kera started to take off but I grabbed her by the shirt and pulled her toward the stairs that led to the second floor.

"Relax, there aren't any cops." I told a scared-looking Kera. "They do this to get everyone out and keep their money. Besides, you're twenty-one—we're fine."

By then we'd made it to a window overlooking the front yard, and there wasn't a police car in sight.

"Hey, can I buy you girls a drink?" some kid in a Penguins jersey asked us. Before I responded Kera grabbed his arm.

"You sure can." She grinned up at him.

Instead of pointing out that since we already had our cups the beer was free, I followed them down to the bottom floor. Apparently, my little friend had been waiting a long time to come out of her shell and had picked tonight to make that happen.

It was funny to see Kera let loose so much. She smiled eagerly and blinked rapidly at Frank, which is what Kera had been calling him, although I was quite sure that wasn't actually his name. I had to pause for a moment and mentally calculate the number of drinks she'd had. If I didn't know her better I might think she was totally playing up the "drunk girl" persona she was putting on, but knowing her as I did, and the sheltered life she'd had, it wouldn't surprise me if she was pretty lit from a beer and a half.

Just when I had decided I was content sipping my beer while Kera lived out her frat party fantasy, I felt someone's eyes watching me. I was sitting on a love seat, which by the way may have been an exact replica of the one in my grandparents' house back when I was eight years old, minus the plastic covering that would stick to my legs. On the couch next to me sat Kera and "Frank", although most of their conversation was (thankfully) out of my earshot as she batted her eyes while sitting on his lap.

I chanced a look at the person currently burning a hole in my head and was pleasantly surprised. He stood toward the corner of the room with two other guys, who appeared to be having an in-depth conversation about something of the utmost importance. If I'd had to guess I'd have said it might have been something like the difference between light beer and regular, or which magazine had the best articles, *Penthouse* or *Playboy*.

That last thought prompted a smile on my face, which he took as an invitation, and he walked over and took a seat on the couch next to me.

"Mind if I join you?" He flashed a confident, toothy grin.

I took a big swig of my beer, secretly wishing I'd had more to drink. As bad as that sounded, a little alcohol goes a long way and helps me not come off so damn awkward.

"You want to watch Kera and Frank make out, too?" I asked with mocked enthusiasm.

"Actually, I came here to save you from watching them make out."

"Good enough for me! You lead the way!" I stood from the couch, secretly patting myself on the back for being bolder than came naturally.

A quick moment of panic filled me as I followed him up to the third floor. Maybe it was too many of those damn videos they showed in high school about avoiding date rape, or maybe it was just my paranoid and overactive imagination. I followed, calculating my exits along the way.

Instead of the sudden death I had anticipated, the staircase led to a tiki-themed balcony that overlooked the street below and a few random people puking in bushes.

"I'm Lucas by the way." He handed me my beer that he had refilled along the way.

"Becca," I said as I accepted. "You go to JWU also?" I asked, hoping our conversation wouldn't be strained and inevitably result in me making up an excuse to go check on my friend.

As it turned out, Lucas, despite his appearance as a clean-cut, preppy, rich kid, actually went to a local art college in Providence and was an artist, or at least aspiring to be an artist. I took his offer to paint me as an icebreaker, although I might have been a little naïve in thinking that. He was pretty good looking, but unfortunately, it was easy to get the impression that he thought he was too, which ultimately just made him less attractive.

Maybe it was the fact that I was bored—or maybe it was the beer—but even though I wasn't necessarily into him, that didn't stop me from a little light making out. When he kissed me the first time we hit teeth, which, let's face it, is like the ultimate indication that the two of us just weren't meant to kiss again. Once more, a signal I decided to ignore. Once our kissing reached a more agreeable pace I couldn't stop my mind from trying to ascertain the familiarity of the orange citrus taste and smell of his breath. He had been chewing gum prior to our make-out session, a fact I realized as he pulled the gum from his mouth and wadded it up before staring intently in my eyes (a lead up I could have done without).

The taste was so familiar—not good familiar I might add—but something I couldn't place.

And just like that, it hit me and immediately I stopped our kiss. The toilet bowl cleaner I always used while cleaning my bathroom. Orange Zest, or something like that.

"I think I better go check on my friend!" I said as I unceremoniously jumped away from him.

Slightly embarrassed, I didn't turn back as I made my way down the stairs. Oh well, I'd likely never see him again, but what actually bothered me was the moment had only made me miss Jameson.

Chapter Fourteen

I jolted awake knowing even before my eyes opened that I'd overslept. I threw my covers off and ran to the bathroom, trying to figure out if I had time to make it to my class or if it was a lost cause. It's funny how alert you can be when you wake up after oversleeping. If only I were that alert every day when I awoke.

Quickly, I decided it was better to be late to class than to miss it altogether. I threw my hair up in a messy bun, washed my face, and grabbed a pair of black leggings and a sweater. I was out the door as soon as the last of the toothpaste was rinsed from my mouth.

As I swung open the double doors of my building I had to push against the strong winds I hadn't realized were present until I made my way outside. Looking up at the dark ominous sky it was apparent a storm wasn't too far away, and I could only hope I made it to class before being stuck in a downpour.

I looked longingly at the people outside at the bus stop and wished I had the time to wait, but I knew it would be quicker if I just walked.

Walking from my dorm to where my classes were was, on a nice day, beautiful. My side of town was hilly, and if you had money to spend, the plethora of stores offered anything you could want and even more things you never knew you wanted. Once you made it downtown it was pretty flat and usually full of people making their way around.

When I was about five minutes from my class the sky opened up and the rain came pelting down, scattering the people that crowded the busy sidewalks. Since I had woken up late and without my normal senses, I had left without an umbrella.

Thankfully, I consider myself more of an optimist, and decided the rain would at least cover up my hair being in such disarray. That is, of course, unless I got struck by lightning. That thought brought my eyes back to the sky, and somehow I convinced myself the high-rise buildings surrounding me offered some protection from such a possibility.

It was a quarter after ten by the time I tried to sneak into my Business

Law class. Of course, everyone turned to look at me and I was relieved to see my professor's face quickly change from annoyance to pity when he took in my dripping wet appearance. I smiled at his reaction to me and took my seat, and quickly pulled my laptop from my completely soaked bag.

I was thankful I'd decided to make it to class. Finals were a week away—now was not the time to be missing classes.

As much as I loved the way Johnson & Wales was spread out across Providence, it was days like today that made me wish the buildings were closer together. But by five o'clock I'd reached to my favorite dining hall, a café of sorts that had around twenty seats. While it was limited when it came to the menu, I preferred it over the other dining halls, which were much more like my high school cafeteria and had an overabundance of people. Usually, I ate dinner with Kera and a few friends but I'd decided it was best that I use the time to study.

The cold rain continued, and as much as I wanted to wait it out so I could walk home it was already getting dark and the rain had begun to change into sleet.

I stepped into the cold air and immediately pulled the neck of my sweater up to try to protect myself from the chill that filled me. Looking at my watch I realized it would be another hour before the next bus would be running.

"Share my umbrella?" I looked up, startled at the voice that had snuck up on me.

I hoped my face didn't show the reaction I felt immediately when I looked toward him. His sandy blonde hair had somehow managed to stay perfectly in place despite the wind and rain. His eyes were a crystal blue and his strong, defined jawline was somehow made even better by the slight stubble across his face.

Suddenly I wished I had spent more time on my appearance today, although the weather would have long since removed all my efforts.

"Yes, thank you," I said, after realizing my eyes had most likely lingered a bit too long on him.

"Where to?"

"Where are you headed?" I asked, assuming I'd walk with him until we headed in different directions.

He looked down at his watch as a smile slowly played across his thin lips.

"Nowhere for about two hours. You lead the way." His smile stayed as our eyes met again, and suddenly my stomach did a little flip. His eyes were trouble. Not the bad boy kind of trouble, but the kind that could easily persuade.

"I live near Brown so just as far as you're going. And thank you for the umbrella." I smiled, chancing another look his way.

"Brown it is then!"

I glanced at him, my face apparently showing the argument lingering beneath the surface.

"No arguing. My mother would never forgive me if I left a lady to walk such a long way in the rain."

I smiled at his chivalry, which seemed to come so naturally to him. It seemed obvious to me when a guy was forcing it just to make himself look good.

"I'm Maddox by the way." He smiled as he switched the umbrella to his other hand so he could hold his right one out to me to shake it.

"Becca." I smiled while accepting his hand.

We began our walk and suddenly my mind filled with worry. It occurred to me in that moment that I had nothing of interest to say, and decided that if it got too uncomfortably quiet I'd make my exit early.

"When I offered my umbrella I assumed it would be a little more helpful in actually keeping you dry," he said, breaking me from my thought process.

We laughed briefly at our predicament when suddenly the steady sideways sleet/rain turned into a complete downpour.

"Coffee?" He eyed the Starbucks just across the street. His face registered shock at the sheets of rain that were succeeding in completely soaking us head to toe.

I gave a quick nod and we both started jogging, despite the fact we were already completely soaked. By the time we reached the entrance, we were both laughing.

Standing beneath the awning I uselessly brushed my arms to get off the excess water as Maddox held the door open for me.

My stomach flipped when I realized, for the second time, that I was too nervous around this man to think of anything meaningful to say. I said a silent prayer that I could just pause my awkwardness for the next half hour or so.

As we weren't the only ones who'd taken shelter inside the Starbucks, the line was long and I motioned to the bathroom in the back.

"Maybe I'll just—"

"Of course, what would you like?" Maddox asked, smiling as he watched me tuck a stray strand of wet hair behind my ear.

"Vanilla Latte," I said, already feeling the warmth it would provide.

"Shit," I said aloud as I took in my appearance. My hair was a disaster with miscellaneous wet strands heading in all different directions. Quickly I pulled the hair tie from my head and flipped my head over, trying to shake out the wetness and bring some life back to it. The rain had brought out the natural curl so I was actually able to leave it down. Taking in my reflection I was thankful I had forgone my normal makeup routine since that only would have resulted in black smudges under my eyes anyway. I pinched my cheeks and was ready to walk out the door when a smell wafted its way to my nose. Mortification struck me instantly as I grabbed my sweater and pulled it abruptly to my face. Yep - I smelled like an old wet sweater. I Quickly pulled it over my head and held it between my knees as I smelled my white tank top.

"Thank you," I said aloud once again, apparently thanking the Gods of Stinky Clothes that my undershirt still smelled of my perfume, and my white shirt hadn't ended up see-through thanks to Mother Nature.

After doing one more once-over in the mirror I made my way back to Maddox who was now seated at a small two-seater table next to a warm fireplace.

He glanced up briefly and then did a double take as I came toward him giving my best fake-confident smile.

"Hi... Hey," he stammered as he stood up, his hand motioning to the open chair across from him.

He gave me a somewhat puzzled look which sent a quick jolt of nerves through me.

"Was there a salon in there?" His eyes darted quickly from me to the bathroom I had come from.

"Stop." I laughed nervously, my hand going to my face and covering my mouth in embarrassment.

As if sensing my discomfort he grabbed a cookie from the plate between us.

"I got you a cookie." I'd daresay his smile was sweet and innocent but taking one look at him I knew better.

"Thank you." I returned his smile and accepted the cookie, breaking off a small piece and putting it in my mouth.

I tried my best to chew politely, a little self-conscious as he watched me.

"So, you go to school in Providence?" he asked, and took a sip of his whipped cream-covered drink.

"Yes, Johnson and…Wales." I paused briefly mid-sentence as he tried, unsuccessfully I might add, to maneuver his lips around the mound of whipped cream.

Apparently my amusement showed on my face as his eyebrows popped up and he watched me speculatively.

"Don't even say it!" he said with laughter in his tone as he set the drink down and grabbed a napkin to dab his face. "So I like the frilly whipped cream-covered girl drinks!"

I laughed quietly at his mock anger.

"I'm okay with that, and felt it was best we got that out into the open up-front," he continued, now trying to pull the laughter from his features.

"It's best you were up-front; I'm afraid for me it's a deal breaker." I kept my face completely straight.

He froze for a moment, watching me as if trying to figure out if I was being serious. Without skipping a beat or looking from my eyes his hand moved to the cookies between us.

"Well then." He paused, briefly keeping his eyes pasted on mine. "You're not allowed to have any. More. Cookie!" He quickly went for the plate and pulled it toward himself.

"You wouldn't," I deadpanned. Mock horror pasted its way across my face.

"You've done this to yourself."

I stuck my bottom lip out and gave him the most pathetically sad face I could muster.

"Oh, that was low."

He shook his head back and forth at me, the amusement showing in his eyes.

"Here's your cookie." His words were slow and defeated as he slid the plate back to the middle of the table.

"Thank you." I grinned triumphantly as I took the cookie, broke off another small piece and put it in my mouth as he watched amused.

Again he shook his head at me, one corner of his mouth tipped up in a subtle grin.

We spent the next half hour chatting about majors and classes while the rain cascaded down and pelted against the windows. Maddox, as it turned out, was a student at Brown, and lived off-campus with his cousin who was much more like a brother to him. Even though he was from Boston, it sounded like I visited home much more often than he did.

The sudden silence caught my attention and my eyes went to the window, where despite the now-darkened sky, it was apparent the rain had stopped.

"I should go while it's not raining." I glanced at my phone to catch the time.

"At least let me walk you. Or drive… my car is just down the street," he said hopefully.

"Your car?" I eyed him suspiciously.

"Yeah… well, I didn't think you would take a ride from someone you didn't know, but now that I've fed you cookies I figure I'm far less creepy."

I couldn't help but grin back at his playfulness and I suddenly realized that my face hurt from the last half hour of sitting across from this sweet, sexy stranger. I hadn't had such a fun, enjoyable conversation with a man in a long time and the thought brought an unwanted darkness to my mood. I looked away quickly, hoping he hadn't caught on to my inner moodiness.

"No, that's okay." I pasted a smile to my face. "I should walk." I started to gather my things. "Thank you for the coffee though, and the cookie."

His hand reached for mine, which was still holding onto my phone resting on the table.

"At least take my number." He paused. "In case the rain starts up again," he continued in explanation.

I thought for a moment before handing my phone over to him. What harm could come from letting him have my number? I could always not answer.

Chapter Fifteen

Needless to say, he did call, and when he did it only took me about half a second to make the decision to answer it. I told Kera about our coffee and she insisted I see him again.

"Any guy who would leave his car and offer to walk you in the rain is a keeper."

She made a valid point. Honestly, it just felt good to feel good again, and I wasn't ready to give that up again so quickly.

Despite my newfound confidence, by ten a.m. on Saturday, I had gotten myself worried and nervous to the point of just not wanting to go on our date at all. I had nothing to wear, and I realized I was in a strange city and knew relatively nothing about the guy. On the upside, when we'd met I looked like a drowned rat so pretty much anything would be an improvement on that. Kera was excited but promised to sneak a picture of his license plate when we left in case I ended up dead. Reassuring.

By eleven a.m. Kera had worked my confidence and excitement up, and so began the eight-hour process of getting ready. To be fair, I did spend four of those hours shopping. Thank goodness for used books—I actually had a little money left in the bank.

I hadn't been this nervous about a date in a long time…probably because I hadn't actually been on a date in a long time. Regardless of the reason, I was having real difficulty calming myself down. There was zero chance I'd be able to eat at dinner.

Thankfully, for December in Providence we were actually having a warm day, and after trying on countless outfits I settled on tan skinny pants with my knee-high brown boots, a white cable knit sweater, and a tan-colored cashmere scarf that matched my pants perfectly. One positive thing about winter is that my hair actually cooperates and on this occasion it was looking good with some wavy curls. I was in full panic mode when I got his call from downstairs. To avoid the whole roommate meet and greet I told him I'd meet him at the entrance of the building.

Maddox somehow managed to look even more gorgeous than I'd remembered him, although I didn't think that was possible. His confident smile showed off his perfect teeth. I didn't actually look around the lobby of my dorm but I could feel the stares from all the women. I had no doubt that had he wanted he could have gotten at least four phone numbers in the two minutes it had taken me to make it down from the fourth floor.

"Hi," I said, nervously smiling as I stood in front of him.

I had no control over my body language and noticed, after the fact, of course, I kind of shrugged my shoulders in my hello as if in an attempt to hide from him, or myself. Hopefully, he didn't notice.

"Don't be nervous," he whispered to me so the drooling girls didn't hear him. "I promise to have you home before you turn into a pumpkin."

Crap, he noticed.

We made our way out of the building and I explained to him.

"Actually, I'm pretty sure it's our transportation that would turn into a pumpkin; I would turn into a lowly servant."

"Oh no, not my Tesla!"

Only once we reached his car did I realize what he was talking about.

"Tesla? You named your car?"

Although if any car deserved a name it would be this one. It would certainly be considered a luxury car. While it wasn't a sports car it was equally jaw-dropping. Honestly, I didn't know what it was, but it looked like it would put a BMW to shame. I reached the passenger side and waited for a moment trying to figure out how to go about opening the door as there was no obvious handle. Before I could make an idiot out of myself he hit a button on his keys which made the door handles pop out. Then he opened the door for me.

He waited for me to get in so he could close the door. In the moment it took him to walk around the car I was able to take in a few things. Firstly, this car was crazy. It had a huge touch screen where the radio would be and beautiful tan leather everywhere. The second thought that occurred to me was that this guy was way out of my league.

"Actually, my car's name is Superman. Tesla is the make of the car." He laughed. "Tesla would be an odd name for a car, don't you think?"

He was doing a good job calming me down, and we spent the rest of the short ride talking about dorm life.

"I gotta say, I don't miss living in a dorm. I'm pretty darn happy sharing a loft with my cousin a little off-campus."

"Oh that's nice; does your cousin go to Brown also?" I asked.

"Actually, he graduated. He is kind of enjoying life right now before he dives into the real world."

We made our way through Providence and a smile immediately came across my face as we drove under the gateway arch into Federal Hill.

"*La Pigna,*" I said slightly under my breath, more to myself than to Maddox.

Maddox turned his head and looked at me questioningly as he navigated the car through the stone arch.

"*La Pigna,*" I repeated. "That little thing at the top of the arch."

"I always thought that was a pineapple; is that not right?" He eyes ping-ponged between me and the road as he drove along the quaint streets lined with various coffee shops, restaurants, and shops.

"It's actually a pinecone, although I think eighty-five percent of the people living here would agree with the pineapple idea. The pinecone is actually an Italian symbol of welcome, abundance, and quality. And maybe one of these days I'll open my own Italian restaurant here with my own little *La Pigna.*

"Oh good, I take it that means you like Italian?" he asked as we pulled into the valet section of Lorenzo's, a beautiful Italian restaurant. The outside was stunning, with a black wrought iron fence adorned with white twinkling lights and a brick walkway through flower gardens. It was exactly how I would picture an old Italian restaurant to look. I noticed Maddox nod to the valet so he could be the one to open the door for me, and I tried to withhold the cheesy grin that threatened my lips.

Holding his hand to the small of my back, Maddox led me inside. The walls were a pale yellow with dark wood exposed beams, wooden floors, and tables were preset with double-layered white tablecloths and oversized back leather chairs. He told them the name for the reservation and the maître d' led us to the back of the restaurant to our secluded table. Maddox was so confident, yet friendly with everyone, and despite having only begun to get to know him I already had a sneaking suspicion I was going to like him.

We ordered dinner—nine courses of the chef's specialties—an

incredible combination of flavors that would leave even a world-renowned chef salivating. Few words were spoken as we sampled and marveled over each dish.

"How could you have known that, while I love all food, Italian has got to be my favorite?"

"I guess I'm just lucky like that. I'm glad you liked it."

"Like would be a serious understatement; it was delectable. The roasted mushrooms were unbelievable. Paired with a fried egg and ricotta salata it could be its own food group."

"I like how excited you get when you talk about food. I have no idea what egg and ricotta salata is but the way you talk about it makes me feel like I'm really missing out." His grin was appreciative.

"Mmm, you are!" I returned his infectious smile, and couldn't help but marvel briefly at how easy it was to be myself with him. I hadn't felt that way with a guy since—I shook away the thought.

With this marvelous meal also came a wine pairing for each entrée. I didn't overdo the drinking, it's just that I don't make it enough of a habit to be able to build any sort of tolerance whatsoever. Honestly though, I was thankful for the buzz to dissolve my nerves a bit. After dinner, we made our way back through Providence so he could introduce me to WaterFire for the first time.

"I can't believe you haven't been here before! We're lucky they are having a lighting this late in the year, usually the last one is in November. So what have you been doing all this time?"

That made me a laugh a little. "I've been going to class and studying!"

"Well, it's about time you live a little." He grinned at me while we walked through the brick walkways and tunnels on each side of the river. In the middle of the river were basin lightings with flames that reached about four feet in the air. The combination of the fire and the lights of the city reflecting on the water was an amazing thing. It was also the perfect romantic scene.

Making our way through the people on the walkways, we spotted a place to sit along the edge of the river. We watched the display and he told me about his involvement with Big Brothers and Big Sisters, and his "little brother" Anthony. With a great fondness, he explained how he hoped his influence would help the boy realize he could do whatever he wants with his life, despite growing up in not the best of circumstances. It was nice to hear him talk about his little brother with such excitement and passion. He had so much hope for this boy and showed a sweet, soft side.

I decided to stand because the thin fabric of my pants was not mixing well with the cold concrete. Maddox swung his legs around so his back was to the river and put his hands on my waist, moving me so I was standing between his legs facing him. His touch brought the nerves I had been feeling earlier back with a vengeance and I couldn't help but smile at him.

"I don't like you at all." I grinned, the lie slipping from my mouth before I really had a chance to think it through.

"You don't?" His grin matched my own.

"No. It's such a relief really, I was kind of worried about it," I explained.

Before I could gauge his reaction to my fib, he stood right in front of me, making the distance between us almost nonexistent. The difference in our height meant that I had to look up at him, and with his two fingers he tilted my chin up and kissed me. This wasn't a hesitant, tentative kiss, but more of the kind of kiss to prove me wrong. Before anything could become inappropriate in such a public place he pulled away, but he held my hand and we walked along the river. Keeping the surprise off my face wasn't a simple thing; he'd literally stolen my breath.

As we walked along the cobblestone, his hand in mine, suddenly a blanket of relief clothed me. Somehow being in Providence felt not only where I needed to be, but where I wanted to be.

All too soon he brought me back to my dorm and walked me to the front door of my building. I wanted to invite him up to "watch a movie" but thought better of it. I was more impressed that he didn't ask to come up.

"Becca, thank you for coming out with me tonight. And I'm glad you didn't turn into a lowly servant after all."

"Thank you, I had a great time."

He tilted my head up again and gave me a sweet peck on the lips before taking a step back. Before I could second-guess myself I grabbed the lapels of his jacket and pulled him to me so I could show him how that kiss should have gone. As our lips and tongues explored, he grabbed me around my waist tighter and pulled me up against him so our bodies became one. With his other hand, he stroked the back of my neck and into my hair, causing my entire body to tingle all at once. This time, I was the first to pull away.

"Goodnight." I smiled and walked into my building.

I tried to play it cool but in my peripheral vision I noticed he was still standing there, unmoving. I reveled in my small victory. It's fun to have the upper hand for once as I generally feel like I'm the one always following behind, guessing what the guy is thinking.

Let him guess.

Chapter Sixteen

With newfound energy, I made my way upstairs and into my dorm.

As soon as I walked in the door Kera jumped up from her bed and the piles of textbooks that covered it.

"Alright, you need to explain that grin!"

Was I grinning? I hadn't noticed.

"Well… how was it?"

"Pretty great, actually."

I told her all about the amazing dinner at Lorenzo's, WaterFire, and the kiss that I'd felt from my very toes to the top of my head.

"Did he say he was going to call you or ask you out again?" Excitement filled her features.

Oh crap.

Maybe I shouldn't have been so excited to leave him wanting more. I'd be lying if I said I played it cool and didn't stress about not hearing from Maddox.

The first postdate stage is confidence. I didn't imagine it, he had a great time too—we definitely had a connection. The second stage is a much more pathetic one. What if that peck at the end of the date was a sign and I totally missed it! I made a complete ass of myself! The third stage is one of self-preservation. I don't like him that much anyway and have totally had my eye on (insert random guy's name) in my (fill in the blank) class. If you do get that much-desired phone call then stage four is one of relief, followed by feeling like a complete ass for being so worried for the last few days.

Stage four came on Monday when he texted me in the middle of my International Cuisine and Culinary Cultures class.

Like a total ass, I stared at his text message with a ridiculously over-the-top ear-to-ear grin. Nothing more than "I had fun, you busy this weekend?", yet I couldn't hide the excitement that radiated through me. Then, as he did every single day, Jameson popped into my mind stealing the smile away. Could Maddox measure up against Jameson? I had to make a conscious effort not to compare the two.

It isn't that I'm the type of girl who can't be alone, the kind that needs a man to keep me happy. The problem was that after my date with Maddox it just felt so nice to be so happy and excited for something. I couldn't help but relish in those feelings, and it didn't help that Maddox was ridiculously gorgeous and drop dead sexy, and all that was wrapped up in such a charming personality.

As the week went by, it seemed just a bit easier to wake up a little earlier than usual to make sure I wasn't running out the door in so much haste that I didn't have time to fix myself up. Also, I'd be lying if I said I wasn't a little more aware of my surroundings as I walked around campus and to my dorm.

By Thursday, Kera and I were both over classes, and although I was looking forward to spending more time with Maddox I was ready for our winter break, especially since I hadn't made it home for Thanksgiving.

"So, when do I get to meet Maddox?" Kera looked up from her phone.

Oddly, as much as I wanted Kera to meet him there was a big part of me that was afraid that I would somehow jinx things if I thought too much about it or made it into a bigger deal than it actually was.

"I'm not sure. I've only been out with him once." I looked away from her and back to my book that sat useless in my lap.

"You want to go get some wings?" I asked, taking the subject away from Maddox and me.

Wings on Thayer had quickly become mine and Kera's favorite place, not only for the wings, but also just a place to go hang out and sadly, take loads of online quizzes to determine our *Love Style* or *Celebrity Soul Mate*. Maybe that's a little lame but I'm proud to admit Zac Efron and I were apparently a "match made in the stars". All joking aside, it was the one place we went where there was no studying and thinking about classes was prohibited.

Located on the main part of College Hill, Wings on Thayer never disappointed in the eye candy department or the food. As we stood at the counter ordering our wings and fried cheese, my attention was diverted to the group of guys laughing in the back of the room.

"Alright, *Which Disney Prince is your Soul Mate* or *Test your Sex IQ?*"

Kera nudged me apparently ready to start the quizzes.I grabbed our tray and followed her to the small table toward the back of the restaurant.

"Wait! I found it!" Kera jumped in before I had a chance to answer.

"Will He Be Great in Bed?" She looked at me, raising her eyebrows playfully.

I couldn't help but laugh as an answer—from the way he kissed I didn't think I needed the quiz!

"This is important. Plus, better to find out before it's too late." Her lips tipped up in a smile.

I had to love Kera's sarcasm and dry sense of humor. It had occurred to me on more than one occasion that people often did not know how to take us; we could go on and on about something completely joking, but never letting on that it's a joke.

"Alright, shoot," I said, putting on my mock game face for the quiz.

"How was your first kiss? A. A tentative peck; B. Attack of the tongue (and not in a good way); or C. Slow at first but left you panting and wanting to rip each other's clothes off?"

"Ha! For sure C! Although, they forgot D. Dude's breath tastes like your toilet bowl cleaner and makes you want to puke."

"What was that guy's name again? I nearly forgot all about that." Kera laughed at my expense.

"Mr. Clean," I quipped.

When she held my gaze accusingly I conceded. "Lucas".

"Poor guy. You could have just told him to get a new mouthwash or something."

"Nah, damage was done."

"How much time does he spend staring into your eyes and holding your gaze?" She continued reading off the questions from her phone.

"What kind of bogus question is that?" I laughed, fishing my vibrating phone out of my purse.

"What kind of person still uses the word bogus?" Kera asked as she peaked at my phone nosily (not that I actually minded).

Maddox and I had been texting back and forth almost constantly about nothing in particular; nonetheless I looked forward to the very pleasant distraction.

Chapter Seventeen

On Friday, Kera and I skipped our last classes so we could take the shuttle to the airport and pick up Sara—and by shuttle I mean we pretended to be hotel guests at one of the city's nicest hotels so we could take their shuttle. On a side note, hotels such as these are a good place to stop when you were fresh out of money and toilet paper, or individual size shampoo and conditioner (not that I've ever done it).

Despite growing up together and making plans to go to the same college, Kera and Sara had ended up getting into different schools. Sara had decided to fly directly to Providence to stop in for a quick visit before she and Kera drove back home together to upstate New York. Oddly, I felt a pang of something like jealousy, secretly worried that Kera having her best friend here would somehow take away from the fact she was *my* best friend.

My attempt at a few woe-is-me moments ended abruptly when Maddox texted me to find out if I wanted to meet up with him and some of his friends that night to hit some of the bars around Brown. Once I told him about Sara being in town we quickly made plans to all meet at his place before heading out.

The snowy weather didn't deter Sara's plane and she arrived on time. As soon as I met her I knew I'd like her. A petite little thing at about five foot four, she had long straight brown hair, bright red lips, and dressed like she was ready for a night on the town, not a few hours in a plane. The first words out of her mouth after saying hello were a suggestion that we all have a drink at the airport bar.

"I think I need to find myself a Providenstonian—a Providenceian?" Sara looked at us questioningly as we gathered her luggage from the baggage claim.

"A Rhode Islander?" Kera asked, laughing at her friend.

"Whatever they are called is not the point. The point is tonight we are going to have some fun." She grinned wildly, her eyes darting from me to Kera in excitement.

We did what any responsible college student would do on a Friday night and spent our grocery money on new clothes. In all fairness, we were days away from heading home for Christmas break anyway so surviving on meal plan food wouldn't kill us.

I studied myself in the mirror, appreciative that the long walks around campus were paying off. The white long-sleeved sweater dress I was wearing came off my shoulders in a fold that fell just below my boobs, cinched in at my waist and clung tightly to my thighs. It showed off more leg than the bitter cold would agree with, and my favorite pair of brown suede boots.

"Fuck it, let the liquor keep us warm!" Sara stood in the door wearing a short red halter dress and black boots that came up to just above her knees.

"Kera!" She yelled across the small place that now felt like home to me.

"She takes forever," she whispered, rolling her eyes mockingly and slurring her words just enough to make me think it probably wasn't her first shot from the bottle that dangled loosely from her index and middle finger.

Once Kera made her presence known, we all took a couple shots, to get the party started early as Sara put it.

We took an Uber to Maddox's place as Kera laid down the law with Sara. Of course, I knew she was the more responsible one between the two of us, but I was beginning to realize that it was a role she probably had with all of her friends. Apparently, Sara was a wanderer, and had on more than one occasion taken off with a "new friend".

"You girls try to stay warm." Our Uber driver, who appeared to be in his late thirties, nearly broke his neck to watch us as we exited his Honda.

From the outside, you never would have guessed the impressive space that made up Maddox and Gabe's apartment. The elevator we took to the third floor was the type I imagined only existed in movies, with the gates you had to pull across to close yourself in. Muffled music thumped through the air from behind the door as I knocked while trying to keep my nervousness under wraps.

Maddox answered the door, and a boyish grin spread across his face as he appraised me briefly before pulling me toward him gently in a sweet, albeit brief, kiss. His hand went to mine as he stepped aside enough for the three of us to enter his place.

"Alright, who's who?" His eyes flickered between Kera and Sara.

We made quick introductions as Maddox led us to the living room where his friends were huddled around a bar which separated the large living space from the kitchen.

I guess I should have assumed Maddox had money based on his car and appearance, but I hadn't expected his place to be so impressive. It had an industrial feel to it—high ceilings, ceramic tile floors that somehow looked like concrete, and exposed brick. The kitchen alone was a dream, with dark granite countertops, stainless appliances, and a stove that any chef would be jealous of.

I had to pull my eyes away from my dream kitchen as Maddox introduced us to his friends.

"This is my cousin, Gabe, and his girlfriend Stephy." I outstretched my hand and Gabe easily accepted it. They both had a somewhat severe look to them, but, like Maddox, when Gabe smiled his whole face lit up.

"Nice to meet you." Gabe smiled and greeted the three of us while Stephy looked more like she didn't want to be bothered with us, her nose slightly upturned.

"And this is my buddy, Dave—"

His introduction was cut short since his buddy was currently chugging a beer.

"Why don't you girls grab a beer while I show Becca around?" Maddox motioned over his shoulder to the mammoth-sized refrigerator before leading me through his place, his hand still in mine.

His living room was the epitome of a bachelor pad for the wealthy. A black leather wraparound couch faced the brick fireplace that matched the walls of exposed brick, and just above that was a huge, mounted flat-screen TV like the ones that decorated the walls of every BW3's. SportsCenter played muted across the screen as we made our way upstairs to a loft.

"And this is my room here," he said as we took the last few steps up his metal stairs.

His room overlooked the rest of the apartment, but the view on the other side was the most impressive. The only light illuminating his space was being provided by the lights of Providence, which was easily within view from his floor-to-ceiling windows.

"Wow," was all I managed as he came up behind me and wrapped his arms around my waist.

"You look amazing by the way." His head dipped down and the words were spoken so near to my ear that the sensation sent tingles across my skin.

I tried to hide my blush as I thanked him and looked around his room. His bed was enormous, and I couldn't help but wonder how it was possible for him to get even an ounce of privacy up here with only a half wall and about thirty feet separating it from the rest of the apartment below.

"Well, let's go be social before I get it in my head that we should kick them all out and stay up here watching movies instead of going out." He smiled before once again leading me around his place by my hand.

The thought of being alone with him in his place had me both nervous at the thought, and thoroughly excited at the same time.

Downstairs everyone was still huddled around the bar laughing at some story Dave was reliving for their benefit.

"I swear to God, this asshole was running around Boston, convinced every cop in town was after him, and he refused to get in the car with us," Gabe added to the story I'd just walked in on.

"And where were you, Maddie? I can't for the life of me remember!" Stephy asked while looking accusingly at Maddox. At that everyone's laughing ceased.

Maddie? I'd known her for five minutes and already I was convinced she was a bitch who might just be a complete pain in my ass.

Apparently, it wasn't just me who thought she was being weird, since Gabe gave her a questioning look, while Maddox's was much more lethal.

Someone quickly changed the subject and we sat around the bar talking and drinking some sort of imported beer before deciding it was time to head to Screwdrivers, a local bar the guys had talked us all into.

"Where's your trash?" I asked as I finished off the last of my Modelo while everyone was putting on their coats.

Gabe motioned toward the side of the refrigerator and I made my way to dispose of my beer when a picture hanging on the fridge immediately grabbed my attention. It was Gabe, Stephy, Dave, a guy I didn't recognize, and Maddox with his arms possessively wrapped around a smiling, gorgeous platinum blonde model type. My gut immediately sunk the second I took in the picture. Just as I was willing myself to look away from the picture there it was in plain sight. Her head rested against him in such a way that I couldn't make out her features, but on the ring finger of her left hand was one obnoxiously-sized diamond that would have been completely acceptable to any celebrity.

I tried to pull myself away, but by then the damage had been done.

"Oh, he hasn't told you about Izzy yet?" Stephy's smile was presumptuous, and maybe if she hadn't snuck up on me I wouldn't have been surprised by what she said.

"Actually—" I started with my head held high in false confidence.

"The car is here." Gabe interrupted what I was about to say before the words were able to leave my mouth.

I walked the short distance to Maddox with my head held high and kept the best fake smile possible plastered on my face as he helped me into my coat. The picture bothered me, but Maddox and I were just beginning to get to know each other so it wasn't like he was keeping it from me. Somehow, what actually bothered me was just that there was someone that was that important to him. Was she still a part of his life, and if not, why exactly was there a picture of her hanging on his refrigerator? With that, Jameson came to my mind so quickly I hadn't even realized I'd gone so long without thinking about him. I pushed the thoughts of him away. There was no going back to what could have been.

When we walked into Screwdrivers it was a relief that the music, as loud as it was, made it difficult to hold a conversation. It seemed Maddox was oblivious to the whole picture thing and I was thankful for not having to venture into that conversation just yet.

We relinquished our IDs and Maddox paid for the three of us girls to get in too, warranting an approving nod from Kera. Sara made a beeline for the nearest bar where people were lined up three rows deep trying to get a drink. To the left a large area of pool tables was overflowing with people and the whole right side of the club was a large dance floor which was already packed, despite the fact that it wasn't quite eleven p.m.

The guys chatted about something I was paying zero attention to, that is until I felt Maddox's hand slowly caressing the small of my back with his thumb. His touch brought about an instant awareness of everything Maddox—the words he was saying, the smell of his cologne, the feel of his hand on me. I had to fight the urge to snuggle closer to him and breathe him in even more. I reminded myself to be careful of this one. He was one of those men who could suck you in before you even knew it.

Before we managed to walk away from the bar Sara insisted we all take a shot and handed each of us one.

"This"—Sara held up her shot—"is to the fact that what happens in Providence, stays in Providence." She paused after apparently thinking that through. "At least for me—the rest of you guys are on your own!" She smiled before tipping her head back and finishing the shot in one sour-faced swig.

We all smiled and followed suit.

"Alright, Sara doesn't get to pick the shots anymore." Maddox smiled through gritted teeth at the bitterness of the shot.

Our laughing was cut short as the bartender handed over our drinks and we headed toward the back of the club where we claimed some high-top tables for our group.

If there is one thing I like about a night at the club it's the sensory overload. It doesn't give you too much time to spend thinking about the things that normally consume your thoughts. The pleasant buzz from a few cosmos warmed my skin and made my lips a little numb as I moved in sync with the thunderous bass that tingled my body with each hit. It was mostly Kera and me dancing together as Sara had been grinding with a guy not too far from us for the last fifteen minutes or so.

"Hey, can I get you another drink?" A guy sporting a Pittsburgh Steelers T-shirt got a little too close to me to make his offer.

"No, I'm good. Thank you, though." I smiled back at him hoping he would go at that. Taking drinks from a random guy at a club isn't very smart to begin with. There's no telling what they might stick in it by the time they'd got it at the bar and brought it back to you.

On cue, Sara came back to Kera and me, tugging her new friend behind her, and she grabbed Kera and motioned for me to follow. We made our way to the edge of the dance floor when she stopped.

"I need another drink, and Chris was telling me about this bar not very far from here. I think we should go." She looked from Kera to me hopefully.

"No honey, we gotta stay here with Becca and her friends." Kera smiled sympathetically.

"I could just go." Sara leaned closer to us to try to keep our conversation from her current companion. Our disapproving looks must have been pretty apparent because she quickly continued. "Chris is a *really* nice guy. In all seriousness, I can just tell that he's a good person," she pleaded.

I had to bite my lip to keep the smile off my face. There was something about how she said it, as if she felt she could look into his soul and make that kind of determination over a couple drinks and words thrown across the blaring sounds of music.

"I'm sure he's great but we have to stay together. You know this."

Sara gave Kera her most pathetic look, when the guy I thought I'd seen the last of interrupted us.

"Hey, I'm glad I found you. I looked up and you were gone," he stated as if it were some great catastrophe that we'd been separated.

"How about we grab that drink?" His tone was hopeful.

I chanced a glance toward the table to find Maddox watching me intently. That should sound a little creepy but it wasn't. Instead, I'd call it attentive, like he was just making sure I was okay. Although there was something else there, maybe a hint of jealousy?

"Come on, I'm harmless, I promise."

I directed my eyes back to him. "I can't, but it's for a reason I think we can both respect." I smiled as he leaned in to hear my explanation.

"The fact is, I'm from Cincinnati, so you and I"—I looked between the two of us indicating his shirt—"I'm afraid we are sworn enemies. If I wasn't here with someone, which I am, and it was any other team... well maybe. But, I'm afraid that just isn't the case."

I smiled and chanced a glance at him to find him grinning down at me. At that I walked around him to go back to where Maddox was sitting but found him instead walking toward me. I didn't turn around to see if the Steelers fan was gone but I silently hoped he was. The smile on his face reassured me Maddox wasn't the possessive type.

"You having fun?" His question was genuine, as was the smile on his face, and I couldn't help but feel a little taller in that moment. Maddox looked delectable in his blue cashmere sweater which showed just a hint of his blue plaid dress shirt at his forearms where his sleeves were slightly pushed up. Somehow, even in the darkness of the club, I could still see the brilliant blue of his eyes.

"I am." My grin was bigger than necessary but the perfect combination of the alcohol brought out a looseness in me, and the fact that Maddox somehow helped me feel bold, made everything in that moment just feel good.

"Good." He pulled me next to him and wrapped his arm around my waist.

"I think it's about time someone kept an eye on you. I'd say Kera has

Sara covered." The words were said against my ear, which felt in part like necessity over the music, but also like an excuse to get just a bit closer.

"Stop giving me goosebumps!" The words came out of my mouth before my brain knew to sensor them and I blushed, giving my slip-up away.

"I give you goosebumps?" He grinned devilishly as his hands played slowly from around my waist to over my ribs.

Wow, something about him saying it while he did that made it that much worse—or better.

I looked back at Kera and Sara to find them chatting with Chris, and when Kera saw me she gave me a quick nod, giving me the okay to run off on my own for a bit. Once I agreed, Maddox led us to the dance floor. We maneuvered through all the people milling around and dancing. As is true with pretty much any club near closing many people still roamed around hoping it wasn't too late to find someone to keep them company for the night, while others had met some wayward predicament, resulting in misplaced false eyelashes and smeared mascara.

Maddox pulled me closer to him as we moved to the now slow tempo, and I couldn't help but be thankful that on this night, unlike so many before it, I was happy.

All too soon they announced last call and it was time to go. Maddox took my hand and led me back to our table where everyone else had gathered.

"You ready to get out of here?" Kera asked.

I nodded in her direction and she stepped closer to me.

"You don't care if Chris comes back to our place, do you? I would have said no under normal circumstances, but it turns out he goes to JWU also," Kera continued quickly with her rationale.

I looked at Sara wrapped in Chris's arms, contentment obvious on her face.

"If you think he's fine I believe you." And that was the truth. Kera was a smart girl, and while she would often see the good in everyone she was also more of a realist.

"What's going on?" Maddox asked, having picked up on our conversation.

I explained that Chris was coming back to our dorm. There was no mistaking the concern on his face.

"You sure that's a good idea? Just because he goes to school with you doesn't mean he's someone you can trust to take home." He spoke directly to me.

"Hey man, you ready to get out of here? Our Uber's here," Gabe questioned as he and Stephy stood up and finished off their drinks.

"You guys go ahead, I'm gonna make sure these girls get home okay."

No further explanation was needed apparently. Gabe smiled and nodded at me.

"See you again, Becca."

As they strode away I wondered for a second if that was a question or a statement. Gabe seemed cool enough, although Stephy might take some getting used to.

Our Uber wasn't far behind and we headed back to our place. Given that there wasn't much privacy to speak of in a dorm room—well that, and the fact there was a full-on make-out session taking place only a few feet from my bed—Maddox and I sat outside my front door in the open hallway.

"Gabe seems nice." I pulled my knees to my chest and sat with my back against the door.

"He's a good guy, and like a brother to me." Maddox mimicked my position with his legs outstretched on the cold linoleum floor. Strangely, it occurred to me that he seemed too perfect to be here, in a grungy dorm room hallway with me.

"It's been nice living with him, despite the fact that he can be a total slob." He smiled at that comment.

"Ha!" I laughed. "You should try the whole dorm thing. My first week, here our reclusive roommate regaled us all with stories of how she used to sell embalming fluid to the local addicts back at home, straight from her parents' mortuary."

"Seriously?" He appeared as shocked as I was when I'd first heard it.

"Yes! Kera and I were convinced she was dealing out of our room, but thankfully she met some guy and now only stops here long enough to pick up clothes and head back to his place."

"Okay, maybe you win." He nudged my side playfully.

"I do! Embrace his dirty socks, because you could be living in a meth lab or something!" I laughed at my own tendency to exaggerate but seriously, he didn't know how good he had it.

"Fair enough. So, did you know anyone when you got here?" Maddox asked with interest.

I looked down before resting the side of my face against my knees. "No." I exhaled. "It definitely wasn't an easy thing, leaving everyone behind and coming here."

"A boyfriend?"

"Well yeah, we tried the whole long-distance thing but that pretty much never works." I trailed off, not wanting to explore that subject, but took a minute too long to make eye contact again.

Jameson.

"Well, I for one am glad you had all that strength inside you. Coming here alone, that took a lot of courage."

I could only smile in response. I didn't feel strong or courageous most days. Often, I'd wondered what the hell I was thinking.

"I'm also glad this restaurant you have in your mind is located here in Providence," he smiled.

"So what about you? What's your story?" I happily shifted the conversation from me to him.

"My story?" He laughed and nudged his shoulder against mine. "I don't know." He paused. "I think I'm still figuring that out."

"Fair enough. So what's your story so far?" Was I really going to come right out and ask him about the girl in the picture? Could he still be involved with her yet be here with me? The question had to be answered but I didn't want to have to be the one to bring it up.

"The plan I guess is to work for my father's company once I graduate." His lips turned down slightly after the words left his mouth, making it pretty obvious that "the plan" wasn't *his* plan exactly. "I've got another year left of school so I've got some time to figure it out."

"So no girlfriend or anything?" I held my breath slightly as I waited for his answer. I wanted to focus on other things but the idea of someone else gave me a necessary bit of tunnel vision.

His eyes grew larger at my question and he tilted his head to the side slightly. "You think I'd be here with you if I had a girlfriend?" His tone was surprised but not accusing.

At the heat of his gaze, I looked down and picked at my jeans. "Well, it's just the picture on your fridge. Stephy said her name is Izzy?" I looked up at him, deciding I should be paying attention to his reaction.

"Oh." Understanding showed in his face. "Izzy is my ex, that's all. It ended months ago. I promise you"—he paused as he tilted his head slightly downward so he could look me straight in the eyes—"that is entirely in the past."

So why's her picture still on your fridge? I wanted to ask that question but I didn't. I believed him that nothing was going on there but couldn't help but wonder if it was her who'd walked away. Why else would he be keeping the picture?

At six a.m. I nearly fell over when the door I was leaning on suddenly opened. Maddox caught me before I collapsed fully into the doorway. Chris, who looked like he'd had both the worst and best night of his life, slowly made his walk of shame down the hallway to the elevators.

"Well, I should probably let you get some sleep." Maddox stood and held his hands out to help me up.

Using more strength than necessary he pulled me to my feet and directly against him so I came up hard against his chest, our bodies flush.

"I had fun." He looked down at me, his thumb gently caressing my neck.

"Me too." I felt the heat find my face, unsure why exactly I was blushing in the first place.

As if I could hide the redness of my face from him I looked down but his fingers quickly found my chin and pulled me back up to his gaze.

"I'll call you tomorrow—or today I guess." He smiled.

I started to pull away from him but he held me tighter, and when I looked up at him in response his mouth took mine in a sweet, tentative kiss. I moaned softly as my mouth found his, and with that he took that sweet kiss and turned it into a mind-numbing all-consuming inferno. In a matter of seconds my body responded, butterflies filling my stomach, and heat touching every inch of my skin. I grabbed onto his solid biceps somehow wanting him closer to me, despite the fact that there was no space between us. His hand found the wall behind me while his other played at the back of my neck into my hairline. Just as abruptly the kiss was over and we both stood there panting.

"Tomorrow then." His index finger touched the tip of my nose briefly before he turned and walked toward the elevator.

I turned and went into my room, fighting the urge to watch him go.

Chapter Eighteen

I lay in my bed thankful the smile on my face was going unnoticed by Sara and Kera, who were both still asleep. Only having a few hours of sleep didn't seem to affect me as it normally would, and I woke up feeling nothing short of incredible.

I hopped out of bed, my current thoughts preventing me from lying still any longer. The sun was shining bright in the sky, despite the cold temperature, and I decided I was long overdue for some exercise. Quietly, I rummaged through my closet and settled on a pair of long black yoga pants, a tank top, and an Under Armour sweatshirt. No point in looking pretty to go for a jog. I brushed my teeth, threw my hair in a ponytail, and was out the door within minutes.

I started off slowly, for once not bothering with my headphones, taking in the sound of my feet hitting the pavement instead. Maybe it had more to do with the lack of music than anything else, but today my mind wandered and kept bringing me back to Maddox. There was something about the way he looked at me that made my skin tingle as if I were back in that moment where he'd wrapped his arms tightly around me. Stupidly, I'd admitted that he gave me goosebumps but his reaction to that confession nearly made it worth it. Not only was there some serious chemistry going on between the two of us, but he was also focused, determined, and seemed like a genuinely good person.

The image of the photo from his fridge popped in my mind. *Izzy.* The petite blonde whose rock-clad fingers were wrapped tightly around him.

It was just a picture.

I tried to convince myself, but why it was still hanging on his fridge brought more questions to my mind than I cared for. My thoughts of Izzy fought their way toward the surface of my mind and threatened to take away from the light, feel-good mood I was presently trying to hold onto. But thinking of Izzy only made me think about Jameson, and while we were never engaged as they apparently were, he was still lingering somewhere in my past. I, like Maddox, still had secrets that weren't ready to be shared.

The new directions of my thoughts brought about a faster pace and I pushed myself to the limit as I ran across a pedestrian bridge, taking me from the city to a small rundown park. By the time I realized I wasn't actually somewhere I wanted to be I'd nearly used all my energy. It wasn't necessarily a bad part of town, but the park itself looked as if it hadn't been tended to in years, with graffiti covering the concrete of the walls of the bridge I'd just run across.

I stopped momentarily to catch my breath and tie my shoes tighter when I noticed a few guys lingering nearby. Deciding it was a better idea not to stick around to figure out if they were up to no good I took off back over the bridge toward my dorm. My thoughts now nondescript I took in the peaceful buzz that running always gives me.

When I returned, Kera and Sara were among the living and ready to head out for lunch. We opted for one of the dining halls across campus as funds were getting pretty low after yesterday's shopping excursion. As it generally is, the dining hall was packed and we made our way to the line. Instead of having Sara pay for her lunch Kera handed over her meal card after she swiped it once for herself. Rarely did either of us use our three daily-allotted meals.

Going to a culinary school came with certain perks, one of those being that the cafeteria food wasn't half bad.

"Seriously?" Kera asked me accusingly taking me by surprise.

"What?" I asked as I grabbed an individual carton of milk.

"Aren't you supposed to have more refined tastes?" She nodded to my overflowing bowl of Cinnamon Toast Crunch.

"Haha, CTC is a classic!" I joked.

We made our way through the dining hall and found a table toward the back with a few people we all knew from various classes. They were chatting about heading home for the holiday and part of me dreaded it because I was finally at a good place here, and excited to see what happened with Maddox. I wanted to believe I was dreading the possibility of seeing Jameson, but the truth was more gray than just black and white. I couldn't deny that the thought of running into him or finding some excuse to see him brought an undeniable level of excitement.

And yes, I recognized how messed up that actually was. Maybe seeing him would make me realize I was over him, or maybe seeing him would bring back everything we had before.

"What's got you all smiley over there?" An acquaintance from my pastry class grinned my way.

I paused for a second, realizing the smile on my face had much more to do with Jameson than Maddox.

"She didn't tell you? She's dating some rich Ivy League guy from Brown," Kera answered for me with a little too much excitement.

"We're not dating, we're just … seeing each other I guess." I tried to explain something that didn't really have an explanation yet.

My phone beeped and I looked down, not realizing how hopeful I was that it was Maddox until I saw it was my dad.

Chapter Nineteen

A million nerves fluttered around my stomach, but I was actually looking forward to being home and seeing Amelia and my family. Although I would much rather deal with a twenty-eight-hour Greyhound bus ride than have to expose myself to the fear flying gives me. For many, it's the takeoff or the landing... but for me it's the takeoff, the landing, and everything in between. If I had to pick a favorite part it would certainly be the landing but that's only because I have some jaded false sense that at least if we're going down in a fiery crash I have a better chance at survival if I'm closer to the ground.

"Not much for flying?" a twenty-something girl seated next to me asked while I was desperately trying to keep up with the flight attendant as she went over seatbelt operations and crash preparation instructions.

"No," I said curtly as I searched the seat pocket in front of me for the laminated instructions.

"Try this," she stated, just as I was frantically questioning my own abilities to handle the responsibility of being seated in an emergency exit row.

I glanced her way and she held out her jewelry-clad wrist and handed me a small individual bottle of Jack Daniels. I looked at her and realized that while we were about the same age she was far more confident and at ease on a plane than I was.

"Go ahead." She shook the small bottle at me.

"It will help quicker than anything else." She extended it to me again.

While I wasn't exactly used to chugging straight Jack Daniels I knew she was right and it would at least calm me down. I took the bottle from her, unscrewed the tiny lid, closed my eyes, tipped my head back, and took the biggest swig I could stomach.

"Damn, that shit burns!" I said through watering eyes and gritted teeth.

"Better with Coke, but it'll do." She smiled before tipping back her own bottle.

"I'm Jessie by the way."

"Becca."

Jessie was a student at another college in Providence and was flying to Cincinnati to spend Christmas with her boyfriend's family. Our conversation and the calming buzz helped the two-hour flight pass quickly, and before I knew it we were waving goodbye at the baggage check.

Seeing my family waiting for me made me realize how much I missed them, and seeing my eighty-year-old Gigi waiting with them nearly brought me to tears.

"Becca, my sweet!" Gigi said as I reached them.

She snatched me up in a hug that seemed far too gripping for the tiny woman she was. Gigi had more fashion sense than most women. Her hair, while it was short, was the thickest most beautiful white hair any older woman would die for. Standing only about five foot two, and weighing maybe a hundred pounds, she was always dressed to the nines, today being no exception. She wore white dress pants and a black and white blouse, with chunky turquoise jewelry covering her neck and wrists. A grin covered her face and, while she hated them, her smile lines showed the happy person she naturally is.

"I'm so glad you're finally home!" My mom smiled and there was no mistaking the resemblance between her and Gigi. Although, unfortunately, neither she nor I were lucky enough to have Gigi's naturally tanned complexion.

The hour drive from the airport passed quickly with all the catching up we had to do. Gigi wanted to hear about all my classes, and was certain my cooking abilities were already going to far exceed her own, which I feared would never be the case. When we pulled in the driveway I felt that sense of peace one only feels at home.

The house I grew up in was a typical trilevel three-bedroom in a residential neighborhood. While modest, it was the perfect place to grow up. Kids played in the street until the sun started to go down and bad things didn't find their way to the neighborhood. Once upon a time we slept with the windows open and picked blackberries from the field behind our house.

If I had to choose a favorite memory though, it would have to be the winter I was eight years old. While snow in Ohio certainly wasn't unheard of, it usually never amounted to more than a few inches at a time. This particular winter we missed over a week of school when two feet of snow dumped from the sky almost overnight. My dad, who was typically always busy working or with his music, also missed work due to the weather, and he created our very own bobsled trail in the front yard. For the next week, every kid in the neighborhood could be found in our front yard competing in mock trials for our very own Olympics.

It never escaped me how lucky I was to have the family I have.

Gigi and Mom went straight to the kitchen and started fixing my favorite food of all time, a börek. How exactly they got the recipe I still don't know, but apparently they went to great measures to snag it from a Greek man who owned a restaurant in Wisconsin where Gigi is from. Generally reserved for Christmas, this delicious cheese pastry is a symbol of my childhood, but also one of the best damn things I've ever tasted.

"You promised you were going to teach me how to make this!" I was partially bummed that I'd missed the process but mostly excited they'd decided to go to the trouble of making it for me.

I pulled at the flaky layers of fried phyllo as the cheese oozed out.

"You can figure this out, Becca. What do you taste?" Gigi asked as she and my mom watched me.

I closed my eyes as I took a bite.

"Well, phyllo dough of course…" I let my senses take over as the ingredients saturated my taste buds.

"Farmer's cheese?" I asked hopefully.

When they didn't answer I looked up to find them waiting for me to continue.

"Parsley?"

"Close your eyes," Gigi instructed, and I did as she asked without giving it a second thought.

"Now open your mouth slightly and smell it."

I heard the plate slide across the bar as she pushed it closer to me. I picked up the plate, brought it closer to my nose and smelled it.

"Now, open your eyes and try just a little bit of the filling."

I took a bite and let the flavors absorb not only my tongue, but other parts of my mouth too.

"There's more than one kind of cheese," I said aloud.

"Good." Gigi smiled approvingly, and somehow that meant more to me than any recognition I'd ever receive in school. Maybe it was something ingrained in me from childhood, a desire to impress or get Gigi's approval, but that was something she was always willing to give. Or maybe, it was just because it was Gigi and seeing that sparkle come to her eyes and her smile wrinkles appear was like bringing light to the dark.

We ate the rest of our böraks, not trying to dissect the ingredients but instead just enjoying each other's company.

***

"Amelia!" When my phone rang I was so excited to hear her voice I nearly fell off the barstool.

She's my very dearest friend and while we both suck at calling and talking as much as we should, when we are together it's as if a moment hasn't passed.

As soon as she got ready she headed to my place so we could hang out some before going out. As per her nature, when she arrived she spent the first thirty or so minutes chatting up Gigi and my parents while I struggled to get ready. For some reason it was taking an exorbitant amount of time to figure out what I was going to wear.

"Why don't I have any decent clothes?" I asked as I threw more clothes from my suitcase to my now-covered bed.

I glanced up to find Amelia giving me a knowing smile.

"What?" I asked.

"Uh huh… Go ahead and pretend we both don't know exactly what's going on here." Amelia slid my clothes to the side and sat on my bed.

As always, she looked like a million bucks in a pair of jeans and a black tank top, cleavage provided by Victoria's Secret.

"What are you talking about?" I dipped into my closet, which still held some of the clothes I'd left at home when I went to Providence.

When she didn't answer I chanced a glance her way. I knew what she was going to say, but wasn't ready to go there.

Instead of being annoyed with me for being knowingly dense she only laughed.

"You gonna be real with me, or keep acting like this isn't about Jameson?" She took the clothes I was holding and started picking through them.

"Maybe I just want to look pretty for you?" I suggested hopefully.

"Wear this one." Amelia handed me a black off-the-shoulder sweater to wear with my jeans.

"I can't do it, Amelia. As much as I want to see him it's just torture. I'm not going to lie and say my feelings for him are gone, but at least not being with him is tolerable. It took a long time to get to this point.

"Leaving like I did was messed up, and then even though he was completely awesome I couldn't do the long-distance thing. We just can't work. He's here, I'm there, and that's just the way it's going to be. Plus, I met someone at school."

Amelia stared at me blankly just long enough for me to remind myself I don't need to keep talking just because someone doesn't respond.

"Is that all?" she asked, a grin hiding behind her eyes.

"Shut up." I gave her a small smile.

"Who's this new guy?" Her sly smile lett me know she was anxious to hear the details.

"His name is Maddox and he goes to Brown. It's a new thing, and honestly, it's the first time I've been able to look at someone and not compare them to Jameson."

"Well, we are a little stuck then because I promised Stan we would at least make an appearance. We'll just go and listen to a set, and then head somewhere else. Maybe we'll even make it out the door before Jameson has a chance to jump off stage and steal you away from this Maddox guy." Her eyebrows rose at the suggestion.

"Don't do that with your eyebrows! You look like a total creeper!" I laughed.

"Would you prefer I wink?"

Ew. Low blow. I rolled my eyes.

"Wait! You promised Stan? Since when are you and Stan making promises to each other?"

What she said had escaped me briefly.

Please tell me she and Stan aren't an item! I don't know if I can handle it if she's dating the drummer for Jameson's band.

"Relax, we just talk occasionally. I'm not shacking up with your man's roommate."

I shook my head at her ready to rid myself of this conversation altogether.

Since it takes both of us entirely too long to get ready to go anywhere, we didn't end up at Iron City until after eleven. As per usual, Amelia dragged me around the long line of people waiting to get in and straight to the front door.

"Say it ain't so!" Jeremy greeted us.

Do people even use that expression anymore?

"Hi, Jeremy." Amelia and I greeted him in unison.

"You remember me!" He held his hand to his chest as if deeply touched that I hadn't forgotten him in the months that I'd been gone.

"Seriously, she hasn't shut up about you since she's been gone!" Amelia gushed at him, and I could have knocked her out for her little lie.

"Well, I guess I'll just have to catch up with you girls inside then." He grinned confidently as he held the door open for us.

"Seriously, you're a scheming bitch!" I said as soon as we were inside and out of earshot.

She laughed in response and I could only roll my eyes for my own benefit since she wasn't paying me a bit of attention.

Music echoed loudly throughout the club and I had to will myself to not allow my eyes to look toward the stage. I knew he was there. I could feel it in my gut, even though I'd never admit that to anyone but myself. Granted, I knew he was going to be here tonight but something about Jameson was electric, and when he was near I felt it before my eyes ever needed to confirm it.

I allowed Amelia to pull me through the crowd and figured she was leading us to the bar, since she knew better than to spring Jameson on me without at least coating my stomach with some liquid courage.

Without even asking me what I wanted she handed me my favorite Rhinegeist beer, and naturally all was forgiven. This beer said "home" to me.

We walked along next to the long bar and far too close to the stage for my current comfort level.

"Millie!" I yelled over the music trying to get her attention.

She looked back at me knowingly and pointed up to the loft that sat high above the stage, before turning around and leading me up the stairs.

Unable to fight it anymore I looked toward the stage, my eyes immediately finding Jameson looking back at me while his fingers moved effortlessly across the strings of his electric bass. *Look away!* I told myself but the words were useless in my mind. My stomach did a flip and an excitement filled me that I wished I could deny. Just being near him made me want to be closer to him, and that disturbing feeling never seemed to dissipate.

Once upstairs I pulled my eyes from him to see we were heading towards a big high-top table with about six people I used to work with at Maggie's.

"Becca!" Katie, a longtime friend and server at Maggie's, jumped up to greet me in a hug.

"How have you been? You look great!" She excitedly yelled over the music.

We chatted briefly while everyone said their hellos. I knew nearly everyone at the table, minus a couple new people who must have started working at Maggie's since I'd left, but it was nice to be back with familiar people at a familiar place. Briefly, the thought of heading back to school made me sad, but I quickly dismissed the thought since I'd just gotten here. Holding an actual conversation with anyone was hard since it was difficult to talk and be heard over the music, so most things were said in clipped sentences.

Despite the reminders I kept giving myself, my eyes kept finding their way to the stage, and to Jameson.

"I can't believe how good they are!" a girl I didn't know but who was seated with us yelled excitedly, her eyes never leaving the stage.

"I knew Jameson played but I didn't know how talented he was!" she beamed.

Oh, hell no.

Amelia laughed next to me and I realized I must have been more obvious than I'd thought when I whipped my head around to get a better look at the girl. I felt the heat rise in my cheeks and had to mentally reprimand myself before my face turned beet red. Why did that just get me so annoyed? I needed another beer.

I hopped off my stool and put on my best fake smile.

"I'm gonna go grab a beer." I pointed to my not actually empty bottle.

Before anyone could mention that we have servers and don't need to go to the bar, I turned and headed for the stairs. This time as I made my way down I didn't let myself look at Jameson. It appeared I wouldn't be getting away from this night without seeing him but at least I could hope to keep it as minimally awkward as possible. Suddenly I felt like I needed air, and instead of going to the bar as planned I walked straight out the side door to the patio where all the smokers convened.

The air was cold but felt good on my heated skin. I looked up toward the sky between the brightly lit buildings.

"Cigarette?" A voice next to me asked.

"No thanks, I don't—"

When I glanced toward the voice I found Stan standing next to me.

"—smoke," I finished.

"Uh huh. Makes hiding out in the smoking patio a little suspect, don't ya think?" His tone was firm but his slight smile lightened the accusation. Or maybe it was his now purple hair that made me take him less seriously.

"I'm not hiding." I looked back toward the sky. "Just needed some air," I said truthfully.

"Good timing."

"I didn't realize you guys were on break." I started to explain, but Stan was the type that didn't beat around the bush and wasn't going to make any of this easy on me. I knew enough about Jameson and Stan to know there probably wasn't much he didn't know about what had gone down between Jameson and me. It wasn't that Jameson was the kiss and tell type, it was more because he was the sensitive and emotional type, and Stan was his best friend.

"What about you and Amelia?" I asked, hoping it would effectively change the subject. "She said she promised you we'd make an appearance here tonight." I added accusingly.

"Yeah, we talk sometimes." He took a hit off his cigarette and slowly exhaled the gray smoke into the sky.

"In fact, I should probably head in and say hi to everyone." He smashed his cigarette out into one of the ashtrays.

"Coming?" he asked.

I just stared at him like a complete idiot, not speaking. It suddenly occurred to me that Jameson was probably hanging out with everyone at our table. What the hell was I going to say to him?

At that, he turned and went inside.

Realizing I was acting like a complete ass, I turned and went in, only stopping at the bar long enough to grab another beer before heading upstairs.

As expected, as soon as I could see the table I recognized Jameson standing with his back to me. Suddenly, as if sensing I was there, he turned around, looked at me briefly then held my eye contact. I wanted to stop, actually I wanted to turn around and go back downstairs and put as much distance between us as possible. Maybe that was a lie. Is it possible to want to run toward someone but also want to run away from them? Has anyone actually proven which is right? The heart or the mind?

"Hey." He smiled his damn gorgeous smile, his white teeth showing past his dark five o'clock shadow.

"Hey." I smiled before briefly looking away from him, as if my smile was giving away everything left unsaid. How was it possible that just being close to him brought about such a profound reaction? My stomach quivered with immediate desire, as if somewhere along the way I'd drank a magic potion. A potion that made his every feature more desirable to me—his soft lips, his piercing eyes—and, as if a day hadn't gone by, I wanted all of him to myself once again. It must have been more than a magic potion though, maybe it was some sort of voodoo spell, because it went so far past just the physical. Every part of him drew me in—his mind, his heart—he was the whole package.

"It's good to see you." He held his arms out silently asking for a hug.

I went to him. *A hug is harmless*, I told myself.

As it turns out, hugs are not harmless. I closed my eyes, rested my head against his chest, and breathed him in. Touching him just reminded me of what had been, not that I needed any reminding, and for a minute I didn't want to let go. Apparently, he wasn't in a hurry either. His arms wrapped around my waist and pulled me in closer, tighter than the average hug would entail.

When I opened my eyes after probably what had been too long I found the eyes of everyone at the table on us. Even though Jameson was still holding me I let go of him, suddenly feeling self-conscious.

I needed to get a grip. I'd moved on, and I wasn't so naïve to think that Jameson hadn't done the same. Women were always interested in him, and being in a band only seemed to intensify his appeal. The thought of him with someone else brought about dual reactions—a pathetically sick feeling in my stomach and some primitive desire to punch whoever she was in the face and get him back.

Without letting me go he looked down at me and I met his eyes.

"Ignore them," he said, as if he was already aware of the way I felt.

I knew who he was talking about, the prying eyes that were trained on us, but somewhere within myself when he said the words I couldn't help but think of Maddox. Was it Maddox that I wanted to ignore right now? I looked away, and pulled back until he reluctantly let me go. Doing my best to regain some sort of composure I took a drink from my bottle and searched the depths of my mind to find something to say, only to find an apparently empty brain.

"Hey Jameson, you doing your song tonight?" asked one of the girls at our table, and I was grateful for the attention on him and not us.

He looked my way at the question, before quickly looking back to her.

"I'm not sure, I guess if someone requests it," he answered noncommittally.

"Well that's gonna happen!" she exclaimed happily.

Why did I find myself wanting to glare at her? I'm the most non-confrontational person ever but how she looked at him made me … jealous.

"Since that night you first sang it people have requested it every time you guys have played here."

"You're singing now?" I asked, that having piqued my interest.

"Just a little." His answer was so modest it was adorable.

Everyone knew Jameson could play, but not everyone knew he could sing. I'd tried to convince him to put himself out there but it had always seemed just a bit out of his comfort zone.

"That's awesome." My smile was genuine as was his in return.

Words passed between us with nothing said. All the conversations we'd had about taking his music to the next level, and the nights he'd sung just for me, echoed through my mind. Had I helped him in some way to overcome that fear? He'd always made me feel braver, like I could do whatever I wanted with this life. Had I given him an ounce of that same strength?

"C'mon, we gotta get back up there," Stan said, interrupting everything unspoken.

"I'll see you around," I said to Jameson.

"You know I always could tell when you were lying to me." He swept his thumb across my cheek, a sad smile playing across his face.

And with that, he walked away.

Once he was gone I did my best to finish off my beer. Why did he have to affect me so much?

The band started playing again and everyone was chatting over the music—until Jameson started singing.

It's still you
You are all it's ever been
Gray eyes seeking out your plight
Never lost, your eyes - they seek me too.

But do I burn too high - I lean your way
Don't melt me down to throw away.
If I reach for you – will I burn out?
I climb higher to touch your face.

My fire burns – just for you.
Can you feel the heat burning through?
You're almost mine, don't look away
How can I make you stay?

It's still you
You are all it's ever been
Gray eyes- yet my reflection fades.

I burn down before you now
Tears of wax – finely flow.
Now this flame just burns my eyes
I see the darkness in the sky
Surely still I cannot let it die.

Just hearing him sing would have been enough to do me in, but the words—was I selfish to feel like he'd been singing it to me? They said he'd been singing it for months, so that would mean it wasn't for me, right? Tears stung behind my eyes and I struggled to keep myself from letting them spill over. Taking a calming albeit shaky breath, I looked up to find Amelia looking at me like she too was about to cry.

"You're ready to go?" she asked.

Thank God she knew me so well.

We said nothing as we made our way to her car, and for a moment we just sat there.

"Tell me that wasn't for me, Amelia," I asked, while messing with the fringe from a small hole in the thigh of my jeans.

She sat there briefly, as if trying to find the right words to answer my question before turning the key and putting the car in gear.

"Do you want me to tell you it wasn't for you, or do you want me to tell you the truth?"

And with that, the tears hiding behind the surface found their way to the edge. Neither of us said anything as I stared out the window at the city passing by.

Unable to take the silence any longer I turned the radio on and let it play softly in the background. Despite the conflicting words and melodies, Jameson's song still tried to play in my mind.

"I just don't understand it, Becca," Amelia said after a few minutes. "I know you care about him and he still cares about you … why are you fighting it so much?" Her eyes glanced to me then back to the highway before us.

"It's not that simple and you know it." Anger fueled my words and they came off more accusatory than I had intended.

"How am I supposed to accomplish the things I need to do for myself with him here and me there? I can't do it, Amelia. I can't just stay here because of a guy, even if he was *the* guy, and give up the chance to get what I want out of life. I won't look back at my life and realize I let someone else change my trajectory."

Amelia watched me unspeaking, as if my words had somehow taken her by surprise. She knew my mom, and while we'd never discussed it, it was no secret my mom blamed the end of her modeling career on the fact that she'd had me. Maybe in part that was where my determination came from.

"Do you have any idea how difficult it was to be there and want nothing more than to be with him? Do you know how it feels to have someone make you feel so content that you could see yourself giving up everything just to be with them?" The tears again stung behind my eyes but I fought their betrayal of my anger. "No, you don't know, because you and I have barely talked since I've been gone!" My words charged her and I knew it had much more to do with everything going on in my mind and less to do with her.

"That's not fair, Becca. That isn't just my fault, and don't forget we were supposed to go together! Do YOU know how hard it is to see you move on and me still here, stuck?"

Her words cut me. I'd been so focused trying to make a life for myself there that I hadn't considered what it was like for her.

"I'm sorry, and you're right." My tone softened.

"I'm not mad at you, Becca, I just don't understand you sometimes. You love him, I know you do."

I looked down at my jeans and resumed picking at the loose thread.

"Did you know I asked him to come with me?" A single tear slipped past my cheek and I swallowed trying to keep the others at bay. It was only my pride that kept me from telling her before now. Something about saying the words out loud and letting someone else know made it sting that much more.

Her face was enough of an answer. Her jaw dropped and she took her eyes off the road to look at me.

"Yeah. So don't be too hard on me, Amelia. I tried, it's just ... It's not meant to be, I guess."

"I'm so sorry, I didn't know. I can't believe you didn't tell me! I guess your quick exit to Providence makes a little more sense now."

"Let's just let it go, okay?" It seemed impossible to actually let it go, even when I was far away he crept into my thoughts. Being here just made it that much more difficult.

"Okay." Her sympathetic smile only made me want to hide somewhere away from my life.

"I'm sorry for being a shitty friend, you know I love you though, right?"

Amelia laughed. "You're not a shitty friend; we could both do a better job. And I love you."

Chapter Twenty

The light shining through the window of my childhood bedroom pulled me from sleep. I covered my face with another pillow and searched deep within myself for the will to move so I could close the damn curtains, but came up empty. On the bedside table to my left, my phone chirped. I opened one eye in response. I could stay here all day and refuse to move, and maybe I could avoid the world. Sadly, the world was safer than what was going on inside my mind. I sat up and fought the urge to pull my feather comforter back to me when I felt the coolness of the air. Rubbing my eyes I tried to pull the sleepiness from my face as I grabbed my phone from the table and unplugged it from the charger.

>Hey babe, how's your trip going?

Maddox. That little text did a good job waking me up.

Staring at my phone I tried to think of a response. Something told me "Oh not great, ran into my ex and spent the night crying," might not be the best thing to say.

>Good! Just getting ready to decide what kind of trouble to get into today! How are you?

That brings up a good point, what was I going to do today?

>Lol hopefully you won't get into too much trouble, Ohio is a bit far for me to come bail you out.

>I'm bored! Not ready to give in and head home just yet though.

>If it makes you feel any better I'm already ready to come back. Lol.

>Come back! We'll make our own trouble.

Hmmm… that sounds interesting.

>As appealing as that may sound I think I'm stuck here, at least for a little while longer.

"Hey, sleepyhead!" Gigi greeted me as I joined her in the living room. She sat on the couch in a fluffy fleece robe with a steaming cup of coffee.

"Hi, Gigi." I smiled and sat down next to her.

"So I've been waiting to hear about school. How is it going?"

"Well…" I pulled my knees to my chest and thought through the last few months and what a whirlwind it had actually been.

"It was hard at first because I met somewhere here over the summer, so leaving was bad."

Gigi always listened to me with so much interest, and not as if she had a hundred other things on her mind that needed to be dealt with.

"Oh, I bet that was hard. Are you still dating him?" she asked with interest.

"No, I ended it shortly after getting to school. I just couldn't do it."

"The distance, you mean?" She took a sip from her oversized mug.

"I don't know… that was part of it. He was just really… intense." Translation, *we* were intense.

"And then a few weeks ago I met Maddox, and he's completely different from Jameson. I mean *completely*."

She watched me contently, waiting for me to continue.

"Jameson is a musician… he's bold but so gentle and sensitive. He says what he thinks, and isn't afraid of what comes from those words. He has so much faith in me, and it sounds stupid, but I feel like he's rooting for me, you know?"

"He sounds sweet. And the other guy?" "Maddox." I smiled. "He's great; we met because it was pouring, and he offered me his umbrella. Come to find out his car was right there but he acted like he was walking so he could get to know me. He goes to Brown and has a really nice apartment with his cousin off-campus."

"So, if all three of you were in the same place who would you be with?" Her question, as simple as it was, was not something I had thought about.

"I don't know." I considered the question.

"That's the great part about being young, you have plenty of time to figure it out. You don't have to know all the answers, just do what makes you happy. One thing I can tell you is that things have a way of working out, and whatever is supposed to be will be."

"Thanks, Gigi." I smiled, and a small sense of relief washed over me. Something about her always made me feel more calm and confident.

"Now go have some fun and maybe later I'll give you your great grandfather's Chicken Valdostano recipe." She raised her eyebrows in playful excitement.

"Thanks, Gigi." I smiled and kissed the soft skin of her cheek before running off to start my day.

As far as Christmas vacations went it was pretty great to spend time with everyone. My mom, unlike Gigi, was quick to make her preference known when it came to the Maddox vs Jameson debacle. While she had an obvious soft spot for musicians, she was quickly Team Maddox after hearing about how we met and the fact that he had a "little brother". It also didn't hurt, I imagine, when I showed her and Gigi a picture of him from his Twitter account.

Gigi was much less forthcoming and said that whatever I decided would be right. I tried to explain to her that there wasn't a decision to be made there anymore, as things with Jameson and me were in the past, not the present, but that didn't seem to make much difference to her.

My dad and I avoided the topic altogether and instead talked about what we always talk about—music. He played me some of the pieces he was currently working on and I let him know the music I was currently obsessing over.

Thanks to the various gift cards we both received for Christmas, Amelia and I spent most of our time shopping and being as girly as possible getting manicures, pedicures, and spray tans. It made me wish even more that things had been different and she'd been able to come to Providence with me. I decided seeing Jameson was not a good idea, and Amelia didn't give me a hard time about that. She didn't say it but I think that knowing I'd tried to get him to come with me made her take some of the blame off me. I was relieved she didn't try to get me to see him. He was like a vacuum, and I was afraid of being sucked back into him.

Chapter Twenty-One

The bottom of my plastic champagne flute fell to the grimy, confetti-covered floor as I looked out over the crowded dance floor. Amelia was dancing with a very awkward and out of place Stan, and I couldn't help but be envious of the two of them. He was making his best attempt at swaying back and forth to the music as Amelia was expertly grinding her body against him. It's not the dancing I was envious of. Despite the fact that Stan couldn't dance if his life depended on it, he was here—because with Amelia is where he wanted to be.

I pulled my phone from my pocket and was thankful for the twentieth time tonight that the slightly poofy skirt of my small black dress actually had pockets.

Seven minutes until midnight and the start of the New Year. Determined not to stand around and watch everyone bring in the New Year with a kiss, I headed to the front of the club and stepped out into the freezing cold air. Despite the fact that there were heat lamps and the area was partially tented off, I wish I'd grabbed my jacket from the coat check.

This night could have gone differently, and, as I always do, I questioned the choices I was making when it came to Jameson. I wish he were here, and somewhere inside myself I knew that if I'd asked, he would have been. I also knew opening the door to him was dangerous territory. I wanted more. I wanted to pursue the dream I'd had since I was a child—to become a chef. I wanted to open my own restaurant and create a place where people come from all over to experience. At this point in my life I just didn't think I got to have both. Maybe if things were different—if school was here, or Jameson was there, maybe—but for now I had to learn to focus and make the life I wanted my reality.

I pulled my phone from my pocket again—three minutes to go.

Maybe it would be okay to send him a message, just to wish him a Happy New Year. Was there really so much harm in texting back and forth some?

I scrolled through the old messages on my phone to find his name and the last message he'd sent me, a message I never responded to.

My fingers started to move as I typed the message, but once my Happy New Year was written I kept going, my fingers typing as if they had a mind of their own, spilling all the details of what I'd wanted to say but hadn't had the courage. Before I finished I deleted it and tried again. "I miss you." It's all I really want to say.

Before I can hit send my phone buzzed with an incoming message and Maddox's name flashed across the top of the screen.

>Happy New Year, babe! When do you get back?

>Happy New Year! I'll be back Thursday.

>Dinner Friday?

Cheers erupted from inside, but a smile came to my lips as I suddenly began to realize that maybe this was exactly what was supposed to be for me. It was time I realized that Jameson was in the past, and we both had futures that may not include each other. Providence was where I needed to be and, while I didn't know what would happen with Maddox, it was time that I started living my life there, not here.

>Sounds good. :)

>:x Happy New Year!

When a text message from Jameson came through I deleted our entire conversation without reading it. I was resolved in my decision as I tucked my phone back into the pocket of my dress and headed inside, back to Amelia and Stan.

Chapter Twenty-Two

Having survived yet another flight I headed back to my dorm exhausted and exhilarated at the same time.

"You're back!" Kera exclaimed, jumping from her bed as I made my way through the door.

"Hi!" I closed the door behind me and dropped my bags on the floor of the hallway.

"Is it crazy that I missed you a lot?" She wrapped me in a big hug.

"Not at all! I missed you, too!"

Kera grabbed my bags from the hallway and started lugging them to our shared room.

"Thank you!" I collapsed on my bed. "I totally intended on leaving them there until I was desperate for more clothes."

It felt good to relax. It felt like I'd traveled across the world based on my current level of exhaustion. Kera came and lay down next to me, our faces only a few inches from each other.

"How was home?" Kera asked easily and with genuine interest.

"Good…"

Wow, my answer doesn't even sound sincere to me.

Kera watched me, also disbelieving of my response.

"Honestly, it was good. Good to see my family and Amelia. We had a lot of fun catching up."

"Did you see Jameson?" She was always one to get right to the root of things.

I looked away from her and stared at the ceiling for a minute before bringing my eyes back to her.

"I did. Only once though."

She seemed surprised, and maybe it was because I said I saw him, or maybe it was because I said only once. If I had to guess I'd say it was the latter.

"And …"

"And … I don't know. It's always the same with him. It's … electric."
I closed my eyes searching for the words that would do justice.

"What does that mean really? I don't think I've ever been with anyone
where it was like that."

I turned to lie on my side and she mirrored me so we were now face
to face.

"I don't know if it's a good thing or a bad thing, Kera. On one hand,
it's amazing like your soul recognizes the person even before you do.
I know that sounds completely insane, but it truly is something more
than just a typical connection formed with someone over time. He just
… understood me, and wanted for me all the things that I want for
myself. The flip side of that though is trying to figure out how to still
be you when you're with that person. It was so intense it was almost
all-consuming. It started making me feel like if he asked me to, I would
follow him anywhere … or worse, I'd follow him nowhere."

She propped her head up on her elbow, still facing me.

"But if he wanted for you what you want for yourself, he wouldn't
have let you be so consumed that you wouldn't achieve what you want
for yourself."

"I don't know. Maybe."

"So what happened when you saw him?"

"It doesn't matter," I said after thinking for a moment or two.

"Jameson and I … we just can't be. I know I've said it before but I
really do have to find a way to create a life for myself here, a life without
him."

Kera frowned at my words, a quick reaction that maybe she didn't
even register.

"Hey, maybe Mr. Right is just waiting to be found." I smiled, hoping
to lighten the mood.

"Maybe Maddox is Mr. Right!" she added excitedly before lying back
down and staring up toward the ceiling.

"Maybe he is… and maybe he has a single brother!"

Chapter Twenty-Three

I couldn't help but be a bit nervous about seeing Maddox again—excited but still nervous. It probably wasn't helping matters that wherever he was taking me was a secret; my mind was imagining skydiving or hang gliding, or something equally terrifying. Do they do skydiving in the winter?

"Where's he taking you?" Kera asked from the open doorway.

"I don't know," I said as I pulled the straightener through my hair. "He said it's a surprise."

"Well now! Try not to look so excited, will you?"

"I'm supposed to wear something comfortable, with nothing too loose or baggy! What the hell does that even mean?"

"I don't know, I think they told my mom that once when she was having surgery. Organ harvesting maybe?" She laughed.

I gave her my best evil look and she ignored it, taking the straightener from me.

"Turn around, I'll do the back of your head."

"Maybe a rollercoaster? That might explain it," she said as she worked on my hair.

"Maybe … I'll guess we'll find out soon enough," I said, equal parts nervous and excited.

Once Kera finished my hair I put on a little makeup, just enough to open my eyes a bit and add a little more color to my face.

"Hey, Maddox," I heard Kera say from the other side of our dorm.

"I'll be out in a minute," I called through the closed door of the bathroom.

A minute or two later I came out to find Maddox sitting at my desk and talking with Kera, a bouquet of pink roses and cream-colored lilies in his hands.

"Hi!" He stood when he saw me, his face immediately lighting up with contagious excitement.

He was wearing dark colored jeans, and I couldn't help but admire how sexy he looked in his black formfitting cashmere sweater that showed off his muscular chest and arms.

"Hi." I smiled a bit bashfully as he held the flowers out to me.

With my mind always a bit overly active I thought for a moment, trying to figure out if he was going to go in for a hug or a kiss, and could only hope I wasn't completely awkward and did the wrong thing at the wrong time.

He smiled as he stepped so close to me we were almost chest-to-chest.

"I'm glad you're back." He gently caressed my cheek and carefully tilted my face up to him so he could give me a small peck on the lips.

He was confident but not presumptuous, and there was something about his ability to take charge I really was beginning to like.

"You should probably let her know where you guys are going, or at least just let her know she won't be relinquishing a vital organ." Kera sat down on her bed with a handful of books and notebooks.

Maddox looked between Kera and myself, a little dumbfounded.

"She's being dramatic." Alright, I'm the dramatic one, but he didn't need to know that yet.

"Uh huh… you kids have a good time." Kera smiled as she opened her book and pretended to start reading.

Before Kera could say anything further I took Maddox's hand and led him out the front door of our place.

I pushed the down button on the elevator, and we stood there still hand in hand.

"Well if you'd like to know where we are going I can tell you … or you can wait and trust me that it's a good surprise."

How could I say no to the sweet smile he was laying on me?

After a short drive, we arrived and Maddox pulled his car around the back of a strip mall to a nondescript looking warehouse. He put the car in park and shut off the ignition, glancing over at me excitedly. I looked from him to the building curiously.

"Ready?" His eyes were wide with excitement as he put his hand on my thigh.

"Let's do this!" Whatever this was.

He quickly hopped from the car and made his way to my side to open the door for me. With his hand on the small of my back, he led me to the door, opened it and followed me in.

As soon as we stepped inside I took in the sight before me. The walls were exposed brick, and there were six stations set up throughout the room, each standing on their own with a bar-like countertop and stovetop. The side wall held lines of ovens, and toward the front of the room was one large station covered with various ingredients.

I looked at Maddox, elation covering my face.

"I thought about making you dinner but realized I can't cook... I think this might be fun to do together... did I do well?" His expression was hopeful.

"You did great!" I was so giddy I had to stop myself from jumping up and down.

"Oh good, Gabe thought it was a terrible idea, me taking you to a cooking class when you already spend so much time cooking," he explained as we waited by the door.

"No, you were right! What are we making?"

"Hello, are you scheduled for tonight's class?" An older woman wearing an apron with various multicolored cupcakes greeted us.

"Yes, under Maddox Spencer."

"Ah yes, Mr and Mrs Spencer. You'll be on station six." She pointed to an open station toward the back of the room.

"I forgot to mention I was planning to take you to a chapel to get married on the way here, but decided that AND a cooking class might be too forward of me."

"That's probably wise. I usually reserve marriage for the third or fourth date," I joked.

I looked over our station as a few other couples came in and were shown to their stations.

"Wait a second, you said I needed to wear comfortable clothes with nothing too loose fitting... for a cooking class?"

"Hey, I was just passing along what the instructor told me when I made the reservation. Well, the second part might have been for my own benefit."

"Uh huh." I shook my head at him.

"Good evening, everyone, and thank you for joining us for our Italian Cooking session." The same woman who had greeted us now stood at the front of the room addressing everyone.

"Today's menu includes Steak Gorgonzola Fettuccini Alfredo, a spring salad with homemade blackberry balsamic dressing, and a simple Italian Anise cookie."

I couldn't help but giggle a bit to myself as Maddox appeared a bit overwhelmed by the instruction sheet.

Once the instructor was finished going over the first set of instructions we were left to collect the ingredients and tools we would need. Once again Maddox looked over the list, a little bewildered.

"Gorgonzola cheese… Anise extract…"

"Why don't you grab the tools and I'll get the ingredients," I suggested.

"Good idea." He handed the list over to me.

By the time I got back with our various ingredients, Maddox was still looking through the cabinets.

"What's a colander?"

"Seriously?" I laughed. "How have you survived this long?" I pulled the colander from the cabinet underneath the countertop.

"Carryout?" He grinned.

I tried very hard to focus on the instructions from the front of the class but found it very hard to do so as Maddox was playing with the garlic press as if it was an instrument from another dimension. When he got the attention of the couple at the station next to us I grabbed it from his hand and set it back down on the counter.

"You better pay attention or we'll be forced to get pizza after this thing is over," I whispered.

"That's why I brought a professional." He grinned and poked me playfully in my side.

Dessert was made first so the cookies would have a chance to bake and cool, however apparently it is not a known fact that when combining flour with other dry ingredients, one should not drop them so abruptly that flour dusts everyone and everything within a five-foot radius.

We both laughed at our flour-covered predicament while the instructor looked down her nose at us.

"Shhh… you're going to get us kicked out of here!" I said as I dusted the flour off of my supplied apron.

By the time we were working on our balsamic reduction and cream sauce, Maddox had fully crossed over into what I now realized was a very playful side.

"You've got flour on your nose." Maddox wiped his finger across my nose and cheek.

"Hmmm... I wonder whose fault that is!" I smiled over my shoulder at him as I continued my constant whipping. "Why don't you start the water for the pasta?"

"Aw, now that's something I know how to do!" He busied himself with his task.

I listened intently while she discussed different wine pairings for traditional Italian dishes, that is until I heard the sizzling sounds the boiling pot of water made as it spilled over the burner. Maddox frantically tried to get it under control as I stepped in, decreased the temperature, and moved it to another burner. I couldn't help but laugh at Maddox's kitchen skills, or lack thereof.

Somehow, we managed to put our meal together and sat down in the separate dining area to eat.

"That was a little more difficult than I expected." He placed his napkin across his lap.

"Nah, it wasn't so bad. You did good!"

"No, but you are pretty incredible. It was nice to see you doing your thing."

"Thank you, but I've still got a ways to go." I carefully spun my fork against my spoon to get the perfect bite.

"I wish I was as confident about what I was doing, I'm just not sure the family business is my thing."

I frowned slightly at his admission. "What is the family business exactly?"

Maddox exhaled and pushed his chair back slightly from the table.

"Basically S.I. was started in the early 1900s by my great-great-grandfather. What began as an engineering and architectural firm rapidly evolved over the years into an international business that does everything from highways, metro systems, power stations to mining and wastewater treatment."

His words were robotic and lacked all passion or interest.

"So that would explain your engineering degree," I said, mostly to myself.

Pushing my plate aside I leaned in closer to him. "Okay, so take all that away, no family business. What would you do?"

Maddox leaned back in his chair, tipped his head back, and looked toward the ceiling.

"That's the thing; there is never one without the other."

I tilted my head to the side and looked at him questioningly.

Now he came alive a bit with the answer, his blue eyes lighting up as he looked more hopeful and excited than I'd seen him before.

"I would want to do more of the stuff my mother does. She's heavily involved at the Children's Hospital, and actually it was help from SI that made it possible for an entire pediatric cancer wing to be built."

Just as quickly his demeanor reverted from excitement and back to business as he continued.

"But that's what you have to do, pay dues and build an empire, then you can truly make a difference."

"I don't know, I think you can make a difference without an empire. Maybe to build an entire cancer wing... but sometimes the smallest things can make the difference."

I could tell from his lack of response that he had resigned himself to the fact that his family business was what he had to do.

"So, what is the plan? Will you travel the world and work on these projects alongside your family?"

"No, that's not really the way things are done there anymore. Basically, I would be joining the board and will help make the decisions as to what projects we accept, and how those projects will be managed."

I nodded in understanding, yet I didn't really understand. He was getting his degree in engineering, and while I'm sure he would be putting it to good use, it seemed as if he were using it for something entirely different, something he didn't really want.

"You ready to get out of here?" He wagged his eyebrows excitedly.

"Sure." I laughed.

As we made our way to the front door our instructor thanked us for coming as Maddox helped me into my coat.

"I really hope you join us again!" She looked directly at me.

"I will say your husband might benefit from some... remedial courses, if that would be of interest." I couldn't help but grin at the way she scrunched up her nose while she spoke the word *remedial*.

"I think I may just leave the cooking to Becca." He smiled as he slipped into his own coat.

"Thanks again." I held my hand out to her.

"Anytime, dear."

Maddox held the door open for me and joined my quick pace to the car. The sun had since set, and the cold night fogged our breath as we exhaled.

"It's freezing!" I said, as he unlocked the car door and ushered me in.

"I'm sorry, I should have started the car and let it warm up." He got inside, started the ignition, and cranked up the heat.

"Oh, it's fine." I rubbed my hands together for warmth.

"Here, let me." He took my hands in his and rubbed them together.

"Thanks for coming with me tonight, although if I'd thought it through I may have picked something I was a little more…experienced with."

"I thought it was sweet." I smiled, keeping his eye contact. "Not a lot of guys would even think of a date like that."

"Well, I guess I'm not like a lot of other guys."

"No, you're certainly not."

Maddox put the car in gear but held onto my hand resting in my lap.

"Sadly, those cookies were pretty disgusting." His eyes went from the rearview mirror to the road.

"Right? I was so surprised!" I agreed.

"So it would appear I still owe you dessert."

"Mmm, dessert. I could never turn that down." I returned his grin as he looked from the road to me.

"Good, I know just the thing." He squeezed my hand.

I was a bit surprised as he pulled into the parking lot of the Super Shop & Stop, having expected we'd go somewhere like an ice cream parlor.

"Stay here, I'll be right back," he grinned as he hopped from the car.

During the ten or so minutes he was gone I halfheartedly browsed my Facebook. A story had caught my attention, so I jumped a bit when he returned lugging five or six bags into the back of the car.

"What all did you get?!" I looked over my shoulder at all the bags.

The first thing that caught my eye was a can of Reddi-Wip and I pulled it from the bag.

"Oh, so *that's* what you have in mind!" I pointed my finger at him with pretend revulsion.

"Ha! Actually, that is for my Oreo sundae but now that you mention it…" He trailed off as his eyes looked me over with promise.

"So, what's in those bags for me?" I asked playfully.

"Besides the Reddi-Wip?"

I gave him a pretend warning glance.

"Well, being that I wasn't sure what you'd like, you've pretty much got your choice of any ice cream flavor or topping."

I smiled to myself. Maddox was almost too easy to like.

***

When we arrived at Maddox's building I tried to help him carry the copious amounts of ice cream and toppings to his place, but he refused, and instead gave me his keys to open up the outer door and his front door.

I followed him to the kitchen, leaning against the bar as he set down all the bags and started removing the contents and laying them out on the bar.

"What happens if I want your Oreo ice cream?" I asked a bit sheepishly, considering all the different options he'd given me.

"I don't think I'll mind sharing." He pulled the lid off the ice cream.

"Here, come sit and you can help me." He patted the countertop with his free hand.

I took off my coat and hopped up so I was sitting on the countertop next to where he stood.

"I might even give you some of my Oreos." He pulled the cookies from the grocery bag.

"Mmm, Double Stuf!" I held my hand across my heart.

"Well, I am a man of sophisticated tastes."

I sat watching him and couldn't help but think that I really liked his playful side. On one hand, he was an educated, strong man, but there was also a real tender, almost boyish side to him that was nothing short of adorable.

"What are you grinning about?" He dipped his professional grade ice cream scoop into the half-gallon carton.

"Nothing…" I said, not wanting to let him on to the fact that at this moment I was finding him pretty damn tempting.

"Want a bite?" He held out a spoon with an obnoxious amount of ice cream on it.

I nodded and he came closer to me so he was standing between my legs. He held the heaping spoon close to me, but then quickly pulled the spoon out of my reach.

"You know, on second thought, maybe I didn't get enough to share." He grinned and shoved the spoon in his mouth; his other hand held the half-gallon to his chest protectively.

Quickly I grabbed the can of Reddi-Wip sitting on the countertop next to me and pointed it at him.

"You better think real carefully about what you do next," I warned.

When he tried to back up slowly I grabbed the bottom of his shirt. "You don't have the guts."

Without really thinking it through I pressed my finger down on the spout and shot Reddi-Wipp, completely covering his shirt and neck.

"HA! That's the last time you test my courage!" I danced in celebration.

Oh shit.

Maddox stood there, void of reaction, his eyes squeezed shut. After a couple seconds of silence, I quickly realized my little joke was a bad idea.

"Hey, I'm sorry…" I started.

"No, it's okay." Maddox extended his arms searching for the countertop, his eyes still squeezed shut. "I think some of it ended up in my eyes, they are burning something fierce." His expression was pained.

"Oh my gosh! I'm so sorry! Come here."

I pulled him toward the countertop and grabbed a towel to dab his eyes.

"Can you open them at all?" I carefully examined his eyes.

"I don't know, let me try."

And with that, his eyes snapped open wide, the can of Reddi-Wip now in his hands. Grabbing me around the waist he pulled my upper body flush against him and held my hands behind my back with one hand.

"That was a *very* bad idea, little girl." His grin was one of mischief and revenge.

I squealed when he held the can less than an inch from my face, and tried without success to squirm free of his grasp.

"I *really* hope you like whipped cream," he said, just before he unloaded a huge dollop directly on my nose.

In the small space that existed between us, I pulled my knees up and pushed against him just enough so he lost his hold on my hands. As soon as I was free I jumped down and started to run from the room but he caught me around the waist. I wiped the whipped cream from my face, turned toward him, and delivered the white creamy fluff right across his face.

"Ohhh, you're in trouble!" he huffed.

Suffice it to say a battle ensued. Countertops were streaked with sticky whipped cream, the floor was a slippery mess, and both of us were covered nearly head to toe. We stood there looking at each other, breaths heaving.

"Well, that was fun." I laughed.

"You've got a little something …" He pointed to his cheek.

"Oh, do I?" My tone was one of shock. "How embarrassing." I brought my hand to my cheek to wipe away the offending spot.

"Here, let me get it for you." He stepped toward me.

Fearful, I looked to the Reddi-Wip that lay on its side on the counter but quickly remembered its contents had long since run out.

A laugh escaped his mouth and he held both his hands up. "I come in peace." He stepped toward me.

Slowly, he lifted his hand to my cheek and gently wiped away a glob of the cream. "See." His eyes held a much different kind of intensity.

My eyes were drawn to his lips and I got up on my tippy toes to kiss him, but my foot slipped in our mess that now dangerously coated the floor. I started to fall backward and Maddox went to grab me with one hand and tried to steady himself on the countertop with his other, which was now also covered in melted ice cream and whipped cream, lost his balance, and we both ended up on the floor.

In his chivalrous attempt to save me he ended up spinning me around so when we fell he landed smack on his butt with me, of course, falling right on top of him. We both broke into laughter.

"Well aren't you just a little hazard." His face inches from mine, he tucked a few stray strands of hair behind my ear.

Before I could respond his mouth found mine as he put his arms around my waist pulling me securely against him. Straddling his waist I deepened our kiss, my lips tasting the sweetness of his mouth.

His lips were firm against mine as our mouths opened, our tongues seeking each other out. Without conscious thought my hips flexed up moving against him as his other hand went to my butt, grasping it firmly with his strong hand.

A small whine escaped my lips as his hand moved under my shirt and felt the soft skin at the small of my back. My skin burned and tingled with a heat that left me squirming under his touch.

When his tongue trailed to my neck I lost all conscious thought, my head dropped back and I closed my eyes as he sucked and licked kisses across my skin.

Wanting to feel his hot skin against my own, I grabbed the bottom of his shirt and pulled it over his stomach. He took it from there, removed his hands from my waist and pulled his shirt over his head. My eyes greedily took in his tanned, muscular stomach before he flipped us over so I was now on my back on the sticky ceramic tile and he was the one on top. His hand went directly to my stomach and snaked its way under the fabric of my shirt across the bare skin of my navel. His mouth once again found mine, our lips and tongues greedy for more. My back arched, pressing him harder against me and he groaned slightly, his hot breath mixing with mine. As his hand continued to move upward from my navel, up my ribs and just under the wire of my bra, I could feel his hard length against my thigh. As much as I knew it was a bad idea to take things so far so quickly, I moved against him rubbing him in just the right place.

"Hey, Mad?" The front door slammed closed and we froze as Gabe crossed the short distance to find us in the kitchen. On the floor. Covered in Reddi-Wip.

In some lame attempt to hide from the situation I pulled closer to Maddox and squeezed my eyes shut.

"Jesus Christ!" He turned around quickly and shielded his eyes simultaneously.

I'm pretty sure his tone indicated both shock and humor, although that was something I hadn't really realized was possible.

"I'll just..." he trailed off before walking away.

A door closed in the distance.

"Oops," Maddox laughed.

I chanced a glance at him and saw him smiling down at me. He kissed my nose and got up, offering a hand to me.

I knew my face had to be the darkest shade of red possible as I straightened my clothes and tried to compose myself.

"I'm just going to run to the bathroom and then I'll help you clean this up." My eyes scanned the disheveled kitchen.

"Nah, it will be easier to just tear it down and rebuild," he said as he scratched his chin.

Chapter Twenty-Four

Big blue eyes watched me as I attempted to reread a chapter, for the third time, from my macroeconomics textbook. I set the book down in my lap and rubbed my hands over my face in frustration.

For the last few weeks we'd made studying together a pretty regular thing, and every Friday he took me to a new, extravagant restaurant. Initially, I tried to get him to stop spending so much money on me but he'd said there was no way he was taking a future chef to TGI Friday's. He'd gone on to explain it was good research for me, and I eventually stopped trying to get him to change his mind.

"Why am I not getting this?" It didn't seem to matter how many times I read and reread the chapter, I wasn't getting it. "And why do I have to understand national trends that affect inflation and unemployment?" I could feel my face redden with a mixture of annoyance and anger. "I just want to cook!"

On that last note, I picked up the book and threw it on the floor, altogether done with the subject.

Maddox moved the laptop from his lap and put it on the side of the bed. "Come here." He held his arms out to me.

I scooted the short distance between us resting my head against his chest.

"If you *only* wanted to cook then those things may not matter, but you don't just want to cook. You want to have your own restaurant, and that information will be important for that." His fingers trailed across my back.

"And, I'll have you know I got a B+ in Macro so I'm happy to help you. You'll get it."

I smiled, although from my current position he couldn't see my face, so I nodded.

"You may need to take a break from it. Sometimes when you try so hard to force it, it makes it harder to take in."

"C'mon, come out with me tonight."

Maddox had told me earlier that he, Gabe, Stephy, and a few others were going out and I should join them, but feeling so overwhelmed with this class I'd initially said I couldn't go.

"Please … it's Saturday night." He rocked his weight against me nudging me gently.

"Alright." I turned my head so I could look up at him.

Most of the time Maddox was really easy to please, and his excited smile was always contagious.

"Since we're done studying … wanna take a nap before we go out?" His expression showed only a trace of mischief as he pulled me down with him so we were lying in my bed.

I'd grown quite accustomed to making out with Maddox and damn, was he good at it. I'd decided pretty quickly I wanted to wait on the whole sex thing, for a while at least. I just wasn't ready for the seriousness that went along with a relationship, and I'm not the type of person who can be that casual about sex. But good God, was he tempting.

Maddox was lying on his side and he pulled me back against him so we were spooning. I closed my eyes and wondered briefly if it was actually a nap he was wanting.

As if on cue Maddox's hand, which was resting on my hip, slowly dipped under the fabric of my shirt and started caressing the skin there. He'd quickly figured out that when he touched me there, shivers erupted across my entire body—a fact that he loved to exploit.

Strong arms wrapped around me and pulled me up his body so that instead of resting my head on his chest we were now face to face.

"That's better," he said quietly in my ear.

His hand traveled higher on my belly until his fingers gently traced my ribs leaving heat behind in their wake.

A purr of a moan escaped me when his mouth found my neck and laid small kisses across it. I squirmed against him, my body unable to stay still.

Something inside me found a bit of courage that I am often lacking and I pulled away from him and got up from the bed. He watched me curiously as if maybe I actually wanted to take a nap after all. I pushed him so he was lying flat on his back and climbed on his lap, straddling him. Grinning with surprise he put his hands on my hips as I leaned forward and kissed him, my hair falling over him as I did so. I set the tone of our kiss, my mouth opening and my tongue sliding gently across his lips. His hands grasped me tighter by the hips and our lips moved together in synchrony. With my legs holding me in place my hands went to his shirt and pulled it up over his pecs so I could feel his chest, which even lying down showed the ripples of his muscles. His tanned chest only had a few speckles of blonde hair and a thicker line ran from his belly button down to where his jeans met his skin. I couldn't help myself as I rocked my hips against his groin and he moaned out in pleasure.

He sat up with urgency and his lips plastered to mine once again. Our kisses became desperate and he pulled my shirt up easily over my head. He lay back down but propped his head with a pillow and pulled me to him, kissing my neck, then my collarbone before his mouth covered my nipple through the slight fabric of my black bra. My hand played with the curls of his hair as he latched onto my breast, sucking at my nipple gently. He pulled his mouth from me long enough to pull the thin fabric away from my breast before he covered the bare skin with his mouth. A moan escaped me before I could even realize it was threatening.

From behind me the clasp of my bra was undone and he pulled it from my arms leaving me bare before him.

He watched me for a moment as if memorizing the sight of me.

"You are stunning." His fingers trailed the line of my jaw, down my neck and between my breasts.

Leaning down I kissed him thank you. After a few minutes we were both grinding against each other and I was quickly beginning to change my mind about the whole no sex thing when we both heard a key in the door.

Frantically I hopped off Maddox and threw my shirt on deciding I didn't have enough time to get both my bra and shirt on. By the time Kera made it to our shared room Maddox looked completely calm and collected as if nothing had happened. I, on the other hand, was completely certain she knew exactly what she had nearly walked in on.

"Hi!" Kera said cheerfully as she set her bag down on her desk.

"Hey," I smiled while willing the blood to drain from my face.

"I gotta go, babe, but I'll pick you up about nine?"

"Yeah, sounds good."

He stood from the bed and pulled me close to him. He kissed my mouth and kept our lips together as he whispered, "That is to be continued." His tone was slightly pained.

Another kiss and he said goodbye to Kera as he left.

"What were you guys doing in here?" Kera teased.

"Seriously? How did you know?" I asked exasperated.

"Ha!" Kera laughed as she sat down on her bed and watched me with humor in her eyes.

"Your face was bright red and your eyes looked like they were gonna pop out of your head when I walked in. Did you ever get away with anything as a kid?" She laughed.

"Damn. And no, I never did get away with anything!"

***

When I'd asked Maddox what I should wear, I, unfortunately, listened to him when he said whatever was fine. So, showing up in jeans and a long sleeve T-shirt with a scarf seemed completely acceptable at the time. As soon as we walked into Ruth's Chris I immediately felt out of place. Maybe it would have been fine if Gabe and Stephy didn't look like they were getting ready to walk a runway, but nonetheless, there I was.

"Why didn't you tell me to wear something nicer?" I nervously held onto Maddox's arm as we walked past the hostess to the bar area.

"You're fine." He didn't seem to think anything of it, which should have given me some comfort, but it didn't.

We approached the high-top table where they were seated. Stephy sat next to Gabe, her short black dress giving the impression that her legs went on for days. One hand held her glass of red wine and the other possessively held onto Gabe.

"Hey, buddy!" Gabe said with a chipper smile as soon as he saw us approach. "Becca, you keeping this kid in line?"

Before I could answer, Stephy's scoff made us all turn to look at her. Whatever explanation she was going to give, if any, died when she looked at me and took in my appearance.

"Oh boy, laundry day?" Her expression showed one of pity and disgust.

Her response could have been taken as just her joking around, that is if you were completely dense, or in this particular situation, a man.

I could already see myself in the middle of the night tonight coming up with the perfect zinger to sling back at her, but as it always seems to work, I had nothing in the right moment.

"Good to see you too, Stephy," was my response, lame as it was. Not that it mattered anyway because she had already turned away from me and back to her wine.

"What do you want to drink, babe?" Maddox asked, and I had to make a conscious effort not to gape at him. Seriously, were men this obtuse, or was it more about not dealing with the things they didn't want to deal with?

"Chardonnay." I put on my best smile as I took off my coat and sat down at the table, thankfully across from Gabe so I wouldn't have to be directly across from Stephy all night.

Despite my best efforts not to allow Stephy's comment to get to me, I was still struggling to let it go. But I smiled, listened, and even participated in the conversation periodically.

"I personally don't understand why anyone would want to backpack across Europe. If you want to go to Europe then go to Europe, but that's what jets are for." Stephy added her two cents to the conversation sticking her nose up periodically.

"I don't know, I think part of it is the adventure. You could fly everywhere but if you did you'd miss the amazing landscape of the countryside and the quaint small towns you may otherwise never get to see," I said as Gabe and Maddox nodded approvingly.

Stephy took a drink from her glass but displeasure was apparent on her face.

"All I can say is June can't come soon enough! No more school and three months across Europe is exactly what I need." Maddox relaxed back in his chair and rested his hand on my thigh.

"You know what we need?" Gabe asked Maddox excitedly.

Maddox gave him a questioning glance as Gabe hopped from the table and headed toward the bar.

"You know, three months is a long time. I may just have to fly you out to come spend a couple of weeks with us." Maddox wrapped his arm around me.

"I don't know, maybe." I grinned as if I was going to miss a chance to spend a few weeks with Maddox, in Europe of all places.

He leaned forward and kissed my lips sweetly. Funny that such a simple, short kiss could bring about such a skin-tingling reaction.

My earlier bad mood was disappearing and my smile was genuine, despite Stephy's obvious distaste at Maddox and me.

"Lookie what I got!!" Gabe excitedly set down four glasses on the table.

"What do we have here?" Maddox asked while Stephy scrunched her nose up, taking a whiff.

"This just so happens to be the best damn bourbon you can get..." Gabe paused for effect.

We all watched him questioningly, Maddox showing the most excitement of course.

"Pappy Van Winkle!" Gabe exclaimed.

"No way?!" Maddox shared in their moment of pure joy while I looked at the two of them trying to figure out what was so exciting.

We all took a drink from our glasses and I watched Gabe and Maddox, who both appeared to be not just tasting it, but experiencing it. That was something I could respect, although with me it was much more about the food and less about the drink.

I fought past the bitterness of it and tried to understand what they seemed to be getting out of it, but I guessed it really was more of an acquired taste.

For the next hour, we sat and talked about various things, although mostly we talked about their backpacking trip and all the things they were planning to see and do.

"One more drink?" Gabe asked, and Maddox looked my way as if to see if I was up for one more. I nodded.

"One more," Maddox agreed.

"What do you want?" Gabe looked at me first.

"I'm still working on my last one." I pointed to my half-full glass of wine.

"Maddox?" he questioned.

"I think I'm gonna have to go with old faithful," Maddox answered.

"Oh wow! I guess there is something you can stay faithful to!" Stephy spit, her expression showing she was pretty damn proud of herself.

"Stephy!" Anger laced Gabe's tone.

What the fuck?

Maddox said nothing as he bore a hole in Stephy's head with his eyes.

"What?" she asked with practiced innocence as she shrugged her shoulders slightly.

I felt the heat rise to my face with a potent mix of anger and frustration. It had been obvious from the moment I met Stephy that she had some kind of a problem with me. Her being obnoxious and unfriendly was somewhat annoying, but at the same time not overly difficult to ignore. But her words did exactly what she wanted them to do—made me doubt Maddox. There was no question he and I came from different worlds, and he often talked about things like money and traveling the globe, as if it were simple, something everybody did. There was a line that existed between us he didn't understand; the line between having things handed to you and having to work for everything.

I finished off the drink I'd been milking for the last forty-five minutes in one swift gulp, probably a tell that I was uncomfortable, but I was past the point of giving a shit. An overwhelming urge to get up and leave ran through me but I fought if off, mostly because I didn't want to give Stephy the impression she was able to get rid of me so easily.

I looked up to find Maddox still glaring at her, things obviously being said without words. As soon as Maddox saw me look up his eyes shot to me and I was surprised at the amount of concern I saw in his expression.

I looked away from his intense gaze. There was no way in hell I was going to have this conversation right now, especially not in front of people. Gabe got up and went to the bar to get drinks as I silently tried to figure out a way to leave without it looking completely obvious I wanted out of this situation.

Holding my phone in my lap I pulled up my Uber app. I might not be running out the door immediately but I arranged for my ride to pick me up in a half hour. In the meantime, I'd figure out a way to make a graceful exit.

Awkward silence existed between the three of us and Maddox fidgeted uncomfortably, a habit I'd yet to see from him. He put his hand on my knee and rubbed his thumb gently against the fabric of my jeans.

Gabe returned to the table overly chipper as he handed everyone a shot. This time I took it without a moment's hesitation. As much as I wanted to appear normal I didn't have it in me to make eye contact with Maddox.

After about ten minutes Maddox spoke up saying we were going to head out. Relief set in immediately that I wasn't the one to have to say I was leaving.

"It was really good to see you again, Becca." Gabe obviously felt bad and verged on being over the top trying to make things better.

"You too." I smiled. He was the only person at the table that didn't currently have my blood boiling.

"Bye Becca!"

Oh my God, I don't think I've ever wanted to slap someone more in my entire life. Is "How to be a smug bitch" a course at every prep school?

"Bye." Damn my inability to be passive aggressive. I could only hope I was successfully pulling off my guise of not giving a shit.

Maddox helped me into my coat and it took everything I had in me to not sprint to the front door. We made it out into the cold air and my lungs welcomed it.

"Becca," he started, reaching out.

"Seriously." I whipped around to face him. "It's fine. I don't want to go there." I quickly looked away from him—his expression of longing and concern was not something I expected.

My breath cast a fog with every exhale and I rubbed my hands over my upper arms trying to warm myself.

Maddox tried to put his arms around me but I stepped out of his reach.

"Just come back to my place, let me explain things."

"Or we can go to your place," he continued when I didn't respond.

"No, I'm good on the explanations for tonight." I turned and started walking to the side of the building. Neither of us was raising our voices but nonetheless, we'd managed to get the attention of the valet parkers.

"Don't make a big deal out of this."

And with that comment, something switched inside me.

I whirled around, nearly running into his chest since he was walking behind me a bit closer than I realized.

"Seriously? First of all, I don't particularly enjoy hanging out with people who are nasty to me every time I see them. And it doesn't help when you tell me it doesn't matter what I wear, and then I show up looking like a homeless person compared to everyone else. And does it concern me that Stephy felt the need to point out to me that you have issues being faithful? A little bit! But you know what? It's not my place to worry about that because you and I are just… whatever we are." I pointed between the two of us. "So whatever, it doesn't matter."

I didn't realize I hadn't remembered to breathe during my entire rant until the huge breath I took once I'd said what I needed to say.

"It does matter! You matter to me." He reached out for me again.

"Look, I just want to go. Okay?" I held his eye contact and gave him my best "I mean business" look.

As if on cue my Uber arrived and I got in, leaving Maddox standing there watching me go.

Chapter Twenty-Five

The buzzer to the front door rang and Kera excitedly jumped out of bed.

"Nobody should be allowed to have that much energy in the morning," I said, pulling the blankets over my head.

"Delivery for Ms. Stanton," a male voice echoed through our intercom.

"Surprise, surprise," Kera huffed under her breath, loud enough for me to hear her.

"Are you going to get up and go get it?" she asked, suddenly standing above me.

"No." My voice was muffled under the warmth of my covers.

"Get up!" She nudged me.

"I want to see what it is this time!" she whined.

"Urgh!" I said, using a bit too much effort to pull the covers off.

Deciding I didn't give a crap who saw me in my pajamas, I grabbed a hooded sweatshirt out of my closet and threw it on over my tank top and boxer shorts. I jammed my feet one at a time into a pair of slippers. I shuffled across the floor, swung the front door open and didn't bother closing it before I made my way to the elevator. Kera was taking far too much enjoyment out of my situation so that was my way of punishing her for it.

I hit the down button repeatedly before I even realized what I was doing. By the time the elevator dinged its arrival I'd given myself a brief, yet silent pep talk and decided I was done letting this situation consume so much of my thoughts.

A delivery guy was impatiently tapping his foot next to the desk as he held an obnoxiously sized brown teddy bear and a huge vase of long stem red roses.

"Hi," I said as I stood before him.

"Good to see you again," he joked, handing over the form for me to sign.

"Try not to forgive him quite so soon, he's a great tipper." He winked.

"How do you know it's someone who needs forgiveness?" I eyed him speculatively.

"I've been doing this a long time, and this right here," he held up the teddy bear and the flowers, "is called trying to make up for something."

"Fair enough." After thanking him I took the flowers and the bear and headed back upstairs.

Kera was already in the shower when I got back and I threw the bear on my bed and set the flowers on my desk next to the ones that had been delivered yesterday. He'd sent flowers, he'd called, and he'd texted, but I wasn't quite sure what I wanted to say, if anything. A big part of me felt that not getting involved with him was the best choice, but in reality, I knew I was already involved.

"What's the card say?" Kera held her towel to herself and rummaged through her closet.

"I don't know. Do you think I'm being too hard on him?" I plucked the card from the arrangement.

"Well, I think you should talk to him, and then decide what you want to do. Right now you're just avoiding it."

"I know, you're right. Why do you always have to make so much sense?"

"It's easy when it's not your own life." She smiled.

I spent a little too much time doing absolutely nothing, so by the time I was willing to get ready for class I was already running behind. I hopped in the shower and my thoughts kept returning to Maddox. Kera was right. All I was doing was avoiding the situation, and refusing to deal with it wasn't making me feel any better. It wasn't really even a matter of Maddox doing something wrong, it was more whether I wanted to willingly get involved with someone who apparently had a past that involved cheating. Why it was so much of a concern for Stephy I had no idea. What I did know was that it was time to stop avoiding the situation and make a decision about how I was going to handle it.

I spent more time than I should have curling my hair so I could keep it down and put on some makeup. Something about the other night made me not want to feel like I wasn't looking my best.

I made it through Macroeconomics, although while my body was physically in class my thoughts were focused on Maddox. Not surprisingly, when I walked out into the crowded street after class, there was Maddox, leaning against his parked car in the fire lane. Unable to control myself, a smile found its way to my lips and relief showed across his face.

"Hey," he said as I made my way to him.

"Hi." I stopped just in front of him awkwardly. Usually, we would greet each other with a kiss but I wasn't exactly sure how to act.

"Don't be mad, I just wanted to see you."

"I'm not mad, I'm just... trying to figure things out I guess." I looked up at him and silently wondered how I was supposed to think straight with him in such close proximity.

Maddox took the bag from my arm and opened my door for me. When I started to get in he kissed the side of my head. Without realizing it I closed my eyes and drank in that moment a bit too much. I hated to admit it, but I'd missed him over the past two days. We'd gone more than two days without seeing each other before, but the idea that what we had could be over left me wanting.

"I get it." He helped me in the car and hopped in the driver's seat. He took my hand and held it as it rested on my thigh.

"I just don't want you to decide anything without talking to me about it."

We spent the ride back to my place in silence, the radio quietly playing in the background as he held tightly to my hand. I could almost see his desperation. While it felt nice to be so wanted, a big part of me was afraid of what would happen if the two of us stayed together.

Once we arrived at my place Maddox got out of the car quickly so he could open my door for me. As soon as I got out he took my hand in his again. We headed down the walkway and into my building. By the time we made it to my room, the tension was palpable. Thankfully Kera was still going to be at her classes for a while which would give us a chance to talk, although now that it was time to talk I found myself wanting to avoid it altogether.

"Becca...come here," Maddox said from his seated position on my bed.

I stopped my needless straightening of my desk and walked over to him. When I got close he wrapped his arms around my waist and rested the side of his face against my chest.

"Just tell me you'll listen to me before you make up your mind, alright?"

I nodded my head, not thinking about the fact he wasn't able to see me.

I sat down on my bed next to him and faced him.

"Izzy is my ex. I dated her somewhat off and on for three years." He exhaled and looked away from me briefly before his eyes returned to mine once again.

"There was just a lot of pressure there. Pressure from her, from my family. Everyone had such high expectations that she and I would end up together, and that I would take over my family's business."

He watched me intently as if trying to gauge my reaction.

"It was just too much, and yes, I made mistakes with her."

"You mean you cheated on her." I wasn't about to let him downplay what he'd done.

"Yes. I'm not proud of it, Becca, and Stephy running her mouth was obviously not how I wanted you to find all of this out," he said after a brief pause, and took my hand again.

"So Stephy and Izzy?" I started.

"Yes, they have been friends for a long time, and Stephy hasn't exactly moved past it."

"What about Izzy ... and your family? Have they moved past it?"

He frowned and in doing so set off an alarm within me.

"Yeah." The pitch of his voice was a bit higher when he said that, and I wasn't sure if it was because what he was saying was a lie, or if he was just trying to be optimistic.

"I mean, my family can be very ... difficult ... but they are starting to understand I'm not going to live my life exactly as they expect."

When I didn't respond he continued.

"Look, the thing is I really like you, and I'd like to have the chance to see where this goes. And back at the bar when you said you didn't know what we were it made me realize I know exactly where I want to be, and that's with you."

I saw nothing but serenity in his eyes, yet there was still a part of me afraid to trust him.

Maddox cupped my face with his hands. "Just tell me you're not going to give up on us so easily, over something that is long in my past."

"Is that where Izzy is, in your past?"

"Yes." He looked at me intently. "I wouldn't be here right now if that wasn't the case," he assured me as his fingertips traced my cheekbones. "Just tell me you want to be with me too and we'll make it official. Just us." He looked so vulnerable, it easily pulled at my heartstrings. The always confident and self-assured Maddox was sitting here in front of me with his heart on his sleeve.

"Alright," I answered, a slow smile stretching across my lips.

"Alright! Not quite the enthusiasm I was looking for but I'll take it." I laughed playfully at his reaction. "You know I want to be with you."

"Oh yeah?" he asked, as his face came closer to mine.

"Yeah." I grinned back at his response.

Before another word could pass between us his lips found mine. It was a tender, sweet kiss, one of his hands going around my waist and pulling me closer to him while the other went to the back of my neck to my hairline. It didn't matter how many times he touched me I always felt it—a near painful want to be closer to him. My body arched, pressing my breasts further against him and, in response, his grasp on my waist became tighter, pulling me against him.

"Oh, no more flowers then?" Kera bellowed with disappointment, startling us. We hadn't even heard her come in.

Both our eyes opened widely but Maddox didn't back away from me, our mouths parted, but our foreheads still touched as he closed his eyes and let out a slow exhale. I loved Kera but in this moment I really wished I had a private room.

"Nah, there's plenty more where those came from." He kept his eyes on me.

"You should come out with us tonight." He backed away just a bit from me and put his attention on Kera.

"We're going out tonight?" I smirked at him.

"We are," he said assuredly.

"Actually, I have a date!" Kera said excitedly.

"What?! With who?" Kera had readily spoken her displeasure at the lack of dating life she'd had lately.

"A guy in my pastry class." She beamed. "He's Italian and drop dead freaking gorgeous."

"Shopping?" I asked, but knew the answer; first dates always required a new outfit.

"Definitely."

"I guess I'll pick you up at eight then?" Maddox asked me as he got up from my bed.

"Eight it is." And now it was me beaming at him.

I stood from the bed and his arms were around me before I'd even taken a step. I looked at him, my chin resting on his chest, and he kissed my nose.

"See you tonight." His words sounded like a promise.

***

I was putting the finishing touches on my makeup when Maddox rang the buzzer from downstairs. I grabbed my gold glittery clutch and headed downstairs to meet him. I was glad he was running a few minutes behind because I'd been able to help Kera get ready after our shopping excursion. I was so happy—happy for her and happy for me. We were finding our way here in Providence, and everything felt good and right.

I waited impatiently for the elevator, not wanting to give my feet any extra reason to hate me tonight in my three-inch stiletto heels. Once again, and thanks to such unpredictable weather, we were having unseasonably warm temperatures for February. I felt amazing in my black backless dress. The mid-thigh length, together with my heels, made my legs look even longer, and what girl doesn't love a flared dress?

When I arrived on the first floor Maddox was chatting with the guy at the reception desk and I came up behind him and ran my fingers across his waist.

"Hey… wow." He spun around and his eyes looked me over, drinking me in. "You look … breathtaking." He shook his head a bit.

"Mmm." His hand went to the small of my back, revealing to him that the entire back was open except for a black ribbon that tied the two sleeves together, then fell all the way down my spine.

"You're very lucky you met me down here instead of having me come up. There is no chance we would have left the room," he whispered against my ear as we walked out into the night.

"I *really* like this dress." He opened the door for me and helped me in before joining me in the car.

"You sure you want to go? We could just head to my place," he suggested with a playful smile.

"You, sir, promised me a night out."

"Alright, but I do think you should come home with me tonight.

Since you're my girlfriend it only seems fair that I should get a little extra time."

"Hmm ... I'll think about it," I teased, already knowing I wouldn't be giving up the chance for a little time with him without roommates around.

***

I didn't quite know what to expect from a cigar bar but when we walked into Cubanos it was like no other bar I'd been to in Providence. Overly dim, the entire wall to the left was a glass walk-in humidor which illuminated the intimate space. The back wall was a long bar with racks of wine displayed behind it. The seating and tables were like those you would find in the offices of high-end executives—dark brown and black tufted leather chairs and love seats with small cocktail tables between them. Seated in front of the bay windows at the front was a small stage where two men sat on barstools. One sang, his voice echoing softly through the place, while the other sat with a cello propped between his legs, the bow fluidly floating atop the strings.

Maddox's hand stayed on the small of my back as he led me to the table where Gabe and a few other guys were sitting. They all stood when we arrived, and one of the guys got up and moved from the love seat and took a chair so Maddox and I could sit together.

Maddox greeted everyone and introduced me to the guys. I was always pleasantly surprised with Maddox's friends; they were friendly but also carried an air to themselves, and came off as much classier than the guys I was used to being around.

"Becca, I hear the two of you made it official?" Gabe asked, seemingly pleased while the other guys chatted amongst themselves.

"We did." I smiled with both satisfaction and a bit of embarrassment because of the attention.

"I'm sorry about Stephy, and I'm glad she didn't scare you away. She can just be a bit—"

"Bitchy," Maddox finished for Gabe.

The comment brought about the attention of the other guys and they all broke into laughter.

"She's not so bad; you'll see that when you get to know her better," Gabe finished.

The thought made my stomach drop a little and Maddox took my hand, lacing his fingers through my own as if knowing I needed some reassurance in the moment.

"What would you like to drink?" he asked as he kissed my knuckles.

I thought for a moment, tipping my head to the side and looking up at him.

"Surprise me," I smiled.

He leaned in close to me so the guys at the table wouldn't hear us. "You good?" His eyes quickly motioned toward everyone sitting with us.

"I'm good." I kissed him chastely on the lips.

The guys at the table, as it turned out, were nothing compared to the claws that came out when Stephy was present. A few of them went to Brown with Gabe and Maddox, all of which were graduating within the year.

"Are you a student at JWU?" one of the guys seated across from me asked. "I'm Chad, I think we might be in Macro together."

As soon as the words left his mouth I recognized him. He was a front-of-the-class, know-all-the-answers type, whereas I was the hiding-in-the-back and hope-to-not-get-called-on type.

"Yes! I thought you looked familiar," I said, recognition showing on my face. "I'm not going to lie, that class kind of makes me regret deciding to go to college altogether," I said, half joking, half completely serious.

"No … really?" Chad asked with a laugh.

"Seriously. I made the mistake of asking Professor Davis for some help, not knowing he's a serious creep."

Chad leaned forward with interest at my last comment. "Oh no, I've heard that before about him. I'd be glad to help you out if you'd like," he replied, just as Maddox got back to the table.

"What do you need help with?" Maddox asked as he sat down and handed me a glass of red wine.

"We were just talking about my God-awful Macroeconomics class. Chad is actually in the same class."

"I was just telling her I'd be happy to tutor her; sadly economics is kinda my thing," Chad joked.

"Oh, that's nice of you," Maddox's fingertips stroked the bare skin of my thigh before resting on my knee and tracing small circles there. "But I think I've got her covered. I also took Macro at Brown."

I brought my glass to my lips to hide the smile that immediately formed across my lips. Was that jealousy?

Chad didn't miss Maddox's hand on my leg and immediately

answered with a, "Sure, I got ya."

I saw Gabe out of the corner of my eye grinning, apparently not having missed Maddox's message.

"What do you think of the wine?" Maddox asked, bringing his attention back to me.

"It's good. I'm not used to something this dry but the flavor is really good."

"You want to try this?" Maddox handed me his short, wide glass of amber liquid.

"Sure." I took a small sip from the glass.

Maybe I look way too much into the little things but something felt intimate in that moment, the way he watched me when I drank from his glass, the way his fingers played across the bare skin of my knee ... everything about Maddox made me want him.

The liquid burned my throat on the way down and I tried not to scrunch my face up at the bitter taste of it.

"The more you drink it the more you'll be able to taste the different flavors of it. Maybe next time we should have you drink it with a little water." He took the glass from me and wiped his finger across my lip where a little of the scotch lingered.

"And when exactly did you start drinking scotch?" I asked.

Both Gabe and Maddox laughed when I asked the question.

"How old were we, Gabe?"

"God, I don't know ... ten?" he laughed.

"Ten!?" I looked wide-eyed between the two of them.

"Yeah, my dad had a decanter in his office and Gabe and I started sneaking in there and sampling the stuff. It didn't go so well the first few times," Maddox laughed.

"Maddox puked all over the floor but luckily the maid had a sweet spot for him so she cleaned it up and put him to bed without letting his dad know."

They both laughed at the memory.

"As we got a little older it started tasting a little better and we improved our methods. Dad was certain Mom was watering down the stuff because she didn't like that he drank it, when really it was us replacing what we'd taken."

"Did he ever figure it out?" Gabe asked, still laughing.

"Not until Maxwell, my brother"—he added for my benefit—"went and ratted us out a few Christmases ago!"

"I bet your dad was still pissed!" Gabe grinned.

"Oh, hell yeah he was! Apparently, it was an eight-thousand-dollar bottle of scotch I puked up all over his floor."

Everyone burst out laughing but I was still stuck on the fact that someone would leave an eight-thousand-dollar bottle of scotch anywhere other than in a safe!

I had to admire the relationship between Maddox and Gabe. It appeared they were very close and had been ever since they were very small. As their conversations often did, it soon became focused on their backpacking trip coming up in the summer. They talked about all the places they wanted to see but my interest was piqued when they started talking about Italy.

"Maybe that's when you should come join us? Maybe get some ideas for your restaurant?"

"That might be hard to turn down," I smiled.

"Why turn it down? Just say you'll come." He watched me but I couldn't commit to something so big without thinking it through.

As we continued our conversation throughout the night Maddox seemed to find every way possible to tease and taunt me with simple touches. He would lean back in the love seat, while I pretty much had to sit up straight or my dress would give a little too much leg away. His hand found the back of my dress, dipping below the fabric at the small of my back and sending chills across my body. While the touch wouldn't have been considered inappropriate to anyone else, he had me squirming silently under the surface.

His hand went again beneath the fabric of my dress and reached my side, sending tingles throughout my body.

"I *really* think you should come home with me tonight." His lips brushed my ear as he spoke.

I nodded yes, still trying to put on the pretense that I was listening to the conversation I was involved in at the table.

He placed a small kiss at the base of my neck when I agreed and a pulse ran through my body. The anticipation of being alone with him was beginning to make me crazy, and this time I thought my goosebumps gave me away.

"Where is the restroom?" I asked, and when someone started to speak up Maddox interrupted them.

"I'll take you." He took my hand as he got up front the love seat.

His hand still clasped in mine, I followed him as he led me down a small side hallway where the restrooms were. While the place was relatively small, all the tables and the bar were completely full with people standing around and milling about. Once we made it to the restrooms we were alone.

"This was a good idea."

"What?" I looked at him questioningly.

"Your guise of having to go to the bathroom so you could get me alone." He gently backed me against the wall, putting his hands on either side of me.

"Oh, is that what I was doing?" I tipped my head up to look at him.

"I'm sure of it," he said, his face slowly getting closer to mine.

His hand went to my side and his thumbs traced over my ribs.

"You about ready to go?"

As if I needed some convincing his lips pressed against mine, his tongue tasting of vanilla and maple.

"Yes," I said against his mouth, our breath entwining.

"Ok, let's go!" He took my hand and started to pull me toward the door.

"Wait!" I brought him to a stop. "I really do have to go to the bathroom!" I motioned toward the door.

"Oh yeah," he laughed. "I'll meet you at the table.

I checked myself in the mirror and messed with my hair that was in loose curls across my shoulders. It was funny how when you felt good you looked better, and I really was feeling like I'd found my place here at school. Once I was satisfied with my appearance I left the bathroom and ran right into Chad as he was coming out of the men's room.

"Oh, wow, sorry!" I said, nearly running straight into him.

"My fault," he smiled. "It was really nice seeing you tonight though, and I meant what I said about the tutoring. If you'd like we can get together after class and I can share my notes with you or whatever. Maybe grab lunch?"

"Yeah, maybe," I said, not really sure how to answer that question. It felt rude to turn down the help he was offering, but I wasn't actually trying to have lunch with him.

As we made it back to the table Maddox was standing and talking with everyone and turned as we approached.

"Great, I'll save a seat for you and see you in class on Monday," Chad said as he took his seat.

Seriously?

"You ready?" I approached Maddox and put my arms around his waist. I'd hoped it would take his attention away from Chad, who he was now glaring at.

When he refused to take his eyes off Chad I moved my hands to his belt buckle, my fingers sneaking just over the edge toward his belly and pulling him just a bit closer to me. That did draw his attention back to me, and he brought his thumb to my cheek and gently caressed it.

"Yeah, let's go." He took my hand.

We said our goodbyes and made our way out of the bar and back into the now chilly air. We hopped into one of the cabs that lined the street, opting to leave Superman parked there for the night.

We said nothing as his hand rested on my leg and suddenly moved higher, until it was under the fabric of my skirt. Excruciatingly slowly, his hand kept going, his fingers tracing small circles against my skin until he reached my inner thigh. Unintentionally I shifted, not being able to stay still with the way his touch made me burn with want, but in doing so my legs came apart just enough for one of his fingers to find the lace of my panties. I had been watching the driver, making sure he wasn't benefiting from our little show, but when he felt his way across the thin fabric of my panties I put my head against his chest and closed my eyes.

Deeply I exhaled against his chest and tried to keep quiet and still so I wouldn't give us away, but really I wanted to straddle his lap and feel him against me.

"Hey."

I looked up at him and he touched his finger to his lips, asking silently for a kiss. I leant up and kissed him; our lips parted, neither of us allowing it to go so far as to get the attention of our driver.

"Grrr," Maddox growled as he pulled his hand from my skirt and backed away from our kiss.

I couldn't help but silently celebrate that it appeared I had the same effect on him that he had on me.

When we arrived at his place he paid the driver and held my hand as we walked into the building. We stood quietly in the elevator amongst the usual metal stripping metal sounds as it made its way to his place.

I followed him inside, then I suddenly felt slightly uncomfortable by our silence and wasn't really sure what to say.

"You seem quiet," I said to his back since he wasn't facing me.

He turned around and looked at me, starting at my feet and slowly drinking me in, taking his time to allow his eyes to wander up my body before meeting my eyes.

"I didn't like Chad." He stepped toward me, leaving only inches between us.

"Really? You want to play jealous boyfriend all of a sudden?" I asked, a bit taken aback by his confession.

"I'm not *playing* anything." His hand went to my upper thigh, lightly grazing over my skin.

I exhaled slowly, trying to find some sort of response in my mind as his hand went higher, until his fingers reached the waist of my panties. His hand felt across the smooth skin of my stomach but kept dipping back down just under the lace fabric, teasing me but never giving me what I wanted.

A hitch in my breath brought his eyes back to mine and kept his hand gently playing against the fabric of my panties, his lips on mine. I moaned slightly as our mouths opened and moved together, his hand rubbing me a little more firmly against my panties. I wanted him so badly my body was near pain, throbbing and wet for him. Finally, he pulled my panties aside and slid one finger through my folds.

"Mine," he said against my mouth, his finger rubbing against my clit.

When that word left his lips I cried out, quite loudly I might add. Maybe I should have been upset that he was, in fact, playing the jealous boyfriend, but instead, the only response that went through my body and mind was that I wanted to be his.

My hands went to his belt as I tried desperately to figure out how to get his buckle undone, despite the fact that my head was tilted back and my eyes were closed, his mouth now focusing on the tender skin of my neck. Selfishly, I was only able to focus on the heat building inside me as his fingers worked across my clit.

"You better take that sweet little ass of yours upstairs before I make you mine right here against the front door." His voice was a half whisper half growl as he pulled his fingers from me and stepped back.

My eyes went straight to the bulge straining against the thin fabric of his gray dress pants, and I couldn't help myself when my hands went back to his belt, slowly unhooking it and pulling the leather from the loops. He watched me as I slid my hand across his cock through the fabric of his pants, grasping him delicately as I felt the length of him. The buckle hit the ground harshly as I let it fall from my hand and drop against the ceramic tile.

His breath hitched in his throat as I grasped him hard and he pointed to the stairs. "Up … stairs," he slowly got out.

I let him go and stepped around him heading upstairs. When I made it to his room he hadn't joined me yet, having stopped to lock the door and turn off the lights.

I pulled my panties off and dropped them on the middle of the floor and, as expected, when he walked in they were the first thing he saw. He stood there watching me, his blue eyes soft with want as he looked me over.

"Lie down," I instructed, and was surprised when he easily complied. He stretched out across his bed, his upper body slightly propped up against the headboard.

"Nope," I said when he started to undo the button of his pants, and he watched me unspeaking with obvious curiosity.

I walked over to him slowly before mounting myself on top of him, knowing full well I gave him a not-so-modest look at my goods as my leg went over him. His hands immediately went up under my skirt to grasp my hips and I unintentionally rocked forward as his hands moved to my naked ass.

I pulled his shirt up over his chest forcing him to let go of me long enough to pull it over his head. My hands ran across the hard muscles and I leaned over and kissed him, teasing and taunting him with my tongue. I felt him grow harder against me and I ground my hips and pushed hard against him in response. He pulled me closer, deepening our kiss as his hands ran up my bare back to the tie at my neck. Slowly he undid it and pulled the front of the dress away, leaving me naked and exposed in front of him, except for the short skirt which pooled across his waist. His hands went to my breasts and I arched my back, stabilizing myself by putting my arms straight back behind me and resting my hands on his thighs. His hips moved slightly against me as he fondled the fullness of my breasts, his thumbs occasionally brushing across my hard nipples.

"You are so fucking beautiful," he said, his voice raspy.

I watched him as he looked at me, his body still moving rhythmically beneath me, grinding us together.

I moved down on his legs just enough so I could get to the button of his pants and slowly undid it, then worked the zipper down. Maddox lifted me with him as he arched his hips up to pull his pants the rest of the way off. I let out a little laugh at that, not expecting him to lift me in the air quite so easily.

Again he took me by surprise when he suddenly moved, pulling me down on the bed next to him.

"This needs to come off." He pulled what remained of my dress down my legs, leaving me completely naked in front of him.

He shifted again so I was on my back and he was on top of me. My hands immediately went to his cock, which strained against the fabric of his black boxer briefs, but he pulled my hands away and held them above my head, effectively pinning me to the bed.

I let out an exaggerated sigh when he didn't let me have what I wanted, but he ignored me as he moved down my body until he was sitting between my knees. He pulled my legs up at the knee so I would spread out before him and I grabbed him, trying to bring him back up to me.

He looked at me unspeaking and then tried again. This time I allowed him to spread my legs pushing my knees in the air. His hand went to my neck, slowing working his way down between my breasts, past my navel, until finally, he slid one finger through my folds. My body arched off the bed slightly and I let out a moan when he found my wet clit.

"Do you have any idea how bad I want you?"

I nodded. I knew exactly how badly he wanted me. I was right there with him, wanting him just as badly.

My hips rocked without my consent as his fingers worked my clit in small circles. I was half-conscious to the fact he was moving further down on the bed, but I was too busy feeling what he was doing to pay much attention to anything else—until I felt his head between my legs. My eyes shot open and an uncharacteristically loud moan escaped my mouth when his hot breath and warm tongue lapped across my clit.

My body moved of its own accord with the pace he set and I had to fight the urge to pull my knees together and bring him closer to me.

A thought came across my mind that I should be embarrassed about not being able to control my body as my hips pressed harder against his mouth, or how wet he made me as his tongue worked me over. As quickly as the thought came it was gone, my body ruling my mind for a change.

My breath came quicker as I felt my orgasm building inside me, and I rocked on the bed grinding myself against him. As he continued sucking and pulling at my clit I felt his other hand sliding against my opening. A slow torturous tease threatening pure ecstasy as his fingers dipped slightly inside me before sliding up and down and away from precisely where I wanted them. I pushed against him, silently begging him to enter.

Moans continued to escape as I got closer and closer, the heat and want ready to explode when he finally slipped a finger inside. Slowly he worked it in and out of me as his tongue drove every conscious thought out of my head. He started to pull back and I cried out at the loss, but my cries became louder as he pushed back inside me stretching me as he slid another finger in. My hands went to his head desperately pulling at his hair, pushing him deeper as I screamed and exploded.

"You liked that?" he asked, satisfaction showing across his face as he pulled his fingers from me and sat up on the bed.

Somehow, despite everything, I still managed to feel self-conscious lying naked before him.

He lay down next to me and I watched him carefully waiting for him to make the next move. Instead, he just watched me tucking my overly tousled hair behind my ear.

I reached for him, finding him hard in my hands.

"We don't have to do anything else, I just wanted a taste."

I smiled, seeing in his face that he actually meant what he said.

"I don't think I'm quite done with you yet," I said as my hand moved across his length.

"Oh yeah?"

"Mmm hmm," I nodded as I pulled his hard cock from his boxer briefs.

A small hiss escaped his lips as he kept eye contact while I stroked him slowly up and down.

There was something seriously intense about him keeping his eyes on mine while I pumped him up and down, my fingers sliding over his head.

"Roll over," I said slightly, pushing him until he rolled onto his back. I sat on his thighs, held him in my hands and worked him slightly, increasing my pace. I edged my way down his legs and bent over him to lick a bead of pre-cum before my tongue circled the head. I slowly started working his cock into my mouth and he moaned my name, tangling his hands in my hair.

"Fuck. You feel so fucking good," he hissed as I tried to take all of him in my mouth.

My mouth and hands worked together as I stroked the underside of his shaft while my mouth worked him up and down.

"Oh my God! You have to stop or I'm gonna come."

I kept moving not listening to his threats.

"Mmm, baby, stop. I want to be inside you."

I continued only a moment longer before climbing up on top of him.

"I'm not trying to rush you." His fingertips traced across my swollen lips.

"You're not rushing me," I whispered as I leaned my forehead against his.

"We can wait." His fingers traced across my jawline.

I shook my head. I knew exactly what I wanted—him, all of him.

He rolled me over and lay on his side as his eyes lazily took in my supine position. My body arched as his fingers trailed up my side and he leaned in and kissed me, a kiss I smiled into. His hard length rested against my leg as his hands tightened in my hair, his mouth claiming mine. I pulled away from him and he watched me carefully. Reaching for his bedside table he pulled a foil packet from the drawer and I watched as he rolled the condom over his shaft.

"Come here." I pulled him toward me and opened my legs so he could settle between them. I held onto him, my hands on each side of his face as he lay on top of me. I arched up and found his mouth, slowly tasting him. There was such tenderness in him, which only made me want him that much more. His hands went down my ribcage to my hips and pulled me against him. Both of us were breathless with anticipation as his fingers went to my wetness, gently dipping inside me. I arched beneath him, unable to control the squirming of my body when he touched me.

"You sure, baby?" He asked again watching me.

"Hmmm … I'm sure." I rocked against him. "I want you." I fought the urge to allow my eyes to roll back in my head and forced myself to look at him.

His mouth was on mine but I felt him shift as he settled himself more firmly between my legs and pull mine around his hips. His cock threatened my opening as he slid himself up and down over my wetness.

My quiet moans pleaded with him, begging to feel him inside me. He grasped his hard length and positioned himself before slowly pushing and stretching my walls to accommodate him. My breath came out with a hitch as he slowly pushed in, deeper and deeper. He pulled back and then slid further forward, my body taking more of him with each thrust.

"You're so wet for me," he hissed, his eyes staring deeply into mine.

I moaned, unable to keep quiet when he said anything dirty to me.

"Mmm, and so tight." He pushed the rest of the way into me.

I gasped at the glorious intrusion and our breath mingled as we stared at each other while he ground himself in and out. My hands were on his back, scratching, pulling him closer to me as the muscles of his chest flexed against my naked skin.

"I want to feel you come, baby." His words brought me even closer to the orgasm boiling just beneath the surface.

I cried out at his words and he quickened his pace grabbing my hips with more force as he pushed inside me.

"Mmm, baby." I pushed him to roll onto his back. We never broke contact as we changed positions so I was straddling him.

I moaned as I worked my hips against him, my hands splayed on his chest. He matched my pace flexing into me with every thrust. Neither of us could stay silent, our moans and heavy breathing blending together as we took each other to greater heights of ecstasy.

The sounds leaving my mouth sounded foreign even to my own ears as I slid up and down on his cock. But when he brought his fingers up to play with my clit there was no holding back. I fell on his chest, moaning and calling his name as he continued to slowly grind himself inside me.

Desperate to bring him to my level of satisfaction I flexed harder against him, my body greedily milking him and begging for release. Despite our position, with me being on top he did most of the work as I stayed splayed out across his chest. When his breathing picked up even more I could tell he was close and I sat up on him, pushing him deeper with every thrust.

"Oh baby…" he gasped, as I quickened my pace rocking up and down on him, my body slapping against his thighs.

He brought his hand to my face; his fingers delicately traced my parted lips. Feeling bold I bit his finger lightly before taking it in my mouth and sucking it. He watched me intently while obviously fighting himself internally, trying to keep us in this moment for as long as possible.

"Mmm, Becca." He grasped my hips tighter and pulled me hard against him.

Again I felt an orgasm building, coming on quicker than before since all of my senses were completely heightened.

Maddox sat up taking me with him and propped himself against the headboard. I sat in his lap facing him as he pushed himself back inside me, making us both moan. His mouth latched onto my nipple as I bounced up and down on him, his teeth gently pulling the sensitive skin.

"Oh baby…" He huffed. "You're gonna make me come if you don't slow down."

I couldn't slow down, I was so close to finding my release once again, and desperate to bring him to his own.

After a few more strokes he twitched inside me violently as he groaned and called out my name with his release. Both of us collapsed against each other, our lungs greedily sucking for air.

"Jesus Christ," Maddox said after a few minutes.

I tilted my head so I could look at him.

"I may never let you leave this house." He smiled.

Never had I had sex with someone who watched me and stared into my eyes like he did. It added a level of intensity, but it also felt even more personal than I thought possible. He watched me with awe and made me feel beautiful.

I started to doze off. Lying there in his arms felt too perfect to be real.

"Wait! What time is it?" I asked, startled as I tried to get out of bed.

"It's late." He wrapped his arms around my waist and pulled me back against him.

"Kera's date was tonight! I'm a terrible friend. I have to talk to her and see how it went."

Without releasing me Maddox sat up and grabbed his pants off the floor to dig for his phone that he'd left in the pocket.

"It's two am, baby. Either she's home and asleep, or it went really well and she's not home at all." He wagged his eyebrows at that last comment.

"There's some girl code here you're not catching on to at all."

"How about this." He repositioned us so my back was against his chest, his arms wrapped tightly against my waist. "Tomorrow morning"—he kissed the side of my neck—"the three of us will go to breakfast"—he paused to kiss the other side of my neck—"and she can tell us all about it." He lifted my hair and kissed the back of my neck.

"It's a little hard to focus with you doing that." I said, unable to get the sated smile off my face.

"I'm gonna take that as a yes." He pulled me back so he could reach my mouth and kissed me, his hands covering my breasts.

"Wait—stop." My plea couldn't have been any more half-hearted. "I at least need to find my phone." I started to get up from the bed.

I looked around for something to throw on so I could run downstairs but my dress was too complicated for such a quick trip so I pulled the top sheet off the bed and wrapped it around myself.

"You better hurry up or I'll come find you."

"Hmmm…" I smiled as I left the room and went to find my purse.

I found my phone and went through my messages to find that Kera had texted me. I frowned to myself for not being home when she got back to hear all about it. I sent her a quick text apologizing and told her we'd be there in the morning and we'd go to breakfast. Kera wasn't exactly the private type so I didn't think she'd mind Maddox being with us.

When I made it back to his room Maddox appeared to be asleep and I looked at my phone and the time trying to decide if I should just go ahead and go home.

Maddox blinked his sleepy eyes open slowly.

"Come here." He reached out to me.

As if I could turn down the beautiful, sultry blue-eyed, tousled-hair Maddox.

Chapter Twenty-Six

The week went slowly, but only because I was ready for the weekend, and a chance to spend more time with Maddox. The one possible thing that could spoil my great mood? Walking into my Macroeconomics class. I was already showing signs of full-on Macroeconomics hell even before walking into class, and despite working on it I was still falling behind and completely agitated.

The last thing you need to be doing when barely passing a class is be distracted by outside things, but when said outside thing is Maddox Spencer … it's a bit easier said than done.

>I think you should come stay at my place tonight.

I grinned at my phone as I slouched down in my chair to hide my indiscretion.

>Oh, do you?

>Yes! I had a terrible dream last night and I'm afraid I won't be able to sleep without your…

>Tight…

I stared at my phone waiting for the next message to come through, my eyes quickly scanning the people seated around me to make sure they weren't getting an eyeful of my conversation.

>Little…

Unnecessarily I glanced around again.

>Airway snoring on my pillow.

And I snorted. Out loud. In my Macroeconomics class.

"Alright, has everyone joined a group?" Professor Davis asked after looking me over with a disapproving tight-lipped frown. I guiltily pulled my phone against the fabric of my shirt, trying to hide what I'd been doing.

As everyone chatted amongst themselves and exchanged numbers Professor Davis stalked my way and leaned in close to me. "It appears we've ascertained the source of your disconnect in my class, Ms. Stanton."

I wanted to argue that I rarely looked at my phone during his class, but I knew it would have been futile.

"We have an extra spot," chimed in Chad, who had apparently been standing behind me.

"Join your group, Ms. Stanton," the professor sneered at me.

This day was quickly turning from excitement to the throes of anxiety with a quickness. In any other class a group assignment wouldn't have been an uncomfortable thing, however I was currently feeling completely incompetent, and that left me with an overwhelming sense of dread. I picked up my things and reluctantly joined Chad and our other group member.

"I think we should do the Australian Economy." Our team member Zack got right to the topic.

"Becca, what were you thinking?" Chad turned in his chair so his knees were facing mine.

I fought the urge to scoot my chair back, deciding the more important thing to focus on at that moment was that I had not only missed the fact that we had a group project, I was also completely clueless on what the project was even about.

"I'm sorry, I kind of missed the discussion on the project—"

My words were cut short by Zack's reaction, which would have been much more suitable for a child who'd just been told he couldn't get a new toy.

Chad's response mimicked my own as he returned his attention to me after taking in Zack's over-the-top reaction. "We have to choose a country and analyze their current economic state, including unemployment, GDP and economic growth, and identify what we feel is the biggest cause of concern of those three areas."

"The Australian Economy is fine with me." Chad turned to face Zack giving his consent.

"Works for me!" I concurred with more sarcasm than I intended. Honestly, I am about as familiar with Jupiter's economic state as I am with Australia's.

"Alright, let's exchange numbers and we'll set up a time to meet and assign roles," our self-appointed project leader said as he tore a piece of paper out of his notebook and began scribbling down his details.

"Does everyone live on campus?" Zack asked, handing the scratch paper to me.

"I'm at Markum." I wrote down my number and passed it to Chad without looking up.

"Federal Hill," Chad responded.

"Alright, I'm in Cranston so we'll have to figure out something," Zack said, putting his laptop in his bag and not looking at either of us.

I gathered my stuff, relishing the fact that at least it was Friday, and I totally got to blame Maddox for the fact that I ended up in a group with Chad.

I made my way out of the building into the corridor through the mass of people who were just as excited about the weekend as me.

As I always do I walked through College Hill, passing by all the various shops and boutiques and windows, browsing along the way. Today, however, I finally had a good reason to stop at Gabby's, a high-end boutique with the most elaborate selection of lingerie I'd ever seen.

Excitedly I made my purchase and tried to imagine his response to seeing me in this. Of course, I did have to push from my mind that the money I was spending was given to me by Gigi. Every month she put some money in my account for "fun" as she put it, and I wasn't supposed to spend it on anything school-related. I'm not sure this was exactly what she had in mind but at least I was following the rules and keeping it "fun".

Once home I opened the door and was surprised to hear Maddox, Kera, and someone else chatting.

"Hey guys!" I said as I entered my room.

Maddox and the other guy stood as I entered.

"This is my friend, Giovanni," Kera grinned at me, and I shook his outstretched hand.

Giovanni's dark curly hair and tanned complexion was just what I'd expected after Kera had told me about her "Italian Stallion".

"Hey Becca, I've heard a lot about you!" He had one of those smiles that lit up his entire face and showed off pearly white teeth. In a style very similar to Maddox, he wore a pair of charcoal dress pants, a button-up shirt and a dark sweater. While they both looked great, I couldn't imagine wearing that much clothing all the time; to me, it just seemed stuffy.

"Nice to meet you. What are you all up to?" I set my bags down on the bed.

"I was just trying to talk them into doing something tonight," Maddox answered as he rummaged through my Gabby's bag and pulled out some of the tissue paper that wrapped up the items inside.

Quickly I smacked his hand and pulled the bag to my chest.

"No peeking!"

"On second thought, maybe you guys should just go." Maddox added playfully.

"Very funny!" I laughed.

Keeping to our normal Friday night tradition, we decided to eat at a place on Thayer Street where I'd not been before. As it turns out Giovanni was completely against eating at any of the dining halls, and either cooked or went out to eat. He was eager to give us his critique on all the restaurants in the area.

"What do you think?" Giovanni asked as I took my first bite of raw beet and cucumber salad.

I let the flavors absorb into my mouth before answering him. "Surprisingly, really good!"

"Right?" he asked excitedly. "It's to die for! There are some aaammmaazzziiinnnggg restaurants all over Providence if you know where to go." He took a spoonful of his tomato bisque. "Have you guys been to Delanie's yet?" he asked as his spoon gently clanked against his soup bowl.

"Yes, we went a few weeks ago." Maddox answered, glancing my way.

"Their lobster bisque is absolutely divine!" Giovanni looked from me to Maddox.

"Maddox has been pretty great about taking me to a new restaurant every week. Our only rule is that we can't order anything we've already had before." I smiled gratefully at Maddox.

"Oh, I love that! We should do that with you guys!" His grin was contagious, and apparently, Maddox felt the same way because he was grinning from ear to ear.

"Agreed!" Kera chimed in cheerfully. "Although I may have to get a part-time job in order to do so."

I put my hand on Maddox's thigh and rubbed my thumb softly across the fabric. I hated that Maddox paid for everything, but at the same time he was insistent on us going out to eat so much, and knew that was something I couldn't afford to do.

"Hey, we haven't hit the pizzerias yet, which is also on our list."

By dessert we'd heard all about Giovanni's real desire to go into fashion, but that he'd chosen his second love—food. Kera watched him excitedly and I was too distracted by his hand gestures to notice anything else. Overall, I really liked him, but I had that lingering question in my mind that I couldn't ignore. He just seemed a bit feminine, but maybe that's how all straight fashion majors from New York acted. I'm from Ohio so what do I know about things like that?

We parted ways after dinner, Kera and Giovanni deciding to walk around Thayer Street and Maddox and I heading back to my dorm.

As soon as Maddox joined me in the car he turned and looked at me with a shocked expression.

"What?" I asked a little alarmed by his demeanor.

"Please tell me you realized that Giovanni is batting for the other team."

"Oh no! Are you sure?" I asked concerned for Kera's sake. "Just because he wanted to be a fashion major doesn't mean he's gay."

Maddox tilted his head and gave me his best "really" face.

"He's colorful... *and* straight?" I asked hopefully.

"No babe."

"Straight men often describe their meal as 'to die for'."

"And roll their eyes back in their head gleefully?" Maddox countered.

I laughed at his reenactment of Giovanni's mealtime production. "Seriously though, how do we bring this up with Kera?"

"I say let her figure it out on her own," Maddox suggested with all seriousness.

"Really? I can't do that! She'll be traumatized if she tries to put the moves on him and finds out that way."

"Maybe just ask her if he's made a move yet and then bring it up?" He glanced from me to the road.

"Alright, that's probably a good way to handle it. Poor Kera," I frowned.

Chapter Twenty-Seven

I opened my eyes sleepily, not completely sure what had awakened me until my tired eyes took in Maddox leaning above me.

"I gotta go, babe, I'll call you later," he whispered before pressing a kiss against my lips.

"Okay," I yawned as I pulled my white feather comforter up to my chin.

The smile found my face naturally as he grabbed his things and closed the door silently behind him.

"Stop grinning!" Kera's voice was gruff with sleepiness.

"I'm sorry!" I pulled up my comforter a little higher to hide my lips.

"Is this really my life?" she frowned, while dramatically throwing her covers off.

Needless to say, she hadn't taken Maddox's observations on Giovanni's flamboyance very well. At first, she'd argued that it was just his personality, but after some hindsight reflection she started to see things a little more clearly.

"At least you didn't put the moves on him and get shot down," I offered.

"True. But seriously, how do I go out on two dates with a guy and not realize that he's not into women?"

"If it makes you feel any better I didn't realize it right away either."

Our intercom buzzing interrupted us.

"Maddox forget something?" Kera asked as I fumbled my way out of covers and to the intercom.

"Hey Becca, it's Chad."

Instead of answering I turned and gaped at Kera.

"Are you guys supposed to be working on your project?" Kera got up from her bed and went to her closet to put something on.

"At"—I turned and squinted at Kera's alarm clock—"ten am? No!"

Without saying a word, I hit the buzzer allowing him to enter the building. I grabbed a hoodie, shuffled my slippers on my feet and headed downstairs, still not sure if I was actually going to entertain the idea of starting this project.

"Good morning, sunshine." The hot cup of coffee he held out to me outshined Chad's overly zealous smile.

"What's going on?" I asked as I pulled the sides of my sweatshirt together.

"Thought we'd get a jump start on our project."

Urgh. He was way too cheerful and the coffee was his only saving grace.

"Alright." I turned and headed back to the elevator, not waiting to see if he was following me and not really caring either way.

"Not a morning person?" Chad nudged my side with his elbow.

"Ha." I rolled my eyes not even trying to make that laugh sound genuine.

"Kera, we have company," I announced as soon as I opened the door to our room, and allowed Chad to follow me in.

"I'm just going to change clothes real quick." I grabbed some clothes out of my closet and snuck into the bathroom.

Kera, damn her, made her exit as soon as I came back, leaving Chad and me alone. I took a seat cross-legged on my bed while he sat at my desk next to me.

"So … what about Zack?" My brain clearing enough to question the obvious.

Chad tapped his pen against his mouth. "Well, I know you've been having a hard time with the class so I thought you and I could get a head start."

While I might not like the fact that Chad had shown up at my place unannounced, the truth was I did need help and didn't much like the idea of looking like I was inept to the likes of Zack.

Over the next two hours, we discussed the project itself, before going into the current economic state of Australia. I had to give it to Chad—this really was his area, and I couldn't help but laugh at how excited he got when he was explaining things to me.

"Alright, I'm starving." He slammed his laptop shut. "Let's break and get something to eat."

I looked away from him briefly. While grabbing lunch was relatively harmless, I didn't think Maddox would see it that way. Silently I smacked myself for not telling him that Chad and I had ended up in the same group, figuring I had a few days before we actually would end up working together.

"Oh come on, your boyfriend can't be that possessive, can he?" His words didn't match the smile etched across his face.

"Maddox is not possessive." The words came from my mouth with every bit of the certainty I was feeling. "Why don't we order something? I'd prefer we just keep working on this until we get to a good stopping point."

"I suppose," Chad huffed.

We continued going over our work until the food came, at which point it became apparent that Chad was incapable of working while eating.

"What if I put the emphasis of my work into the unemployment rates and projections over the next few years?" I asked while picking through my Mongolian beef.

"So how long have you and Maddox been dating?" he asked, before taking a bite out of his egg roll.

I made a conscious effort not to roll my eyes as I set my takeout container on my desk.

"A little small talk won't kill us."

"Sorry, I'm just worried about this class and this project is a big part of our grade," I said in explanation.

He ignored me.

"It's been a few months," I replied.

"So things going pretty well?" he asked, with something in his eyes that looked like hope.

A knock at the door pulled both of our attention in that direction and I hopped up to get it.

"Hey, babe!" Maddox said as I swung the door open.

My mouth opened slightly as if I was going to say something, but instead I let it hang slack for a moment before closing it abruptly.

"Hey!"

Shit, that sounded a little over the top cheerful.

Maddox watched me speculatively for a moment before making his way through the door I was holding open for him. How exactly had he bypassed the front desk?

"Oh, hey Maddox." Chad peaked around the corner carrying his Chinese takeout box with him. He smiled ruefully as he dropped another bite into his mouth from his chopsticks.

My eyes flew to Maddox afraid that he was about to completely lose his shit. In his defense, it did look kind of bad, Chad standing there relaxed, shoes off. That shit-eating grin on his face wasn't helping things either.

"Chad and I were assigned to do a group project together, we were just getting a head start on it." The words left my mouth at an unusually fast pace.

Maddox walked down the hall ahead of me and I cringed inwardly at the entire situation.

"You guys about done? I thought we'd spend some time together today since I had to leave in such a rush this morning." He planted a quick kiss to my lips.

His eyes stayed on me but I didn't miss the fact he was making sure Chad knew he'd slept here.

"I think we're good for now," Chad answered as he started packing his things into his bag. "We'll have plenty of time to work on this."

"Good to see you, Maddox," he said, receiving only a nod in return.

"Seriously?" Maddox looked at me accusingly as soon as the door clicked closed.

"You know this is actually entirely your fault." I pointed a finger at Maddox and eyed him playfully.

"Oh really?! You want to explain how that's possible?" He was playful in his tone but there was seriousness in his eyes.

"Yes! I was in class when you messaged me, thoroughly distracting me I might add, and I missed it entirely when Professor Douche bag let us know to get into groups for a project—"

"Uh huh ..." He came toward me with mock seriousness.

"—accusing me of snoring, which I don't do by the way." My eyes were wide and lethal as I pointed at him.

"And I missed getting in a group and was assigned to Chad's. See? Your fault!"

I couldn't contain my giggle as he wrapped his arms around my waist and pulled me so my back was against him.

"You know I don't like that guy," he said against my head, his tone now level and serious.

"I know," I responded, a bit deflated. "I'm not overly fond of him myself but I don't get your level of distaste toward him."

Maddox backed up and sat down on my bed taking me with him so I was sitting in his lap.

"Turn around."

I did as he asked, now straddling his lap.

"You are missing something with him that's pretty apparent to me." One of his hands wrapped around my waist holding me steady while his other tucked a stray strand of hair behind my ear.

"What am I missing?" I asked cocking my head to the side a bit in disbelief.

"He's got a thing for you, Becca, it's pretty damn obvious. And I wish you would have at least told me you two were working together and that he was coming here today." I looked into his stormy blue eyes and was surprised that what I saw in them was tenderness.

"I didn't mean to not tell you." I ran my thumb and forefinger across his jawline which was showing just a bit of blonde stubble. "This all happened yesterday, and he just kind of showed up here this morning. I didn't know he was coming."

Maddox tilted his head, his mouth displaying a thin, crooked smile. "Uh huh," he nodded. "That's exactly what I'm saying. You ever have someone you're in a group with just show up to start working on it without telling you first?"

I looked up at the ceiling as if I was pondering his question but of course, he already knew the answer was no.

Using his thumb and forefinger, Maddox tipped my head back down so I was looking at him. "That's what I thought."

I let out a frustrated breath.

"I'm not saying you did anything wrong, I'm just saying you need to watch out with him, he's got a motive."

"But I kind of like you," I said in a hushed tone as I leaned toward him resting my forehead on his.

"I kind of like you too, which is precisely why I want to kick his scheming ass—"

Deciding it was best to not let him continue with his current train of thought I held my hands on each side of his jaw and kissed him. He stood up taking me with him and backed me against the wall as I wrapped my legs around his waist. In one quick movement, he pulled my shirt over my head, his mouth now meeting the thin fabric of my bra. It was supposed to be a quick distraction but maybe that was something else about Maddox I needed to consider ... him as a distraction was never a quick thing.

Chapter Twenty-Eight

I tried to focus on my paper but my thoughts were distracted by Maddox. He seemed to make everything about being in a new place interesting instead of foreign. His level of excitement toward life was contagious, and any bit of free time I had was spent with him, trying new things and seeing new places. I couldn't help but envy him in a lot of ways; while he did have to buckle down and focus during the last few months of school, it appeared his classes came easier to him. He also seemed to have a magical bank account that never ended and was getting ready to spend his summer backpacking across Europe, while I, on the other hand, made the decision to take on a full class load and stay in Providence. I wanted the break, but my desire to get finished with school and make a life for myself outweighed my need for a summer vacation. Besides, it wasn't like I was going to have a lot going on with Maddox out of the country.

It wasn't easy but I did manage to get through my classes, specifically Macroeconomics, with an acceptable GPA, and at least my summer classes were going to be a little less difficult.

"You ready?" Kera hopped up and down excitedly.

"Yup!" I said, taping off my last box of belongings and looking around our now empty dorm room. I was surprised to find I was actually going to miss my dorm, but taking classes over the summer meant finding a new place to stay. Getting an apartment with Kera was a no-brainer.

***

After I'd finally unpacked enough to find my essentials, I lay on my bed and stared up at the ceiling, sleep refusing to let me have a reprieve.

Maddox's family was in town, so I was spending my first night in my new place without him. I couldn't decide if I should feel bad that he hadn't asked me to go to dinner with them. A part of me thought that may not be a good thing, but another part was just relieved I got to put off the whole meet the parents thing a little bit longer.

Something didn't feel right though, and I couldn't quite put my finger on what it was. Shadows from passing cars danced across the walls of my room, and I forced my eyes closed and tried to will myself to go to sleep. I felt homesick, but that didn't seem like the right description because I wanted to be here. An empty feeling filled my belly and doubt assigned to some unknown source filled my mind. Silently I convinced myself that it was just nerves over being in a new place and meeting Maddox's parents, and I eventually drifted off to sleep.

***

There were many things I'd grown accustomed to over the previous few months—Maddox's hand at the small of my back when I walked into a room, the sweet yet masculine smell of his cologne that lingered on my pillow after he'd gone, and the vanilla taste of his lips after he'd had a drink. However, there were still times when I found myself in a place I wasn't accustomed to, and I had to fight past the awkwardness that tried to consume me.

Before we even made it to Maddox's family home I already knew it was going to be one of those times. Maddox steered his car down the long, tree-lined driveway to his family's estate, which could not be seen from the road. Once we reached the circular drive in front of the house Maddox squeezed my thigh reassuringly. I know better than to compare myself or my family to someone else, but there was no denying we were from very different worlds.

I'd met his parents briefly at the graduation ceremony and, while his father was friendly enough, I couldn't seem to dispel from my mind how dismissive his mother was. I shook the thought from my mind and took a deep breath as I looked over their impressive home.

The house, if it was even fair to call it that, was a three-story white and tan brick monstrosity. In the middle of the circular driveway was a green space with perfectly trimmed hedges outlining a massive flowerbed which had every color and type of flower you could imagine. I tried to swallow my nerves as Maddox pulled the car around the back of the house and in front of one of the five garage doors. Catering vans filled most of the spots, and seeing them there actually brought a level of excitement to me, since I am always curious about trying new things.

"Ready?" Maddox turned to me with something that looked like anxiety in his face.

"I am!" I smiled while attempting to look excited. I may have been a little more convincing had it not been for the shakiness of my breath.

I straightened my dress as I stepped from the car and held my shoulders high as we walked in through the garage to the house. This time I hadn't bothered asking Maddox what I should wear; I'd just assumed it would be a dressy event. I felt great in my gold off-the-shoulder dress with chiffon pleats and cinched waist. It had just enough gold beading on it to make it sparkle, but not so much that it was over-the-top. Of course, as I walked in the door it was very clear that the occasion was far more over-the-top than under.

"Mother," Maddox said to get her attention, as she was directing the staff to where she wanted things.

Rita Spencer looked much more mother of the groom in her white long-sleeve laced dress. It fit tightly against her body, with a cream-colored bow that sat off to one side on her waist. Her hair, not unlike my own, was up in a tight twist, and I couldn't help but draw the parallel to the tight lines of her face. Maybe it was the plastic surgery she had undergone that kept her face from revealing genuine emotions, or maybe it was just her uptight personality. I was guessing the latter.

"Maddox, you're early." Her eyes took in his perfectly tailored black tuxedo.

"You know the guest of honor never arrives before his guests," she scolded. "Make yourself scarce." She shooed us away before turning back to the staff and the ever so important task of aligning the tall vases of irises with the lines of the windows.

As Maddox led me into the foyer I looked around the impressive first floor, at least what I could see of it as he led me up the curved staircase. The place was gorgeous, from the marble floors to the perfectly tailored curtains that hung from the windows. Immediately I was reminded of the litany of antique stores my mom and Gigi had dragged me to over the years, and all the furniture that was for looking, not actually touching.

"I should have offered to help your mother," I commented as we reached the second-floor landing. Not that the woman had even acknowledged my presence.

"She would have seen that as odd." Maddox turned to look at me as

I trailed behind him. "She's more of the planner and dictator."

Of course, I should have realized that, but it was just one of those things that came naturally—when you arrive at a party you offer to help.

Maddox swung the door open and led me inside. I stepped into the impressive room and walked around taking in the atmosphere. The dark wood four-poster bed and matching bedside furniture gave it a darker effect.

The door clicked as he closed it behind me, and I turned and glanced over my shoulder as he walked up behind me with a mischievous look on his face.

"We have about forty-five minutes." He placed a wet kiss on my neck. "What should we do with our time?" He held me just below my breasts.

I felt that familiar butterfly feeling in my stomach and heat beneath the sheer fabric of my panties.

"Be good," I said, but not before letting out a little sigh thanks to the sensations he was causing.

My eyes shot open as I realized how easily he was able to persuade me. I pulled away from him. He let go reluctantly as I turned to face him and backed up slightly.

"Have I mentioned how much I can't wait to see what you've got on underneath that dress?" He stepped toward me and closed the slight space that existed between us.

"We are not having sex in your parents' house! Not to mention the fact that people are already arriving!" I whisper-yelled, despite the fact that nobody could hear us where we were.

"There's not enough time for that anyway." He pulled off his tuxedo jacket and stood eyeing me up and down.

I could feel the blush creep across my cheeks as he watched me, his eyes dark with heat as he stalked toward me.

"I only want a taste." His mouth was on mine and there was desperation in his kisses I couldn't help but relish.

His hand traveled down my back and lingered briefly before he grabbed my ass and pulled my leg up so it was wrapped around his waist. In doing so my dress came up giving him easy access to me. His hand quickly took advantage as he tugged at my panties.

"Maddox," I pleaded halfheartedly, my body and mind conflicting.

"Uh huh?" He pulled my leg off his hip so he could slide my panties the rest of the way off.

Before I could argue he was on his knees in front of me taking one of my legs placing it over his shoulder as I clung to the wall to keep from falling.

"Mad—" I started my argument, but as soon as his tongue licked across my wet folds in one long stroke I lost my words.

One of my hands instinctively went to his head as the other tried to focus on not falling over with only one heel-clad foot on the ground.

He took his time lapping slowly as his other hand slid up the inside of my leg to my inner thigh. The moans escaped my mouth without an ounce of control as his tongue picked up its pace and found my clit, wickedly flicking back and forth over it. A finger teased my opening and my hips rocked against his face, begging silently to feel him inside me. I watched him from my position as his hot breath and wet mouth worked me over, only making me want him even more. His eyes went to mine, and despite the fact that I knew I should probably be embarrassed that he caught me watching I didn't look away as he held my gaze.

He took that opportunity to slide one of his fingers inside me while he continued to lick and play with me. A moan escaped me as my hips rocked into his intrusion and his mouth pulled away from me briefly before he slid a second finger inside.

"Turn around." I did so without thinking twice.

I felt his hands on my shoulders and the zipper being pulled down but just when I went to object his mouth went to my neck and for the millionth time since knowing Maddox, I lost all conscious thought.

He turned me around so I was facing him and backed me up slowly until my back hit the wall. His mouth went to my breast and he latched onto my nipple sucking it hard and making me gasp. It wasn't until I heard his zipper go down that I realized what he was up to. The unwrapping of a foil packet and our heavy breathing filled the silence of the air.

He picked me up and I wrapped my legs around him.

"I want you so fucking bad." He pushed inside me in one hard thrust making me groan in a mixture of pleasure and pain as he stretched my body to its max. His reaction was much the same as my own as he tried to control the guttural noises that escaped his mouth.

He kept the pace fast and hard as he rocked in and out of me. I held onto him with one hand while my other gripped the wall behind me. Quickly, my moans became uncontrollable as I felt my orgasm reaching the surface. Maddox coved my mouth with his own muffling the sound as my body took over for me, clutching and pulling against his hard cock.

"Mmm, baby," he said through gritted teeth trying to maintain control as my release begged for him to follow.

His mouth went to my neck and he groaned into my skin, sucking and biting lightly as he found his release.

We stayed there for a moment breathing into each other as our bodies tried to come down from the intensity that rocked us both.

"Mmm…" I could feel the smile on his face as he hummed into my neck.

Thankful for his ensuite bathroom, I grabbed my dress and scurried inside to check the damage from our mind-blowing quickie.

"Shit," I muttered out loud as I took in my disheveled appearance.

Maddox pushed the door open and joined me in front of the double sinks, a look of pure satisfaction and mischief on his face.

"You are terrible," I grinned back at him through our reflections in the mirror, unable to keep the sated smile off my face. His shirt was still unbuttoned and his belt hung unfastened at his waist. His hair had sustained most of the damage from my endless tugging and pulling.

"Your idea." I pointed at his reflection in the mirror as he wet his hands and attempted to tame his wild hair.

"It was a *really* good idea."

"This is not good." I motioned to my hair as I pulled out the clip letting the messy tangles fall around my face.

"You're beautiful," he said approvingly. "But you may want to hurry," he added playfully as he quickly ducked out of the bathroom.

***

My hair did not fully recover from our little romp but my mood was much improved as we made our way downstairs into the throes of the party. I eyed Maddox a bit nervously as he held my hand and was greeted by person after person who'd come to congratulate him. He introduced me to everyone with a confident ease, whereas I, on the other hand, was trying to tell myself that not everyone knew what we'd been up to.

Slowly, we made our way outside where a huge patio was covered with tents. A production this big was far from your average backyard barbecue, and looked much more what you would expect at a wedding. Floral arrangements adorned the elegantly decorated tables and white twinkling lights lit the expansive space. I grabbed a glass of champagne from one of the tuxedo-clad servers and took a sip in hopes of calming my nerves.

Everyone Maddox introduced me to was kind, and genuinely seemed happy and proud of his accomplishments. When there was a long enough break in people coming up to him, we took a seat at one of the tables and I looked out over the endless yard and the pond that sat just behind the patio area.

Maddox opened his mouth to say something, but we were interrupted by his mother catching our attention and motioning for him to join her.

"I'll be right back." He kissed the top of my head and rose from his seated position.

I tried my best to appear to be having a good time as Maddox made his rounds throughout his party, but when over thirty minutes had passed I started feeling stupid for sitting with a fake smile on my face. I figured if I smiled at least I would appear to be having a good time, but people were probably starting to assume I was suffering from some mental health issue sitting by myself for so long with a stupid smile on my face. Deciding I couldn't sit here any longer, I got up and followed the path from the patio to the gazebo that looked out over the pond.

A fountain shot water through the center of the lake creating a pleasant splashing sound that was barely audible over the sounds of the party. I could imagine how pleasant it would be out here on a normal night and tilted my head to the sky to take in the stars that shown brightly above.

My phone beeping caught my attention and, thankful for the distraction , I peered down at the screen to see a message from Amelia.

>Thought you'd like to know Jameson and his band got signed. Love and miss you!

I stood there for a moment and couldn't help but feel completely excited for Jameson. He deserved every bit of the attention he received, and it was about damn time he realized how talented he actually was. A part of me wished I was there to celebrate with him, but I quickly dismissed that thought and berated myself for even thinking it. What was wrong with me? Maddox stepped away to greet his guests and I was already having thoughts like that.

The clicking of heels against the gazebo floor got my attention but

I kept my eyes to the sky, unsure if those footsteps were headed to me specifically.

"Amazing, isn't it?"

Stephy.

I didn't actually want to turn to look at her because our interactions were rarely pleasant, but my manners got the best of me.

"It is," I said, making eye contact with her before looking out over the lake again.

"It must be hard not knowing anyone here." She shook her head back and forth with mock concern and I felt the corner of my lip tip up trying to stifle the laugh that wanted to leave my mouth.

"It's one of those strange things really."

I looked at her to see where she was going with her thought.

"People know their own, or in your case, they know when someone doesn't belong. Maddox is having his fun but don't be such a fool to think that someone like you will end up with a Spencer." Her spiteful eyes looked me up and down with apparent disgust as she turned on her heel. Did she just say "A Spencer"?

"What is your problem, Stephy?" I called after her, and she stopped in her tracks and glanced over her shoulder.

"Give it a few weeks and I doubt I'll have any." Her smug grin showed before she turned, leaving me to absorb her words.

I watched her walk away. What had I done to deserve such hatred from her? I felt my face redden with anger and wanted to kick my own ass for never being able to keep up with her snarky comments. People who come from money have to be careful that the people who surround them are actually there for the right reasons, but Stephy made it sound like being with "A Spencer" was some status symbol beyond my realm of possibilities.

I tried to distract myself from my thoughts of wanting to find Stephy and give her a piece of my mind, so I scrolled through my phone and opened Instagram. The first picture that came up on my feed was one of Jameson. He was on stage, not looking at the camera, his dark wavy hair hanging slightly over his face while he looked down at his guitar. My eyes were drawn to his muscular tattooed arms and, in my mind, I could see the vividness of his hummingbird tattoo. I glanced at all the comments from various people congratulating him, including people who didn't appear to know him but were commenting on the fact they'd seen him recently at a show. Without giving it a second thought I flipped back to my text messages and sent him one congratulating him on being signed. I waited for a moment and realized how much I was looking forward to his response. For the first time, it occurred to me that maybe Jameson was just done with our little back and forth and that prospect upset me. On more than one occasion it was me who didn't reply to his messages; why did I regret that decision now?

I walked toward the house trying to not allow my now sour mood to show on my face. I spotted Maddox talking with some people as I walked across the patio through the crowd and grabbed another glass of champagne from a passing server.

I made a quick entrance into the nearest bathroom and smiled at the attendant who stood ready to hand me a paper towel or some other such task given to bathroom attendants. The main part of the bathroom was decorated with a chaise lounge, huge mirrors, and a double sink, which was currently set up with various bottles of perfume and makeup items.

Staring at my reflection I tucked a few wisps of hair that refused to cooperate behind my ear, frowning absently at myself for not being absolutely perfect at an event that called for nothing less.

"If you are sad, add more lipstick and attack." I looked at the reflection of the woman whose hand was currently outstretched and offering a black tube of lipstick. Was that a Coco Chanel quote?

It seemed a bit odd, but she was nothing short of stunning so listening to her advice seemed like a good idea in the moment.

Her smile appeared genuine, but it didn't reach her pale blue eyes, and it made me pause for a moment questioning how it was possible for someone so beautiful to be sad. Her hair was just a bit blonder than my own but, unlike mine, was perfectly tucked up into her updo. Her dress was a short, pink and V-neck, and despite the fact that it was loose fitting it didn't diminish her petite figure. All of her features were beautiful, but her high prominent cheekbones, pink lips, and big blue eyes made her breathtaking—even if those blue eyes held an abundance of sadness.

"Thank you." I handed her lipstick back to her. She tucked it into her purse and left the bathroom with a smile.

She carried herself with a level of confidence I wanted to find within myself, and I held my head higher as I left the bathroom shortly after her.

Maddox caught my eye as I walked across the patio toward him.

"This is my girlfriend, Becca." Maddox introduced me to the

middle-aged couple before him. It felt good to be with him and hear him introduce me to others as his girlfriend, and I basked in that moment. They spoke briefly before moving on and Maddox wrapped his arms around me.

"I'm sorry, baby. I tried to get back to you it's just been a little crazy." He tucked my hair behind my ear he kissed the back of my neck.

"Maddox, have you said hello to JC and Meredith?" Mrs Spencer asked, pulling our attention to the couple standing in front of us. A smile plastered to my face I looked up to find the couple standing before us, along with the woman I'd met in the bathroom.

"Izzy and her parents are like an extension to our family." Rita showed the warmest smile I'd seen cross her face as she linked her arm with Izzy's.

My heart fell into my stomach and I could feel my face redden with every negative emotion possible—anger, frustration, and humiliation. I stood there frozen, the only consolation, if there was one, was that Izzy appeared to be as taken aback as I was. I didn't look at Maddox. Despite the fact that I should have wanted to see his reaction, I didn't. My face was hot, and I tried to discreetly exhale after I realized I'd been holding my breath.

"Thank you for coming, Mr and Mrs Marcum. Izzy." He shook hands with the Marcums and nodded to Izzy.

They spoke. I was keenly aware there was a conversation happening in front of me, and while I tried to act normal I wasn't actually able to hear anything they were saying. Why? Why would it be that the one person at this entire party who was friendly to me had to be Izzy? Why did I have to have the reaction I had when I met her? Why had I already decided she was some extraordinary being, and why did I have to question if the sadness in her eyes was due to Maddox?

I tried, God knows I tried, but I felt the stinging in my eyes, and I wasn't about to stand there and let this happy little family see me cry.

"I'm going to grab a drink." I pulled away from Maddox. He tried to hold my hand, to keep me next to him, but I pulled away, unable to be in that situation a moment longer.

I wanted to run, where to I couldn't say, but I wanted to get away. I blinked repeatedly, trying to keep the tears from spilling down my face. I tried to calm the thoughts racing through my brain. It wasn't like anything overly horrific had occurred, but I couldn't deny the overwhelming sense of not belonging. Maddox's family seemed to know the inevitable from the very moment I met them—we were different. While it wasn't an ongoing problem between Maddox and me, it was still some invisible divide that existed beneath the surface, waiting to make itself known and separate us.

I grabbed another glass of champagne from a passing server and headed at a leisurely pace, despite my inclination to run, to the gazebo, which currently stood empty.

Feeling as if I didn't belong was not a bad thing. I'd learned at a young age that while I may want to be liked by everyone, life doesn't work that way. Aside from that, being liked by someone generally means there is some sort of common ground. Maybe the people I want to like me aren't the kind of people I want to associate with, so why let their disapproval seem like a bad thing? Still, here I was back in school and being the kid nobody wanted on their team; knowing it shouldn't bother me didn't make it hurt any less.

I looked out over the water, and for the first time in a long time I didn't have any idea where I wanted to be in life. Home was safe but complicated. School was feeling more and more like a means to an end— somewhere I had to be if I wanted to attain my goals, but not somewhere that made me feel warm and fuzzy.

I pulled out my phone with every intention of texting Amelia. She always seemed to offer something that made things better, whether it was good advice or just saying something to make me laugh, I could count on her. Instead, when I pulled out my phone my heart dropped as I saw Jameson had texted me back.

>Thanks, although it's not a done deal. We're still working on the logistics. I just want to play music.

I smiled to myself at his humility, which was perfectly Jameson. He was never in it for the fame or money, he was just doing what he loved. What he loved and was exceptionally good at.

>Be proud of yourself, whether it happens or not you deserve it and you've earned it.

>Thanks, your opinion has always meant a lot to me, even if it was sometimes biased.

>Biased?

What did he mean by biased? With my dad being a musician I'd grown up around music and felt like I had a good ear.

>;) you really want me to answer that?

Oh! After thinking for a minute, I realized what he was saying. Could I really have an unbiased opinion after sleeping with him?

>Ha! I got ya. No need to elaborate.

>I'd be happy to if you're needing a reminder...

Damn his words for making me remember, and damn the smile for refusing to leave my face. There didn't seem to be an appropriate response to that so I didn't respond. After a few minutes through my phone chirped again.

>How is life in Providence?

>Complicated. :/ I guess wherever you go there you are.

>You know you can always talk to me, right?

I could always talk to him, but as much as I wanted to let him be my friend it just didn't feel right to talk to him about Maddox. It would be wrong to complain about my relationship to someone I walked away from and it would be wrong to do that to Maddox. For what seemed like the hundredth time I had to berate myself for having feelings for Jameson. They were never gone, and I was never so deluded to believe that they were. A tear slid down my cheek as soon as I was brave enough to admit that to myself.

"You alright?"

I jumped at Gabe's question, not realizing he'd snuck up on me. I wiped the tears from my cheeks and put my phone back in my purse before turning around to face him.

"Yeah! Fine. I'm fine." Crap, my upbeat tone didn't come off as believable as I stuttered and fidgeted through my answer.

Gabe eyed me speculatively, having not believed a word I'd uttered. He took a step forward so he was standing next to me and leaned on the rail overlooking the pond.

"They aren't easy people, Becca." He let out an exasperated sigh and glanced at me before his eyes returned to the pond. "Want to get some cake?"

I couldn't help but let out a laugh at his brief pep talk, which ended with an offer of cake. Obviously, he'd either overheard everything or Maddox had said something. I'd already decided it was time to put on my big girl panties, and for Maddox's sake put all the thoughts in my head on hold. None of it was his fault, and acting like a brat at his graduation party wasn't an option.

Chapter Twenty-Nine

Kera ended up being able to make the tail end of Maddox's graduation party and her arrival couldn't have come at a better time. Initially, she hadn't thought she would be able to go because of her work schedule, but when she got off early she decided to make the drive. We stayed until the party was over and having her there gave me a much-needed distraction. I smiled and laughed my way through and played the good girlfriend. When it was time to leave I insisted on driving Kera back, claiming I was worried about her making the drive after working all day. The reality was much more pathetic—I just wasn't ready to be an adult and talk to Maddox.

I told Kera everything and she laughed and cursed at all the right times. More than anything I just wanted someone to tell me what to do because I couldn't find the right answer within myself; like so many things there was no obvious right answer.

Despite my real desire to avoid the situation all together I didn't actually want to walk away from Maddox. There was no denying the fact that something about Maddox drew me in, and while a part of me was afraid of trying to be with someone I couldn't end up with, it wasn't so easy to walk away.

I paced my small apartment, having already completed all the mundane tasks I could come up with. My brain never stopped playing scenarios but at least my baseboards were now sparkling clean. Maddox was due here soon and the thought occurred to me that he could be coming over to end things with me and that caused a sense of panic to run through me. I felt like I'd done a pretty good job of acting like everything was fine at his graduation party, but I was pretty sure he was able to see right through my smiles.

A knock sounded on the door and I stopped uselessly straightening the magazines on the table and took a calming breath.

I swung open the door. "Hey."

"Hey," he said, and while he smiled it didn't reach his eyes.

I stepped aside so he could come in and he put his arms around my waist and kissed my head. The silence was palpable as he and looked around the living room and for the life of me I couldn't think of anything to say in that moment.

"School going well?"

I laughed a little at his question just from the sheer awkwardness of the situation. You'd have thought it had been weeks since we'd spoken instead of just a few days.

He glanced up at my laugh and smiled; this time it showed in his eyes as well.

"This is awkward, right?"

"It is." I laughed.

"Who goes first?" I was thankful he left that part up to me; if he was going to end it I would rather he do it before I say all the things I wanted to say.

"Please." I sat down on the love seat.

Instead of sitting on the couch across from me he sat next to me, helping alleviate some of my nerves. If you're going to break up with someone usually a little bit of distance is nice.

"I'm sorry about the graduation party and my family ..." He sighed and rubbed his temples. "There's a reason I didn't rush you into meeting them and it had nothing to do with you. I know how they can come off. I didn't want to scare you off and it appears I've still somehow managed to do that." His expression was pained and it seemed apparent from his expression that he was concerned as to what my response was going to be.

"It's okay, Maddox." I turned slightly so I could face him.

I thought carefully, trying to find the right words for what it was I wanted to say. "Sometimes I feel like you and I are just ... different." I looked up at him to gauge his reaction and his eyes saddened with defeat.

"Different isn't a bad thing." He grabbed my hand and laced our fingers together.

"No, it isn't, but I don't enjoy feeling like I don't belong." I looked down, the words difficult to say out loud.

"You belong." He tipped my head up so I was looking at him. "You belong with me."

He searched my eyes looking for affirmation while stroking my jawline gently with his fingers.

"If you don't want to be with me then tell me, but don't let other people push us apart."

I looked down, the intensity of his gaze difficult to face straight on.

"Please, tell me what you're thinking." His tone was pleading as he tipped his head so he could look into my eyes.

"I want to be with you," I answered. "I'm just scared."

"Come here." He pulled me onto his lap so I was straddling him. He held onto my waist tightly wrapping me in his arms.

"There's nothing to be afraid of, Becca. I'll always take care of you."

The honesty and purity of his statement was etched in his eyes and I kissed him, longing to feel that closeness that I always felt when we were together. Maddox's breath caught in his throat and he stood up abruptly taking me with him and backed me against the wall. His hands grasped me tightly, his kisses showing an urgency that had never existed so greatly between the two of us.

He pulled both my T-shirt and my bra over my head in one impassioned moment and my hands fumbled with his belt and jeans desperately wanting to feel him inside me.

We never made it to the bedroom. Instead, we gave our passion control and took exactly what we needed, against the living room wall.

***

"Let's go to Newport this weekend!" Maddox said excitedly as he hopped out of bed with way more energy than should be legal on a Saturday morning.

The warm weather and Maddox's high from graduating made it difficult to focus on my classes. Minus the weekends, I was doing a pretty good job turning down his outlandish offers of taking off to the nearest beaches and spending the summer lounging.

He couldn't have been more tempting if he tried, with his black boxer briefs and that damn sexy V of muscles—it was like a traffic light always stuck on green.

"I can't, remember? I'm cooking tonight at Open Doors." Open Doors was a soup kitchen I'd found shortly after arriving in Providence, and while most of the time I volunteered there involved serving and cleaning up, tonight would be the first time I'd be acting as the main chef.

A look of reproach and annoyance flashed across his face before he turned away.

"What?" I asked defensively as I sat up in bed.

Still looking away from me he shook his head as he went through his drawers and pulled out his swim trunks.

"You obviously have something to say so out with it." I got out of bed and stood next to his dresser.

"I just don't understand why you'd put so much effort into that kind of a charity." He stopped what he was doing and eyed me, letting his words settle.

My mouth dropped open slightly as I stared at him trying to find the meaning in his words.

"What are you talking about?" I stared at him incredulously. "You volunteer for Big Brothers and Big Sisters."

"Exactly." He slammed his dresser drawer closed and headed to his bathroom.

"If you want to help someone, start with those who cannot help themselves, not a bunch of lazy people who refuse to work or do anything to improve their situation."

His words literally stopped me in my tracks as anger reverberated through my system.

"How about if you want to have an opinion on something, why don't you get some facts first!" My tone was now heated, having heard about as much as I could handle from him. "I'll have you know that many of the people who come to Open Doors are Veterans! Are they not worthy? Or the women who have escaped situations of violence and abuse ... or the countless people who are there because getting back on their feet is exactly what they are trying to do?"

I could feel my face heated and red with anger as he turned around to face me.

"Do whatever you want to do, I'm simply saying you might be better served putting your talents elsewhere. It wouldn't hurt to do something that will actually help your chosen career when you go to open your restaurant."

I didn't even try to hide my shocked expression. This was a side to Maddox I'd not seen before and I couldn't believe that I missed such a glaring flaw.

"Why is it people ask you to tell them what's on your mind and then get mad when it's not what they want to hear?" he continued when I said nothing.

"I'm sorry, I didn't realize the only charity work you were interested in doing was for the notoriety of it." Without waiting for a response, I turned and headed downstairs to check on my sauce, which had been cooking over the last two days. In the background, I heard the bathroom door close and the water turn on.

When I got to the kitchen I jumped when I found Gabe sitting at the table. He was rarely home anymore and his presence startled me at first, and then disturbed me when I realized he'd overheard our entire argument.

"Morning." He grinned apologetically as he used his fork to kick around the scrambled eggs on his plate.

"Morning … and sorry about that." I pointed toward the loft as I halfheartedly stirred the overabundance of sauce. Due to the amount of food I needed I also had one at my place that Kera was watching for me.

"Don't mention it."

We kept each other company in silence as I added some additional seasonings to the sauce and prepared to put it in containers.

"That smells amazing by the way." Gabe got up from the table and washed his dish in the sink.

"Thank you! It's my grandmother's recipe so I'm still figuring it out." I smiled as the memories of the many times we made it together flashed through my mind.

Gabe stood next to me and leaned over the pot inhaling deeply, his eyes closing as he did so.

"You want to be my taste tester?" I was excited for someone to let me know what they thought of what was easily one of my favorite dishes.

I stopped stirring and held the wooden spoon over the pot so he could take a taste, and just as he did so Maddox walked into the kitchen.

"Did I interrupt something?" Maddox's tone was full of venom as he stared me down.

"Honestly that's the best sauce I've ever tasted," Gabe said, looking at me and ignoring Maddox.

"You going to get dressed or are you just going to stay down here all day cooking in your pajamas?" Maddox leaned on the doorway, still staring me down.

"Maddox!" Gabe challenged as I looked down at myself in confusion.

I was wearing my pajamas but they consisted of a pair of shorts and a gray V-neck T-shirt. While it wasn't formal it certainly wasn't inappropriate.

Maddox and Gabe stood staring at each other, and without a word, I made my way upstairs, hastily grabbing my stuff and throwing it in a bag as I put my jeans on.

I heard a hushed conversation downstairs but at this point I didn't even want to know what was being said. The front door slammed and secretly I hoped it was Maddox who'd left. I was out of words for him today.

I returned downstairs to an empty kitchen. Taking only a few minutes, I packed up my sauce and was out the door. Having had a chance to think about things only made me more confused. I knew Maddox cared about his little brother, and didn't see himself as someone who had ulterior motives for helping someone else. That only led me to the conclusion that, like me, Maddox was feeling some sort of disconnect between the two of us. I didn't know if it was Maddox that felt wrong but I couldn't deny that something in my life felt extremely off.

When Kera pulled in the driveway my hands were strained with the overabundance of stuff I was carrying, so much so that when my phone rang I didn't even bother to check to see who was calling; whoever it was could leave me a message.

"Thank you." I smiled at Kera, who looked as if she had just dragged herself out of bed and come immediately to pick me up when she got my text.

"No problem," she said as we both got into the car.

"What happened?"

I sighed aloud, not in the mood to repeat my whole argument with Maddox. Maybe it was stupid but I didn't want to paint him in the light he'd managed to put himself in. I knew he wasn't the asshole he'd just made himself out to be, I just didn't understand what had set him off.

Delaying my answer, I checked my phone and saw that my missed call was from my dad.

"Hang on," I said as I dialed my voicemail.

His voice was cryptic, his tone lined with anxiety and tears. "I've got some bad news, Becca. Call me as soon as you get this."

"Oh no," I uttered out loud, and Kera took her eyes from the road briefly with alarm.

"Something's wrong." I quickly dialed my dad who answered on the first ring.

"Dad, what's wrong?" There was no chance I could hide the alarm in my voice. I closed my eyes waiting for the bomb I knew was about to drop.

"It's Gigi, Becca. She passed away last night."

Everything inside me stopped—my heart, my breathing, the world. I tried to breathe, to say something, but nothing came to me. I squeezed my eyes shut as the tears escaped. The only sound that left my mouth was ragged breathing and a sob.

Kera's arm went to my shoulder as she tried to soothe me, at this point not even knowing what happened.

"I'm so sorry, Becca. We got you a flight home, we can get through this together as a family." His words were pleading, and I hated not being there to hug my dad. All of my life he always made everything better, but it seemed hard to imagine that anything would ever be okay again, not without Gigi a part of this world.

I listened as he gave me details, but nothing he said registered. I was in a fog and wished more than anything I would wake up and this would have all been a dream.

Once I hung up with my dad I told Kera that Gigi was gone, which ultimately resulted in me sobbing for the next several hours. I lay in my bed and willed sleep to find me, which of course it never did. Kera immediately took on the task of getting some of our friends together to serve dinner at Open Doors, and while I was grateful, the fact that tonight they'd be eating Gigi's sauce only made me cry more.

The door opened tentatively and Maddox's sympathetic eyes landed on me. Without a word he got in bed, wrapped his arms around me and pulled me tight against him. We said nothing as he held me, gently wiping away the tears that refused to subside. Kera must have called him; I couldn't even find it within myself to text him.

Chapter Thirty

I blink my sleepy eyes repeatedly in an attempt to wake up. I'm seven years old but I'm not one of those kids that wakes up ready to go. My mom threatens to leave me in bed and just go to work and leave me there all day and let me miss school. Whenever I tell her that's fine she always changes her mind. But it's summer now and I'm at my grandparents' house like every summer. It's different than home. I can't touch anything and unless Poppy takes me fishing I'll have to go with my mom and Gigi to the stores where I'm not allowed to touch anything there either. If they put a bench there, you'd think that would mean I could sit on it, but no.

"These benches are not for sitting," Gigi would answer.

"Then why do they have benches?" I'd ask, but she'd never explain.

I hoped today would be a fishing day.

Poppy and Gigi's house is not like mine. There are couches you can sit on and ones you cannot. Cabinets full of teacups that would make for the perfect tea party, but they are not for drinking.

The bed squeaks when I get out and if it wasn't for the smells of the kitchen I would have stayed in the big bed with the endless quilts. But I'm hungry and ready for Gigi's eggs she makes for me every morning. The smell that's filled the small cabin for the past two days is Gigi's famous spaghetti and meatballs, which we won't get to eat for another day. I make my way down the small hall which leads to the open kitchen and living room. My Poppy built this house with the biggest trees on the land. The water tastes and smells like rust but I'm not supposed to mention that. I didn't know that it was a secret. Gigi is in front of her old stove that is so old there's no way to know how to make things in the oven. My mom wants one but I don't understand why since ours is much newer and fancier. Gigi is different than my other grandma who wears an apron, bakes cookies and sews clothes for my Barbies. With Gigi we go to fancy places every night and they take hours to get ready in her tiny bathroom. Then I have to keep clean, which is hard because Poppy says I have to play outside and his TV doesn't get cartoons. Gigi looks my way,

"Good morning, sweetie."

She pulls out my chair and I climb into my seat to wait for my breakfast.

"Today I'm going to teach you how to make my gravy."

"We're having biscuits and gravy?" I ask excitedly.

"No sweetie, the spaghetti sauce," she explains.

This makes no sense to me but I decide to not ask. Instead I ask my Poppy hopefully, "Can I go fishing with you today, Poppy?"

"Not today, today is not a kid day." He kisses Gigi on the cheek before the screen door bangs closed and he crosses the gravel driveway to his truck.

I slowly eat my eggs while Gigi gets out all the spices in the cabinet. She shows me all the spices and lets me dump them in the pot with the bubbling red lava. She doesn't use the spoons like Mama does. I use the big wooden spoon to stir all the colored flakes into the red sauce and the scent fills my nose. I can't wait 'til Mama gets up so I can tell her I made Gigi's spaghetti.

***

For a minute after I woke up I couldn't figure out how it was possible I could still smell Gigi's spaghetti sauce. Before I could fight them off, the tears filled my eyes. If I allowed myself to think about it, it would be an overwhelming feeling of dread. She was the reason I came here, the reason I fell in love with cooking. I couldn't make sense of any of it so I did the one thing that did make sense, the thing I'm good at. I cooked.

I was so thankful there was some of Gigi's sauce left over from the dinner for the homeless; strangely it felt as if there was something left of her for me to hang onto. Again I was thankful for the reprieve cooking gives me. It's a sort of obsessed bliss—nothing else matters. I sliced my mushrooms and peppers and happily listened to French music. I don't speak French but there's a sort of connection I find between the music and cooking. I would be leaving for home in two days but I wasn't going to focus on that. I focused on Maddox's face and the reaction he'd have when he tasted my Gigi's sauce.

My phone buzzed at me alerting me to a text message but I kept chopping. It could wait. I knew that on the other side of my kitchen the sad reality awaited—a reality without Gigi.

"This is not fair, when do we get to eat the famous spaghetti I can't stop smelling?" Kera asked, startling me out of my cooking-induced zone.

"Actually"—I tasted the sauce from my wooden spoon—"I think it's almost done."

"It's still missing something," I said, more to myself then Kera. "I can't quite tell."

"Well, it smells fabulous. I'm ready to be your official taste tester," Kera added while throwing her books on the counter.

"It will be ready in twelve minutes." I tossed the spaghetti noodles into a huge pot of steaming, boiling water.

Once the noodles were done cooking I fixed Kera a big bowl of Gigi's spaghetti and meatballs. I grated fresh Parmesan on the top and handed it over to her.

"You're not having any?"

"No, I'm going to wait for Maddox, he should be here in about an hour."

Anxiously, I awaited Kera's first bite response. No matter what I cook, how often I make it, or how many people I cook for, I never get past the first bite nerves.

Kera dutifully spun the noodles around her fork and included a piece of meatball in her perfect bite. Obviously, she'd spent enough time around us culinary folk to pick up a thing or two. She put the bite in her mouth and closed her eyes. For a minute, I watched her as if I could determine from her reaction-less face what her thoughts were. Not to let me down she said, with the pasta still in her mouth,

"Oh my God, Becca … soooo good. Seriously, amazing."

"I know, right?" I beamed. "I don't have it down yet, it's still missing something."

I stuck my finger on the hot spoon that had been resting in the sauce to take a taste.

"I don't know how you do that! You're going to burn your finger and your taste buds off." Kera teased. She took her bowl from the table and sat on the counter next to the stove. I can always tell when she has something to say that's important to her. Her face takes on a serious, contemplative look and I can see the thoughts move around in her head while she pauses.

"Are you doing okay?" she finally asked.

"I'm okay."

As long as I stay busy and avoid thinking.

She gave me that smile, the one that is shared a million times over when someone dies. That sympathetic look alone can bring out the waterworks.

"How's your mom?" She tilted her head to the side as she asked me, but she already knew.

"Not well. I haven't talked to her, just my dad. He says she needs me there."

"When are you guys leaving?" Her question took me aback for a moment. I knew this was coming and I knew exactly how she was going to react.

"I leave tomorrow." I tried my best, stern, ask-me-no-questions look but apparently, it doesn't work.

"Maddox?" She deadpans.

"I didn't ask him to go."

"You didn't *ask* him? You shouldn't have to *ask* him. Money bags can take a few days and be there for you!"

She hopped down from the counter, leaving her mostly eaten spaghetti and meatballs behind as if she needed to step away from the situation.

"*Seriously*, Becca?"

We were interrupted by a knock at the door. I quickly looked at my watch as I hadn't expected Maddox to be there for another forty-five minutes. Given Kera's feisty mood I opted to get the door to keep her and her quick mouth away from Maddox.

"Hey babe," Maddox greeted me as soon as I open the door.

"Hey," I smiled up at him. He was looking more relaxed than usual in his jeans and fitted sweater.

"It smells amazing in here." He made his way to the kitchen and to the bubbling sauce on the stove.

"Let me just throw some noodles in and I'll fix you a bowl."

Stirring the sauce he scrunched up his face. "Ew, mushrooms. Babe, you know I don't eat them. Besides, I already ate with Gabe."

He kissed my cheek.

"He and Stephy are at it again. I swear if he wasn't so afraid of upsetting his mother…"

As he was talking I could feel the disapproval radiating from Kera behind my shoulder.

"So when are you guys leaving for Cincinnati?" Kera interrupted.

I could feel my face heat and I knew better than to think I could hide my reaction. Whether it was one of embarrassment or anger I couldn't tell you.

"Babe..." Maddox looked nervously between Kera and me.

Kera walked to the connected living room and flipped open a book. I knew better than to believe her show of not paying attention.

"I'm sorry, it's just with this trip coming up there are a lot of things that need to be taken care of."

I felt the tightness in my throat and the tears that wanted to start their retreat once again, so I headed to my room and pulled my suitcase from under my bed.

"It's fine," I told him. "I know you have a lot going on right now."

"Thanks, babe." He flopped down on my bed and opened up his phone. While he put all of his focus into it I packed and tried to figure out what I was going to wear to what had to be one of the saddest days I'd had to face.

Hours later Maddox was asleep next to me, Kera having long since retired to her room. My thoughts, however, were preventing me from even drifting off, and the room was far too quiet. Every time I closed my eyes I saw her face.

My phone vibrated and lit up on the bedside table.

Jameson.

>I just talked to Amelia, are you okay?

I looked over at Maddox, who was deep asleep and unmoving. Why exactly did I feel guilty talking to him while Maddox was asleep next to me?

I grasped my phone close to me trying to find the words.

>No, not really.

>When will you be here?

>My flight gets in tomorrow at 2:50 p.m.

>I can pick you up?

Again, I looked over at Maddox. A sting of guilt went through me, but I could really use the level-headedness of Jameson right then.

Before I could come up with a response my phone lit up with another message.

>I figured your family has a lot going on right now.

I thought for a moment trying to ascertain if he was making a good point or if I was just looking for an excuse to be around him. I knew it was wrong and I knew I was being selfish but at that moment I was just tired of trying so hard not to care.

>That would be great, thank you.

***

I'd boarded the plane and fastened my seatbelt as tight as the thing would possibly go. This time around I knew better and I'd downed a couple Dramamine with my Merlot, which I decided was the best idea I'd ever had because the pain was buried just deep enough that I'd been able to not cry for a good forty-five minutes. Determined to maintain my current dry state, I tried to find that happy line between sober and slouched. I was pretty much off in la la land when the person seated next to me, who had been silent up until now, asked,

"So what's in Cincinnati?"

"Jameson," I responded without thinking. I realized what I said immediately and felt like an asshole. "I mean a funeral—there's been a death." I tried to show my most serious face.

Alright, so maybe my Dramamine and red wine cocktail wasn't the best decision in hindsight and all that.

"I'm sorry to hear that." She opened her book to continue our flight in silence. If I could I would pay someone for gene replacement therapy. Apparently, I failed to get the "how to act appropriate and less awkward" trait from my father's side.

I managed a quick snooze before the ding of the seatbelt sign and the descent of the plane woke me. Suddenly, I was thankful for the new security precautions at airports that made it so friends and family can't meet at the gate. I was pretty sure the crusty stuff on the side of my face meant I'd been drooling all over the window and could use a makeup refresher.

As the plane descended I was suddenly faced with the situation I was about to walk into, and all the nerves I could possibly muster found their way to the very pit of my stomach. Jameson picking me up was a bad idea. A temporary lapse in judgment undoubtedly brought on by a combination of grief and lack of sleep. I hadn't seen him in six months, and we didn't exactly leave things in the best of terms. And Maddox! I really cared about him and doubted he'd appreciate Jameson picking me up. Not that he knew who Jameson was, but that wasn't the point.

Walking through the gate I nearly yacked all over myself. Not good. The dizziness I felt was either motion sickness or my ill-fated cocktail. Thankful to be deplaned I headed straight to the bathroom. Good mother of God, I looked like straight up hell-in-a-hoodie. My outfit may have been another factor I'd failed to consider. I had a typical flight outfit which consisted of layers of clothing to combat motion sickness, hot flashes, and my strange need to cocoon myself while flying. Like a child, I somehow feel like hiding from the plane will make it less real. But the jeans, tank top, hoodie, and ponytail combo isn't a sexy look for me. With that thought, I reminded myself that looking sexy for Jameson shouldn't be at the forefront of my mind. I touched up my makeup pretty unsuccessfully and when a giggle escaped my mouth I realized I was overly buzzed. Fuck it, time to face the music.

I followed the signs through the endless terminals and felt all the air leave my lungs when I spotted Jameson leaning against the baggage collection area. He didn't see me right away and I just watched him looking around at all the people passing by. He looked nervous as he fidgeted with his perfectly messy wavy hair, and checked his watch at least twice. His jeans fit him loosely and the fabulous ink that decorated his forearms stood out in contrast against the black of his T-shirt. It appeared as though he was getting ready to move from his location to find a better place when he spotted me.

He stopped immediately, and for a moment neither of us moved. The people passed between us rushing through the airport and moving on to their next destination while we were lost in time for a moment. He was the first to make his way through the crowd of people to stand before me. I was holding my brown leather backpack by the top strap and just dropped it to the ground and grabbed him for a hug. If I had taken the time to think about what I was doing I probably wouldn't have done it. For once, I'm glad I didn't think first because he held me, and that was exactly what I needed. He let me be the first to let go and only the realization of Maddox back in Providence brought that embrace to a halt.

"I see you are properly cocooned for the flight." He knew me too well. "What will it be, Skyline or White Castle?" he asked as he picked my backpack off the floor.

Only someone from Cincinnati would understand the withdrawal that came from leaving and starting a new life in a city that didn't have Skyline or White Castle. Generally, my answer would have been Skyline, but nothing is better than White Castle when you've got a good drinking buzz.

We made our way through the aisles of parking to his old red jeep. As I sat in the passenger seat I couldn't help but think about all the time we'd spent driving around and talking.

"Just to be clear," he said to me with a level look, "you won't be getting out of any explanations while you are home, but at this moment you are off the hook."

"Thanks, Jameson." I put my hand over the top of his which was resting on his thigh. He immediately looked down at my hand resting on his and it surprised me that the familiarity that was still there. It wasn't just that it was familiar, like a pat on the back from my father, but the feeling that had always accompanied his touch was also still very much there. The electricity ran through my body, and my tendency to stop breathing without realizing it was also very much alive inside me.

We talked about his possible record deal briefly, but his demeanor changed somewhat when I broached the subject.

"We'll see where it goes," was pretty much the only response I got out of him.

Once we reached White Castle he perked up again, insisting I get a little bit of everything since I'd been deprived over the past year. We sat in silence until we got to my parents', but when it was time to get out of the car I couldn't do it. We sat in the driveway for an hour and talked before I finally headed inside to face my new reality—a life without Gigi.

My mom was in bed when I got there, and despite the still early hour, I wasn't surprised. I knew she would be devastated, and when things went badly in life that was where she went to retreat. My dad and I talked for an hour before I went back to her room to let her know I was home. We lay in her bed and cried, watching Lifetime movies until we both passed out.

Chapter Thirty-One

I shouldn't have come here. I know this yet here I sit outside his house. *Don't go in, put the car back in gear and leave.* I say this to myself halfheartedly. I know I will go in and I know what will happen. He is gravity and I'll lose control of all sense. I think of Maddox back at school and a sudden guilt floods me. I look down at my hands and notice the white-knuckle grip I didn't realize I had on the steering wheel. It strikes me odd how sometimes our bodies fight in different directions to our minds. While my brain is telling me to bail, my stomach is filled with the white heat of butterflies, and my heart begs for just one more moment of fullness, one I can only get when I'm with him, a fact I've hidden somewhere deep, pretending it doesn't exist. The battle of my wills dies abruptly when I see him. He opens the door and stands on his front step looking at me. In this moment, I'm confounded. I stare at him blankly wondering how it is possible that I might be the only person on the planet that knows how amazing he is. No man should be this sexy, smart, and funny. Before I realize that I'm acting like a complete stalker he walks over to my open window.

"Coming or going?" he asked with a nervous grin.

"Huh?" I responded with zero grace.

He nodded his head in the direction of my white-knuckled indecision. Abruptly I slid the car into park.

"Coming." I quickly looked away to hide my embarrassment. Why did that answer have to feel dirty?

Smiling, and not at all oblivious to the direction of my thoughts, he held the car door for me and I slid out. For a moment, I just looked at him, somehow yesterday felt as if it had been erased from my memory and I was seeing him for the first time. Despite the fact that having been apart from him for so long I was immediately reminded of how hard it was to be without him. As if the universe had erased everything that occurred, what had been done and undone, my gut reaction was to kiss him. Bad, bad, bad idea.

"Can I get a hug?" he asked, interrupting my thought process.

"Of course." I wrapped my arms around his waist at the top of his jeans. As he rested his chin on the top of my head, his arms pulled me against him tighter and he just held me there. He didn't let go, and I closed my eyes and breathed him in. I could have stayed there forever and I tried to convince myself I didn't ever have to let him go.

"I've missed you," he said, barely above a whisper.

I didn't say anything. I didn't know why exactly but the words I wanted to say never left my throat. Instead, I kept my head against his chest and tried to hang on to the moment. He smelled incredible, but I was keenly aware that any other man wearing this particular cologne still wouldn't have such a profound effect on me. It was him. It was Jameson.

He let me go and I tried to make sure I let go appropriately, instead of doing what I wanted and continuing to cling to and smell him.

He took my hand and led me in silence up the driveway to his little house.

"How's school going?" He held the door for me and, with his hand on the small of my back, led me into his living room.

"Good! A bit overwhelming at times, but good. Providence is amazing, so much culture. My favorite part has to be Federal Hill, which has incredible five-star restaurants with world-renowned chefs. You need to see it. It just makes me feel like I made the right decision going to school there. It also helps keep me focused when I'm surrounded by exactly what I want."

"I told you going there was the right thing for you to do. I'm proud of you." He smiled and again I wanted to kiss him.

I walked around his living room to distract myself as he grabbed a couple beers from the refrigerator for us.

He slid into his couch, propped his feet on the coffee table, and patted the cushion next to him.

"Come, tell me about your year."

I told him about Kera and how we became fast friends. I told him about my first failure as a wannabe chef and he laughed when I told him about my first experience at a frat party. I told him how much I enjoy walking to all my classes so I can window-shop at all the stores that border the JWU and Brown campuses. I didn't tell him about Maddox, funny considering I'd always considered evasion a lie. He didn't laugh when I mentioned that it was just window-shopping as any purchase would greatly impact my strict ramen noodle budget. Instead he looked at me with an overly serious face and lectured me on how unsafe it was for me to walk around the city by myself, in the dark.

"Just don't walk around after it's dark, alright?"

He was looking at me, inches from my face, and all the words he had just spoken were completely lost. Instead, I was keenly aware of the left side of my body. Of my feet resting on the table in front of us. I was completely aware that even though our legs were covered in jeans, they can't block the heat that simmered between us. Suddenly the room felt warmer but there was no way I was breaking the connection of our bodies.

Jameson looked at me and I felt like he saw completely through me and into my soul. I wanted to touch him and run my finger across the small white scar by his eye. Relief filled me when his feet hit the ground and he turned his body towards me again. Finally, I would again get to feel his lips on mine again. Arching my back I leaned toward him and closed my eyes.

"Hey, Becca! No freshmen twenty! Way to go!" shouted Stan as he walked into the room. I wasn't sure what was more alarming—him busting into the room a nanosecond before my lips were on Jameson's, or that he was now sporting a bright green Mohawk.

I jumped from the couch and gave him a hug. It probably had more to do with the fact that I felt like a teenager getting busted by my parents, and less with the need to hug him.

"I'm not a freshman," I said while poking him in the rib.

"Yeah, well, same thing."

Stan had always liked messing with me and had always treated me like a sister. Jameson got up from the couch and gave Stan that half shake / half hand slap thing that men like to do. I was still hugging Stan when Jameson stood next to me and put his arm around me, pulling me discreetly away from Stan's half hug.

"You get a hug—I had to ask for a hug," he told Stan. "I had to ask." He looked at me and gave me a wink.

"I'm meeting up with the guys at Mad Frog, you guys should come out," Stan said.

"Probably not tonight, we've got some other stuff going on."

I wasn't completely sure, but I thought that I heard Stan say "I bet you do" under his breath. We said our goodbyes and Stan was out the door, drumsticks in hand.

"Want another beer?" asked Jameson, making his way back to the kitchen.

"Sure," I said, curling up on his couch.

"How about we watch a movie?"

"You pick," I responded.

He picked something funny which I was thankful for. He was doing well distracting me from what was going on at home. I realized it was selfish but I needed this tonight. I needed this escape from reality and I needed him. As if reading my thoughts, he pulled me from my couch cocoon so my head rested across his lap, letting my feet lie across the armrest on the opposite side.

"Your mom okay?" he asked knowingly.

"No," is all I could manage. I closed my eyes but my grandmother's face didn't escape me. "I wasn't here." A single tear escaped the corner of one of my closed eyes.

"I know," he said sadly while playing with my hair splayed across his legs.

"Feel free to keep doing that," I told him, feeling more relaxed than I'd felt in months. Jameson leaned down and kissed my forehead.

"You feel free to take a little nap." He let his fingertips run across my cheek.

"I'm not tired," I lied. Suddenly the beer, sleepless nights, and emotional ride I'd been on had hit me.

***

I woke suddenly in the exact same position but with the sun shining in my eyes. My phone was doing that annoying text reminder thing, vibrating and beeping every few minutes. You'd think I would have woken up confused, but I wasn't. I was with Jameson, and wherever I was I'd be okay as long as I was with him.

Why did this have to feel so good? I always did sleep better with him next to me. A twinge of guilt surfaced at the thought—what was it about Jameson that felt like home? Not just a place, but a complete sense of security.

I sat up, stretched and noticed that Jameson was also in the same position he was in last night. Feet on the coffee table, his head against the cushion.

"Hey," he said, blinking awake with his sleepy smile.

"There's no way you were comfortable!" I said, feeling guilty for passing out on him.

"I'm okay." He grinned, looking too sexy for this early hour. "But I really have to pee."

I couldn't help but laugh at the pained expression on his face.

"I've been holding it for six hours, couldn't get this clingy girl off me!"

"Very funny!" I said while trying to land a friendly swat strategically aimed for his bladder.

"Gotta be quicker than that," he said, catching my hand. He took it and kissed my palm before heading off to the bathroom. I was thoroughly enjoying watching him go when my text reminder went off again. I grabbed my phone from the table and reality hit when I saw three missed calls and three text messages. My dad was responsible for the missed calls and two of the messages, the last text was from Maddox.

I quickly searched through my purse to find something to conceal my morning breath, then Jameson came out of the bathroom.

"There's a new toothbrush in the bathroom if you want it."

I was in the middle of brushing before it occurred to me that he kept a new toothbrush in his bathroom for houseguests. I opened the door so I could yell at him.

"Seriously? You give all your women toothbrushes? Is that like a consolation prize?" I joked.

"No, but I like the fact that you referred to yourself as my woman."

Pulling my hair from my face with one hand I spat toothpaste into the sink.

"I bet that's what you tell all your bitches!"

"Do you have to go?" His tone was regretful as he leaned against the doorframe. One hand was braced against the top of the door causing his shirt to pull tightly against his skin. I instructed my eyes not to look at the bare skin of his midriff.

"I do. I shouldn't have stayed, but thank you." I redirected my eyes to my mirror and wiped the little bit of makeup from under my eyes.

"But I made you breakfast." He disappeared into the kitchen. When he returned he was holding a small plate with a sandwich. I took the plate from him and inspected the sandwich.

"Peanut butter and jelly?" I asked.

"It's all I have in this place ... should probably hit the grocery."

"Thank you," I said. "For the sandwich and for last night."

"You don't have to thank me, Becca. I'm glad you came. If you want, I'll go with you tomorrow. I do actually own a suit, but I'm not shaving." His face was serious as he warned me of the latter.

I couldn't think of a thing to say so I just hugged him.

"Thank you," I said, my face still buried in his chest. He smoothed the hair on the back of my head soothingly.

Chapter Thirty-Two

I hate funerals. Sure, everyone hates funerals, but everything about them makes me nervous. I hate the stuffy clothes you have to wear, and somehow, I know I'll be hot regardless of the temperature. I also get carsick so sitting in an overly packed limo sounded incredibly annoying. I'd much rather follow the procession in my own car, crying in peace to Sarah McLachlan; she could make you cry on your happiest of days. But to be honest, what I dreaded most was how my mother would handle all this.

I was extremely close to Gigi, but my mother had made Gigi her entire world over the last few years. I reminded myself how poised and put together Gigi always was, so I planned my outfit to be as perfect as she was. I picked a black satin dress with a scoop neck and short sleeves. The top was fitted and tapered at the waist, and the skirt was slightly flared to just below my knees. The best part, as it usually is, was the shoes—a matte black heel with an oversized black satin bow across the top of the toe. My hair was in an updo, because she would have seen that as elegant and appropriate, with two black satin ribbons across the top of my head.

Amelia was already at my house, appearing to have shared my thought process since she was wearing a long black dress with black lace across the top of her chest. We both squeezed into my parents' bathroom to finish off our makeup.

"It's too bad that Maddox couldn't be here, I really wanted to meet him."

For obvious reasons I didn't tell Amelia *why* he couldn't be here, she never would have accepted his excuse. I didn't accept his excuse either, but putting too much thought into that whole mess was just too much.

"It's okay." I contorted my face into the appropriate expression in order to properly apply my mascara. "Jameson is coming with us."

She didn't have to say anything; the way she stopped mid eyeshadow application to stare at me was enough to tell me exactly what she was thinking. Before she could begin her tirade, the doorbell interrupted us. We made eye contact long enough for her to give me a knowing "Uh huh", but she was grinning.

Just when I thought I couldn't be any more attracted to him, there he was in black suit pants, a white dress shirt with the sleeves rolled up to expose his tattoos, and his suit jacket hooked on his finger and hanging over his shoulder. His hair was neatly combed back and while my mother may not approve of the beard, I couldn't care less. I liked the fact that he looked like a sexy rock god. But in all reality, I wanted him here because he understood the relationship I had with Gigi, and how much she inspired me to pursue my dreams. I almost felt as if he understood better than anyone what a significant loss her death is to me.

"You clean up nice," I said, pulling at the tip of his beard gently.

"You look gorgeous," he replied, eying the length of me.

Just then Amelia appeared at the top of the stairs above the entrance of the front door and they made their hellos.

The funeral itself was bittersweet. While it was terrible to say a final goodbye, it was also amazing to see how many people had come from all over to pay their respects. As my family and I, with Jameson at my side, made our way to the casket we looked at all the flowers that had been delivered in her honor. Maddox had sent the largest of all the floral arrangements with a card that simply read:

For Becca's Gigi~
A woman I've never met,
but one I've heard so much about,
and have so many reasons to be grateful for.

~Maddox Spencer

The sweetness of this gesture did not go unnoticed by me, or my family and friends. My mother noticed the card and pointed out to me how sweet my boyfriend back at school was, right in front of Jameson. I knew I should have mentioned Maddox to him by now but there was no erasing the fact that I hadn't. Jameson, being Jameson, didn't comment, but I knew this would be added to that list of things that would be discussed between the two of us.

Jameson sat next to me while we listened to the eulogy my mother tearfully gave. She expressed the joy she'd had over the last few years having Gigi in Cincinnati, and of all the years we vacationed in Northern Wisconsin at her cabin. The memories of those summer vacations flooded me, and the tears that had been sitting at the surface for days spilled over into my current reality. Jameson held onto my hand and handed me a handkerchief from the inside of his suit pocket. I knew it was wrong, but I was so thankful he was here with me. Once again, I needed his strength to get me through this. My father, seated next to us, cried the first tears I'd seen him cry since the passing of his own mother.

***

The days following the funeral were no different for us than for anyone else who has lost a loved one. Dealing with attorneys and wills was basically the last thing any of us wanted to be doing. My ideal situation during a time like this would be having a cup of tea and staying in bed watching movies. But as much as I wanted to bring those things to fruition it was more important for me to be present for my parents.

Jameson came with us to most things and held my hand when I began to feel overwhelmed by this hand life had dealt us. People always say that losing a grandparent isn't as difficult as losing a parent, or sibling, or God forbid a child—a theory I'd always thought made sense. Until I lost Gigi. It didn't matter that she was old. I was glad she hadn't suffered for too long, and while that brought me peace it didn't lessen the pain I felt. What matters is the relationship you have with that person, the closeness. Maybe if she hadn't been such a huge part of my life, and maybe if she hadn't helped mold me into the person I was, maybe then it wouldn't have hurt so badly.

We'd just finished up meeting with the attorney when Jameson and I decided to break off and do our own thing. He suggested a movie and the idea of jumping into someone else's life sounded exactly like what I needed. I let him pick the movie and he settled on a comedy.

He grabbed my hand as we walked through the crowded parking lot and I fought off the butterflies that filled my gut, telling myself it was just because of all the cars, and the fact that I've been in a daze over the last few days. His hand still grasped mine as we made our way up the stairs to the theatre. Why was it that my heart refused logic and still sank whenever our skin made contact? Guilt flooded me and I let go. He glanced at our hands and then my face.

"So what movie did you say we are seeing?" I quickly questioned, as if to take his mind away from the situation.

"It's a Farrelly Brothers comedy, should be pretty good," he smiled hopefully. "The better question is do we want popcorn, candy, or both?"

"Both!" I exclaimed. "And an Icee!"

"Now you're talking!"

Theaters are so much more comfortable than they used to be. It had been forever since I'd been to a movie but I know I would have remembered the reclining red leather seats if they had been there before.

"I'm so tired!" Jameson faked a yawn and did the fifteen-year-old boy method of putting his arm around me while stretching. Then, of course, he laid on the sweetest grin and sly wink, so even if I'd wanted to reject him I wouldn't have been able to. I wouldn't have rejected him anyway.

I guess his teenage gesture set the tone for the evening because I felt like an inexperienced high school girl again. I was completely unable to focus on the movie and instead was focused on the proximity of his body to my own: how close our legs were to each other, our hands resting next to each other's on the armrest—I caught myself looking at them thinking of how I'd like to hold his hand. Then came the inner torment of what the hell it was I was actually doing with him. It felt like living two separate lives—Jameson at home and Maddox at school. If I didn't think about it too much I could actually begin to pretend this was all okay.

As if he knew where my thoughts were heading, Jameson picked my hand off my hand rest and brought it to his mouth, then kissed my palm before bringing our hands back to rest in his lap. I could chastise myself all day long, I could feel like a terrible person, but nothing was going to remove my hand from his in that moment. Right or wrong, Jameson made everything that was wrong feel more tolerable.

Finally, I had found some sort of relaxation in my life. Gigi was still gone, but for an hour or so I felt at peace. For a moment, I let go of all the wrongs currently filling my world. The wrongs of death and the unfairness of life, and the fact that I was being a person I couldn't respect, caught between two men.

I had let go of that and was feeling pretty great for the first time in forever when we walked in the front door of my parents' house. As the door opened an overwhelming feeling of serious trouble hit me, so tangible you would have thought this feeling of dread was an actual physical person. It was Maddox, on the couch, sitting next to my mother.

"Becca!" He stood from the couch simultaneously straightening his dark charcoal slacks. Without looking at Jameson he came to me and picked me up in a hug.

"Are you surprised?" Maddox's eyebrows rose complimenting his cheerful expression.

"Shocked, actually! I thought you'd be on your way to Europe in the morning."

"I am, but I left a day early to come and see you and your family."

Jameson walked to the couch to sit with my dad, opposite my mother. It wasn't like I'd expected him to turn around and walk straight out the front door, but I had thought he'd find a way to leave, not just make himself comfortable as if he were here to stay for the evening.

"I was just telling Maddox how lovely the flowers he sent were. Easily the most beautiful arrangement at the funeral," my mother beamed.

"Yes, that was so thoughtful, thank you." I smiled up at him.

"Well…" Jameson slapped his hands on his thighs and stood up. *Thank God.*

I never thought I'd be so happy for Jameson to leave my house.

"Becca and I were just about to go get some ice cream."

Oh shit.

"Maddox, care to join us?"

I looked from Jameson to Maddox. "No, I don't need ice cream, and Maddox only just got here."

"Don't be shy, Becca, you were just saying after the movie how much you wanted ice cream."

I eyed Jameson, willing him to just stop talking.

"Well, what do you say, Maddox?" Jameson asked.

Maddox returned Jameson's cryptic gaze. "Yes, ice cream sounds good."

God help me. I looked to my parents for help but my dad just appeared highly entertained and was having a difficult time hiding his grin, while my mother looked utterly disgusted and was giving me her signature "don't screw this up" look.

Maddox had a two-seater rental so we opted to take my car and I had to actively ignore both of them trying to get in the front seat with me.

"So we haven't been properly introduced." Maddox's leather jacket squeaked as he leaned through the center console to speak with Jameson in the back seat. "I'm Becca's boyfriend, Maddox."

"I'm Jameson." He stuck his hand out to shake Maddox's. "I don't recall her mentioning you."

To that, Maddox said nothing and faced the front of the car.

God help me, I could think of nothing to say, although I wasn't sure any amount of words could have cut the tension anyway. Thankfully the drive was short and we exited the car in what was most likely going to be the most interesting and terrible ice cream trip known to man.

We made our way through the turnstile line, not unlike an amusement park. Maddox led the way as he talked about his backpacking plans and I could almost feel the eye rolls coming from Jameson behind me.

"Oh, that's right, the backpacking trip. That's why you couldn't make it to the funeral," Jameson quipped.

"So you have heard of me?" Maddox challenged.

"I heard about *that*, I must have forgotten."

"I'm sure you did." Maddox scoffed. Its deeper meaning did not escape Jameson, or me for that matter.

"Should I get chocolate or strawberry?" I asked, a little louder and shakier then intended. Lame, I know, but it was literally the only thing I could think to say on the fly.

"Which one of us are you asking?" Jameson's daring tone couldn't be missed.

"Just stick with your usual, babe," Maddox said, kissing the top of my head.

The usual. Interesting choice of words when we'd literally gone to get ice cream on only one other occasion.

"On second thought, ice cream isn't sounding so appetizing." With that Jameson turned to me, paused, and walked out the door. I turned to follow him, not to make some grandiose gesture and choose between the two of them, but because he was my friend and he'd been there for me through a lot. Before I could take a step Maddox grabs my arm.

"Becca, no," he said, half pleading, half demanding.

"He doesn't even have a car here, I'm just going to make sure he's okay."

"He's fine, Becca, he's a grown man."

His eyes said more than the words that left his mouth, and a mixture of loyalty and guilt gripped me. He had come all the way from Providence to meet my family and be with me after Gigi's funeral. He was, in fact, my boyfriend, whereas Jameson was just an old friend. It felt strange to refer to him as an "old friend"; obviously, he was much more to me than that. But for all intents and purposes, it was what he was. I was with Maddox, not Jameson. So, I stayed.

We made our way to an open table in the half gas station, half ice cream parlor toward the back of the room. He held out my parlor-style chair for me.

"You have something you need to tell me, Becca?"

This was not exactly the type of conversation you have while licking an ice cream cone so you can imagine how awkward it was to be asked that mid-lick.

"What do you mean?" I asked innocently.

"You know what I mean, Becca. Is something going on between you and Bad Boy Jameson?"

That little nickname kind of made me smile, which then turned to an awkward laugh, resulting in a not so appreciative expression from Maddox.

"No, nothing…" I didn't even convince myself with that untruth. "We had a past, though."

"And you thought it would be a good idea to spend a bunch of time— and go to the movies—with someone you had a significant past with?"

"I didn't say it was *significant*. You weren't here, Maddox. Do you have any idea how much Gigi meant to me, how difficult it was to lose her?" I got angrier as each word left my mouth. Suddenly having this conversation just pissed me off more that he hadn't been there.

"You never asked me to be here, Becca—"

"I shouldn't have had to *ask*," I interrupted.

"Well, I'm here now. I should have been here, okay? I realized that a little late but I came because I wanted you to know how much you mean to me. I was wrong."

He put down his sundae, grabbed ahold of my free hand and caressed the tops of my fingertips.

"Come to Europe with me. We can spend some real time together and you'll get along great with the guys."

"Thanks, Maddox, but now isn't the best time for me to up and leave the country and be out of contact with my family. Besides, it would be nearly impossible for me to get a ticket at this point."

"Expensive, not impossible. I got you, baby."

I gave him an apologetic smile. "As much as I would love to go with you, I just can't right now. It means a lot to me though that you'd take me along on your trip."

"Becca, you're going to have to tell me that you're going to stay away from Jameson for the rest of your trip. I trust you, but I don't trust him at all. It's pretty obvious what his motives are."

"It's not obvious. You're being paranoid. He's a friend, he's been a friend for a long time."

"Becca, I love you, but you're being really naïve here. Trust me. You need to back away from Jameson; nothing good is going to come from that."

"I promise." Technically there were only two days left of my trip here, and did he just say he loved me? Does *I love you, but…* mean the same thing as just an *I love you?*

That night we hung out with my parents and talked. There was no question that my mother was now infatuated with the "very impressive" Maddox. Thankfully, she deviated from her normal repertoire of telling all my boyfriends about my "chunky years", or the time they found me naked in the neighbors' koi pond (I was five years old by the way). She even managed to leave out my first prom, when my then boyfriend, Cody, got carsick in the limo and puked all over my dress. She left out all my cringeworthy stories and instead worked unnaturally hard to make me look appealing. I'm pretty sure at one point she used the line "a real keeper", so to be fair she did, in fact, have a few cringeworthy moments.

"Except for that whole *culinary* program," she slurred, distracting me from my thoughts.

"If she wanted to be a cook she could have stayed right here in Ohio instead of wasting a bunch of money on useless pursuits."

At that, my dad took her wine glass from her. "Alright, Marie, it's been a long day. How about we go to bed?"

"I'm sorry, dear, it's just hard without you here, especially now. I don't know what I'm going to do when you go back to school," she said, tearing up a bit.

"I know, Mama. You can always come visit me, anytime."

"Yes, in fact, I haven't discussed it with Becca yet, but I've been thinking she and I should get a house off campus. It would have a guest room and we'd have more than enough room for you guys to come visit."

I had nothing to say to that. I'm not sure who was more shocked, my parents or me. My mother looked overjoyed, of course. My dad looked a combination of confused and annoyed. Likely because I'm his only daughter.

"So, what do you say, Becca? I was going to wait until I got back from Europe but, if you'd like to, you can look for places while I'm gone."

I turned my knees toward him so we were facing each other. "I don't know, Maddox, I'm not really in a position to pay to live off campus. Most of the money I make goes toward tuition."

"No worries, Becca, I got you." He cupped each side of my face and looked me in my eyes.

Before I could quantify a single one of the fifty thousand thoughts running through my head my dad stooped as he helped my mom from the couch.

"Let's hit the hay, Marie. It sounds like these two have a lot to talk about." He nodded our way.

"At least let me make you breakfast in the morning. What time do you need to leave for the airport?" my mother asked.

"I'll need to leave by nine am."

"Alright, breakfast it is."

And with that, my parents were off to bed. There had been far fewer verbal casualties then I'd expected, but there was always breakfast!

***

I woke early the next morning. In truth, I wasn't completely convinced my mother would be able to drag herself out of bed so early. She hadn't always been this way but over the last few years she hadn't quite been herself. Part of loving someone is protecting other people's perceptions of them. I wasn't embarrassed by her by any means, but I didn't want other people seeing a side of her that was less than perfect.

I shuffled my sleepy self upstairs to figure out what I could pull together for breakfast. Coffee first. Once the machine started its joyful percolating sounds I hit play on the iPod which was already hooked up, and an upbeat Beach Boys song started playing. Dancing my way around the kitchen I prepared bacon, mushroom and spinach frittata, baked apple roses, and individual muffin pan potatoes. I was just about finished when my mom came into the kitchen, freshly showered.

"Oh, thank goodness; I was going to feel bad sending the man off with only Cheerios in his belly," my mom joked.

"Hey, benefits of having a daughter in the *culinary* program!" I quipped.

"Ahh, there's the Becca I know and love." My dad entered the kitchen and kissed me on the forehead. "So what's this about you two moving in together? Are you sure that's what you want?"

I opened my mouth to speak.

"Of course that's what she wants! That Maddox is a real catch. Smart, gorgeous, and from the sound of it, filthy stinking rich!" My mother half whispered the last part.

"Can we hold off on this conversation at least until he's gone?" I asked, exasperated.

"There are more important things than money, you know that, Marie," I heard my dad say as I walked downstairs to find Maddox. I stopped first in the bathroom to make sure I hadn't also frittata'd my hair in the cooking process. Apparently, no amount of professional training was going to teach me how not to also wear whatever it is I prepare.

I looked at myself in the mirror, wondering for a moment what type of person I was. Specifically, the type that would end up with a Maddox, or with a Jameson.

As if in reply, Maddox came up behind me and wrapped his arms around my waist, pulling my oversized sleep shirt taut. Looking at me through our mirrored reflection he whispered, "Good morning, beautiful," and kissed the side of my neck. It wasn't the "good morning, we're in your parents' basement" kind of kiss, but the "please remove my sleep shorts as quickly as possible" kind of kiss. Before I knew it he had picked me up, turned me around and sat me on top of the vanity before his lips found their way to my mouth. Just as my fingers had found their way to his chest ready to unbutton his dress shirt he stopped.

"Let's go see what your mom made us for breakfast."

"You dirty tease," I scoffed.

"This looks amazing, Marie," Maddox complimented, taking his seat at the table between my dad and myself.

"I get no credit; Becca gets all the glory for this one," my mom added proudly.

"Yes, if Marie had cooked we'd all be gathered around bowls of

Cheerios," my dad added.

"Well it looks amazing," Maddox said, offering the first plate to my mother.

"So Maddox, what do your parents do? I was talking all night and never gave you a chance to speak!" my mother laughed.

"My mother is now retired, although I think she spends more hours with her charity than she ever did when she was working. My family owns an engineering and architectural firm; my father is the CEO, and my brother is the Chief Financial Officer. My mother has been trying to get him to retire for years but I'm not sure he ever will."

"So you have a brother? Any more siblings?" my mother asked, batting her eyelashes a bit too obviously.

"Just my brother Max—well, Maxwell—and myself. But I'm very close with a cousin who may as well be my brother—Gabe. He graduated a year ahead of me.

"Are you planning on staying in Providence?" my dad asked.

Maddox looked my way before responding.

"I am."

I was thankful Maddox had managed to make it out the door before my mom felt the need to point out my "childbearing hips" or offer the family pet as my dowry. There was no question who she thought I should end up with.

I busied myself clearing the table from breakfast.

"I knew I missed you; I've been doing these dishes alone ever since you left for school."

Doing dishes with my dad had been our nightly ritual for most of my childhood. My mom subscribed to the belief that the cook doesn't do the dishes. I would say I agree with that, but the number of dishes I use when cooking can be a bit overwhelming, usually resulting in my feeling too bad to make the recipient of my culinary experiments clean up after my mess.

"So, what exactly are you doing, Becca?" he asked bringing up the ten-foot elephant in the room.

Knowing my dad hadn't missed a thing that had played out over the past couple of weeks, there was no point in trying to deny.

"Honestly, I have no idea," I huffed, drying the plates he handed to me. "How am I supposed to know who I'm supposed to end up with when I'm not entirely sure who I am just yet?"

"You know who you are, Becca, and I'm sure you'll make the best decision for you. But you do need to make a decision; you can't have both. The longer you take making up your mind, the more likely you are to lose both."

"I know this!" I said, taking my drying towel and covering my face with it. "Honestly, I feel like I'm in two different worlds. Whichever one I choose will take me in a completely different direction."

"All you can do, Becca, is choose the one who treats you the best and brings out the best in you. It's impossible to say where your heart and your head will be five years from now, so, for now, you just have to follow your heart."

Follow my heart. Funny, that statement didn't narrow things down for me more. On one hand being with Jameson made me feel safe and at home, wherever I was. But when I was with him I was at home, so maybe that feeling is more related to proximity than anything else. I felt like a kid, but at the same time I felt like I could do—and be—anything.

Maddox made me feel alive and excited, and ... taken care of. He and I shared a level of ambition that Jameson might have been lacking.

After we'd finished up the dishes I sat in the middle of my bed staring at my phone. I knew I had to say something to Jameson but the words had definitely escaped me. Somehow, I didn't think it was the best idea to send him a message saying "Hey, thanks for spending so much time with me and taking care of me over the last couple weeks. Sorry I ditched you when my boyfriend came to town unexpectedly".

Wow, I really am an asshole.

I dropped my phone on the bed, curled into a ball and went to sleep, hoping that somehow things would be clearer to me after a good nap.

When I awoke I did the best I could and sent a simple text.

>I'm sorry.

>To be clear, which thing specifically are you apologizing for?

>All of it?

>I don't know what to say here, Becca.

>How would it ever work for us, Jameson? I still have a year left in Providence.

>If you want to be with him just say it, Becca. Don't pretend it's the distance you can't handle.

>I don't know what I want but I know I can't be this person.

>For once Becca, say what YOU want.

Say what I want. I couldn't say what I wanted when the damn truth was that I wanted them both. I am not a person who would allow myself to be selfish enough to keep them both, but the thought of losing either one of them was too much to bear. And, with that, the floodgates opened and I allowed myself to partake in the pity party that had been months in the making. The unfairness of losing Gigi, a relationship I wished I could have with my mother, and losing touch with Amelia, who had been like a sister to me. Suddenly returning to Providence was too difficult to imagine.

Chapter Thirty-Three

I felt the pain of losing Gigi even more the last few days I was home. There was no more Jameson to cheer me up and keep me distracted, and no more surprise visits from Maddox. I was just another sad person in a house that didn't feel like home.

Going back to Providence this time around was much harder. What once held promise of the life I'd always wanted suddenly seemed pointless. I hadn't talked to Jameson since that last text message he sent me, Maddox would be in and out of contact over the next two months, and even though I knew I should concentrate on my classes it was the last thing I wanted to do. Without Gigi here I felt myself questioning my whole life plan. It all seemed so good at the time, but now nothing felt right.

The summer rain was relentless, keeping me cooped up most days. Maddox called sporadically to tell me he was having the time of his life, but bad connections and distractions (on his end, of course) never made the time right to unload my problems onto him. He did suggest I check out some houses for rent so we could move in together when he got back from his trip. Maybe that would help pull me out of my slump; certainly things would get better when he got back. I'd set up a few showings for the following week, and honestly was pleasantly surprised Maddox was showing such a level of commitment and excitement about living together.

Since my mood was crap I decided to do what any rational woman did when upset—I went shopping. On my way out I stopped at the community mailboxes to find an envelope had arrived from Maddox, postmarked Rome, Italy.

Becca,

I know things must be difficult for you right now being back at school. I wish you'd taken my offer to come with me. Rome is amazing, as are all the other places I've been, and I know you would love it. If you change your mind, know that the offer still stands. You say the word and I'll have a ticket waiting at the airport for you. If nothing else you could call it culinary research. I think of you every time we go somewhere to eat and can imagine you figuring out the ingredients with every bite. I miss you and hope you are looking for a place for us when you're not busy with school.

Not to worry, I'll be sending you lots of goodies back from my trip but here's a little something to get us started on our new place, or whatever it is you might need right now.

Miss you,

XOXO

Maddox

Man, I have good taste in men! It immediately reminded me of the knives Jameson sent me. Why exactly did that thought have to enter my mind? Maddox was amazing and it was time to stop comparing him to Jameson.

Maddox's letter and the money he enclosed changed my shopping trip from one of window-shopping for clothes to actually looking for stuff for our place. I was glad Kera had some time off to spend the day with me and finally get some girl time.

We walked through the stores that lined the infamous Thayer Street, browsing at everything and nothing in particular.

"How did the funeral go? Your mom doing alright?" Kera asked.

"It sucked. I mean the funeral was fine, it just sucks that she is gone."

Kera stopped thumbing through the printed art posters that had held her attention to put her arm around me.

"I'm sorry, I know what your Gigi meant to you. You know she was proud of you though, Becca. And maybe it will help you become closer with your mom. I don't know." She frowned. "I wish I could have been there with you. Maddox should have been there."

Kera walked toward the side of the store to smell the individual candles that lined the wall.

"Was it terrible?" She looked over her shoulder at me.

"Well…" I wasn't exactly sure how to explain that one.

"I spent most of the time with Jameson. He went to the funeral with me, the attorneys, the movies." I said that last part under my breath a bit. Before she could comment on my last remark, which I knew she would, I added, "And Maddox did come to see me, before he flew to Europe."

"Are you freaking kidding me?" she asked, her jaw slack, nearly dropping her Yankee Candle.

"Not kidding," I deadpanned.

"Just tell me they didn't meet."

I didn't need to get the words out because my face said it all. Immediately Kera put the candle back on the shelf and ushered me out the front door to a row of benches on the sidewalk. She pulled me toward the bench and before we were completely seated she said, "Alright start at the beginning; what exactly is going on?"

"I don't know, Kera, I'm so confused. Jameson texted me when he heard about Gigi, which of course was at the same time Maddox didn't offer to go with me to the funeral. I was upset. So, Jameson asked if I wanted him to go to the funeral with me and I said yes."

"Were you trying to get back at Maddox?"

"No, honestly it wasn't about that. I just didn't want to have to go through it alone. And Jameson has a way about him that just makes me feel like I can be strong. I knew him being there would get me through it more than anyone else could."

"Even Maddox?" She raised her eyebrows slightly with the question.

"I'm not sure. It's not really a fair thing to say since I've never really been through anything like this before."

"You hadn't been through anything like this with Jameson before either. But anyway, continue your story."

"So I spent the entire time with Jameson, including the night Maddox showed up. We walked in the door from the movies and Maddox was there in my living room impressing the shit out of my family, well, more specifically my mom. If she had a say I'd be wearing an apron and pregnant with his baby by now."

"And Maddox and Jameson…" She was way too excited to ask the question.

"Yeah, not good. Jameson was completely confrontational and Maddox didn't back down at all. Jameson ended up leaving the ice cream parlor and didn't even have his car there."

"Wait—you Jameson and Maddox all went to get ice cream together!"

She was smiling at this point.

"It's not at all laughable, I assure you."

"Needless to say, Maddox wasn't pleased, but he was surprisingly cool about the whole thing. I haven't talked to Jameson since that day though."

"And now Maddox is ready for you two to get a place together? Sounds like he's trying to put you on lock. If you were trying to make him jealous and get him to take things to the next step it worked."

I thought for a moment about what she was saying and had to question myself in that regard. I'd never been the type to play a game to get what I want. Was living with Maddox what I really wanted? Suddenly I felt overwhelmed about everything. The things going through my mind I couldn't say out loud, not even to Kera. I missed Jameson and felt partial relief that Maddox was gone, but part of me missed him too. I couldn't help but think I'd be more excited if it was Jameson and I that were moving in together, and that thought alone brought the first tear to my eye. Kera noticed it right away and pushed the red hair from her face as if to get a better look at me. She turned her knees toward mine and put her hand on my leg.

"I'm so sorry, Becca, I didn't mean to upset you. I wasn't implying you are playing games with Maddox, I was just saying—"

"No, I know what you were saying. It isn't you or anything you said. I just don't know what I'm doing. I don't know what I want, or, even worse, *who* I want. I'm so confused. How ridiculous is it that I can't even determine what my own mind wants?"

"It isn't ridiculous." She looked me in the eye. "Sometimes our minds and our hearts want different things. That's when we can't figure out what we want, and when we get ourselves in trouble."

Somehow that made perfect sense to me.

"But if you're not one hundred percent into moving in with Maddox, don't do it. You don't want to find yourself in a position where you are more stuck than you already are right now."

"So I should wait. Maybe once he's back things will be easier to figure out and we can discuss it then," I said, more to myself.

As fate would have it, Maddox called me later in the night and immediately pointed out that I sounded *different.* He called my bluff when I said everything was fine, and when he finally pried it out of me that I wasn't completely sure about moving in together he jumped on the defensive. Instead of being able to talk it through, he assumed my "newfound indecision" was due to my time with Jameson. I denied that, not really knowing which of us was right. Regardless of the reason, I didn't think it was a good idea to go into something so big when I wasn't completely into it. By the end of the conversation, he had declared that he and I needed some space. *Some space?* Not sure there could be any more space between us. Somehow that just seemed to me like a good excuse for him to live it up when he was on his trip, which I immediately realized made me seem like a huge hypocrite.

All I needed to do was make it through this year and I'd be done with school. I could stay here, go back to Ohio, or move somewhere I've never been to open my restaurant and begin the life I'd always wanted for myself. Now, why didn't that prospect excite me?

I'd managed to go from being completely fulfilled and ambitious about my life to this new place of doubt and hopelessness. I regretted being away from Gigi, and wished I could have somehow known I was going to lose her; I would have done things differently. Now my indecision about living with Maddox had equated to possibly being without him altogether. And as he always was, Jameson was a million miles away. I sat on my bed cross-legged with a box of tissues in my lap, finally giving up and allowing myself to have a good cry. When was it exactly that my life started to completely fall apart? Maybe it was never going as well as I thought it was. I lay down on my bed and opted for cheesy Hallmark movie because it matched my crying mood.

I awoke, disoriented, to the chirping of my phone. Before reaching for it I looked around my room, taking in the darkened windows that let me know I'd slept longer than expected, and the plethora of tissues that let me know that my pity party had been even more pathetic. I glanced at my alarm clock and decided I wasn't ready to face the world and my life. As it was after ten p.m. the pressure of being productive was not an issue.

Squinting at the brightness of my phone in my dark room I paused when I saw I had a text message from Jameson.

>Hey.

Oh crap.
Part of me knew responding was a bad idea. The only thing I had

successfully done for my life as of late was confuse everything. With that being said I also owed Jameson more than that.

>Hey.

>You doing alright?

>I suppose, you?

>I'm ok. I just wanted to check on you. I feel bad about walking out on you at the ice cream parlor.

>You feel bad? I feel bad. I wanted to go after you but I was just in a bad place since Maddox had come all the way to see me.

>It's ok, a lot of it was my fault. I didn't care for your boyfriend though. I'm sorry for saying that but it's the truth.

>He's a good guy, Jameson. But I think I managed to mess that up pretty well. I don't know what I'm doing here anymore.

>I think maybe coming here was a mistake. Being away from Gigi just kind of nailed that thought home.

>What did you mess up with Maddox? And going to school there was not a mistake, Becca. You're going to be an amazing chef and have your restaurant like you've always wanted.

>I don't know anymore. All I can feel right now is regret. I miss Gigi and I know my family needs me right now.

>What are you saying, Becca? You seriously thinking about coming home?

>I don't know. Possibly.

**

Business Law was actually one of my favorite classes that didn't necessarily directly apply to my major. The class itself was small, which was nice, because I had more one-on-one contact with my professor, but at the same time some of my classmates reminded me of being back in high school. Take Juicy for instance. Obviously, that wasn't her name, but it was one I gave her since most of the time she was wearing sweatpants with 'Juicy' written across her ass. She sat there most days either messing on her phone or doing her nails. I'll never understand why someone would pay so much money for an education they obviously weren't interested in getting.

Today, however, I wasn't one to talk and found myself a million miles away from anything happening in this classroom. I had to literally remind myself to focus every few minutes, my mind suddenly filled with a fog that wouldn't dissipate. Every fiber of my being wanted to be somewhere else, but for the life of me I couldn't figure out where that was.

Honestly, my depressed state of mind surprised even myself. I was so ready to just give up trying to become this person I had envisioned in my mind. Somehow everything that had once meant so much to me seemed unrealistic and stupid.

I yawned as I tried to pay attention to the professor, despite the millions of thoughts running through my mind. Jameson had ended up calling me the previous night after our text conversation and we'd stayed up talking way too late, hence my inability to stop yawning. Usually, he was able to pick me up pretty easily but—and maybe it was because of Gigi's death—for once he hadn't been able to pull me from my depressed mood. Now I wanted to kick myself a bit for being so vulnerable with him. Sometimes you have to smile through the tears and put it out there to everyone that you're okay, even when you're not.

Focusing on my class was important, but my thoughts were already too far-gone to care when my phone vibrated with a text.

>Did you know Jameson is playing a gig in Boston this weekend?

Boston?! It takes less than an hour to get from Providence to Boston, how could Amelia have known this and I didn't? I would normally have been thrilled to see him, but now it was agitation that filled me. Would he seriously be this close to me and not bother telling me?

Instead of responding to Amelia's text it was Jameson I messaged.

>*A little bird just told me you are* going to be in Boston this weekend?!

>I am, who is this little bird?

>Who is the bird?!? You weren't going to tell me?

>No, I wasn't.

What the hell? It was a bit staggering how much that statement and the omission hurt me. He knew I was having a hard time here so why would he come so close and not even tell me?

Betrayed. That's how I felt, even if it stung admitting it to myself. After a few minutes of not answering him my phone vibrated with a new text.

>I was going to surprise you.

Oh. I covered my face slightly because I couldn't stop the smile that was out of place with the lecture I was enduring on business ethics. Although, I couldn't really claim to be enduring it since I wasn't actually paying a lick of attention. Ethics are ethics, right? I should be fine.
>Really?!

>Yes, I'm gonna have words with Amelia.

>When will you be here?

>Early Friday but the show is that night. We got a lucky break and are opening. Your ticket is at the gate, just pick it up and head backstage, let them know you're with me.

I could barely contain my excitement as I sat there, now actually trying to pay attention to the lecture. I couldn't ascertain what exactly had me so excited. Maybe just the excitement of watching someone as they achieve their dreams. Maybe it was because I was having a hard time and needed a friend. And maybe it was because it was Jameson, and at that moment there was nobody I would rather see.

Thanks to this new piece of information it wasn't as challenging getting through the week of classes. Suddenly, I had something to be excited about, something to look forward to. I told myself maybe that was all I'd needed all along, and whether it was Jameson or someone—or something—else, it didn't really matter. I also tried to convince myself that a thrill didn't run through me when he said for me to tell them I "was with him".

***

I took the train to Boston and arrived too early to actually show my face. As I stood outside the venue I knew he was probably already inside, but decided it would be best to walk around or grab a beer as opposed to coming off as eager as I actually felt.

I opted for a bar down the street and made my way to the bartender despite the fact that the place was overflowing with people. I had taken one sip of my beer when I got a text message.

>When are you going to get here? I'd really like to see you before the show.

I smiled at his message and was glad it wasn't just me feeling antsy.

>I'm just down the street, be there in a few. Nervous?

>Excited. :)

My heart dropped with excitement when I read his response but I quickly realized he was talking about his show. It didn't change the way I felt though, and while I would never admit that to him, I was at least able to admit it to myself.

Skipping my beer, I headed back to the venue, a large outdoor amphitheater. Just as he had said, when I gave my name to the person at the ticket booth they had a ticket held for me, as well as a backstage pass. I sent a quick text to Jameson to let him know I was here and headed toward the front of the stage. Somewhere in my mind I had assumed this would be a smaller venue, and wasn't prepared when I realized this was not at all unlike the many concerts I'd been to over the years. It didn't start for another hour yet but there were already thousands of people milling about the lawn area. Closer to the stage there were actual seats, and if I had to guess I would say the entire place could hold twenty thousand people. I clutched my backstage pass as hordes of people passed me, clad in concert T-shirts featuring the headlining band.

My stomach felt hollow with nerves as I headed to security. However, before I'd even made it to them I saw Jameson coming toward me.

He walked past security and grabbed me in a hug.

"Oh my God, Jameson, I can't believe you are about to play for all these people. This is insane!" I exclaimed, even before he let me go.

"Yeah, you're telling me!" He grabbed my hand and led me up the stairs behind the stage.

"Are you afraid?" I asked. "I would be afraid."

Jameson watched me momentarily before answering as if considering. He took my other hand so he was facing me and held both my hands.

"I just pretend I'm only playing for someone I care about. I know the music and will just have to let it speak for itself."

"I know you are going to do great." I meant it—I could feel it.

He kissed my forehead before leading me down a hallway to a room that had their band's name affixed to it.

When he swung it open my eyes immediately landed on Stan. He had a mohawk so naturally he was the focal point in most situations. He saw me and smiled excitedly.

"You believe this?" He got up from the couch and grabbed me in a hug.

"It's crazy!"

"Are you hungry? 'Cause all this shit is for us." He pointed enthusiastically to a large table full of food and various drinks. "They've got hamburgers, chicken, pizzas, pop, beer..."

I laughed at his exuberance and was glad he wasn't one of those people that started acting like an asshole once they got even a hint of fame.

"I'm okay."

Suddenly I became aware Jameson was still holding my hand and I hoped he wouldn't let me go. It felt so right to be with him, and inherently I knew it had nothing to do with the situation. It didn't matter to me if he was rich or famous, I just wanted to be with him, exactly how he was right then, exactly as he was a year ago.

Jameson sat down on the couch with Stan and pulled me with him so I was sitting on his lap. I gave him a shy smile even though I wasn't embarrassed. I knew the guys in his band and had been around all of them enough to not feel out of place. Honestly, at that moment I wanted to be even closer to him and wondered briefly what was going to happen after the concert. Was he going to leave right away, or hang out with everyone? Or would I get to steal him away for a while?

All too soon the band had to head onstage and I was so nervous for them that I felt like I, too, was going to be on that stage. I wanted everyone in the crowd to get it, to see how incredibly talented they all were. I wanted to find a Metaloids T-shirt and wear it proudly, although I'm not actually sure they even had T-shirts yet.

Jameson let out a deep breath, the only thing so far that hinted at any kind of nerves. Delicately he placed his palms on either side of my face, concentrating on me. "I'll just play for you." He said the words as if it was what he needed to do for himself to make it through.

I nodded in agreement. "Play for me."

Before either could have another thought of us, he pulled me toward him and kissed me with a hungry need and an urgency I don't ever remember him having. His hands grasped my hips and he pulled me against him, and it was either the best second first kiss, or a goodbye I would never forget.

The roar of the immense crowd was deafening by the time they walked out onto the huge stage. I sent up a quick prayer that all who heard them would appreciate their unique sound. Jameson's eyes stayed on me for the most part as I stood just in front of the stage with the other VIPs. I didn't think I'd ever get used to seeing him on stage; every time it felt like the first time. There was no mistaking the fact he belonged up there, and that music brought out something magical in him. Thankfully, there was a special roped off portion for us before the first set of seats. Even though everyone had a seat, it didn't appear a single person was seated; everyone was on their feet. Each song ending brought about a fury of noise from the crowd, and I was elated for the guys.

Their set only lasted about an hour before the main act came on and I met them backstage as they were exiting.

"What a fucking rush, man!" Stan hugged Jameson and he patted him firmly on the back.

Jameson's eyes never left mine as several of his bandmates and crewmembers came up to him. It was nice to see that he was so intent on making his way to me. Seeing him after a performance reminded me how he looked after sex. His hair fell into his face a little more from the dampness and he wore a look of pure elation and contentment.

"You don't want to hug me but you better give me a kiss." Jameson had finally made his way to me. Not unlike the other guys, he was a bit of a sweaty mess from the heat of the lights, and the fact that it was still eighty degrees even though the sun had already gone down.

I grabbed him by his belt and pulled him to me, too excited for him to care about a little sweat. Besides, it wouldn't be the first time…

"You were amazing!" I said as he touched his forehead to mine.

"I'm just glad you were here." His fingertips ran across my chin.

"Me too." I closed my eyes and didn't realize he was going to kiss me until I felt his lips on mine.

I took a seat on the couches while Jameson went back to shower and couldn't deny the deep feeling of guilt that found its way to the surface. That was the second time I'd kissed Jameson today, and I honestly didn't even know where Maddox and I stood. I could pretend our last conversation made this all okay, but my conscience knew better. Maddox had been frustrated with me for a while for not being more eager to join him on his trip, and the fragmented conversations we had been having due to bad connections had worn my nerves thin. But those things didn't make what I was doing feel any more justifiable.

Jameson entered the room and seeing him nearly erased all the second thoughts that had filled my mind in the short time he was gone. His hair was still wet from his shower and its natural curl made it hang in short waves. He was wearing a pair of jeans and a black T-shirt, and somehow could make something that simple look sexy. Maybe it didn't matter what he wore because the colorful tattoos on his muscular forearms would always be the focal point.

"You ready to go?" Jameson asked as I stood from the couch.

"Sure." I smiled. "You don't want to stay with the guys?"

"Nah, it's not very often I'm in your neck of the woods. Why don't you show me around Providence?"

"Yes!" I grinned with excitement; there were so many things in Providence I wanted him to see.

Jameson had rented a car when he got here since his original plan was to surprise me, a surprise I had ruined by getting pissed at him. Once we were on our way I knew I needed to talk to him about Maddox and I wrung my hands in nervous anticipation.

"Out with it," Jameson said, calling me out on my inner turmoil.

I exhaled and looked at him with regret. I didn't want to have this conversation any more than he probably wanted to hear it.

"Maddox, right?" he asked, this time not pulling his eyes from the road.

"Yes. I don't know where he and I stand right now exactly but I do know it's wrong that I kissed you."

"I kissed you, technically."

"Yeah, well ... I didn't exactly tell you to stop either."

"Did you want me to stop?" Jameson asked, this time studying my reaction.

I closed my eyes briefly. The question was unfair and he knew it. There was no doing the right thing in this situation. I owed it to Maddox to be faithful to him, at least until we'd had an actual conversation and defined where we stood with each other. At the same time, Jameson had been amazing to me since the beginning and I was the one that had walked away from him without much of an explanation. Somehow I felt like I owed him my honesty if nothing else.

"My answer doesn't really change anything; the situation is what it is." I hoped that would make him drop the question but knew better.

"I'd still like to know the answer."

"No, I didn't want you to stop," I frowned.

"Don't be sad." He took my hand from my lap and laced our fingers together before letting them rest together on my leg.

"It's just good to be near you, we don't have to do anything but just be together."

I smiled at his suggestion and relaxed a bit. Maybe holding his hand wasn't such a fragile line.

We spent the rest of the ride to Providence in a comfortable silence and watched the city lights come into view.

"Is that a pinecone?" He craned his neck looking at the arches that lead us into Federal Hill.

Directing him to Federal Hill was a no-brainer. I wanted to show him all the amazing restaurants and get his ideas on the one I was planning on opening.

"It is!" I said, impressed at the fact that he actually knew what it was since most people assumed it's a pineapple. "*La Pigna*. It's an Italian symbol of welcome, abundance, and quality. I can totally see myself opening a restaurant here and somehow incorporating that symbol."

Jameson pursed his lips as if in thought. "You should make it a family style Italian restaurant."

"I'd not considered doing it that way but I like that idea."

"It makes sense with the *La Pigna*. What says welcome and abundance better than a family Italian dinner?" Jameson pulled the car into a spot.

My head swam with ideas as to how to make that a reality. It would be a great homage to Gigi to model the style of the restaurant on her kitchen. Large wooden block tables and large bowls filled with different types of pasta.

"I really like that idea." I smiled as Jameson walked around to my side of the car and took my hand, lacing our fingers together once again.

Pretty much everything was closed save for a few bars, but neither of us much felt like being inside a crowded, smoke-filled bar. Instead, we just walked around and talked about the restaurant I was going to open. The night, despite being a bit warm, was beautiful and a slight breeze blew through the air.

After nearly two hours of wandering aimlessly and talking we circled back around to the car and hopped in.

Along the way back to my place we passed a gas station and Jameson ran in to pick something up. When he came back to the car he was holding a plastic grocery bag behind his back and grinned at me wildly.

"I got you a present."

"Oh really?!" I teased with excitement.

"Well don't get too excited but it was pretty much the nicest thing that can be found in a Seven Eleven." He pulled the bag out from behind his back and held it out to me.

He watched me with humor in his eyes while I felt the bag as if trying to figure out what its contents were without actually opening it.

Finally, I pulled from the bag a miniature replica of *La Pigna*, complete with the arches.

"You can put it in the kitchen of your restaurant … it will bring you good luck and abundance, and a little something for you to remember me by."

I pulled the little statue to my chest and could have seriously cried. Without thinking I leaned toward him to kiss him but realized what I was doing before our lips met. Instead, I lifted off my seat enough so I could kiss his forehead. My thumb rubbed across his cheek as I thanked him.

To many, it was just a cheesy tourist trinket, but to me, it was so much more. It was a gesture that reminded me how much Jameson listened and cared about me and my hopes and dreams. I realized that when I was with him it not only made my dreams seem feasible but also made me want to work that much harder to attain them.

When we got to my apartment I felt the butterflies in my stomach and promised myself I wouldn't let anything happen between us that I would regret. Kera was already retired to her room and most likely asleep as we tiptoed through the living room and headed to my room. I closed the door behind us and stood silently as he looked around at the pictures that decorated my walls. When his eyes met mine he smiled sympathetically.

"I don't have to stay if you would prefer I didn't."

We'd already discussed him staying with me for the night and as badly as I wanted him here I was afraid of what I might do.

"No, I want you to stay," I answered, although my voice even sounded uncertain to me.

"I'll sleep on the couch, you don't have to worry about me." He attempted to be reassuring.

"It's not you I'm worried about," I said quietly as my eyes went to the floor.

He closed the small distance between us and rubbed my arm, starting at my hand and moving up to my shoulder. "Don't say things like that to me."

I looked back up into his smoldering eyes. "Okay! I'm going to change clothes." I nervously stepped away from his hold and went to my drawers to pull out a pair of pajama pants and a tank top.

He watched me fumble nervously before I excused myself to the bathroom. I stared at my reflection in the mirror and reminded myself to stick to my morals. It didn't matter that it was Jameson, I was perfectly able to maintain my composure. I took my time changing and brushing my hair and teeth before heading back to the bedroom. Jameson was lying across the bed still in his jeans and T-shirt but had kicked off his shoes.

"You gonna sleep in your jeans?" I laughed.

"Well, I didn't bring any pajamas."

I knew from experience that he usually slept in his boxers and grabbed an extra blanket from my closet.

"You're alright, but you get your own blanket." I tossed the blanket at him with a little more force than necessary.

I looked away from him as he took his jeans and T-shirt off and slid under my sheets and big down comforter. Jameson lay on top of the blankets and like a burrito, I was trapped under my blanket unable to move. I struggled to pull my arm out of the blanket and we both laughed.

"Okay, you can get under my covers but you still have to use your own blanket."

He smiled as he hopped off the bed and slid back under the covers, carrying his personal blanket with him.

"Better?" He smiled, our faces directly next to each other on our pillows.

"Better." I smiled.

I'd lied. Having him this close to me, again, was better than better. I could feel the heat from his body and smell the sweet scent of his cologne.

His arm was out of the covers and I took it in my hands wanting to distract myself and get a better look at his tattoos.

"You told me that one day you'd tell me what this one means." I traced the colorful hummingbird that was perfectly vivid on his right forearm.

"I guess I did tell you that, didn't I?"

I watched him, expecting him to give me the details but instead, he said nothing.

I sat up in the bed bringing his arm closer to me. "Out with it!" I insisted playfully throwing his expression back at him.

He let out an exhale before beginning, his reaction letting me know it was something that was not easy for him to talk about.

"You know, of course, that I was raised by my aunt."

I nodded as he continued and traced the vivid colors of the tattoo.

"My mom's nickname as a child was Hummingbird. From what my aunt tells me mom was always energetic and excited. She had a real zest for life and found excitement in everything she did. Of course, in the few shorts years I lived with her I don't ever remember seeing that side of her."

Again, he paused and I waited for him to continue, his pulse increasing slightly beneath my fingertips.

"I don't remember when it happened but at some point when I was very young she started using heroin, and it was something she could never stop. Child Services got involved after it was discovered I'd been left alone for three days while she was out getting her next high. I was four years old."

I watched him as he closed his eyes briefly as if reliving that time in his life.

"Shortly after that my aunt got custody, but she said it was only supposed to be temporary. I don't know how much I believe her but according to my aunt, my mom tried to get clean. She said she fought with everything in her to stay away from the drugs and get me back. She had been clean for two months when she relapsed. One more slip up and she was gone, overdosed. Just for irony's sake, it was three days before anyone found her."

"You don't believe your aunt that she was trying to get clean so she could get you back?" I asked, wanting to better understand him.

"I don't know," he uttered after a brief pause. "Part of me thinks it's something you tell someone to make them feel better about the shit they get dealt."

"I think she was trying to get back to you, and I think you know that, too." I traced the thorns wrapped around the hummingbird. "You know it because you put this on your body. The thorns represent her addiction, right?"

Unspeaking he looked at me and nodded in agreement.

"We don't always have the luxury of getting the answers we need but sometimes we just feel it inside ourselves. I don't think you should doubt what you feel."

Raw emotion showed on his face and, while it made me happy that he'd opened up to me, I felt bad for bringing something so painful to the surface.

"Thank you for telling me, and I'm sorry for what you went through. I can't imagine how difficult that would have been."

Jameson laced his fingers in mine and cleared his throat before continuing. "It's okay, all in all I've been really lucky. My aunt is and always was amazing. She went to every game, concert, function, and disciplinary action throughout my entire life." His eyes gleamed with mischief as he added that final one.

"What about Popeye over here?" I rotated his arm and pointed out the small blue cartoon character.

"I yam what I yam," he said with his lips tight as if he was holding an imaginary pipe in his mouth.

We laughed at his impression and I leaned back so my back was resting against his chest. The thought occurred to me briefly that he was doing a crappy job making sure his blanket separated us as I could feel the warm skin of his chest against my back.

"I know I said I would be good, and as much as it pains me, I will." His fingers gently stroked my neck, pulling my hair to one side.

"But there are some things I need to say to you."

I closed my eyes and forgot to breathe for a moment, afraid in so many different ways of what he was about to say. In the brief silence that followed I tried to determine what would be worse—him not wanting me, or him wanting me.

His fingers continued to stroke my neck and my upper back and I thought for a moment that maybe he'd decided against saying whatever it was he was planning on saying.

"Look at me, please." His voice was pleading, and I was afraid of what would happen when our eyes met.

I turned around so I could rest my head on his chest and look at him at the same time.

"I just wanted to say I should have fought harder to keep you. I should have come up here with you."

My heart thudded against my chest at his words, and I blinked repeatedly, trying not to let the unshed tears fall.

"I'm afraid I'm always going to regret that decision." He pulled me even closer against him.

I wanted to tell him I was sorry, too, that I should have tried harder to make the long-distance thing work, but I was too afraid that once I opened my mouth the tears would take over and the words wouldn't come anyway.

"And I know it isn't fair for me to say, and I know that you're with someone else, but I want you to know that I've never stopped loving you."

I felt his words in my chest, a pain not unlike the one I'd felt when I told him we were over. An audible hitch in my breath was my only response before the tears began to fall from my eyes. He pulled me up so I was now lying on him, our faces only inches apart.

"I'm sorry, I didn't mean to upset you." He wiped the tears from under my eyes. "I just couldn't ... I need you to know where I stand."

I rested my head between his shoulder and his neck and just held onto him tightly.

"I still love you too," I whispered into the crook of his neck so quietly I wasn't sure if he'd been able to make out my words. Until I felt his arms pull me to him even tighter.

For what seemed like forever we both lay there, awake but unspeaking.

I breathed him in and tried to memorize the way his body felt against mine. As much I wanted to kiss him and feel his lips on mine again I stayed in that position unmoving, knowing the words already spoken were enough of a betrayal, and not wanting to add to that.

Jameson stroked my hair gently, our breathing in sync as I lay against his chest. Absently I noticed his phone had gone off several times and felt bad as it was most likely his bandmates giving him hell for running off with me instead of being there with them to celebrate. Selfishly, I couldn't be more thankful that he was here.

Eventually, his breathing evened out and he was asleep, maybe it makes me a bit of a creeper but I couldn't help but watch him as he slept.

Somewhere between three and four a.m. the decision tormenting me seemed easier than it ever had before. I didn't care anymore that Jameson and I might not be able to be in the same place at the same time. I didn't care if the idea of groupies made me jealous, or if the majority of our relationship over the next year would have to be done through Skype. It didn't make a difference that he was more grounded in Ohio and might not want to come to Providence to be with me. I wanted Jameson, and I wasn't going to pretend for another day that that wasn't the case. I would find a way to finish school and be with him, and if it failed, at least I'd have done everything I could to be with the person I loved.

I watched Jameson expectantly, somehow thinking my thoughts would wake him so I didn't have to wait another minute before telling him. Not surprisingly, he remained asleep, his eyes slowly moving back and forth against his lids as he was deep within a dream.

Giving up on that idea, my thoughts turned to Maddox. Admittedly, I was an asshole. It wasn't that Maddox wasn't a good person, and it wasn't his family, even if I did feel like a carnie sometimes compared to them. It had always been Jameson. Maddox, no matter how great he was, could never be Jameson. Maybe Maddox and I had done for each other exactly what we needed to and our time was just done. He'd certainly made my adjustment here in Providence an easier thing. Because of him I'd explored more and ventured outside my comfort zone. I couldn't say that I'd served some sort of purpose for him but I hoped I had made some sort of positive difference in his life.

The question at this point was how exactly was I supposed to proceed? It felt wrong to have yet another broken phone conversation with him, telling him it was, in fact, over. I owed him more than that.

At the same time, was it fair to leave our relationship in some sort of limbo while he was gone?

Finally, I closed my eyes, both excited and guilt-ridden. I had a brief one-sided conversation with Gigi and hoped she would help me to make the right decisions in my life before I fell off to sleep.

Chapter Thirty-Four

Sleepily, I blinked slowly and felt the bed for Jameson. I'd fallen asleep on his chest but at some point in the night I'd awakened and realized we were both covered in sweat. Jameson had got up and gone to the bathroom but when I checked on him he said he was fine and told me to go back to sleep.

I looked around the room and found him sitting at my desk staring at his phone as if in deep thought.

"Hey," I croaked sleepily.

"Morning." His smile seemed forced as he looked up at me from his phone before tucking it in his pocket.

I got up from the bed before I was really ready and shuffled over to him. "You feel okay?" I asked as I swiped my thumb across his cheek affectionately.

I felt his forehead with my hand. "You feel warm," I said.

"I'm fine." He pulled my hand away from his forehead and kissed my palm sweetly.

His phone beeped in his pocket again, which only seemed to annoy him as he grimaced in response.

Somewhere inside me I was concerned he might be coming down with something, or that I should be worried there could be someone else since his phone had been going off so much, but the excitement I felt at having finally figured out what I wanted was ripping at the seams ready to come out.

"Come, talk to me." I pulled at both of his hands so he'd sit on the bed with me.

He was reluctant at first, making me work a little harder to pull him to me before he finally relented and sat down on the bed next to me.

"I spent all last night thinking. About everything. I realized I don't want to be without you, Jameson." I watched him excitedly for his reaction but as of yet his face was fixed, calm, without reaction.

"I was wrong before, and I don't care what we have to do to make it work, I want to be with you."

And ... nothing. His lack of response resulted in me filling the silence with nervous chatter.

"If we have to do the long-distance thing that's okay. I don't have much longer left at school and I can be back in Cincinnati. I'm not saying we have to get married or anything but we can be together," I rushed.

"I can open my restaurant there, there is nothing saying I *have* to do that here—"

"Becca, stop," he said as his head dropped, his eyes trained on the floor.

My mouth slightly agape I stopped talking and gauged his reaction. This was not at all how I had imagined this going in my mind. He was slumped over, his head down; it almost felt as if he was trying to hide from me. I wanted to ask what was happening but I couldn't find the words past the dryness of my mouth. Instead, I felt my skin prickle with heat—so much heat, in fact, that I almost felt light headed. Had I totally misread everything? Did he not just tell me last night that he still loved me?

I tried to get his eyes to meet mine but he kept his gaze fixed on the floor.

"We were right to be apart, Becca. It was wrong of me to come here." All emotion was detached from him, the monotone words coming from his mouth even sounded foreign.

"I"—I had to clear my throat, the rest of the words stuck there—"I don't understand." Damn the tears that debilitated my vocal cords. "You love me, I know you do! I love—"

"You should be with Maddox." He stood, his eyes still refusing to meet mine.

His words hit me, knocked the breath from me just as it had when I fell from the swing set as a child.

My mind raced with a thousand different questions, yet somehow, while my insides were ready to fight, my body was stuck motionless.

I watched him as he grabbed his wallet off the bedside table and checked his pocket as if making sure he had his phone. Was he leaving?

My heart thudded in my chest and the only thought I was capable of processing was my repeated mantra. *DO NOT CRY. DO NOT CRY. DO NOT CRY.*

"I'm sorry, Becca." He kissed my forehead and walked away. His voice seemed to crack when he said the words but never once did he look at me.

My tears held themselves respectfully until he walked out the front door, leaving me there on my bed, a rocking, crying mess.

Chapter Thirty-Five

Several Months Later

Time kept moving despite my own protests for it to stop, so that I could stop—stop wondering and questioning everything. I did try to call and text Jameson but never received anything in return. Not a single answer, not a goodbye, not a fuck off, nothing. Refusing to come off as some scorned female I gave up ever trying to understand what had happened. In reality, I just gave up asking the questions but never truly gave up wondering.

Maddox and I talked very little before he came home, and I fought off every urge to keep him, knowing that doing so was completely wrong considering where my mind had been while he was gone. Ultimately, I think he fought his own demons with Izzy, and maybe his willingness to understand where I was coming from was more telling than I even realized. He was my friend though, and from time to time he'd send me a text just to say hello. I knew a part of me would always appreciate him for the amazing man he was.

To say I was lonely would be an understatement. With Kera gone most days with either school or work, the only thing I allowed myself to dive into was school. I refused to allow myself to think about what would happen once I was done. I would make those decisions when the time came.

The holidays came and went and my fragile heart turned more to anger as the days progressed. With spring break coming I thought momentarily about going home just so I could yell at Jameson. He deserved it, that much I knew, but again my will to come off as strong and unaffected by his words prevailed. What I soon realized was worse than the holidays was Valentine's Day. If that isn't a day to make single people depressed I don't know what is. When my phone beeped with a text message I almost didn't want to look at it, to watch it be someone like my mother; mothers should know better than to text their single daughters on Valentine's Day.

>Plans tonight?

Maddox. Well, that was a bit unexpected. Should I lie? How pathetic was it on a scale from one to ten if I admitted to my ex-boyfriend that my Valentine's Day plans consisted of eating ice cream and watching the Hallmark Channel … alone?

>Thinking of buying my first kitten. Big plans are being set in motion to become a cat lady.

What's the point in lying?

>It's settled then, let's go to dinner.

Dinner? I actually hadn't seen that one coming. Going out to dinner with your ex on Valentine's seemed like a recipe for disaster—although the sex was always good—still, bad idea. I shook my head at my phone.

>C'mon, we'll go as friends.

I thought about it for a moment before another message came in from him.

>I'm saving you, you don't even like cats.

I giggled out loud at his last comment. There was no shame in going out to eat, and I needed to get out of my pity party before I decided to take up permanent residence there.

>Alright, but if it doesn't go well you'll have to drop me off at the animal shelter on the way home.

Laughing at my own pathetic joke I hopped off my bed and bounced to my closet to find something to wear. Knowing Maddox, I needed something a little classier then the sweatpants and tank top I was currently sporting. I rummaged through my clothes before switching to Kera's closet in hopes she had something fabulous I could borrow. That's the thing about ex-boyfriends—even if you don't want them back it doesn't stop you from wanting to look so incredible the thought never fails to cross their minds.

As my heels clanked across the hardwood floors heading downstairs I was satisfied with my decision to keep it casual, yet classy. I wore a pair of skintight skinny jeans, a cream cashmere sweater and my favorite knee-length tan pea coat. The soft curls of my hair blew in the cold breeze as I met Maddox outside.

"Good to see you." Maddox smiled widely and put his arm around me as he kissed my cheek.

The man did always know how to dress, and today was no exception. The blue sport coat he wore brought out the color of his eyes and his tan skin was in stark comparison to his white dress shirt. Somehow, he seemed even more sure and confident, as if graduating had added yet another level of sophistication to his already impressive air.

There was no denying the fact that he and I felt natural together, and not a second thought was given as he reached for my hand and laced our fingers together as we walked to the car.

"I was thinking Lorenzo's," he suggested as we both fastened our seatbelts. He was watching me knowingly as if waiting to see if I was going to point out that that's where we'd had our first date.

"Hmmm ... Lorenzo's." I tapped my finger against my lip as if deeply contemplating. "I don't think I've been there before."

I managed to keep a straight face for a good twenty seconds as he stared at me with a shocked surprise.

Finally, I let out a giggle and the relief showed on his face instantly.

"That wasn't very nice." He tried to look affronted but the smile that slowly spread across his lips gave him away.

I couldn't help but return his smile—the way his eyes lit up made it impossible not to. He stared, though, for a moment too long, and I felt the butterflies flutter through my belly. Was this truly just friends spending some time together or was there more to it? Before I could question any of this he turned over the ignition and drove toward Federal Hill.

A flood of memories came back as we were led to our table, Maddox's hand on the small of my back. The good memories of my relationship with Maddox far outweighed the bad.

"I'm sorry for not taking you someplace new. As much as I'd like to have returned to our regular Friday night ritual I thought this would be best for tonight." He glanced down at his menu.

As his eyes scanned the menu I watched him momentarily, trying to ascertain if his words meant something more.

"What are you getting?" he asked, apparently noting the fact that I'd not even begun to look at the menu.

We made our selections and sipped our wine as we waited for our food to arrive.

"Listen, Becca." He held his hands out to me from across the table.

Reluctantly, I pulled my hands from my lap and accepted his offer, letting his thumbs run across the tops of my fingers.

"I think you and I should give us another chance," he said after taking a calming breath.

He chanced a glance at me before continuing. "You can't deny we were good together, Becca, just give me the chance to show you I can be the person you believe I can be."

I couldn't help but melt a bit at his words. Maddox could be larger than life, and I believed that if he found it in himself to stand up to his father's wants and went his own way he could do amazing things.

"I need to think about all this, Maddox," I answered honestly. God knew men didn't come much more appealing than Maddox Spencer, however, I still needed to figure out what was right for me.

We spent the rest of dinner talking about school and how everything had been going for him since graduation. As miserable as the last few months had been for me it still felt like very little time had passed since we were sitting in these chairs on our first date.

As we walked to the car contentment filled me and I realized Maddox was somewhat of a safe haven for me.

"You look beautiful tonight," Maddox said as he went to open the car door for me. He paused, the door slightly agape. "I've really missed you." The look of sincerity on his face warmed me and I brought my hand to his face, caressing the slight stubble that had started to show on his chin.

He held me there for a minute penetrating my gaze before I hopped in the car and he joined me.

I looked out through the windshield as Maddox maneuvered the car through Federal Hill and stared up at the night sky, the lights of the small city drowning out the small lights from the stars.

"I'll never understand the point of the pineapple," Maddox said, shaking his head at the arches and *La Pigna*.

Seriously? Heat rose to my face as I contemplated his words. We'd had several conversations about *La Pigna*—it was somewhat the foundation of the restaurant I want to open in Federal Hill!

"Please tell me you're kidding." I watched him in disbelief.

"What?" His eyes rocked back and forth between me and the road, and there was no mistaking his expression, he seriously had no idea why that would bother me.

How could something that means so much to me have been so easily forgotten? Had the conversations we'd had held any meaning for him, or had my words always fallen on deaf ears? Was I crazy here, or were those the kinds of things that separate the people in your life who really get you, from the ones who are just there for a specific period in time? Jameson. He understood me, he heard me, and he valued the things I said. He wanted for me what I wanted for myself. He even bought me a damn touristy *La Pigna* for when I opened my restaurant.

"Stop here, I need to get out." I tried to keep my words even toned but wanted to be out of the car.

"What? What's going on?" Maddox's reaction was one of confusion and alarm but he did as I asked and pulled to the side of the road.

I opened the door and stepped out onto the sidewalk as Maddox watched me from the driver's seat.

"I'm sorry, Maddox." I leaned into the car, ducking my head so I could look at him.

"This was a mistake. You are an amazing person but you and I ... we just aren't meant to be." I tried to smile and didn't want him to take my rejection too harshly.

"There's just something I have to do ... right now."

"Alright." He nodded somberly and when neither of us said anymore I backed away and closed his door.

I watched him drive away before I pulled my phone from my pocket and stared at the screen trying to think of what to say. I knew there was no point in calling him because he wouldn't answer. But I was done being proud and pretending I was fine. Maybe I was a fool and he would get to know that, but I wasn't letting him walk away from me so easily.

He loved me, I knew it, and I loved him too. As much as I'd racked my brain over the last few months, nothing ever made sense as to why he'd changed so much overnight. How he could go from telling me he'd never stopped loving me, to telling me the next morning that I should be with Maddox? None of it made sense and if he refused to talk to me I would show up at his place and demand answers.

>I don't know what words I need to say that would grant me a response but you are done avoiding me. You either say something or you can tell me to fuck off to my face.

Come on, Jameson, say something!
I willed him to answer me as I stared at my phone, tapping my heels against the cold pavement.

>Don't come here, Becca.

Don't come here, Becca? I sneered at his response, a response I'd been waiting for for over six months.

>Alright, we'll play it your way.

Ha! I wondered if he thought that would keep me away? My family was in Cincinnati; it wasn't like I was crossing the country to play stalker. Even if I was, I at least had a good cover. With that settled, I marched my way back to my apartment, thankfully already completely used to walking across Providence, even in three-inch heels. Tonight I would pack and in a few days Jameson could tell me to my face what the deal was.

Chapter Thirty-Six

The funny thing about time is that it passes much easier when you're on a mission. I didn't allow my brain to think ahead to what Jameson's reaction to me might be. I even tried to convince myself that it wouldn't matter. Plain and simple, he owed me an explanation, and I was going to get it. It didn't matter to me if I looked a little crazy showing up at his doorstep; he was the one who was refusing to talk to me.

The nerves did find me, however. Once I boarded the plane, the reality of the situation hit home. The truth was I had absolutely no idea how this was actually going to go. Maybe it was naïve of me to think Jameson would talk to me just because I showed up, and a certain fear gripped me that I might not want to know what he had to say. Maybe he'd met someone and was in love with some girl, but that still didn't explain his little erratic incident while he was visiting me. I tried the whole calming breath thing but knew better than to believe that the anxiety would go away, at least not until I did what I had to do.

Once again, my conversations with Amelia had been few and far between. She was busy with work and some guy she was seeing so there were no hard feelings there, but I still hadn't gotten the chance to tell her I was coming home for spring break. I sent her a quick text before the plane took off and let her know about my little plan of confronting Jameson. Knowing Amelia she would be over-the-top excited about it but unfortunately I had to turn my phone off before she could respond.

I'd like to say I'd grown accustomed to flying by then, but that would be a lie. Once the plane was safely on the ground I fought the urge to kiss the pavement and met my mom in the baggage claim. Slowly, she had begun to look more and more like herself again but was still having a really rough time since Gigi's passing. Her eyes at least appeared to hold a bit more life and she was slowly beginning to do more things outside the confines of her bedroom.

She was disappointed to hear Maddox and I had broken up, but didn't exactly have the strong reaction I'd expected her to. She was smitten with the idea of him, and me ending up with someone who was "well to do", but I think losing Gigi had given her some sort of realization that life was short and the most important thing was to be happy.

For whatever reason, I didn't tell her about my plan of confronting Jameson. While she knew he was important to me I never really gave her all the details, and I was afraid she would try to talk me out of it. At this point, I had myself so freaked out I was too close to chickening out to let that temptation exist. Instead, we talked about school and what had happened at home since I was here last.

I was so busy chatting with my mom I didn't turn my phone back on until I got home, at which point I was greeted with a slew of messages from Amelia.

>Call me!

>Why aren't you answering your phone?!

>Seriously, Becca. Call me before you go see him.

I checked my missed calls and sure enough, she had called me three times since I'd sent that message to her. *What the hell?*

I threw my bag on the floor and sat on the bed in my childhood bedroom, a sense of panic filling me as I dialed her number.

"Hey!" Her tone was one of relief after she answered on the first ring.

"Why weren't you answering your phone? I called you like three times!"

"I was on the plane, what's going on?"

"Where are you now?" Amelia asked, the panic evident in her voice.

"I'm home, start talking, what's going on?"

An audible exhale sounded through the phone before she continued.

"Ok, don't be mad ... I wanted to tell you, I swear, but Jameson and Stan made me promise not to."

I didn't speak, instead I waited for her to continue, willing her to cut the theatrics and come out with it, whatever *it* was.

"Jameson is sick, Becca. Like sick, sick. He doesn't want you to know, and as much as it killed me to keep that from you, I didn't feel like it was my thing to tell."

"Wait, what do you mean? What's wrong with him?" I stood from my bed and paced at the news. I felt sick.

"He needs a kidney."

"A kidney?"

"Yeah, it doesn't look good, Becca."

She tried for a brief minute to convince me not to show up at his aunt's, where he'd apparently moved after getting sick. She gave up after I made it apparent that it didn't matter what she said, I was going. I'd only been to his aunt's once before but decided I could figure out which house was hers and I grabbed the keys to my mom's car and was out the door within an hour.

Jameson had taken me to meet his Aunt Kathy that first summer we started seeing each other. She was a sweet woman and it was obvious she treated him as if he was her own son. I remember she had one of those amazing smiles that could light up a room and that ability to make everyone around her feel at ease. I scanned the houses on the street and prayed she still had the white wicker swing with the red cushions on her front porch; unfortunately that was the only thing I could really remember about the outside of her house.

I stopped the car abruptly in the middle of the road when I saw the outdoor furniture and silently said a thank you to whoever up there was listening. I parked my car on the street in front of the house, got out and wiped my sweaty palms on my jeans.

I felt sick and terrified at the same time. Terrified he would turn me away, and terrified about how sick he might actually be.

I knocked on the door and prayed they were home, a prayer that was quickly answered when his aunt opened the door.

"Becca!" Her face lit up when she saw me and relief at her reaction flooded me. I wasn't quite sure what I was expecting since she'd always been so welcoming before.

"Come in! Jameson didn't tell me you were coming!" She pushed the door open allowing me to enter the living room.

"Oh, give me a hug!" She held her arms out to me.

I smiled and hugged her in return, but couldn't help but notice that while she was warm and accommodating she didn't look quite like I remembered her. Her eyes looked tired with a few more wrinkles creating crow's feet.

"Here, have a seat." She pointed to a brown sectional couch that sat in front of the fireplace.

I started to argue—all I wanted to do was see Jameson for myself, and see that he was okay.

"He's got his nurse in there, they are just getting ready to start his dialysis, honey. Give them a few minutes to get started and you can go in. He usually doesn't like visitors when he's all hooked up but I guess he made an exception." She said that last part like I was something special, someone Jameson didn't have any rules for, which made my heart drop a little since that wasn't the case.

"Actually, he didn't know I was coming," I confessed, squirming a little bit in my seat.

She pursed her lips in reaction and I was afraid for a moment that she would ask me to leave, until the look transitioned into a sly smile.

"Well, you know how men are," she said as if that was explanation enough.

"I'm glad you're here. I'm afraid he hasn't been doing very well. I keep telling him it's best that he let his friends in but he just won't hear it."

"What happened? He was fine—"

As soon as the words left my mouth a realization struck me. Had he known he was sick when he came to see me in Providence? Is that why he left and said all the things he'd said?

"He was sick, honey. It took them a while to figure out what it was, but once they did most of the damage had already been done. It's called Goodpasture's syndrome, and suffice it to say it's done some real damage to his kidneys, so much so that he needs a transplant." Her tone grew graver as she continued. "I'm not a match. He's on the donor list, but despite having come close once he's still waiting." Tears lined her eyes as she sat next to me on the couch, grabbing my hand for support.

A door opened and closed and Kathy's face quickly changed to show a happy, confident facade. A woman in scrubs came into view and smiled once she saw the attention we were giving her.

"He's all good, I'll be back in a few hours," she smiled while waving her exit.

She said so little that I could only assume this had become common practice for them.

"Let me just go tell him you're here," Kathy said, standing from the couch and going to his room.

I could hardly breathe, afraid he would turn me away before I even got the chance to see him. I caught myself wringing my hands together with anxiety and attempted to be calm, knowing that if I did get to see him I'd have to figure out how to control my reactions. I didn't have a lot of experience around people who were sick, but I had faith in my ability to keep a level head when needed.

I heard hushed voices from behind the door, and when it slowly opened Kathy appeared smiling.

"Come on, honey," she said happily as she waved me into the room.

I walked the short distance from the living room to where Kathy was standing and she gave me a reassuring smile as if sensing I needed some encouragement.

Unsure of what was behind the door I swung it open, a confident smile pasted to my face. There was Jameson, seated in a reclining chair next to the bed and some huge machine with IVs attached to it. I tried to avoid looking at the machines and instead focused on him.

"I told you not to come." The curtness in his voice hurt me but I decided to ignore it.

I closed the short distance between us and took a seat on his unmade bed. I don't know why but it made me feel better that it wasn't a hospital bed; maybe it wasn't so bad.

"I don't always follow instructions well I guess."

We watched each other for a moment and I prayed that for once I was able to not wear my thoughts on my face. It was Jameson, but at the same time, it wasn't him. He was easily twenty pounds lighter and somehow looked older. His eyes were drained of the life that normally shined through and there was a pasty paleness to his skin.

"Who told you?" His tone was filled with a mixture of defeat and anger. Stalling for time I allowed myself to glance at the IVs that went from the machine to him.

I tried to avoid his question. "Actually, I was already coming here before I knew something was wrong."

"Does it make a difference that I don't want you here?"

"No, not at the moment." Heat rushed to my face as I stared back at him.

I stood from the bed and walked around his room, suddenly unable to sit and endure his pressure.

"Why didn't you tell me?" My voice sounded desperate as my eyes found their way back to him.

Despite his agitated front, I could see compassion in his eyes, that was until he turned away from me.

"I don't want you to see me like this, Becca. What we had is done, you need to go live your life."

"Why? Why can't I be here with you? And why did you leave me like that?" My voice cracked as I asked that last question, my anger melting into hurt.

He closed his eyes and I immediately felt like an asshole for yelling at someone connected to a machine with IVs going in and out of them.

"I can't do this, Becca. I'm sorry."

"Well I'm not leaving, so I'm sorry." I crossed my arms over my chest and sat down on his bed like an insubordinate child.

Anger filled his eyes as he glared at me. "Becca, GO!"

I tried not to jump at his words and realized it was the first time he'd ever really raised his voice at me. A bit stunned, I didn't react right away, which only made him angrier.

"Get out, Becca."

There was no arguing with him or the fact that he truly wanted me gone.

"I'll be on your front porch." I exited his room, only then did I let the tears fall down my face.

I bypassed Kathy who stood just outside Jameson's door, the sympathetic look on her face nearly breaking what little resolve that remained. I went straight for the front porch, and my lungs greedily sucked in the fresh air.

I couldn't say what is worse—seeing Jameson like this, or his obvious distaste for my being here. I paced the short distance of his patio trying to figure out what to do. I should probably respect his wishes and not be here, but the thought of leaving caused a real, physical pain in my chest. I couldn't leave him.

I took a seat in the swing that hung from the porch and held onto the squeaky chain as I swung gently back and forth. Maybe if I stayed a few hours he would realize he did want to talk to me; it would be terrible if I left, and then he decided he wanted me here. I would just stay a few hours.

Chapter Thirty-Seven

It was three days. Three days I waited with Kathy, eyeing her hopefully every time she came out of his room for some sign that he wanted to see me too. He knew I was there but each time anyone left the room their avoiding eyes let me know he didn't want me here. I didn't know what was making me stay at that point. It was obvious Kathy was enjoying my company, sharing meals with me, and making me a spot on the couch. If it hadn't been for that I would have left simply because I wouldn't want to inconvenience her. The few times I did leave it was to get clothes or something from home, and I was only able to do so after Kathy convinced me to. What was I waiting for exactly?

The porch quickly became my favorite place to sit, despite the fact that Ohio couldn't decide on the weather and went from sixty degrees to snow within a matter of hours. Something about that porch was welcoming as I snuggled against the big red cushions with the book I had randomly grabbed from a shelf inside the house, and since I had nothing else to do I didn't even bother reading the jacket and just dug right into it.

When the door opened I didn't pull my eyes away from the book. That was how my relationship with Kathy went. It was a comfortable silence where we could sit next to each other for hours and say nothing. Other times we would talk for hours but being around her was never uncomfortable and it was never work.

"Still here, I see."

I nearly dropped the book when I heard his voice. He leaned weakly against the frame of the door as he watched me with weary eyes.

I froze momentarily, afraid of saying the wrong thing and having no idea what the right thing was. I started to get up as he slowly shuffled to where I was seated but his eyes let me know he wasn't going to have me acting like he was incapable.

"I got it," he said firmly, slightly breathless.

He wore a pair of grey athletic pants and a black Under Armour T-shirt, and for the first time I was able to see how slight he looked, his clothes baggy against his pale skin.

"It might take me forty-five minutes but I got it." A hint of a smile appeared across his face as he made his way to me and sat down heavily.

It took a minute for him to catch his breath and he closed his eyes as if he was in pain. Damn me for being here three days and not once trying to figure out what I'd say when he finally did want to talk to me. Not being able to find any words I looped my arm around his and leaned my head against his shoulder.

"I'm sorry for not doing what you wanted, I just couldn't leave." The sound left in a whisper.

He exhaled and rested his cheek against the top of my head.

I wanted to ask if he should be outside without a blanket, or if he needed to have on his oxygen they sometimes had him wear. I wanted to yell at him for not telling me he was sick, and for leaving me like he did in Providence. I wanted to tell him I loved him, and I was wrong to ever let him go, but even as the words danced around in my mind I said nothing. What was the right thing to say? What could I say that would make it so he wanted me to stay?

Instead, I closed my eyes and allowed myself to just be content in that moment. With my eyes closed, it was just him; he smelled of the same sweet cologne even if he did seem a bit smaller in my grasp. Maybe if I kept them closed long enough I could pretend nothing was wrong with him, with us, and I could go back to that summer when all that mattered was him and me.

My daydream was cut short when a car pulled up and the same nurse from a few days ago made her way up the stairs to the porch.

"Good to see you up and about!" the woman said cheerfully. "Now get your bony butt inside so we can get the fun stuff started," she said before the front door closed heavily behind her.

"She seems nice," I smiled optimistically at Jameson.

"Yeah," Jameson agreed as he slowly got to his feet.

I fought the urge to help him walk and instead walked slowly behind him as if I could catch him if he started to topple over. Once inside his nurse was there to help him back to his room and I walked to the living room, prepared to begin the whole waiting around process once again.

"You coming?" Jameson called softly over his shoulder, and it surprised me so much I looked around to make sure it was me he was talking to. I went to his room and quickly took a seat on his bed before he could change his mind. He sat in his recliner and pulled his T-shirt off revealing a port in his neck where a small tube was. She wore a mask as she connected the tubing from the machine to Jameson's port and started the machine, flying through the motions automatically as if it was a simple routine action like tying your shoes.

I tried to pay attention to what she was doing but at the same time wanted to show no reaction. Jameson watched me closely and I was afraid if I acted the wrong way he'd decide he didn't want me here.

The machine began the audible pumping of his blood and she walked out of the room leaving the two of us alone. His eyes were now closed and a stress line appeared across the top of his forehead.

I pulled off my shoes and made his bed neatly before I sat back down and leaned my back against the headboard of his bed so I was sitting closer to him.

"Does it hurt?" I focused on the lines on his forehead.

"It's not bad." His eyes now open, he turned his head so he was looking at me. "It's more how it makes me feel." He paused before continuing as if trying to find the right words. "It makes me feel sick sometimes, can give me headaches and muscle cramps ... other times it's not so bad."

I ran my fingers across his forearm that was resting against the chair. "How did you get the scar by your eye?" I finally asked after a few years of wondering. The question seemed safe since it didn't have to do with his current predicament.

His smile reached his eyes this time as he watched me carefully.

"I was working at Maggie's at the time actually. I was working, going to school, and playing gigs, and just wore myself completely down. I was driving home and was on River Road."

I nodded as soon as the street name left his mouth. I knew River Road well, it was one of the roads I like to drive on during a warm spring day. The trees shaded every twist and turn of the road. It was also the place all the high school kids would go because there was one particular bridge that went over a set of railroad tracks, railroad tracks that many believe were haunted. The legend went that if you shut your car off and sat quietly in the middle of the night you could hear a woman crying.

"Yeah, I know River Road," I said, letting him know I was familiar with the road.

"So you know how curvy it is. I guess I just fell asleep; don't remember anything until I woke up in the hospital."

"This nasty thing," he traced his finger of the hook-shaped scar by his eye, "is from hitting my head on the steering column."

"I like your scar," I said, smiling a bit too broadly.

"You do?" he asked with a smile, cocking his head to the side a bit as if in disbelief.

"I do." I reached my arm to him and traced my finger over the scar. "It kinda makes you, you."

"Does it make me look like a badass?"

I couldn't help but laugh at his hopeful expression.

"Yes, and maybe the tattoos and muscles help a bit," I regretted what I said as soon as the words left my mouth. He was still him, but there was no question being sick had thinned him out dramatically.

Not surprisingly, a frown found his face as he looked away from me.

"Not exactly the person I used to be."

"Yes, you are!" I answered without missing a beat which brought his attention back to me. "I know you, you're the same."

"Yeah, I guess you do."

"Speaking of, grab that book off my bedside table." He glanced over to the table, currently full of a combination of pill bottles and books.

I leaned across the bed and grabbed the book he requested and handed it back to him.

"What?" I asked while taking in his devilish expression.

"Can you also grab my water bottle?"

Without thinking twice about it I turned around to grab his water from his bedside table when I felt his hand go to my ass, slowly feeling his way from my cheek to between my legs.

Heat pulsed through my body at the familiarity of his touch. The sensation that always reverberated through my body when he touched me was still there, maybe even with greater intensity.

"Hey now!" I laughed as I turned around with his water.

"Oh, thanks. I don't actually need that though." He smiled.

I shook my head at him, happy to see his boyish grin again for the first time since I'd been here.

"What's in the book?" I asked.

"If there's one upside to all of this it's that I've actually starting writing down the things that have been in my head for years." He handed the book back to me.

I opened the book and flipped through the pages. Each page was handwritten music and I ran my fingers across the notes, my mind unable to comprehend how all the parts together would sound.

"You wrote all of these?" I stopped when I found one with the lyrics handwritten below the notes.

"Yeah, they've been playing through my head for a long time, figured it was time I got them out."

Goodbye to May
Looking ahead - tomorrow may bring
Dreams wrapped in gold, or on a string
Thanks for the love wrapped in a song
You got it all – even if I got it wrong

Goodbye to May – Summer's in the air
With each passing day – a memory takes me there.
A kiss in the wind, warm on my face
Your sweet caress – Goodbye to May.

I left no stone unturned – moved a mountain too
The mysteries I thought, were solved when I had you.

So bring the summer on – June and July
No sense looking back, never ask why.
That smile on your face, I remember it well
That memory is ours, but I alone will tell.

Goodbye to May – summer's in the air
With each passing day – a memory takes me there
A kiss in the wind, warm on my face
Your sweet caress – Goodbye to May.

I read the words and selfishly wondered if they were written for me.

"I want you to take this … I mean when…" He struggled with the words immediately letting me know what he was saying.

"No!" I slammed the book together harder than I had intended. We were not going to talk about him dying.

"Becca." He grabbed my hand and held me there with more strength than I imagined he had.

"If you're going to be here we're going to talk about this."

I looked away from him, the tears springing from my eyes so quickly you'd have thought they had been there waiting at the surface.

"I don't want to." I shook my head and avoided looking in his eyes. "We don't even know yet!" The words refused to leave my mouth but consumed my thoughts.

"Becca, look at me." His tone was firm, and as much as I wanted to deny him, my betraying eyes landed on him.

"I've already been matched twice but neither of them were viable. I'm not going to get another kidney. And this," he motioned toward the dialysis machine, "isn't really working out for me."

His expression was one of sympathy but he wasn't feeling sorry for himself, it was as if he was sorry for making me cry.

"But you're still on the list, so you don't know, right?"

"Yes, I'm on the list but—"

"But nothing!" I interrupted. "You can still get a kidney." My words didn't sound as confident and determined as I hoped they would, instead they came out in gasps and through tears.

I fought the urge to get up and walk around. I felt that need to move but the knowledge that he couldn't have followed me if he'd wanted to stopped me.

I wiped the tears from my eyes and tried to compose myself. How selfish to sit in front of him and cry when he was the one that was going through so much. When my eyes went back to him his expression was pained as he was looking down toward his stomach.

"Can you … go get … Jackie?" he gritted out.

I jumped up from the bed and came flying out of the room so quickly Jackie was already running in.

"Give us a second, baby." She closed the door in my face.

I stood there a moment staring at the closed door and feeling completely helpless before giving up and going to sit on the couch. I tried to think of a solution but could only pray that a match would be found. I looked at my phone making sure the thing was still working. Yesterday I'd left under the pretense of getting some stuff from home, but actually I'd gone to the hospital. I was still waiting to get the results but it only took two different tests to determine if I could be a donor.

After an hour or so of sitting in silence, praying and begging my phone to ring Jackie came out of his room closing the door silently behind her.

"He's alright," she encouraged me when I nearly jumped on her as soon as she left his room.

"He's sleeping now but you can go on in. He'll be out for a while."

Without waiting for further information, I snuck into his room and found him completely out. I tiptoed to his bed, climbed in next to him and held his hand which stuck out from beneath his red Navaho blanket, then went to sleep.

Chapter Thirty-Eight

My eyes opened and slowly adjusted to the darkness of the room, taking in Jameson's face piece by piece. His fingers gently ran through my hair as I yawned sleepily and looked up to his drowsy smile.

"Hey." His voice was gravelly.

"Hi," I smiled, and for fear of morning breath I backed my face away so I wasn't quite nose-to-nose with him.

"Where do you think you're going?" His arms wrapped around my waist and pulled me even closer to him.

It was scary easy the way I gave into him, how I always had; of course he never asked for anything I wasn't ready and willing to give.

"Tell me about your restaurant," he prompted, his words creating warmth across the top of my head.

"Oh, I don't know," I answered, which was funny because I actually thought about what my restaurant would be like all the time.

"Yes, you do! Where is it?" His open hand rubbed gently across my hip and on each turn reached my skin and caused the shivers to run through me.

"Well I thought it was in Providence, Federal Hill specifically, but sometimes I think maybe it should be here, maybe Over the Rhine."

"I like that, OTR needs some authentic Italian."

"And think about all the amazing buildings; I could get an apartment in one of those beautiful old buildings."

"Or maybe better, you could live above your restaurant." His addition made me smile.

"I like that idea." I smiled against him.

"So what about the inside? You planning on going with the red and white checkered tablecloths?"

I hated that he sounded a little out of breath when he spoke in full sentences, and it made my heart flicker a little bit with anxiety and a warm nervous heat flooded my skin, a fact that I tried to hide.

"I was thinking white linens and round tables," I said as I tried to push my anxiety to the side and just live in this moment. "Brick interior walls and dome lights that hang from the ceiling," I said, my smile now more genuine.

"You gonna name a dish after me?" I could tell from his words that a smile was on his face.

"Of course! What dish should be yours?"

We sat in silence for a few moments while we both thought it over.

"I've got it! I know the perfect one."

"What?" I smiled and turned my head toward him so we were now looking at each other.

"Cincinnati's biggest cannoli!" He grinned wildly.

We both laughed at his suggestion and spent more time talking about the restaurant and what it would be like. Of course, now there came the mission of what Jameson's dish would be because I definitely had to name something after him. We'd been lying there for a few hours just talking when Jackie arrived. He didn't have dialysis today but I didn't ask questions when she kicked me out.

I joined his Aunt Kathy in the kitchen as she gathered ingredients to start lunch.

"You should let me cook for you," I said, clearly startling her slightly as her eyes darted to my position in the doorway.

"Sorry!" I said, immediately feeling bad for sneaking up on her. "What are you making?"

I joined her at the countertop full of ingredients.

"You're fine, honey, my mind is just elsewhere." Her thin-lipped smile didn't reach her eyes and I could see the worry that resided there.

"I was just going to make some sandwiches." She frowned as if she should be offering something more elaborate.

"Take a seat, I'll make these." She started to argue but I interrupted. "Please, it's the least I can do for you allowing me to be here."

She conceded and took a seat at the small kitchen table. The kitchen, like the rest of the house, seemed to fit Kathy well. The whole place was warm and welcoming and the cherry theme fit her happy personality to a tee. Today, though, it seemed like a few more wrinkles had formed and no amount of makeup could hide the darkness of her swollen eyes.

"I'm so glad you're here, and I'm glad you didn't let him push you away." She smiled at me as I busied myself making our lunch.

"He wanted you here, I know he did. He's just... proud," she said thoughtfully. "He didn't want you to see him like this."

I only nodded to show her I was listening, my mouth going dry once again as I swallowed back the tears.

My phone ringing interrupted our conversation and the knife I was holding nearly fell to the floor when I saw that the call was coming from the hospital. I dropped what I was doing and answered, quickly heading to the front porch so I could take the call in private.

I listened carefully and wanted to rush them along as they verified that they were speaking with the right person.

"We appreciate the fact that you underwent the necessary testing and your interest in becoming an organ and tissue donor."

C'mon! I screamed in my head, unable to breathe.

"Unfortunately, you are not a match for the patient associated with your paperwork."

I didn't hear anything after that; in fact I may have hung the phone up while she was still talking. I covered my face with one of the red throw pillows on the swing after I nearly collapsed onto it. I lost all control as the sobs left me, the pillow muting the noise. I hadn't realized how much hope I'd put into being Jameson's donor until I knew I couldn't be. For the first time since finding out about Jameson, it felt like I was losing him and there wasn't a damn thing I could do about it.

The unfairness of everything consumed me and created an anger that was foreign to me. Never had I ever felt so betrayed—by God, by life. What was the purpose of him dying so young? He wasn't even being given a chance to live and become who it was he was supposed to be. And why couldn't I be a match? What was the purpose of everything happening? Selfishly, I was mad at God for taking away my Gigi, and now I was losing Jameson too.

I was sobbing so hard I could barely breathe and tried unsuccessfully to get myself under control when Kathy walked outside.

I tried twice to tell her that I wasn't a match but my voice didn't want to work, my mouth opening and closing wordlessly.

She sat down on the swing and wrapped her arms around me tightly, holding me there in a hug.

"I'm—"

"I'm not—"

"I'm not a m-match," I finally got out between sobs.

"Oh sweetie, God love you for trying." She ran her hand across my back soothingly.

I tried to say more but my body wouldn't allow it and instead I just sobbed against her shoulder until the tears ran dry, leaving behind just the pain.

At one point she went back inside and came back with a sandwich. I wanted to eat it, at least for her sake if nothing else, but I was physically unable to eat. We sat in silence now as I stared off into space before finally deciding to take a walk and try to find someplace deep inside myself to hide the anger and sadness that consumed me.

After about an hour of walking around a neighborhood I didn't know, I got back to the house. Jackie's car was gone and I was ready to see Jameson, after having convinced myself that I could put on a brave face and be there for him. No more wasting time thinking about what could happen.

Kathy smiled at my return as I walked straight into Jameson's room.

"Hey." He smiled broadly with sleepy eyes when I opened the door.

The room smelled like fresh cotton and linen and I smiled at the scent mixed with the sunshine streaming through the windows.

"Hi," I smiled.

He was lying atop the covers with his back propped against the headboard. He was dressed in a pair of black Under Armour sweatpants with a gray T-shirt, his hair still wet from his bath.

"You getting tired of hanging out with me in this damn room yet?"

"Not even a little bit," I smiled as I climbed on the bed and snuggled up next to him. "You tired of having to put up with me?" I rested my head against his chest careful to avoid the port that was hidden under his shirt.

"I've never had a stalker before who pretty much moved in with me, so it's different." I felt his chest move slightly under me as he laughed to himself.

"Very funny!" I tipped my head up so I was looking at him, happy to see the joy in his eyes despite the illness that lingered beneath the surface.

"I'm kidding. I'm gonna miss you when you go back to school." As soon as the words left his mouth I looked away from him. I knew this conversation was going to happen sooner or later and knew it wasn't going to go well.

"I'm not going back."

"Becca?" he asked and I knew he was waiting for me to look at him.

"Becca." His tone now firmer I gave in and looked at him.

"What do you mean you're not going back?"

"I'm just not." The words felt childish leaving my mouth, but I didn't want to have the conversation and hoped he took the hint.

"Why?"

"What do you mean *why*?" A deep exhale left my chest at my words.

"You are not going to give up on what you want because of me."

I didn't respond. I knew better then to think there was something I could say that was going to change either of our opinions.

"Look at me." He lifted me slightly off his chest and I sat cross-legged next to him.

"I'm not leaving you, okay? There's nothing you can say here that's going to make me change my mind so just accept it."

"This is exactly why I didn't want to tell you." The exasperation was apparent in his tone.

"Yeah, well that was fucking selfish!"

"*Selfish?*" His expression was startled as he watched me wide-eyed.

"Yes! How do you think I would have felt if you … you died and I never even knew you were sick? I never would have had the chance to tell you the things I needed to say. Or get to see your face."

Fuck, the tears came again and my voice quaked in response.

"Didn't you think about me enough, or think enough *of* me to realize how much that would have destroyed me?"

"Becca…" He wiped the tears from my cheeks and his previously annoyed expression was quickly replaced with one of regret.

"You're all I ever thought about."

"I just wanted … I wanted better for you."

"Better? You don't get to decide what is best for me, I get to decide that."

He paused and I watched him desperately, hoping there was something he could say here that would make me feel better about him trying to shut me out.

"When I was there in Providence … I never wanted to leave. I promised myself I would never let anything come between us again. But when I got that call, when I found out about the road that lay ahead for me … I knew that I couldn't do that to you."

The phone calls? Suddenly my mind went right back to when he was in Providence and I remembered his phone going off all the time. Of course, I would never forget him telling me he didn't love me.

"That's what happened?" I wanted to say more, I wanted to ask if he meant what he said when he told me he didn't love me anymore, but I couldn't handle hearing that more than once. "How could you handle that on your own, how could you not tell me?" I couldn't imagine getting news like that, and maybe I was the selfish one, but I would have told him immediately had it been me.

"You were in a place where your life could go one of two directions. I just wasn't the right direction."

And there it is, proof that you can actually want to slap someone and kiss them at the same time.

"Don't you understand you were the *only* direction? Just because we weren't together doesn't mean I wasn't right here with you."

More tears. I never could have imagined one person was capable of crying this much.

Jameson held my face with his hands, his thumbs gently wiping the tears from under my eyes.

"What you said that day … when you left Providence—" I couldn't get the words out.

"Becca, I lied!" He held my face firmly, pinning me down with his eyes and forcing the words through me. "I love you, Becca. I've always loved you." His eyes continued to penetrate mine as he enunciated every word.

I was frozen, stuck in some place of elation, love and fear.

"I just … I thought it was better for you if I let you go. Never for one second did I want to be without you though."

"You never were," I cried.

He pulled me to him so I was sitting in his lap, his mouth on mine before another word or thought could pass between us. It started slow as if the kiss was meant to prove his love and the truth of his words, and maybe it was our time apart or the desperate passion that existed between us, but the kiss quickly morphed into a desperate, greedy, lip biting frenzy.

"God damn this fucking dialysis." He pulled away from me, both of us huffing for the air that we'd neglected our lungs.

"I'm sorry, did I hurt you?" I asked frantically looking him over, and silently berated myself for not being more careful. I started to get off his lap but he pulled me closer against him, shifting me so I was now straddling his lap.

"No! Not at all. It's just … the things I would do to you." He rested his forehead against mine.

"Do you know how bad I want you?" he asked, and glanced down so our eyes met. "What I wouldn't do to be inside you again."

Nothing had changed for me since we'd been together that summer, or even the first time we'd met. I had always wanted Jameson, and while I never really allowed myself to admit it, I'd even wanted him when I was with Maddox. Time had done nothing to lessen the love I had for him and his illness certainly did not, and I'd be lying if I said that I didn't want to be with him right now in that way as well.

His hands, which were resting on my hips, skimmed up my waist across my ribs and rested there just beneath my breasts.

"Something to look forward to." I said confidently.

"Becca—"

"We will wait until you're better," I interrupted, tired of him telling me there would be no future.

Chapter Thirty-Nine

Some prayers, I guess, are answered, while others are not. I may never understand why things happen the way they do; why some people get to live long healthy lives and why others do not. Why is it exactly that a drug addict seems to have an unlimited number of lives and people who take care of themselves are taken so swiftly? I'd like to believe I'll live a long life and on my deathbed I will have no fear, and total faith that there is a heaven above where I'll be reunited with the ones I love. Even more, I hope that when I do die I have some sort of absolute clarity where I instantly understand the why's in life.

On this day, though, I was lost and sadly consumed with the why's and what if's of the world—well, more specifically, my world. I'd prayed every day for that phone call to come, to see Kathy running in the room to tell Jameson they'd found a viable donor. Sadly, the call hadn't come and he seemed to be slipping further and further away. It seemed that he had to wear the oxygen more and more, and most of the time he was struggling to stay awake. When he was awake he tried to tell me to go back to school; wasted words because there wasn't a chance that I was leaving him.

Hollowness had found its way to my belly, an empty, burning feeling that wasn't going away. I had to fight past the anxiety that filled me for both Jameson and Kathy's sake. I wasn't giving up hope, that was certain, but I couldn't fight the fear that I was losing him.

Jameson shuffled slightly and I pulled my eyes from the muted television I wasn't actually watching anyway.

"Hi." He smiled sleepily at me from behind his darkened eyes.

"Hi." I matched his smile and ran my hand over his blanket-covered shoulder.

Wanting to be closer to him and take advantage of his waking moments, I lay down next to him so we were eye to eye.

"How are you feeling?"

"Ew, don't even ask, I'm sick of hearing myself complain." Somehow behind those words was typical Jameson, not wanting to feel sorry for himself.

"Can I get you anything?" With the closeness between us, my voice was hardly more than a whisper.

"No. Just you being here is enough." He pulled his arm from under the blankets and took my hand in his, lacing our fingers together.

"You know I've been thinking a lot about my dad; I wish I'd gotten a chance to meet him. Maybe who he is in my mind is better than who he actually is though."

"What do you know about him?" My wheels began to turn, wondering if I could find his dad for him.

"Not much, really. I know Kathy knows more about him but until now I guess I never felt like I needed to meet him. I know he and my mom were a lot alike, both into drugs and partying. I guess they both wanted to keep the party lifestyle and went their separate ways after I was born. I was lucky to end up with my Aunt Kathy, that's always been enough."

"She is pretty great." I was truly thankful for Kathy and how amazing she'd been taking care of Jameson and somehow always keeping her happy, upbeat demeanor in front of him. I always felt like I was one step away from crumbling and couldn't imagine how she felt.

"Yeah." He blinked his sleepy eyes heavily, and before too long was off to sleep, his hand still grasping mine.

As much as I didn't want to let go of his hand I was now determined to try to find his dad, although I could decide if, once I'd found him, trying to get them to meet was a good idea.

Kathy wasn't so keen, but she also wasn't about to turn down something Jameson wanted. Reluctantly, she gave me his name—Michael Cooper. I could kick myself for not just coming up with it on my own, since Jameson's middle name is Michael. Even more helpful was the fact that she recalled that before they'd split up, she'd had to drive all the way to Chippewa Falls, Wisconsin to pick up Jameson's mom who had moved there to be with his dad, despite the fact that they had no place to live. From everything Kathy had to say it seemed as if Jameson's parents were a toxic pair, both too entrenched in drugs to function in any sort of normal behavior.

Secretly, I hoped that if I found his dad, maybe he'd be a possible match for Jameson, an idea that Kathy quickly shot down. As if she could read my mind she quickly pointed out that while a parent can be a match it is much more likely to come from a sibling. Aside from that, the years of drugs would most likely mean that even if they were a match the kidney would not be viable enough for transplant.

Unwilling to lose focus on my new goal I trudged on, determined to find an answer for Jameson. As it turned out, the answer wasn't too difficult to find, at least in the form of a Facebook page. There wasn't a wealth of knowledge to be gained there; so far I'd figured out that he really liked online poker and fishing. The only picture was too grainy to really see the details of his face, the obvious focus of the picture being a huge fish he held proudly by the mouth. I strained my eyes to focus, trying to find some similarity to Jameson. The only thing I could really pick out was the waviness of his hair.

I snuck out of Jameson's bed and headed through the house with my laptop in hand looking for Kathy. After an unsuccessful sweep of the house, I found her sitting on the front porch reading a book.

"What are you up to?" she asked as she looked at the laptop I held awkwardly in my hands.

"I think I found him," I said with a mix of excitement and uncertainty as I sat down next to her on the swing.

She took my laptop from me and studied the picture closely without speaking. I watched her expression carefully, trying to gauge whether or not this was really him.

"Well," she said, handing my laptop back to me, "that's him alright."

The air escaped my lungs in a huge breath of relief as I stared at the picture wondering what happens next.

"What do we do?" I asked Kathy, suddenly unsure of what the next step should be.

"Well, I think you leave that up to Jameson. I'm trying not to be biased here but it's hard to forget some of the things that happened all those years ago. I just hope he isn't a disappointment to Jameson."

"Understand. I'll talk to Jameson."

I walked back to Jameson's room thankful that I'd talked to Kathy about it. I couldn't say for sure what Jameson wanted and I would hate to deliver heartbreak to him.

Like a stalker I watched him as he slept, memorizing every detail of his face as I thought about how to tell him I'd found his dad, and, more importantly, how he would react.

More and more it seemed that whenever he woke up, if I wasn't sitting right next to him, his eyes would dart quickly around the room as if seeking me out. Part of me liked that his first reaction seemed to be to find me, but at the same time it made me worry about him more. Was he afraid of being alone?

When he awoke I was just outside his room, having gone briefly to the kitchen to get a drink, when I heard his raspy voice croak out my name. There was a hint of urgency or uncertainty in his voice that made me rush to him, but when I opened the door I was greeted with a smile.

"Hi." His smile was big as he adjusted himself so he was sitting up with his back resting against the headboard.

"Hi." I returned his smile as I sat down next to him on the bed with my closed laptop on my lap.

"What have you been working on?" He motioned toward the laptop.

"Actually…" I scooted closer to him and opened up my laptop. I took a deep breath and rushed ahead, afraid I was going to lose my nerve. "I was thinking about what you said about your dad, and decided I would look for him." I turned the computer to face him so he could see the Facebook page I had found.

The look of shock was unmistakable as he pulled the laptop closer to him and studied the picture.

"I can't believe you found him." His eyes never left the screen and I silently prayed it was happiness that had put him into such a stunned silence.

"Is it okay? I mean, I wanted to do something nice … but maybe I should have checked with you first." I fidgeted through my rant until he grabbed a hold of my hand.

"Thank you." He leaned forward and kissed my forehead sending relief through me.

"I didn't call him or anything, I talked to your aunt and we figured it was best for you to reach out to him if you want to."

"My aunt knows about his?" His shocked expression didn't come as a surprise given the way she'd reacted when I told her.

"She does, she just wants you to do whatever makes you happy."

"I want to meet him." His eyes studied the picture.

"Yeah, we can call him. I bet he'll come out here to meet you."

"No," he interrupted. "I don't want him to know what's going on. I want him to know me for who I am, and not what's going on."

I eyed him with question unsure how exactly we could pull that off.

"Just hear me out." His eyes pierced into mine as I waited for him to continue.

"Why don't we just go there, you and me?"

I watched him, my mouth slightly agape at what he was asking.

"Seriously? You think your doctors will approve that? He's in Wisconsin, it's not exactly close." I found it hard to believe that he felt like he was up for it, or that anyone would allow him to travel so far.

"No, they aren't going to approve it. The way I see it it's a few hours by plane and I won't even have to miss dialysis … and if I needed it it's not like it would be hard to find a clinic." His tone was pleading but as much as I wanted to agree I couldn't imagine putting him in danger like that.

"I don't see how it's possible—or smart—to do that. Why don't we just wait a little?"

"Wait for what exactly, Becca? I'm not getting better! I know you want to believe this is all going to get better, but it isn't." I looked away from his unwavering eyes.

"I want this. I want to meet him but I want it to be on my terms." He grabbed my hand and squeezed it, watching me intently as he waited for my answer.

"What if something happened?" I said, my eyes pleading as I tried to will the tears to stay behind them.

"It's not Alaska, there are hospitals everywhere. If something happens we just go to the nearest hospital." His tone was much softer now as he stroked his finger across my knuckles.

"Oh my God, Jameson, I don't know," I said, shaking my head back and forth.

"Just tell me you'll think about it," he yawned.

I nodded my head yes, although in my mind I couldn't imagine how it was possible to make this happen.

"Come here." He held out his arms to me and I lay down with him, snuggling against his chest.

His breathing evened out and he was asleep within a minute. I, on the other hand, knew sleep would evade me as I tried to figure out a way to give him what he wished for. I stared at the ceiling for what felt like hours, watching the lights from passing cars dance across the walls. Selfishly, I thought about the people in those cars, going about and living their lives, and anger filled me. Why couldn't it be us out and about, having fun instead of being faced with what lay ahead of us?

***

My eyes fluttered open at the feel of delicate fingers running across my face. As soon as the blurriness from my sleepy eyes receded it was Jameson's face I took in.

"Morning," he smiled, and my sleepy eyes popped open wider.

"You look so good!" I sat up, my body now wide-awake with adrenaline.

"Oh my God!" Using the palms of my hands I felt his forehead and his cheeks, shocked to see the color had returned to his face and the dark circles missing beneath his eyes. Even the heated clamminess of his skin was gone. He watched me with a slow amused smile, his eyes dipping to my lips every once in a while.

"You're okay!" I nearly jumped into his lap but he was there ready to catch me, his strong arms holding on to me tightly as he lazily dragged a fingertip across my cheek.

"Thanks for not giving up on me." His expression was now serious as he eyed me with appreciation.

"I would never give up on you." My tone was soft under the heat of his gaze.

Strong lips found mine as he grasped on to my hips tightly, pulling me tighter against him. As our lips and tongues moved together he pulled me so I was straddling his lap. God, I missed this! I missed him so much. It was impossible to deny the fact that we were both desperate for each other as he pulled my T-shirt over my head, his hand immediately going to the cup of my bra and pulling down the fabric to expose me to him.

A cry escaped me when I felt his warm tongue against my nipple and I rocked my hips against him involuntarily, grinding our bodies together. I felt him beneath me, rock hard and wanting me as badly as I wanted him. I grabbed on to his dark, curly hair, pulling him closer against me as he took my nipple in his mouth.

I closed my eyes and my head fell back, both my body and mind completely sated simultaneously at the feel of Jameson touching me, owning me, once again. I heard the clanking of his belt buckle being removed and my body reacted to just the sound of it. I couldn't wait to feel him against me once again. When my eyes returned to him he was looking down but his blonde hair was wrong. Jameson's hair isn't blonde.

"Maddox?" My voice was filled with the shock that was currently riddled through me.

"What? What's wrong?" Maddox stopped what he was doing as he eyed me with question.

"Where's Jameson?" A mix of panic and confusion fueled my words.

"Jameson? He's gone." He didn't need to elaborate; I knew it, felt it in my heart. Jameson was gone.

***

I woke up abruptly, a gasp that started on my lips in my dream turned into a sob once I was back in reality. I got out of bed, my hand covering my mouth and the sobs that I hoped hadn't awakened Jameson.

What the fuck was that? As soon as I made it outside I tried to suck up the fresh air as if it would somehow make a difference. That dream was so wrong in so many ways I couldn't decide which part was worse. I sat down on the swing and dropped my head between my legs trying to calm my own anxious breathing. It was just a dream, it didn't mean anything, yet I couldn't stop feeling the heartbreak that I felt in the dream when I realized he was gone. Allowing myself to think about the possibility of him ... dying ... was too much. Maybe that was the reason I never allowed myself to go there. Agreeing to take him to meet his father seemed like it teetered some dangerous line. If I didn't take him, he could die never having achieved that last thing he wanted, but taking him could push him too hard, or deny him of medical attention when he needed it.

Standing from the swing I wrung my hands together and tried to shake off the unpleasantness of my dream. The only thing I knew for certain anymore was that I was going to make the time I did have left with Jameson meaningful.

Chapter Forty

My hands white-knuckled the handles of the wheelchair as we waited in line to go through security at CVG Airport. With each step, we progressed I was more and more certain that we'd already been figured out. Jameson, under the pretense that he wanted to look at all of his options, had gotten a copy of his medical records before we left. It was one of the few demands I'd had in case something happened. I wanted us to have everything we needed to bring to a hospital with us. I wanted to cry every time I let myself think about Kathy. We'd told her I was taking Jameson to the park down the street, something that in itself was a monumental feat. I could see the fear in her eyes when she agreed and her smile-clad face walked us outside, obviously facing inner turmoil much as I was now. The obvious difference, of course, was that I was the one currently causing her turmoil. I glanced at my watch and cringed at the fact that it had been two hours now since we'd left her standing there on her porch. Without question, she would already be out of her mind with fear, but Jameson and I had agreed we wouldn't message her until the plane was in the air.

Jameson's hand covered mine as we approached the TSA officer. I loved how he was always so attuned to me, even when I was being completely irrational. I put our carry-on luggage on the belt and we took turns going through security. Jameson even had a note from his doctor explaining he was safe to travel and outlining his current medications that he needed with him on the plane. The letter, of course, was not actually written by his doctor but Jameson assured me airport security wouldn't be calling his doctor over a few days' worth of Vicodin and the litany of other, non-controlled substances.

We turned down their offer to take us to our gate on one of their courtesy carts, primarily because I was certain once again they were going to figure us out and not allow us to board the plane. Instead, I pushed him to our gate, doing my best to make idle chitchat along the way.

"Stop worrying." Jameson grabbed my hand and squeezed it reassuringly.

Thanks to advanced boarding we were already in our seats while everyone else slowly boarded.

"I'm not worried." I gave him my best forced smile. It wasn't that I wanted to lie to him, but I didn't want my own fears rubbing off on him. I'm not so dense to believe he wasn't afraid as well. Not only was he leaving Cincinnati against his doctor's recommendations and his aunt's knowledge, he was meeting his father, a man he'd virtually never known.

I looked over at him again, my smile this time much more sincere. I knew he had to be afraid but without question, Jameson was the bravest person I'd ever known.

"Alright, I'm a little worried," I conceded with a smile. "I keep waiting for someone to come tackle us and pull us off the plane." I slid closer to him as I whispered the words.

His mouth pulled up in a smile as he laughed at me and my admittedly over-the-top imagination. I watched his expression, overjoyed to see, for the first time since we'd found each other again, hope in his eyes.

Jameson slept most of the three-hour flight while I sat there watching him and silently talking to Gigi nearly the entire time. My list of prayers seemed to be getting longer and longer and the fear inside me was so strong it had passed the point of being mental. My stomach burned as I prayed I hadn't made the wrong decision. I prayed that Jameson's health would hold up through our trip, that meeting his father would be a good thing, and that somehow, someway, Jameson would get the transplant he so desperately needed.

It was late evening by the time we arrived in Eau Claire, Wisconsin, and we picked up our rental car before heading to our hotel for the night. There was a light rain falling and I squinted through the glare that obscured my vision.

"I guess we should probably find a hotel, huh?" Jameson looked out the passenger window.

"Already done, we've got a reservation at a place"—I paused while glancing at the GPS on my phone—"five minutes from here."

"I'm really glad I put you in charge of this little venture." His smile was appreciative as he reached over and took my hand.

My response came out as a nervous hitch in my breathing and I squeezed his hand. Despite the fear that filled me, his hand on mine and the way his thumb ran across my knuckles warmed me with a sense of peace.

"I really hope my dad isn't a complete asshole or I'm gonna feel pretty shitty about taking off." A nervous laugh escaped his lips.

"It's your aunt I'm worried about, she's likely to strangle us both for taking off and not telling her what we were doing!" It was a true statement but one that I said only because I had no idea how to reassure him about his dad.

"Yeah." He pulled his phone from the pocket of his hooded sweatshirt. "I suppose it's about time we called her."

"We're here," I said as we pulled into the parking lot of our small hotel. "Let's get inside and we'll call together," I suggested as I pulled up to the front entrance. I left the car running as I hopped out, and ducked my head as I ran inside trying not to get completely drenched in the process.

As far as hotels go, this one was … different. The upside was the price and the convenient location near to Jameson's dad's place. While many might consider the fact that they hadn't updated the décor in well over thirty years a downside, Jameson and I were excited to enter the time warp.

"I think the red heart-shaped hot tub really ties the room together." Jameson flopped down on the plain white sheets, after I insisted on removing the comforter of course.

"Ha!" I laughed. "For me, it's got to be how the mustard yellow and green wallpaper really ties into the orange shag carpet."

"Also a good selling point. I take it they didn't have any pictures on their website?"

"Only of the hot tub." I wagged my eyebrows suggestively at him.

An alarm went off on my phone and I tried to discreetly check the list I'd made of all Jameson's meds and when they were due.

"Medicine time!" I danced around excitedly as he watched me with amusement.

"Did you create a spreadsheet?" he chuckled as he looked at the table where I'd tried to stash it.

Ignoring his question I eyed him teasingly and dug through his bag, pulling out his prepackaged nighttime meds, snacks and water.

"Does it say there what time you'll be tucking me in?" His teasing expression quickly morphed into a more serious one with his eyes showing a longing I too felt.

When I eyed him without answering he patted the bed next to him so I would lie down. Worrying had zapped all the energy from my body but somehow the worry remained despite the exhaustion that had set in. Overall, Jameson had done fine so far. He'd slept most of the flight and since he'd had dialysis before we left he'd be okay going without it until Wednesday. I had tried to educate myself as much as possible on end-stage renal disease and I knew I was far from capable of truly taking care of him if I needed to.

"Tell me you'll let me know if you're not doing okay," I pleaded, as I kneeled on the bed before climbing over to him and resting my head on his chest.

"I promise." He tucked the stray strands of hair behind my ear, his delicate fingers tracing across my warm skin.

I closed my eyes briefly allowing myself to feel his gentle touch.

"I think it would be best if I talked to my aunt alone." There was uncertainty in his voice and I knew he was worried about hurting Kathy.

"If you think that's best. I'll be right here." I reluctantly got out of bed and gathered some things from my bag so I could take a shower. It felt like the cowards way out not talking to Kathy, but at the same time I wanted to respect what Jameson wanted.

I closed the bathroom door but stalled getting in the shower in case he decided he wanted me to talk to her. I stared at my phone for a moment before turning it back on. As Jameson and I had agreed, we'd sent Kathy a message once the plane was in the air and then turned our phones off. Neither of us doubted the fact that our phones were going to ring non-stop and decided it was best to turn them off while we were here except when checking in with family. The pings of numerous text messages and missed calls echoed through the small lime green tiled bathroom and I tried to mentally prepare myself for the outraged messages that were undoubtedly waiting for me.

The messages from Kathy didn't come as a surprise, the first ones fueled with anger while the later ones laced with fear. I felt like a complete asshole for putting her through this, and the more I listened the more I feared she could be right, that I was completely irresponsible for taking him out of the care of his doctors for a foolish trip. With Jameson out of eyeshot, I didn't have to be concerned with concealing my tears any longer and let them fall.

What did come as a surprise were the messages from Amelia. Apparently, Kathy had reached out to everyone trying to find us, including Amelia. Kathy had suspected we were going to find his dad, and for the first time, I was told I was doing the right thing for Jameson. If I'd had my way I would have flown his dad to Ohio, but felt that it was best to do what Jameson wanted. I prayed repeatedly that it was not his last wish I was trying to help grant him, but if it was I felt like he deserved it.

After showering in record time I stood clad in my towel listening through the door. I no longer heard mumbles from the room and peeked my head out to see Jameson sitting on the edge of the bed, his phone at his side.

"How'd she take it?"

Jameson's posture slumped as he looked up. "I was just getting ready to come tell you."

I gave him my best smile, trying to hide how much it hurt me that getting up and walking such a short distance had to be so difficult for him. I closed the short distance between us and sat down next to him.

"Well … she's pissed. She said to do what I need to do and get my butt back on the plane Wednesday. Oh, and if I miss dialysis she's going to kill both of us."

"There's no missing dialysis," I agreed with Kathy on that one, and I knew Jameson knew better than to miss it as well.

"Are you tired? You should get some sleep." I grabbed my pajamas out of my bag and stood in the bathroom with the door still open as I quickly slipped into my clothes.

"Nope." He grinned that same sweet grin he'd always had, the one that was somehow sweet and up to no good at the same time. "You're so damn sexy." His eyes traveled lazily from my feet, up my legs, and lingered a moment on my chest before meeting my eyes once again.

I wanted to laugh at him for telling me I looked sexy standing on orange shag carpet, wearing a pair of boxer shorts and a plain white tank top, but the look in his eyes caused me to briefly forget where we were.

Propped on his side he watched me minimize the distance between us, the all too familiar want in his eyes still there after all this time.

"It's warm in here."

Panic must have shown on my face as I immediately went to him to check and see if he had a temperature.

"I'm fine," he added quickly. "I was just thinking you should take that off." His eyes went to my tank top, lingering at my breasts.

Without saying a word I pulled the towel off my head letting the wet waves fall over my shoulders before taking off my tank top. I stood there silently, mere inches separating us as his eyes drank me in.

"You're so beautiful." His fingers touched the skin by my navel trailing slowly up.

My eyes closed on their own volition, my skin tingling at his touch as want pooled in my lower abdomen.

His grasp closed more firmly on my hip, pulling me towards him as he adjusted so he was sitting on the bed, his back against the headboard.

"Come here." The words left his mouth with a growl, his eyes darkening with want.

I straddled his legs and he settled his hands around my waist, my breath hitched slightly at our close contact.

"Do you have any idea how much I love you?" His warm palm went to my heart.

"I love you." My eyes looked up towards the ceiling quickly, emotion taking a hold of me making it difficult to keep the contact. "I love you ... so much." My voice hitched.

His hand left my heart and traveled up my neck to my cheek where the pad of his thumb caressed my skin softly.

"I want you to know that if I could go back to that summer ... I would have gone with you."

"I never would have left you." I shook my head back and forth.

"You have so much you have to do, and I don't want to come in the way of any of that."

I looked at him with question, unsure what he meant.

"When I'm gone I mean, I don't want you to be so sad you forget to carry on."

I looked to the ceiling again, unable to stop the tears from falling down my cheeks.

"Finish school and get your restaurant, Becca."

I tried to pull away from him but he held on to me with the little strength he had left.

"I don't want—" I couldn't get the rest of my thought to leave my mouth, sobs threatening the surface.

"I'm not going anywhere right now, Becca, but you need to let me say this in case I don't get another chance." With one hand he held my waist, his fingers gently strumming across my skin as his other hand held my face.

I closed my eyes briefly before opening them again and holding his eye contact.

"The days I've been lucky enough to spend with you were the best days of my life. Even now, in this moment, somehow I can't deny the fact that I'm one of the luckiest people alive; in this shitty, old hotel room in the middle of nowhere," he said, glancing around the room.

I couldn't help but laugh through the tears at his last words.

"And when I die, if I get any say at all, I'll never leave your side."

I wrapped my arms around his neck and pulled him tight against me, resting my head in the crook of his neck. No words could leave my mouth, all I could do was hold on to him as sobs rocked through me.

"Please ... don't leave ... me." The words left my mouth staggered and breathless.

His hands fanned across my back trying to soothe me as he tried to quiet the sobs that shook me.

We stayed there in that position, skin to skin, heart to heart, for what seemed like forever. Eventually, my breathing slowly began to match his, our bodies finally in sync with each other. I pulled away from him, trying to find the words to tell him everything I felt inside.

Before the words could find their way to the surface his big hands held my face once again, and as he brought our bodies closer together again his lips found mine. They touched softly against each other before his tongue slowly licked across my lips. I opened my mouth to him and breathed in the warm air that passed between us. His hand inched up my back to my head while he deepened our kiss. I moaned slightly as our tongues mingled together, and arched my body against him. His mouth trailed down my throat, to my neck and my collarbone as I pulled away from him just enough to give him access. One of his hands went to my ass and tugged on my shorts so he could slide his hand under its sheer fabric. Automatically I arched back into his grasp and his mouth went to my breast and gently sucked at my nipple. Unable to be still beneath his touch my body rocked against him, grinding our hips together.

His mouth left my breasts and he pushed me back enough so that I had to prop my hands behind me next to his knees. I wanted to protest, missing his mouth on me, but nearly shot off the bed when his hand went between my legs, and pulled my shorts and panties to the side so I was exposed to him. I stilled, however, once he began to massage my clit through my wet folds.

"That's my Becca, nice and wet for me."

I moaned at his words as sensations filled my body. I wanted him so desperately I could feel my climax building the second his fingers made contact. He pulled his legs apart slightly, forcing my body to open up even more for him as he flicked his finger across my opening.

"Please," I begged, unable to take his teasing and wanting to feel him inside me.

He slid one finger inside as his thumb grazed against my clit. At an excruciatingly slow pace his finger pumped in and out creating a heat that permeated through my body.

I fought against the involuntary movements of my pleasure, afraid of hurting him but also too caught up in bliss to think of much else.

"You're so damn sexy." His voice was gruff and sexy with desire.

I opened my eyes and our gaze locked briefly.

"Mmm, that's right, look at me."

I tried to keep my eyes on him as he asked but the urge to allow them to roll back in my head was a constant battle.

I bucked slightly when he slid a second finger slowly in, stretching my walls as his fingers twisted slightly.

Moans escaped my mouth when his thumb slowly started working circles against my clit, my hips bucking slightly against him involuntarily.

"Come for me, baby, I want to watch you come on my hand."

His mouth was slightly agape as he watched me and there was no denying the desire in his darkened eyes. Watching him and hearing his words brought me closer to the edge but I wanted to taste him and feel his soft lips against my own. Unable to pull away from his masterful fingers I was paralyzed in the pure pleasure he afforded me.

He skimmed his other hand across my navel and up my ribcage before squeezing my breast. I moaned when his fingers squeezed my nipple and tugged slightly at my hard nub.

My body stilled, my release so close I wanted to freeze that moment and feel it forever. I bit my lip to try to silence the moans that filled our small room but when I exploded against his fingers there was nothing

I could do to silence the unrelenting spasms of pleasure.

I panted, stuck in my position as the aftershocks worked their way through my body.

"I missed seeing you like that—watching your face and hearing those moans…"

I was surprised to see that he seemed so content, as if he too had derived so much joy from the experience.

His hands wrapped around my waist and pulled me closer to him, his head dipping to mine his lips landed on mine once again. This time his kiss was slower, almost lazy as he tasted my mouth as if savoring the moment.

Worried that I would hurt him, straddling his waist as I had been for so long, I scooted so I was lying next to him on the bed, my head resting on his chest. We had never discussed his health conditions and the treatment he was going through and if it affected him sexually. As much as I wanted to touch him I was afraid that I would make things uncomfortable for him, or even worse, hurt him. A big part of me felt like I was being selfish by not initiating anything with him in return.

"We should sleep since we're going to leaving early in the morning." He saved me from the questions that were lingering in my mind.

"You're right," I huffed. With all my energy expelled I dreaded having to get up to turn off lights and set some things out.

When I started to move away from him he held on to my waist. "Don't put anything on, okay?"

I laughed at his request but obliged, getting up only to run to the bathroom and shut off the lights.

When I got back in bed we pulled the meager sheet over us and I rested in my favorite position with my head on his chest.

"Are you nervous?" I asked, my words cutting through the stillness of our room.

I could feel the steadying breath he took before he answered, "A little."

"Good or bad, I'll be right there." I wanted to be more encouraging but I had no idea what his dad would be like, or even if we would be welcomed.

"I love you, Becca." His words were barely above a whisper as he stroked my back delicately.

"I love you more," I smiled, shifting my head up so I could look at him through the darkness.

Chapter Forty-One

I awoke before Jameson and felt his chest moving up and down against me with each relaxed breath. Neither of us had moved all night, his arm still wrapped around me, now resting against my back, my arm wrapped around his waist. We had been sharing a bed for so long now I couldn't imagine sleeping without him. As if I needed a reminder that he wasn't well, my alarm went off on my phone letting me know it was time for his morning medications.

The alarm having awakened him he pulled me back when I tried to get out of bed.

"I'm going to need you to stay just like this for at least a few more hours," he requested sleepily.

"Believe me, I'd love to," I confessed. "*But* we have stuff to do today!"

After bringing him his medications we both wanted a shower, something I wasn't overly comfortable with him doing by himself despite his insisting. It wasn't that he wasn't able to get around on his own, he did okay with short distances. Longer distances left him breathless and unsteady. A little more complex than I understood was the fact that the problems with his kidneys could affect his lungs, so much so that he'd actually been in the hospital for fluid building up making it difficult for him to breathe. I knew I was in over my head bringing him here but couldn't deny him something I knew he wanted so badly.

I listened with hypersensitivity while he was in the bathroom, and tried to busy myself straightening up the room we'd hardly used. When the bathroom door opened I breathed a sigh of relief.

"You look amazing," he smiled as his eyes surveyed my long, navy blue tank dress. It was simple but the wide brown belt brought some minor flair to it.

More than anything I couldn't take my eyes off him. Naturally, I was used to seeing him in shorts or athletic pants, and it was the first time in a long time I'd seen him dress up. Of course, by dress up, I meant dress up *for him.* The light denim jeans, black collared short-sleeved shirt and his wet, towel-tousled hair made him irresistible.

"You!" I smiled. "You look really good." I tried to downplay my reaction somewhat; I didn't want him to feel like he didn't look good every other day of the week.

"You ready to go?" I asked cautiously.

A nod was all I got but I decided against reading too much into his reaction. The paranoid part of my brain watched his every move, constantly concerned that something was wrong and he didn't want to tell me. That morning though, I knew that no matter how I tried I couldn't put myself in his shoes. I couldn't imagine what it would be like, the courage it would have to take, to meet your father for the first time.

We drove the short distance to his father's house in near silence, his hand firmly holding mine. As we turned onto the street the sound of the turn signal seemed overwhelming. I wanted to say something, to encourage him, but no matter what I thought of in my mind nothing seemed right.

I watched the house numbers decrease as my anxiety level increased. The numbers drew closer before finally, we arrived. The narrow, one-car driveway was full of cars. A work truck with "Ander's Landscaping" neatly adhered to the sides took up the space closest to the street, with a van closest to the house and a smaller S-10 truck behind it.

"It looks like coming early was a good idea," I observed aloud.

His answer came in the form of a long exhale.

"This is going to be good." I squeezed his hand encouragingly and gave him the most confident smile I could muster.

Slowly we both exited the car but instead of going on ahead of me he met me at my door, taking my hand once again. We walked along the narrow path of the driveway not obscured by vehicles, under the tall leafy tree that, not unlike the house, was probably older than both Jameson and me. Tulips and little green flower stems poked through the ground around the front of the house, eager to announce the coming of spring. I smiled to myself as I looked at the glider on the concrete porch, decorated only with red cushions not unlike the ones that currently sat on Jameson's own front porch.

We stood at the front door momentarily and I waited patiently as he took his time before knocking lightly.

Jameson turned his face toward mine, the insecurity in his expression heartbreaking and unfamiliar to his features.

The sound of the deadbolt being undone brought our attention to the door and my hand squeezed his reassuringly in response.

The door swung open and a guy who appeared to be just a few years younger than us stood shirtless in a pair of low-riding red plaid pajama pants.

"Hi," he squinted, the word coming out more like a question.

Jameson seemed partially frozen, no doubt taking in the striking resemblance between the two of them. Both of them had dark, wavy hair, their chins both having that distinguished, square shape to them. Most likely it had even more to do with the fact that they both had tattoos decorating their arms.

"Hi, we're looking for Michael Cooper," I said, missing only a beat.

"Which one?" he said, still squinting and leaning against the doorframe.

"There's more than one?" I asked in confusion, which brought about a quick snicker from both Jameson and the guy before me.

Thankfully my own confusion seemed to quickly lighten the mood and snap Jameson back into the present.

"I'm guessing we're looking for your dad," Jameson answered, bringing some clarification to me in the process.

"Sure, just a sec." Leaving the door open he turned and yelled "Hey, Pop, door's for you," as he disappeared into the house.

It was only another moment before we heard someone grumbling in the background.

"Who the hell is here at eight a.m. on a Tuesday?" The question was not directed at us but apparently the older Michael Cooper knew the answer as soon as he made it to the door and stopped dead in his tracks.

Unspeaking, Jameson and his dad stared at each other, both of them frozen, their eyes searching each other out.

He appeared weathered and older than I expected, fine lines slashed across his forehead and around his mouth. He was not quite as tall as Jameson, and had a little bit of a belly hiding beneath his tan "Ander's Landscaping" polo shirt.

Mr. Cooper opened his mouth to speak but closed it abruptly and cleared his throat.

"Jameson?" His tone was disbelieving and shocked, but lacked any negative connotations, and I breathed out a breath I didn't realize I had been holding.

Jameson nodded his head before also clearing his throat.

"Come in, come in." He shuffled back as if suddenly realizing he had forgotten his manners.

We stepped inside the living room and Junior sat up from the couch abruptly, an obvious confusion bringing out the lines on his face as he pulled his eyebrows together. Apparent Green Bay Packers fans, the couch was covered in team blankets.

"Kara?" He hollered into the hallway as he pulled some TV remotes, magazines, and what appeared to be a pile of junk mail off a pair of reclining chairs and offered them to us.

"Kara?!" His voice grew louder as he called her name. With the magazines and papers overfilling his hands, his eyes darted around the room frantically as if he had no idea where to set everything.

"Pop?" His son eyed him with question before he headed down the hallway at a determined pace, leaving his son's question to linger.

After a moment, Junior got up off the couch, eyed both of us speculatively and took off to where his father had gone.

Jameson looked my way, obviously still in suspense as to how this whole encounter was going to go.

Never in my life had I seen so many mounted fish hanging from one wall. A few deer heads and geese also eyed us but the fish were the most overwhelming.

"You okay?" I whispered, well aware that just as we could hear them speaking in hushed voices in another room, they would be able to hear us as well.

He nodded his head letting me know he was okay when Junior, his father, and I'm guessing Kara came back into the room.

Kara watched us and her shocked expression matched the one that still donned Michael's face. Having apparently been pulled from bed, Kara's hair was standing on end and I felt a little bad for her, knowing the reaction she would have when she caught her reflection in the mirror. Polka dot pajama pants and a sweatshirt completed her morning ensemble.

"Let me fix you guys some coffee," she said while fidgeting with her hands and looking desperate for something to keep her busy.

As soon as she rounded the corner of the small living room and disappeared behind a small dining room table we heard, "Well shit." A smile tipped my lips up—undoubtedly, she'd seen her reflection.

"I can't believe it's you." Mr. Cooper appraised Jameson.

I wondered for a moment if he knew that Jameson was sick. I guess to someone who didn't know what he looked like before, they might think this was him. He was pale, yes; his walk was slower, and he was missing that normal light in his eyes, but I guess his dad wouldn't have a way to know it was ever there before.

"I'm sorry about your ma, son. Your aunt Kathy been good to you?"

He already knew more than I thought he did, and I wondered how Jameson would react to all of this? Would he be mad that he knew about his mom yet never reached out to him?

"Yeah, really good." Those were the first words he'd muttered the entire time and I hoped he would find his voice and say the things he needed to say.

"I didn't think you would want to see me." The regret showed in his weathered face and he looked down, his head hanging in shame.

"For a long time I didn't want to." Jameson paused as if choosing his words carefully.

"I don't know what changed but I'm glad for it."

I watched Junior, surprised at his lack of a response to all of this, the only plausible explanation being that he already knew about Jameson.

"Coffee's done!" Kara came from the kitchen carrying two mismatched mugs from each hand. She now wore a ponytail and an overly enthusiastic smile as she handed each of us a mug.

I eyed Jameson very briefly knowing that he wasn't supposed to have anything with caffeine and he nodded slightly at my silent plea.

"I'm sorry, this is my wife, Kara, and my son JR," Michael rushed, realizing he'd failed to introduce us.

"This is my girlfriend Becca." We all nodded our delayed hellos.

"Now tell me everything, Jameson. Michael here talks about you all the time," Kara encouraged.

A smile moved across Jameson's face but he paused, most likely trying to figure out how to sum up so many years.

"Let's start with a simpler question, what do you do for work?" Michael suggested.

"He's a very talented musician," I quickly added when the question stumped him.

"Really now? Isn't that something? What do you play?" Kara who was now seated next to her son leaned forward with interest.

"Electric bass, mostly."

"And he composes music—everything from the lyrics to the bass, guitar and drum lines."

I looked at Jameson as I spoke. I'd always been in awe of his talent and wasn't about to allow him to cut himself short.

"Well, I'll be. Must be from your ma's side." Michael appeared to be just as taken by Jameson's talent.

"You still live in Ohio?" JR asked, joining into the conversation for the first time.

"Yeah." Jameson shook his head as he answered.

"That's a long ways away, what are you doing up in our neck of the woods?"

Jameson and I both looked at each other as soon as the question left Michael's mouth, our lack of an answer resulting in realization playing across their faces.

"You here just to see me?" The question left his mouth as if he was afraid to believe it.

When Jameson nodded the answer Michael hung his head, his hand covering his eyes.

"Oh Michael." Kara got up from her seat and hurried over to where he was seated across from us.

Rubbing his back she looked our way, frowning as if she was feeling the emotional pain for him.

"He's just talked so much about you."

"I'm alright, I'm alright," he said, mustering his courage. Moisture showed under his eyes as he wiped the tears from his face.

"What made you come all this way? After all this time?" Michael asked.

"I guess I just wanted to know you." A simple answer yet somehow it was so profound. Jameson and I didn't discuss if he was going to tell his dad he was sick, and something about how Jameson carried himself here made me think he wasn't going to. He sat a little straighter and seemed to concentrate more when he had walked the short distance to their front door. I knew better than to pretend I knew what was right in this situation.

"Give me just a minute." Michael took off down that same hallway and after a moment called for Kara to join him.

"Pop always talked about you, I knew about you since I was about five."

"That's right," Kara interrupted when she walked back into the room. "He used to have this imaginary friend—"

"Ma, seriously?" JR barked in embarrassment.

"Well, ya did!" She pointed to him accusingly. "Anyway, he had his little imaginary friend and we started to get worried after a few years of it so we started telling him it was time to let his little friend go and meet some kids around the neighborhood. So, he tells us it's his brother he's playing with, talking 'bout you."

My emotions started to get the best of me and I fought back the tears that wanted to let themselves be known. Through my nearly teary gaze, I looked over at Jameson who somehow looked more pale and ill at ease.

"You okay?" I whispered, suddenly concerned that it wasn't the situation that was causing such a reaction.

He swallowed a few times before speaking, "I think I just need some air."

"Of course, you make yourself at ease." Kara smiled as if she understood the situation might be uncomfortable for him.

When he went to stand his feet didn't seem to want to hold him and he fell back into the chair, his breathing too labored. Concerned, Michael and Kara stood up and came towards him.

I stood from my chair and crouched in front him. "What do you need, Jameson? Tell me what to do." Feeling panicked I tried to keep myself level headed as fear engulfed me.

"Air," was all he said and I thought of the inhaler in his bag I'd left in the car.

"Don't leave him. I'm coming right back, Jameson." I took off running to the car parked just on the other side of the street, hitting the trunk release button before I'd even reached it. Thankfully, I'd kept all of his medical information and medications in one bag snatching it from the trunk and closing it nearly without stopping.

I had the bag open and his inhaler in hand before I even reached him. "Here, take this," I said, handing it to him. At the same time, I pulled his oximetry probe from the bag and stuck it on his finger. I didn't know much about putting him on oxygen but I knew that when they'd done it previously it was because his oxygen levels were reading in the eighties instead of the mid to high nineties where they were supposed to be.

"I'm okay," he got out with effort. "It's just my head. I'm dizzy."

"You want to go outside?" I asked.

He nodded his head and I held him under his arm helping him stand. Despite the short distance, JR took him by his other arm and together we led him to the glider on the front porch.

"Grab that blood pressure cuff … from the bag." Still he struggled with his breathing but I did as he asked and slid the cuff up his arm, tightening it before hitting the button to get it started.

Nervously, everyone looked on, watching him for any indication of what was wrong.

"220/170," I read aloud before flipping the thing over to see where I had written the normal ranges. *Oh shit*. Normal was supposed to be less than 120/80. "Okay, time to go," I said cheerfully while stuffing the cuff back in his bag.

"No, I'm okay," Jameson interjected.

"No, Jameson! You promised me!" I held his gaze, my eyes piercing through him letting him know it wasn't negotiable. "We either go now or I'm calling an ambulance. It's up to you," I continued after he said nothing.

Reluctantly, he nodded his consent and we got him to the car. I didn't intend to leave his family hanging but as I pulled away I could think of nothing other than making sure he was okay. I pulled my phone from my pocket and used my GPS to find the nearest hospital. I was relieved to find it was only a few minutes away.

"You okay?" I glanced toward Jameson, and while he appeared mostly calm I could see the fear in his eyes.

"I'm alright." He put his hand on my leg as if to reassure me, and I hated that I wasn't doing a better job being the one to reassure him.

I breathed an audible sigh of relief when we turned the corner to find the hospital entrance.

"You're going to be fine, maybe it was just too much at once meeting your dad," I suggested while squeezing his hand.

We pulled under the covered entrance of the Emergency Room and I reached around to grab the bag that contained his medical records and medications before hopping out of the car. I hightailed it to the waiting area and grabbed a wheelchair, and was surprised when I came out to find Michael and JR helping Jameson out of the car. In the rush to get him here I hadn't even realized they had followed behind us. Nobody said anything as I wheeled Jameson inside and up to the check-in desk.

"Jameson Cooper, he has end-stage renal failure and is currently on dialysis. He flew here yesterday and today he is complaining of weakness, headache and dizziness. I took his blood pressure and it was 220/170." I took the nurse by surprise as I rushed through his history, doing so before she'd even looked up at us.

"Oh, and here are his medical records and medications," I said, throwing the bag down on the countertop in front of her with more force than I intended.

Jameson smiled. He smiled! I was going through a full-on breakdown and he withheld a laugh.

The nurse smiled and nodded at Jameson. "Been through this before, huh?" Her blonde hair was in a high ponytail and she was dressed in red scrubs, and she struck me as overly cheerful for the type of work she did.

"I've seen a few hospitals," he affirmed.

"We're going to go ahead and take him back to see a physician. We can come get you after he's been checked."

"I can't go?" My voice deflated; I had not expected that I'd have to leave him and felt a pain in my chest at the realization.

"We'd just like to get him triaged first and then you can see him." She took the handles of the wheelchair from me and started to head through the swinging doors marked "Emergency".

"I'll just be right here," I said as I walked along with them.

"It's okay," he said again, and the nurse stopped long enough for me to kiss his forehead before they left me on the wrong side of those swinging doors.

I stood there unmoving for a minute, trying to watch through the narrow windows where they were taking him. I wanted to ignore the nurse and march through the doors anyway but getting pulled out of there by security was enough of a fear to keep me compliant.

Strong arms clasped my shoulders. "C'mon, Becca. Let's take a seat over here."

It didn't occur to me who was speaking to me and the truth was I didn't really care. I was frozen.

I allowed myself to be directed to the small waiting area where JR and Kara were already seated, Michael never taking his hands off my shoulders.

"Sit, sweetie. When they come to get you this is where they will be looking for you," Kara offered.

Since that actually made sense I took a seat in the minutely padded chair and dropped my head, looking down at the multicolored Berber carpet. Hospitals were the worst. The sterile smell burned my nose as people hacked and coughed around us. When someone was called back complaining of a cough and sore throat I wanted to yell at them to go somewhere else! If anyone got in front of Jameson and kept him from getting the attention he needed I would lose my mind.

Seated directly across from me, JR got my attention. Now dressed in a pair of work jeans and a sweatshirt, he had one foot resting across his other knee, his boot repeatedly tapping the floor. Kara was rubbing her open hand across Michael's back as he too watched the floor unmoving. They didn't ask any questions but I knew they overheard when I spoke with the nurse about Jameson's history

It's strange the things you realize you're willing to live without once you want something so badly you'd trade every dream for it. I don't know that God accepts barters but it didn't stop me from asking. If He'd heal Jameson I don't have to get my own restaurant. I don't have to have kids. I always thought I would have a family but I could trade that if He'd let Jameson stay. He could take ten years from my life if He'd give ten more to Jameson. I prayed He'd take Jameson's pain away for a while and give it to me. Maybe I could carry it for him.

My mouth was dry, all the water in my body having escaped from my eyes. I looked around for the vending area and found a sign pointing down another hallway. No way was I going that far from where they took Jameson.

Following my eyes, JR looked toward the same hallway.

"You want something to drink?"

I liked JR. He couldn't be more than twenty-two yet he seemed older somehow. Something about the way he handled us showing up today piqued my interest. It was almost as if he was waiting for the day his big brother would show up. Of course, the story about how his imaginary friend was actually Jameson was more than endearing.

"Yes, coffee please."

As I reached for my purse he pulled a couple singles out of his pocket. "I got it."

My knee now hopped up and down as I waited impatiently, looking over my shoulder at the closed doors willing someone to appear.

When JR returned he handed me a cup of coffee and pulled from his sweatshirt pocket two handfuls of creamers, sugar, sweeteners, napkins and stir sticks. I smiled as I took the coffee and piles of condiments from him.

"How long does it take them to *triage* him?" I asked impatiently while glancing at my watch. It had already been over thirty minutes and if he was waiting back there on some hospital bed by himself I would go off on any and everyone.

"So, what can you tell us?" Michael asked, pulling me from my nearly imploding rage.

I thought about it briefly as I didn't feel like any of it was my story to tell. But really, they had already overheard everything when we came in so I didn't see what it would hurt.

They listened intently while I told them everything I knew. Michael and Kara cried with me when I told them about the transplant he needed, and the two almost transplants that ended up being unviable just before taking place. What got all three of them in tears was when they asked what brought us here and I confessed to going against Jameson's aunt and his doctors to help him get here.

I checked my phone repeatedly, wanting to let Kathy know he was in the hospital but afraid of telling her when we didn't really know what was happening yet. Rationalizing I decided it would cause her more stress waiting to find out what the doctors would say.

Unable to sit still in longer I walked up to the front desk again to find a different nurse sitting there.

"Hi, Jameson Cooper was taken back about an hour ago and we'd like to know how he's doing." I explained.

"You are?" The heavier set nurse responded without looking up from her computer.

"His girlfriend." I dropped my head to the side trying to gain her eye contact which worked after a moment.

"I'm sorry, we are not able to release any information to anyone other than family members." Her smile was snide and I wanted to punch her.

"Where is the other nurse? She said I could go back as soon as they figured out what's going on."

"She's gone for the day." She looked up only briefly before going back to her solitaire game or whatever it was she was doing at the moment.

"I'm his father and I'd like to know his status," Michael said from behind me.

HA! I nearly yelled at her.

"I'll let the doctor know," she said before getting up from her rolling office chair and disappearing down the hall.

"Thank God you're here!" Tears stung my eyes at the thought that they could have just completely denied me all information on Jameson.

Michael grabbed me in a hug and led me back to the waiting area with JR and Kara.

After only ten more minutes of waiting a doctor surfaced and brought us to a private waiting area. It was small with a couch along the wall and a table with four chairs in the middle of the room. A private coffee maker and complimentary snacks adorned one countertop immediately making me panic. Surely people didn't get their own private waiting room when the news was good.

"Why don't we have a seat?" The doctor appeared to be in his forties and was dressed in pale blue scrubs. His eyes seemed kind but soft, again making me think that whatever news he had couldn't be good. Dutifully, we all took a seat at the table and waited silently for him to let us know what was happening.

"As you already know, Jameson is a very ill young man. Despite the fact that he is currently undergoing dialysis there are cases where the patient does not respond as we would like them to. In his case, a kidney transplant will most likely be the only way to save his life. Right now, we have his blood pressure under control and are waiting on some lab results to come in. We'd like to keep him overnight but with the condition he is in we will respect his wishes to leave the hospital."

"What does that mean? Is he okay to go home?" I asked, confused by his last statement.

The doctor watched me with kind eyes before continuing. "There is nothing we are able to do for him but keep him comfortable, and a hospice facility could do that either from his home or in one of their facilities."

He continued to speak but while his mouth moved, no sound made its way to my ears.

I'm not ready! How can this be happening?

"Can I see him?" I said, jumping up from my chair no longer able to sit still.

"Yes." The doctor confirmed. "Go right through this door and turn left, he's in room 103."

I nearly ran from the room and didn't stop until I made it to his room. Slowly I opened the door and pulled the curtain back to find him lying there, a small smile showing on his face when he saw me.

"Jameson..." Damn the tears that fell. Why couldn't I be stronger for him? I walked the short distance to him and when I went to sit down next to him he kept a hold of my arm pulling me closer to him.

"I don't want to hurt you," I said when I realized he wanted me to lay in the tiny hospital bed with him.

"You won't hurt me."

Without giving it another thought I climbed in bed with him and lay next to him, my head resting on his chest.

"We have to call your aunt," I said into his chest.

"She's already on her way." His hand stroked the top of my head.

Chapter Forty-Two

The next week was spent trying to find a way to get Jameson home, a task that wasn't easy considering it was recommended he not fly or spend that many hours in a car. Together, Kathy and I worked trying to figure out a way.

Despite their insisting, Jameson refused to stay with his newfound family. He was too worried about disrupting their lives. Instead, he was transferred to a hospice facility not far from where they lived. All the nurses taking care of him were amazing but nothing could take away from the fact that hospice is where you go to die.

Not once had Kathy said an unkind word to me, but there was a thickness between the two of us that couldn't be denied. When Jameson slept we worked to find a way to bring him home, and when he was awake we talked, and Kathy told stories about his mom and all the crazy things they had done together as kids.

The door to Jameson's room swung open and it was no surprise to find Michael, Kara, and JR standing there. They came at least once a day to see him and often joined in telling stories and anecdotes.

"He's sleeping?" Michael asked with a hushed tone as he pulled up a chair next to the bed and took a seat.

"Not really." Jameson's eyes popped open surprising all of us.

"Good! We've got some news!" Michael stood now, and Kara came to his side and wrapped her arm around his waist proudly.

I looked to JR who stood at the door leaning on the frame. Like his parents, he gave nothing away.

"What's going on?" Jameson asked as we all eyed them speculatively.

"That first night at the hospital I got tested to find out if I could donate one of my kidneys but unfortunately I wasn't a match."

"Dad, you didn't have to do that." It was the first time any of us had heard him call Michael "Dad".

"I wanted to be able to do that for you, son. I know I owe that much to you." His voice broke with the words and he took a moment to compose himself.

"But my boy here"–he said, pointing toward JR—"My boy is a match and he's going to help his brother."

Kathy and I both gasped and grabbed each other's hands.

"Wait. You mean you had all the tests?" Kathy asked in disbelief.

"Yes, ma'am. The doctor we met with said the next step is heading to Milwaukee and getting it done."

"Oh my God! OH MY GOD!" Kathy gasped, as she let go of my hand and practically knocked JR over in a hug.

Stunned I finally gained enough of my senses to go to Jameson. His eyes were fixed on JR, who held his steady gaze.

"You're sure?" Jameson croaked.

"It's not a big thing," JR said. "People can live their whole lives with one kidney." He said it as if that was enough of an explanation.

Breaking his trance, Jameson looked toward me and I nearly jumped in bed with him. I took his face in my hands and held his cheeks. "You're getting a kidney, baby!" Like a mother who'd found her lost child, I placed rapid kisses all over his face while tears fell down my cheeks.

Jameson laughed at my show of affection and everyone came to the bed, where we wrapped our arms around each other for an enormous group hug.

"Come here!" Jameson said to JR, pulling him closer and hugging him.

Everyone cried and held onto each other, even the nurses joined in on our love fest—a happy ending was not something they were accustomed to seeing.

Chapter Forty-Three

One Year Later

The ripping sound of the packing tape echoed through the now bare apartment as I finished closing the last box. Getting to my feet I looked around the living room, both sad to leave it behind but also excited for the next chapter of my life. I'd finally done what I'd set out to do and graduated from school. Getting to this point had been so much more of a journey than I could have ever imagined, but somehow that made the victory that much sweeter.

The choice as to where the next chapter of my life would take me was much easier than I imagined it would be. I love Providence, and while opening a restaurant in Federal Hill would be amazing, it wasn't home. If the last year or two had taught me anything it was that home isn't a location, but the place where your heart resides. My heart was with my family and friends in Ohio, so that is where I would be too. And so it would be there that I would open Gigi Anthony's, an Italian family-style restaurant.

The door opened and closed, the sound echoing through the empty rooms.

"Babe, it's a physical impossibility to fit another box in that U-Haul." Jameson stood in the living room wearing a pair of red basketball shorts and a black Under Armour T-shirt, a combination of the warm summer temperatures and all the heavy lifting causing perspiration to bead across his brow. I could stare at him forever. Thanks to his brother JR, Jameson was given back his life. Within a few months he was nearly back to his old self, and while he would he would need to take medication for the rest of his life, it was a small price to pay.

I gave him an apologetic smile as I glanced toward the last two remaining boxes.

"I promise, this is it!" I said, holding up my hands.

"It better be. You find any more stuff and you'll have to ride on the roof!"

"Oh, you'd put me on the roof, huh?" I pointed my finger at him.

"Yup." He came toward me and grabbed me around the waist.

"You know what?" he said seriously.

"What?"

"We just might have to do that after all!" He picked me up and threw me over his shoulder.

I screamed but then realized the most appropriate thing to do in this situation was slap him repeatedly on his sexy butt.

"You wouldn't!" I laughed as he carried me through the apartment into the kitchen.

He set me down on the kitchen bar and stood between my legs.

"I'm going to miss this place." He looked around the place where we'd spent the last several months.

"Hmmm. I don't know ... floor to ceiling windows looking out over Cincinnati, your own music studio ..." I reminded him.

"Your restaurant buzzing with people coming from all over the world to try your amazing food ..." he added, giving me a sweet kiss on the lips.

"I don't know about people coming from all over the world." I laughed.

"Mmm, they will!" He tipped my chin up and kissed me again.

Together, we'd found the perfect name for the restaurant, Gigi Anthony's. A tribute to both Gigi and Jameson's brother, Michael Anthony Cooper "JR". Despite living in Wisconsin we'd already visited them twice and they were making plans to come down for the opening of the restaurant.

He grabbed my waist and pulled me closer against him.

"You deserve the world." He kissed my forehead.

"You are my world." I smiled.

The End

About the author

Not unlike many of her characters, Lora Logan is attracted to tough, tattooed men, and is lucky enough to be married to one! The mama of three Maltese puppies, she is an animal lover and can be found most days snuggling with them while reading or writing.

While Lora begins every story with an outline, her favorite part of writing is the fact that her characters usually steal the show. She happily follows behind with a pen in her hand as they choose their own trajectory.

For upcoming releases and more information on Lora, check out her website at www.loralogan.com or follow her on social media.
https://www.facebook.com/authorloralogan/
https://www.instagram.com/authorloralogan/
https://twitter.com/LoraLoganAuthor

More of our titles

Their Lady Gloriana by Starla Kaye
Cowboys in Charge by Starla Kaye
Her Cowboy's Way by Starla Kaye
Punished by Richard Savage, Nadia Nautalia & Starla Kaye
Accidental Affair by Leslie McKelvey
Right Place, Right Time by Leslie McKelvey
Her Sister's Keeper by Leslie McKelvey
Playing for Keeps by Glenda Horsfall
Playing By His Rules by Glenda Horsfall
The Stir of Echo by Susan Gabriel
Rally Fever by Crea Jones
Behind The Clouds by Jan Selbourne
Trusting Love Again by Starla Kaye
Runaway Heart by Leslie McKelvey
The Otherling by Heather M. Walker
First Submission - Anthology
These Eyes So Green by Deborah Kelsey
Dark Awakening by Karlene Cameron
The Reclaiming of Charlotte Moss by Heather M. Walker
Ryann's Revenge by Rai Karr & Breanna Hayse
The Postman's Daughter by Sally Anne Palmer
Final Kill by Leslie McKelvey
Killer Secrets by Zia Westfield
Crossover, Texas by Freia Hooper-Bradford
The King's Blade by L.J. Dare

www.blackvelvetseductions.com

Uniform Desire - Anthology
Safe by Keren Hughes
Finishing the Game by M.K. Smith
Out of the Shadows by Gabriella Hewitt
A Woman's Secret by C.L. Koch
Her Lover's Face by Patricia Elliott
Love Times Infinity by K.L. Ramsey
Naval Maneuvers by Dee S. Knight
Love's Patient Journey by K.L. Ramsey
Perilous Love by Jan Selbourne
Patrick by Callie Carmen
Love's Design by K.L. Ramsey
The Brute and I by Suzanne Smith
Love's Promise by K.L. Ramsey
Home by Keren Hughes
Worth the Wait by K.L. Ramsey
The Christmas Wedding by K.L. Ramsey
Only A Good Man Will Do by Dee S. Knight
Secret Santa by Keren Hughes
Killer Lies by Zia Westfield

Our back catalog is being released on Kindle Unlimited
You can find us on:
Twitter: BVSBooks
Facebook: Black Velvet Seductions
See our bookshelf on Amazon now! Search "BVS Black Velvet
Seductions Publishing Company"

www.blackvelvetseductions.com

www.ingramcontent.com/pod-product-compliance
Lightning Source LLC
Chambersburg PA
CBHW050712180626
46814CB00002B/391